Strange Days

A Short Story Collection

Andrew C. Piazza

with select stories as:
Christopher Andrews

Other Books by Andrew C. Piazza:

One Last Gasp
The Messiah Project
Resurrection Day

writing as "Christopher Andrews":

Doctor Insanity vs. The Sparrow

Discuss, read author commentary, and more at
www.AndrewPiazza.com

Andrew C. Piazza

Originally published as "13" Copyright © 2014 Andrew C. Piazza

Copyright © 2018 Andrew C. Piazza

All rights reserved.

ISBN-10: 1986108538
ISBN-13: 978-1986108539

DEDICATION

This book is dedicated to those who can't stop searching, can't stop striving, and can't stop helping. Maybe we are all headed to the dust in the end, but in the meantime, we might as well fill our days with acts based on hope, not hopelessness. The only risk of altruism is if Life really is meaningless, and you'll only know if that's true once you die… and therefore you'll never have a chance to feel dumb about being altruistic anyway.

CONTENTS

As Andrew C. Piazza

1	The Sound Of Snow Falling	1
2	The Long Drive Home	49
3	A Fine Cigar	61
4	Kept Secrets	91
5	Shards Of Glass	109
6	Independent Study	209
7	Promises, Promises	249
8	The Last Pencil	263
9	Harry's Ride	281
10	Tracks In The Snow	303

As Christopher Andrews

11	Alley Cats	381
12	A Little Vampire Story	405
13	The Death Of Armadillo Boy	423

As Andrew C. Piazza

The Sound Of Snow Falling

The Long Drive Home

A Fine Cigar

Kept Secrets

Shards Of Glass

Independent Study

Promises, Promises

The Last Pencil

Harry's Ride

Tracks In The Snow

The Sound Of Snow Falling

I've always thought of racism as being similar to rage in that it is a dark, raw, base, unthinking emotion. It doesn't make any sense in the light of logic and reason; it's only when we allow ourselves to fall into a more primal, unthinking state due to fear or jealousy or hate that the illogical impulse to dislike that which appears different begins to surface. That's why it seemed interesting to me to use the werewolf, a monster lost to primal urges, as a vehicle to explore racism…particularly the hidden, quiet, smoothed-over racism often lurking forgotten in the hearts and minds of those who would never suspect something so dark lies within them.

Andrew C. Piazza

Some sounds have a certain feel to them. The sound of a clothes dryer rumbling feels warm, cottony, and cozy. The heavy rumble of a Harley-Davidson's engine feels like steel chains and heavy muscle. The sound of a wolf's call feels like a long drive at midnight.

The sound of snow falling has a certain feel, as well. Not like rainfall, which is tap-tap-tapping and pat-pat-pattering; the sound of snow falling has more of an ambient quality, a soft white noise which seems to creep up on you. All of those millions of fat snowflakes piling up on top of each other... the sound of it seems to clog up your ears, just a bit, with a tone that comes from everywhere and nowhere while creating a strange sense of urgency. It feels like a pent-up breath.

It feels like something is about to happen.

It felt like the sound of snow falling just before they shot old Ben Tyson, after a few hours' worth of standoff at that house of his out in the woods.

Out in the woods. Hell, everything's out in the woods here in the township of Rambling, better known...to me, at least... as

Shithole, Pennsylvania. And I suppose I should say "we shot" rather than "they shot", even though it was a State Trooper that nailed him and I'm just a plain old sheriff's deputy.

I guess they didn't have a choice. He'd really lost it; screaming about how his live-in girlfriend and her twelve-year-old son were demons, horrible monsters, all that sort of craziness. Every time he shouted to us, you could hear him trying to work up enough nerve to shoot them. It was in between the words, almost imperceptible, but it was there, and once he reached a critical mass...

He never had a chance to. A rifle bullet took him in mid-rant, and we deputies had to clean up the mess, while Sheriff Bradley drove the girlfriend and son away from the scene of their all too real nightmare.

The state troopers didn't stick around for long, either. They went back to patrolling highways or whatever else it is they do, leaving the scut work to us deputies; logging personal effects, taking lots of pictures, filling out paperwork.

Us deputies. There's four of us, including the Sheriff; I'm the only full-time deputy, the others are strictly part-time. Jimmy and Tiny both worked at the same garage, and worked the police department for extra cash... and, in the case of Jimmy, for the thrill of living out his "Cops" TV show-induced fantasies. Usually, it was just the Sheriff or me on duty, with Tiny or Jimmy filling in a couple hours here or there to make our lives a little easier.

We don't get a lot of psychos or shootings out here in Rambling; in fact, I think this was the first person killed in anger in ten or eleven years...maybe more. So I guess we were covering our butts by making sure every single form in the station was filled out, in triplicate. In fact, we were doing so much paperwork, that the evening was turning into quite an anticlimax at the station, when Scotty Pembleton came crashing through the front door with the Sheriff hanging on to him for dear life.

Sheriff "Bear" Bradley was a mess; soaking wet, shivering with the late January cold in his bones, looking like he'd taken the beating of a lifetime.

"What the hell happened?" I asked Scotty, who was barely able to keep on his feet under Bear's weight.

"Unh?" he asked, finally noticing the rest of us once he had manhandled the semi-conscious Bear into a chair.

"Did you find him like this?" I asked slowly, hoping the words would penetrate Scotty's thick skull. Scotty's not a bad guy; his synapses are just a little slow to fire.

He gave me that look, that look I get all the time, courtesy of my status as the only black man in the very, very white town of Rambling. It's not quite a challenge, not quite a gape, but no matter how many times the people around here see me, they always seem to want to pause and ask, "Aren't you a.... black man?" I usually try to play it off with a joke, leak off a little of the uncomfortable pressure that way, but it always seemed to eat away at me, just a little bit, like chipping tiny pieces off of a sculpture.

I gestured for Scotty to answer, and he finally did. "Yeah, um, I mean, yeah, just like this..."

"Where?"

Scotty paused, as if he had to think it over. "Up on the, um, Candy Road."

Candy Road was about five miles long. "Where on Candy Road?"

"Oh, uh, about half-mile past that up around the old mill. You know, where the..."

"I know."

"Well, he came, you know, runnin' outta the woods like all soakin' wet and blue-lookin' and running around talkin' all stupid..."

I fixed him with a stare. I call it my Sheriff Stare. Bear had taught me that, just one of the many lessons Bear Bradley had imparted over the years, out of a seemingly endless supply of small-town cop wisdom he constantly shared with me. I'm not sure why he took such a shine to me; I'm not just the sole minority in Rambling, I'm not even from around here... I grew up in Erie. So I can't figure out why he took such a personal interest in my training as a peace officer. It's just his way, really. In any case, I owed him, so I wasn't about to let Scotty talk about Bear that way.

"I don't mean stupid," Scotty added quickly, once he caught my look. "I mean, he was going and talkin' all... not making sense."

Gee, what's that like, Grammar King? I wondered, taking a heavy, navy blue wool blanket out of the hands of one of the other deputies.

"Figure too far for the hospital, so took him here," Scotty nodded feverishly, almost shaking his ridiculous DayGlo orange ear-flapped hunting cap off of his pointy head. "I didn't know, you know, where to go to take..."

"You did fine, Scotty." Sometimes, you have to stop Scotty in mid-sentence, before his unconventional grammar sucks your mind in like a boot lost to swamp mud.

The chief was still trembling uncontrollably, shivering inside the heavy leather police jacket soaked with river water. It had to be river water; there's a creek that runs almost parallel to Candy Road, and it was snowing tonight, not raining.

"A-A-A..." the sheriff tried to speak, but his jaw was shaking, preventing his blue lips from forming the words properly.

Still, it looked like he was coming around somewhat. The glaze had left his eyes, and when he looked at me, I knew that he knew where he was and the date and that the color of the sky was blue and all those other questions you're supposed to ask a person who's taken a hit to the head. He was starting to look like Sheriff Bradley again, the same Sheriff Bradley who hired me seven years ago and taught me how to be a small-town cop worth his salt.

"Jimmy," I said to the pock-marked, skinny deputy on my left, "go on and get up to Candy Road and get the sheriff's cruiser. Take Scotty's wrecker. That okay with you, Scotty?"

"Hey, now, I gotta to the wife is gonna be pissed when it I get home that late," Scotty managed to get out.

"You're not going anywhere with the whiskey I smell on your breath," I said, my eyes still on Sheriff Bradley.

"Why do I have to..." Jimmy began to protest, until I gave him a dose of the Sheriff Stare. "Yeah, okay."

We took off the sheriff's soaking wet jacket to wrap him with the wool blanket, and that's when we saw the cuts and gashes on Bear's chest.

"Looks like he got attacked by an animal," Eddie McCreary, Rambling's fourth and final cop, frowned as he looked over the sheriff's face and body. He was big and round like the chief, the opposite of stick-thin Jimmy, and sported a bushy mustache which made him look more like an overweight Seventies porn star than anything else.

"Sure does, Tiny," I agreed. Nobody called him Eddie.

Sheriff Bradley's eyes went wide, with either terror or understanding, I'm not sure which. He still couldn't quite speak, but his plate-sized eyes darted from Tiny, to me, and back again. Something about it made me think Scotty shouldn't see it.

"Tiny? Call Doc Penny and tell him to get over here pronto, then find that first aid kit we've got around here somewhere. Hold it...leave the coffee. And Tiny? I want you to put out an APB on the sheriff's cruiser, see if any State Bears are around to help Jimmy find it. Then put out another APB out on Sarah Parks and her kid."

"Sarah Parks?" Tiny asked. "You don't think..."

"Bear was giving them a ride, the last time we saw him. Whatever or whoever did this to him..."

"...might've taken her and her kid. Right," Tiny nodded. "But no way a person did that to Bear."

I tended to agree. "Scotty, go plant yourself out in the front room while we sort things out here."

He looked about to protest, but a shot of Sheriff Stare made him change his mind.

The room cleared out, and after wrapping his hands around the steaming coffee cup for a minute, Sheriff Bradley took a sip and spoke. "A-A-Andy..."

"Yeah, it's me, Bear." I never called him 'Bear' in public, and almost never in private either, but it seemed appropriate just now. "We've got help on the way. Who did this to you?"

He worked his lips together, as if trying to get them ready to speak again. "B-B-Ben..."

"Ben Tyson? He didn't do this to you, Bear, couldn't have; he's dead, remember? They shot him dead four hours ago."

He shook his head irritably. "B-Ben r-right."

"Ben right? Ben... Ben was right? Right about what? About Sarah cheating on him?"

The cheating issue seemed to be what had set Ben off earlier that night.

Bear shook his head again, took another sip of coffee, and another, and waited to warm up a bit so he could speak more clearly. "Ben w-was r-right. W-watch yourself, Andy. They ain't human."

"What was that?" I asked, frowning. I wished Doc Penny would hurry up. The shock of the cold and the attack that had so battered and bruised Bear was obviously taking its toll.

"Suh-suh," he stammered, then got it right. "Silver. I have a set of silverware, top quality, at my house. Five minutes from here."

"Bear, what are you talking about? Who..."

He cried out, and the coffee mug exploded in his hands in a sudden spastic grip. Some of it splashed up into my face, burning me, and I called for Tiny to get his ass in here with the first aid kit.

"Andy!" he grabbed me by the arm, hard enough that I winced. "You listen! You take this..."

He handed me his weapon. I could smell a wisp of cordite coming off of it... the gun had been fired.

"Bear..."

"You take it! And now this is..."

He grimaced, and his body began to writhe around, as if wracked with a terrible infection.

"This is the hard part," he got out once it passed. "Lock me in the holding cell."

"Whoa..."

"You do it! I don't have... I can feel it in me, in my blood, I don't have much time..."

"Bear, calm down, you're not making any sense..."

"None of this makes sense!" he whispered harshly, his grip on my arm getting unbearable. "Forget sense! Believe your eyes! Lock me up now, before it's too..."

He cried out, and then, his entire face twisted into a ferocious snarl.

"I said lock me up!" Bear said, grabbing me by my shirt with both hands, tight enough to pinch the skin. "What the fuck is wrong with you? Listen to me!"

He dragged me to my feet. One second, he's trembling like a frightened kitten; the next, he's strong as an ox.

"Bear," I gasped, "Bear, ease down, you're hurting me..."

"Hurt you?" he snarled, eyes blazing. "Yeah, I'll fucking hurt you, you little bastard! You do what I say! I'm your goddamn boss, boy, what the fuck..."

"Sheriff? Hey, Sheriff?" Tiny said once he was by my side, trying without effect to take Bear's hands off of me. "What are you doing?"

Tiny's eyes really went wide when the sheriff started to shake me like a rag doll, screaming obscenities, demanding to be obeyed, raving like a madman. It was quite a shock; Bear never so much as raised his voice, *never*, and now...

"Tiny!" I cried out. "Help me! We have to get him into the cell!"

Tiny looked at me like I just ordered him to shoot the sheriff. His eyes kept hopping from me to the sheriff and back again, as if he were mentally adding up how much loyalty he had to each of us.

"Do it!"

Bear fought us tooth and nail. He had just asked me, begged me, to put him in the holding cell, and now, he fought us like a wild animal refusing to go into a cage. Maybe he just got caught up in the struggle, maybe not; all I know is, Bear had lost his mind.

"You motherfuckers!" he screamed at us, once we had slammed the cell door shut with him inside. "I'll tear your guts out! You cocksucking nigger! You've always had it in for me, you always wanted my job!"

The room went dead silent. The sheriff had attacked us, called us motherfucker this and sonofabitch that, but I could tell by Tiny's wide-open mouth that everybody involved considered the worst insult possible was just thrown.

But Bear wasn't through with spewing out racism just yet.

"Why don't you go back to Africa, you spear-chucking jungle... bunny?" Bear shouted at me, saliva frothing on his lips, his palms slamming against the bars with the last two words. "Unh? What's wrong, didn't get enough white pussy yet?"

I couldn't breathe. The air seemed stuck in my chest; I couldn't force it in or out.

Sheriff Bradley had never said a racist word in his life. He was the kind of guy, if he heard somebody use the word 'nigger', he would administer a quick and decisive lesson on the proper and polite terms with which one is to address the African-American ethnic group. With his fists, if necessary. Now... now he sounded like a rabid Grand Wizard of a KKK rally.

"Or maybe you're not looking for white pussy?" he snarled, lips curled back over his teeth in a sneer. "Maybe you're one of those *faggot* niggers? Is that it? You lookin' to get that black ass of yours filled up with white..."

"Bear!" Tiny finally squeaked. "Jesus Christ, what's wrong with y..."

"You shut up, you fat tub of shit!" Bear slammed his palms against the bars again. "You're just like him! You probably want to get ass-slammed too! Come on! Jiggle your fat ass over here, I'll take care of business!"

"Tiny," I said quietly. "Shut the door."

He must've thought I was going to shoot Bear. "Andy..."

"I said, shut the door! I don't want Scotty to hear him like this!"

"Yeah, shut the door, fat shit!" the sheriff shouted. "Hop to for this spook! Move, boy!"

Bear said more, much more, much worse, before his screaming focused into a physical assault on the steel bars of the cell. His rants became senseless gibberish by the time Tiny and I left him in there and ducked into the sheriff's office to escape the violent tornado he'd become.

Once we were in the office, Tiny said, "Andy..."

I almost laughed in his face. Almost.

I mean, what did he think? That this was the first time I'd ever encountered racism? It's there every day for me, on the faces of those I'd sworn to protect and serve. Did Tiny think I was stupid? The rooms that suddenly got quiet when I showed up, smiles fading into guilty downcast glances? Looks like Deputy Andy walked in on another black joke. Sidelong looks from bystanders when I'd flirt with Jenny Locke down at the diner? I know what they're thinking... looks like Deputy Andy's looking to get himself a piece of white ass. It's written all over them, all over their faces, all over their looks; not quite full blown racism, certainly not an old-school lynching, but prejudice, yes sir, deep, dark, nasty fucking prejudice, the kind that *really* sucks because the people *with* the prejudice don't even realize they have it. I'm sure Tiny or Jimmy or Scotty or any of the other shit-kicking people in this white jerkwater town would bristle and snarl at any accusation of racism. They'd never, *ever* deny a black person a job or an education or a chance at the American Dream. But they sure do love their black jokes, probably Hispanic or Asian jokes too, and any time I smile and joke with a white woman, I know they're all thinking "Jungle Fever" in their heads.

God! I wanted to scream all that at Tiny, let it all out on him, let out the pent up rage I felt from being held at arm's length by the people of this town. My raving would've been far worse than Bear Bradley's; the entire station might've been destroyed by it.

"Andy," Tiny said again.

I tried to just shrug it off, like I shrug off all of the sidelong looks and snippets of whispers behind my back. At least these people kept a lid on it… it wasn't like that everywhere.

But this was Bear, *Bear* for Christ's sake, the kind of man that a town prays to have as a sheriff, the kind of man who is an automatic father figure to every other person around him, regardless of age, or race, or background, or anything. He'd treated me like a son, and God damn it all, I loved the man.

So I couldn't stop the tears from welling up or spilling over; all I could do was turn away from Tiny. Damned if I'd let anybody see that shit get to me.

"Andy, he didn't mean it," Tiny finally managed to get out. "There's something wrong with him, maybe a tumor…"

I couldn't hold back a sharp and bitter bark of laughter. "A what?"

"I heard sometimes people get tumors, you know, brain tumors, which make them say all kinds of shit. Awful things, terrible things, from good people."

A wipe at my eyes, and my voice managed to stay even. "Kind of a heavy coincidence, don't you think, Tiny? A brain tumor kicking in after he's been mauled by an animal, the same night another raving lunatic tries to kill his cheating girlfriend and her son for being monsters?"

"I dunno, Andy," Tiny sighed. "But you and I both know the sheriff don't *ever* talk like that. The man loves you."

Tears again, and we stood there, me staring at the wall, trying to force back the floodwaters with a levy of rapid blinking, Tiny silent and brooding with white guilt. We stood there for quite a while, I guess, until Jimmy got back with Bear's cruiser, and the night turned even stranger.

*   *   *

"Look at that," Jimmy shook his head, pointing into the cruiser. "What the hell could do that?"

We were outside in the snow and the cold, looking over Bear's cruiser. Doc Penny was nowhere to be found; not at his clinic, not at his house, not even at The Shackleford, the watering hole in which Doc Penny preferred to drown his sorrows. It was probably just as well. I had a feeling a lot more was going on with Bear than cuts and bruises.

Snow was tickling my cheeks in a faint caress; their light, whispery touch somehow erased the physical memory of Bear's assault and allowed me to concentrate on the new mystery of Bear's cruiser.

The wire mesh separating the front seat from the back was torn up... no. Punched out, that's more accurate, punched *through*, a man-sized hole right through the wire. The wire curled away from the hole, sharp claws ringing it, reminding me of a cartoon cannon which backfired and exploded into a reverse flower-petal.

Tiny's breath streamed silver through the falling snowflakes. "Looks like something broke in to get Sarah and her kid."

"Not in," I shook my head, running the beam of my flashlight across the broken edges of wire. "Out. The wire is pushed forward, out of the back seat into the front."

"Why the hell would..." Jimmy shook his head, unable to even finish his sentence.

"Let's look at the tape," I said.

Two years back, Rambling's tiny police department received a windfall of funding. I don't know what it was, or where it came from... a private philanthropist, a government program, beats me. What it boiled down to was, we got a boatload of high-tech equipment none of us could really justify. New guns... no more clunky revolvers, now we had Glock nine millimeters, seventeen shots in the clip, God only knows what a small town cop needs *that* for. Bulletproof vests, which we never wore; Tiny's didn't fit, and Jimmy's made him look like he was stuck in an over-sized turtle shell. Two new cruisers... and in those cruisers, camera set-ups, the ones that record what's going on in front of the vehicle.

Bear never did give up his old gun, but he did take the new cruiser, with the camera set-up and all. Now, I was hoping the tape would shed a little light on the situation.

We were all glad just to get back inside; it was getting bitter cold out, and the snow was starting to fall in fatter and fatter flakes. How on earth Bear didn't freeze to death, after falling in the creek...

Just another mystery. I had plenty to spare.

"Silverware," I mumbled, while Jimmy set up a TV to run the tape.

"Unh?" Tiny asked.

"He was saying something about his silverware earlier. Why would he bring that up?"

"He said a lot of things, Andy," Tiny reminded me with a sympathetic look. "I'd rather chalk it all up to raving."

"This was before all that," I shook my head, and then Jimmy announced the tape was ready.

We weren't ready for *it*.

At first, it was just the image of Candy Road, lit up by the cruiser's headlights. The falling snow made the picture look as if static warbled across its surface. The white-washed landscape rolled by, nice and steady, and then, without warning, the image shifted left.

Bear had taken a hard left turn, toward the edge of the woods, and overcompensated, skidding to the right, left again, and then finally plowed into a shallow ditch. The camera's forward motion stopped with a jarring shake.

Then, the audio kicked in... Bear must've tripped his mike.

"...et off! Jesus! Jesus!" he shouted, but that wasn't all.

Snarling, growling, hissing, something that sounded like a wildcat's screech. The sound of the wire mesh getting mauled. A door opened, and a second or two later, Bear dashed in front of the camera, in front of the cruiser, holding one hand to his side and gripping his gun in the other.

He ran almost out of the camera's eye, to the right edge of the screen, when they came into view. Two of them, one tall, one short.

"Jesus," Jimmy blurted out. "What are those, bears?"

"No kind of bear I've ever seen," Tiny grunted.

They stood erect, like apes, covered in fur. The camera quality was poor, and they were only on-screen for a second or two, but their faces reminded me of a leopard or a mountain lion... blunt, heavy, predatory.

They charged the sheriff, and he shot at them, pop pop pop, and then all three players dashed off screen. Bear's mike cut out shortly thereafter.

"Mountain lions?" Jimmy tried out.

"You ever see a mountain lion stand upright like that?" I snorted, rewinding the tape. "And what made Bear drive into a ditch? From the wire being punched forward, and the tape, I'd say those things attacked him from the back seat."

The tape ran forward again... swerve left, swerve right, swerve left again, bam! into the ditch. Audio kicks in, shouting, snarling. Bear runs into view, chased by his attackers, and...

I paused the tape and ran it frame-by-frame. Bear's heavy revolver leveled at his attackers, and fired, once, twice...

Stop. Pause.

"He hit them."

"What?" Jimmy asked.

"He shot them, the bullets hit... see there?... and they just kept coming," I said, running the video through again.

I knew it then, knew the answer to the riddle, but I had to run through the facts, spell them out, lay them carefully in a row, so that there was no mistake. Sometimes, we know the answer to the mystery, and yet, our mind refuses to accept a leap of logic. Our sane cerebral cortex needs our deep and dark instincts to plead its case, with plenty and irrefutable evidence, before it is willing to accept the outlandish.

Plus, I had two other deputies to convince.

"Where's Ben Tyson's gun?" I asked.

"Hunh?" Jimmy asked.

"His gun," I repeated, answering my own question by searching through Ben's recently-catalogued personal effects.

A flick of the wrist popped open the .357 Magnum's cylinder, and a tilt spilled a few long cartridges out onto my palm. The noses were a little off, a little off-color...

"What is it?" Jimmy asked.

"Ben Tyson said Sarah Parks and her kid were monsters," I said, scratching my thumb along the tip of one of the bullets. "Bear said earlier that... that he was right."

"You think *Sarah*..." Jimmy began.

"Did it scratch?" Tiny asked, his eyes on Ben Tyson's bullets. "Did it scratch like lead?"

I shook my head no.

"Silver bullets," he said.

A nod yes from me.

"What are you talking about, silver bullets, what..." Jimmy began; then his eyes went wide. "What, *were*wolves? Are you nuts?"

"Have you seen the same things I have?" I asked him. "The tape, the gun, the cruiser..."

"Bear going nuts," Tiny said, nodding at me.

"All the werewolf movies I've seen, it's all about losing control to animal urges. I'd say Bear's earlier rant qualifies."

"*Bear?*" Jimmy said. "How's he..."

"He got hurt by them, remember?" Tiny said. "Isn't that how you're supposed to catch it?"

Jimmy shook his head. "This is f..."

A wildcat's roar split the air, stabbed our hearts, made us all jump like frightened rabbits. It came from the room where we'd locked up Bear, and was followed by the banging of steel bars.

"Okay," Jimmy nodded. "What do we do?"

Practically on cue, the phone rang. Tiny answered it, listened for a minute, and turned to me.

"State police just reported Sarah Parks and her kid showed up at Matthew Gaul's house. Two minutes ago. They're on the scene."

"Matthew Gaul, the guy she was having the affair with?" Jimmy said.

"What do you want me to tell them, Andy?" Tiny asked.

"Tell them..."

"Line just cut out," Tiny said, frowning at the phone.

The hairs on the back of my neck started to rise. "Call them back."

A few seconds of waiting.

"Nothing."

Something clenched inside of me. "Try their radios."

There was no response.

I began to pace. It was a useless ritual; I knew what I had to do, but once again, I had to convince myself to do it.

At last, I spilled the silver bullets out of Ben's gun, loaded three back into it, and handed it butt-first to Jimmy.

"What?" he asked.

"Take it. I'll get Bear's gun; it's the same caliber. Three bullets each. We're going to Gaul's."

"What about me?" Tiny asked.

"No, no!" Jimmy shook his head. "Screw all that! I'm just a part-timer, remember? I didn't sign up for this funky paranormal shit! We need to call..."

"Who?" I interrupted. "Call who, exactly? And tell them what?

Maybe we could convince them, with the tape and all that, but by the time we do..."

"Bear will be one of them," Tiny finished for me.

I nodded. "That's right. All the stories say it takes a little while to change. They also say it can be stopped."

"By killing the werewolf that bit you," Tiny nodded again.

"What, we're banking on cheesy movie quotes now?" Jimmy yelped. "Hey, how about this? Maybe *none* of that crap is true! Maybe..."

"Maybe," Tiny said quietly. "What do you want me to do, Andy?"

"You reload, right?"

He nodded. "Shotgun shells. Making them is cheaper than buying them."

"Get your reloading stuff. Then go to Bear's house, break in if you have to, and get his silverware. We'll need an acetylene torch to melt it down, and something heavy to melt it in."

"Cast iron skillet?"

"Good enough."

"How do I make the pellets?" he asked.

"Let me worry about that. While you get all that stuff here, Jimmy and I will go out to Gaul's place, see if we can catch them there."

"I don't know..." Jimmy shook his head.

I turned on him. "Did you ever wonder what I was doing here, Jimmy?"

He shrugged.

"Sure you did. Only black man in an all-white small town? Why would I do that?"

I popped open Bear's gun and dumped out the empties. "We're out of time, so I'll give you the short version. I'm working in a dead-end diner job in Harrisburg, thinking about dropping out of school, no life, no future, no hope. Bear comes in one day to my Criminology class at HACC... he's visiting folks he has down there... and does a little guest lecture on small town law enforcement. I was in a shitty mood, so I tried to make an ass out of him, ask him a bunch of questions, put him on the spot, make him trip up.

"He didn't trip up. He challenged me. Next thing I know, I have a real... dream, I guess. A goal. It just seemed right, like you look at a car and know you'll love to drive it. I knew I wanted to be a cop in a small town. And Bear... rather than being pissed at me for trying to show him up, he offered to show me along the way. One conversation, one goddamn conversation, and he'd turned me around, he'd given me a goal... he'd given me hope."

I thumbed a silver bullet into the revolver. "At first, I thought maybe he was just talking noise, just another white guy trying to be my guidance counselor. But he was for real... because when I called him on it, he delivered. So here I am."

Another bullet went into its hole. "I owe him. I owe him big. And I'll tell you something else... I love that man. So if there is any way, any chance, any hope, that I can get him back..."

"Okay," Jimmy said sullenly, looking at the silver bullet-loaded revolver in his hand. "Okay, it's just..."

"Bizarre," I finished for him, pushing the third bullet in and snapping the cylinder shut. "I know. So let's go before we lose our nerve."

Tiny took off on his errands, and Jimmy zipped outside to get a cruiser warmed up. I stayed behind a second, in the room with Bear's cell.

He was huddled into a back corner of the cage, shaking, looking at me like he either wanted to run away from me or tear me apart. As hard as I tried, I couldn't see my father figure behind those feral eyes.

"Bear," I said softly to him. "Bear, if... if part of you is still in there, I want you to know..."

The words didn't seem to want to come out right. "What you said before, I know it wasn't you. I don't blame you, or hate you, or..."

Damn. Tears again, and blinking which was largely insufficient to hold them back. "It's okay, Bear. It's okay, I'm going to take care of it. I'm going to make it right. I promise."

I was almost out the door when Scotty popped up in front of me. "What for you I want to do?"

No use in even trying to translate. "Scotty, raise your right hand."

"Hunh? Oh."

"Do you swear to serve the laws of the state, and, um, and do anything I tell you to do?"

Sue me. I don't know the official words.

"Um, I was yeah, okay."

"Good. You're deputized. Don't let anybody in here, and don't let Bear out, no matter what he says. Got it?"

"Yeah, I will do the..."

I didn't wait for his grammatically challenged response, I just got out to Jimmy's cruiser, climbed in, and told him to haul ass.

It took him a few minutes to ask the question. "Did you... was that true, what you said back there, about Bear giving you a dream?"

"No," I snapped, "I made it all up."

He looked at me sheepishly, then suddenly began to laugh. I couldn't help joining in; it was infectious.

"Dickhead. Did I mean it. Of course I meant it."

"Sorry," he giggled. "It just sounded..."

"Unreal?"

"Maybe."

"As unreal as werewolves?"

We didn't laugh at that. In fact, it shut us up all the way to Gaul's house. There was only the scrunching of our tires on the white road.

That, and the sound of snow falling.

*   *   *

Gaul's house was a hell of a lot like Ben Tyson's... stuck out in the woods, accessible only by a short private drive. There were two State Police cruisers out front; I figured they had stopped by to question him about any possible affair with Sarah Parks. We parked next to them, and sat for a moment, staring at the house, unwilling to step out of the warm car into the freezing night.

"What, uh," Jimmy started, "What do we do if they aren't all, you know..."

"If they look normal?"

"Yeah."

I didn't really have an answer for that. "I don't know, Jimmy. Guess we'll just have to play it by ear."

Out and into the cold, then, and for the first time in my life, a voice spoke to me. You know how sometimes you get a feeling, vague, nameless, faceless, but nothing absolute? This time, it was an actual, audible voice in my head, telling me what to do… or rather, what not to do.

Don't go in that house, it said. *Don't you dare go in that house. In there is Death.*

A shiver rippled through my shoulders, which I blamed on the cold to re-assure myself. Bear's gun was in my hand, and a glance at it got me back on track. Whatever was in there, however dangerous it may be, it had Bear's soul… and who knows how many others.

"Let's go," I said, concentrating to keep my voice even.

We took it easy, and walked right up the steps onto the porch and peeked in the window, flashlights in our free hands. There was a possibility nothing had happened to the State Troopers… lines go dead all the time out here, from tree branches falling on the lines after breaking under the weight of heavy snow. And the radios… well, radios aren't as foolproof as we'd like them to be. No sense in us charging in there, guns drawn, and maybe getting ourselves shot by our own troops.

The window fogged instantly in response to a touch from my breath, but it was plain to see there was nobody in the living room. A carpeted floor, a weathered sofa, two easy chairs, a TV… but no mangled bodies.

"Andy," Jimmy said, the word streaming silver out of his mouth to form into mist on the glass.

I followed his pointed finger, through a doorway, into the kitchen. Blood.

A spray of blood, thrown against the wall like a careless splash of paint slung by a careless hand. It was about five feet up from the floor… just the right height for a neck wound.

"How, uh, how do you want to play this?" Jimmy asked.

"Nice and easy," I said. "All we've seen is a bloodstain. For all we know..."

I couldn't finish that without sounding hopelessly optimistic. "We'll just walk in the front door, say 'Police', and see what we see. Don't pop off... Jimmy."

"What?"

"Get your finger off the trigger. Index it along the trigger guard, like you were taught. We've only got three shots each; I don't want you to waste a nervous shot into my foot."

"Right. Sorry, Andy."

"It's just another call, Jimmy... just another call," I said, but we both knew it was a lie.

Jimmy opened the door and we stepped inside. It was like a soundproof room in there; not just quiet, but silent, like somebody swallowed the house whole or buried it alive. When the door slammed shut behind us, it crashed in my ears as loud as a gunshot, and ten years fell off of the end of my life from fright.

"Jeesh!" Jimmy whispered, trembling a bit.

"Rambling Police Department," I announced loudly, to break the silence as much as to identify myself. "Is anybody here? State Patrol? Hello?"

Nothing. Of course nothing.

We traded a look and headed down the front hall, guns in the low ready position. The house settled a bit, creaking and groaning under the assault of the howling wind and the cold. Thank God. Better that than the quiet.

We came up on the kitchen doorway. Jimmy set himself on the left, I got on the right, we nodded to each other, and turned the corner.

It was a disaster zone. A bloody tornado had torn through the room, ripping up the table, spilling over the chairs, and slinging a slaughterhouse's worth of gore over the counters, the floors, the wall, everywhere.

"Andy." Jimmy's revolver was shaking.

"I'm going to check the living room, make sure it's clear," I said, and tried to pick my way through the room without stepping in the intricate pattern of pooled blood.

The living room was empty, like before. No bodies in either room. No signs of a... wait. There, in the corner, a spent shell casing.

"There's a handprint on the fridge handle," Jimmy said, reaching above the bloodstain to pull on the door gingerly with two fingers. "Do you think... JESUS!"

He jumped back, as a severed arm fell out of the refrigerator and thudded to the floor. It had been torn out of its socket; there was an ivory gleam where the bone was exposed. A State Trooper's uniform, or the sleeve of it, was still on it, and the hand still gripped a standard issue pistol.

"Fuck, fuck it!" Jimmy shouted, backing away and against a counter. "Can we call somebody now, Andy? I mean damn, what are we doing here?"

I couldn't stop staring at the arm, even though the more I looked at it, the more I felt like I would shake my own nerves loose. "Nothing... nothing's changed, Jimmy. We call, and wait, and maybe they get away."

"Yeah, well, we stay here, and maybe we end up like that," Jimmy said, pointing to the arm.

"Hey, relax, Jimmy," I tried to joke. "It's always the token black guy who gets killed first, remember?"

He didn't even crack a ghost of a smile. "This ain't funny, Andy."

My eyes picked up a wide streak of blood, leading into a small room just next to the kitchen, with a door that led into the back yard. A mud room, some people call it. The streak led right up to the door, and my bet was, out of it as well.

Jimmy followed me into the mudroom, looked at what I was looking at. "Dragged 'em out?"

"Yep."

There was a switch on the wall for an outside spotlight, but a couple of hopeful flicks didn't bring any reward. It figured.

"Great," Jimmy swallowed hard, switching on his flashlight. "Just great."

We let the cold and the snow into the mudroom, and sure enough, the blood trail led outside and into the wide yard behind Gaul's house. Against the pale white background of the fallen snow, skeletal black hints of the trunks of trees came to within twenty yards of the house. The woods out here are deep; I don't think anybody lived for a good many miles in that direction.

"Forget it, Andy," Jimmy shook his head. "They're gone, they're long gone in those woods, they're nowhere near here."

I took a step into the cold. "We can track them in the snow."

"Oh, f... fine!" Jimmy snapped, stomping impetuously out and into the yard, along the track of bloody snow left by a dragged body.

"Jimmy!"

"What?" he shouted at me, arms held wide. "You want to track them through the snow, sure, let's go track them through the snow.

Who cares if it's suicide? Let's go tramping through the fucking forest hunting fucking werewol..."

A loud growl, and a furry shape dashed toward Jimmy, visible against the white ground. A quick patter of pawed feet, and a leap...

Jimmy screamed. His gun was up and BOOM! BOOM! two orange blooms of fire blossomed from the darkness, lighting up his terrified face like a pair of flashbulbs. The shape hit him all the same, knocking him to the ground and the gun from his hand.

"Get it off!" he shrieked, punching at it, hitting it with his flashlight. I was by his side in a second, weapon trained on the creature, until my flashlight beam hit it.

"Jimmy! Jimmy! Settle down! It's dead!" I shouted at him, dragging the carcass off of him clumsily. "It's dead."

"Son of a bitch," he gasped. "Son of a bitch. Fucking werewolf."

"Not quite," I answered. "More like 'fucking German Shepherd'."

"Oh, f..." he began to swear at his mistake, and honestly, I felt like I was about to bust a gut in nervous laughter, when the howling started.

I've heard wolves before. Their calls sound lonely, remorseful, like someone who knows they'll never see the love of their lives again, and the only way to let out that ache is to howl until their lungs collapse.

This howling was nothing like that. It was... mocking. Have you ever seen a documentary, in which an injured animal is laid up on the Serengeti Plain, and all around in the darkness, hyenas are twittering and laughing? Their voices seem to mock the doomed animal... and this howling seemed to mock us.

"Andy," Jimmy whispered hoarsely, "Andy, I only got one more bullet..."

"Stay close to me," I said lowly, shining my flashlight around wildly, looking for those mocking voices. "Stick close and make that shot count. We're going back toward the house, nice and easy."

We backed along the blood-stained track, fighting down the urge to turn our backs on the howling voices and flee in a panic back into the house. Then, just when I thought I couldn't stand the howling any longer, it stopped, like the sudden cessation of native drums in a jungle safari movie.

"Andy," Jimmy whispered.

"Just get inside," I said, covering his quick steps up and into the house.

There was a chattering, banging sound coming from the front of the house. We'd stepped out of the mudroom, and into the kitchen... after latching the mud room door, of course... before realizing what it was. The front door was open, and the inside screen door was banging against the jamb in the wind.

"We closed that door," Jimmy whispered to me.

He was frozen in place, and probably would've stayed stuck in place all night if I hadn't nudged him. He stirred a bit, and started down the main hall, but I stopped him.

It was almost imperceptible, but in the brief pause between Jimmy's whisper and my movement, it was there. Breathing. Heavy, labored, anticipatory, animal breathing.

"They're in here," I whispered, right into his ear, and felt him stiffen.

"Don't go down the main hall," I added after a moment's thought. "Stay here, I'll go left, clear the living room."

The reason was simple. We go down the main hall to the front door, and we've got to deal with threats from three possible angles... left to the living room, right to the den, and up from the stairway leading to the second floor. If I went left, through the kitchen, I could deal with one avenue of attack at a time.

Ever try to walk completely silently across a wooden floor? Give it a try some time. Every single floorboard wants to creak, and in the quiet, it sounds as loud as a slammed door. I picked my way past the streaks of blood, past the trooper's severed arm, barely daring to breathe.

Just as I started to get an angle on the living room through the kitchen doorway, I heard it again... the sound of somebody out of breath or terrified trying to muffle their breathing. It was a choppy, huffy sound, and as I took my next step, I clicked back the hammer on Bear's revolver.

A thunderclap of monstrous proportions, as the mudroom door crashed in on Jimmy. He spun too late, just in time to catch a downward swipe of a hairy forearm that tore skin and tissue from his face and neck. His gun went off, and I turned to face him, and that's when the little bastard hit me.

It went like this. I twisted to cover Jimmy. Two of them were on him... I didn't get a good look, just saw human-sized, human-shaped hairy things with the faces of leopards pick Jimmy up and throw him to the red-streaked floor. Little tassels of torn flesh swung from his lacerated cheek as he hit, and they were on top of him in a flash.

My boots slid on a patch of blood as I twisted toward him, and that's what saved me. The little one hit me from the side, from the living room, as I stumbled. It was like pushing open a heavy door when somebody's pulling on the other side without your knowing it... you stomp forward, off balance. The little one hit me, expecting resistance, and since I was already falling, he slid off of me and slammed up against the wall.

I ended up on my back, and I swear, that bastard was up and on me almost before I hit the ground. My legs lashed out as he leapt... he was terrifying, a nightmare come true, but he was still the relative size and shape of a twelve year old kid, so I was able to shove-kick him up and away from me with a heave. He flew back, slamming up against the wall with arms wide, almost spread-eagled.

Jimmy had just started screaming my name when I drowned him out with thunder. BOOM, the gun kicked and I saw a hole smash into the young werewolf's chest. A second to control the bucking weapon, and BOOM, another hole plowed through him, blowing bits of tissue against the wall.

Stop! my mind warned. *You'll run out!*

I twisted on the floor, ignoring the dim realization that I was sliding on a slick of blood. One of the adult werewolves was tearing at the back of Jimmy's thighs with its teeth, and the other... I swear, he looked up at me and smiled as he did Jimmy in. One of its hairy legs pinned Jimmy's lower back to the floor, and with its brawny arms, it reached under Jimmy's shoulders, leaned back, and pulled with all its inhuman strength. Jimmy shrieked; his arms flailed, and then, his spine cracked audibly and his limbs began to jerk spasmodically.

"Son of a bitch!" I screamed, thumbing back the hammer as Jimmy's body fell forward. My finger was squeezing even as I realized I was letting my last one fly.

The werewolf flinched, twisting inwards at the hip where the slug hit him before he fell to the floor. It took me a half-second to recognize my predicament... no bullets, two werewolves left, no backup. The second werewolf, the unwounded one, looked up at me and saw... the dead son lying on the floor.

I can't describe the expression its face held. Fear, hate, rage, loathing, horror, disbelief, mourning, all at once, all multiplied a thousand-fold. It made me think of the ferocity with which female animals will defend their children in the wild... and then those eyes glanced over at me.

I scrambled up and off of the bloodstained floor, somehow getting my feet under me and dashing through the living room for the front door. She was coming after me, fast; I caught a glimpse of movement out of the corner of my eye as I fled the kitchen. My shoulder blades pinched together; the skin of my back tensed in anticipation of claws shredding my flesh to bits.

I made the open door and flew through it like a freight train. A quick glance back... the mother had paused for an instant by her dead son. It was a short reprieve, and it was already over. She rose to her feet and charged me.

They don't know you're empty! my mind said, and I pointed the gun at her and shouted.

Nothing. She tore through the living room like a shot. I threw the gun at her and bolted across the porch and towards the cruiser.

Thank God we'd left it unlocked. Thank God I've got keys for both of our cruisers on my keychain. The werewolf's paws crunched on the snow just behind me; the stench of her breath was in my nostrils as I pulled open the door and ducked behind it as a shield.

She plowed into it with the force of a three hundred pound linebacker, glancing off of it and away. The impact drove me back into the car, and I pulled my legs in and shut the door just as she regained her feet and smashed into the door again.

I screamed involuntarily, digging at the keychain on my belt. The door buckled inwards slightly; then again under another battering ram assault. The car shook on its shocks with each hit.

Then, some sort of thought or reason dawned on her, and she smashed in the window with a blow of her arm. Glass flew over me; but I had the key in hand. The ignition had just spluttered into life when her clawed paw came in at me. She misjudged the distance; I was able to shrink away, and she shredded the seat rather than my stomach. I lashed out with my boot; knocking the paw away for the half-second I needed to kick the cruiser into Reverse.

Her arm slipped out of the shattered window and away. *Don't back into a drift!* my mind screamed. *Don't get stuck!*

She came on, leopard face contorting in a snarl, easily matching the cruiser's slow backward pace. A leap, and she was on the hood, scrambling forward toward the windshield.

Sarah Parks it's Sarah Parks it can't be Sarah Parks, raced through my mind. I shoved down on the accelerator, glancing back to make sure I wasn't going to end up off of the road and in a creek like Bear.

Hit the brake. Hit the brake and tumble her off. No sooner thought than done, and the she-wolf tumbled off the slippery-smooth hood and into the snow.

Now I was out on the road, and in a quick move, I shifted into Drive, and tore off as quickly as I dared.

She chased me, for a bit. The car was faster, even with the snow and the winding curves twisting through the trees, and she finally disappeared from my rear view window.

You can probably guess how shaken up I was. Head all fuzzy,

shivering here and there, a little dissociation, that sort of thing. The good news was, my nerves had settled themselves somewhat by the time I made it back to the station.

*   *   *

"What the hell is on your happened to you?"

You know it's a bad sign when you start understanding Scotty Pembleton.

"It's not my blood, Scotty. Is Tiny back?"

"Yeah he's put in the other room."

A big part of me didn't want to go back there, through the room in which Bear was caged up like an animal. That part of me had seen enough of the results of the Werewolf Effect for one evening, and dreaded another raving outburst.

I managed to put that part aside. Bear was lying on the metal bench inside the cell, breathing slow and deep. Asleep, I assumed, and walked past him toward the office.

"Andy."

It came just as my back was to him. His voice was quiet, almost a whisper, but it stopped me in my tracks. My breath paused in mid-inhale... please God, just let me get past, just let him keep quiet for a little while longer.

"Andy."

His voice was different than before... calm, even. No traces of maniacal rage or uncontrolled racism. I turned slowly. He was sitting on the edge of the bench, leaning sideways against the bars, looking like he'd just run a marathon.

"God, Andy. The things I said..."

"Bear?" It was too much to ask, that he'd be okay.

He blew out a long, tired breath. "It's settled in me for a bit. I don't feel out of control, but... damn, Andy, I said those awful things..."

"It's okay, Bear, it's okay," I said, walking to the cell and kneeling to his level. "Is it... is it over?"

He looked at me. "Andy, listen to me carefully. You may not believe me..."

"I know about the werewolves. Sarah and her kid."

Bear looked like I had just pulled a hundred pounds of lead off of his chest. "You watch for them, Andy."

"I killed one of them, Bear. Maybe it was the one who hurt you, maybe you're okay..."

"No," he shook his head. "No, I can still feel it in me, still feel it in my blood."

"Are you sure?"

"Yeah. It feels like... I don't know, like when dirt gets all churned up in water. It feels like that in me, except I can feel it getting worse, speeding up. I think my coming around is the eye of the storm. It feels like it's coming back with a vengeance. It feels like... like..."

"Like the sound of snow falling," I finished for him.

He looked at me with the wide eyes of someone who's just had a person put their finger on it for them. "Yeah."

Tiny's voice came from the office doorway. "Andy?"

I patted Bear's hand, the one on the bars. "Gotta go, Bear. I have to go and stop this thing. And I will stop it. I swear I will."

"Silver, Andy," he said.

"I know," I nodded, and stood to join Tiny.

"Love you like a son, Andy," he said behind me.

A few blinks to keep my eyes dry. "I know that too, Bear."

"Where's..." Tiny began, one we were in the office.

"Jimmy's dead. They broke his spine."

"Jesus."

"I shot one of them dead, the kid."

"So there's only one left?"

"No, two. Sarah Parks and Matthew Gaul. Gaul's got a bullet in the hip, but he's alive."

Tiny had to take a couple seconds to take that all in. "I got... I got the silver and all that."

"Where's the skillet and torch?" I asked.

He showed me and I put him to work. Tiny was no dummy... he had reloaded two dozen shells as far as he could without the pellets... powder, wadding, that sort of thing. Thank goodness. We were short on time.

"How do we make the pellets?" he asked.

It's really pretty simple. Melt the silver with the torch. An iron skillet is thick enough to hold the molten remains of silverware without melting itself. Then, use a ladle, or spoon, and shake droplets of molten silver into an ice cold pitcher of water. The droplets hit, hissing, and float down the length of the pitcher, cooling into hard little spheres by the time they hit the bottom. It's usually done with lead, but I figured it would work with silver, too.

So, that's what I did, melting and dripping Bear's silverware into shotgun pellets. Tiny watched the drops of silver sink and solidify, enraptured.

"Damn, Andy, where'd you learn that?"

"Black Panthers."

He looked at me in alarm, but I couldn't keep a straight face, and let out a little giggle. "Kidding."

He smiled and shook his head in a *You Dickhead* gesture. "Very funny. Seriously, where?"

"Saw it in a movie once. Is that enough for one shell?"

"Should be."

"Okay. Let's drain off this water and load one shell all the way; at least we'll have one if they show up."

Tiny shot another look at me. "You're out of silver bullets?"

I smiled a wide Aw-Shucks grin. "Did I not mention that?"

"Jeez, give me that stuff!" he groaned, taking the pitcher of water and pouring it off, catching the pellets in his hand. Tiny wouldn't ever be a ballerina, but his fingers were as nimble as surgeon's.

I dropped pellets into another pitcher while he worked. It didn't take long for him to crimp together a silver shotgun shell on his reloading press, and he loaded it into one of our pump-action shotguns straight thereafter.

"How are we going to find them?" Tiny asked. "I mean, they're long gone by now, right?"

I checked the time. Only two-thirty a.m. Unbelievable. It felt like it had been days and days since this all began.

"Andy?"

"We won't have to find them. I shot her son, Tiny. She came at me like a she-bear protecting her young. They'll come here for us."

He let out a long moan. "Hurry up with that, will you?"

"Grab a spoon and join in."

He did. For a little while, there wasn't any other sound except for the hissing of the hot droplets hitting the water and the muted clinks as they piled up on top of each other. They drifted through the water like fat snowflakes in calm air.

When we'd piled up a significant layer, we drained the water off and Tiny did his thing on the reloading press again while I dripped silver a little more.

"How many do we have now?" I asked.

"Including the one in the gun? Seven."

"That's all?"

"Couldn't use all of them... too misshapen, too small, that sort of thing."

I got up and took four of the shells and loaded up the slide of one of the shotguns... the one which already had a round in the chamber.

"Five for me. That's two for your riot gun there, and keep at it to load some more in. I'm watching the front door."

Tiny licked his lips nervously. "How long do you think we have?"

"I didn't think we would have this long," I said, and wandered out to the front of the station.

Bear was asleep again in his cell, and the station was as quiet as Christmas Eve. I double-checked my shotgun before taking up position... right next to Scotty Pembleton.

"Scotty, get out of here. Go home."

He shook his head vigorously. "No, no. You're gonna I heard all about the things you said about them werewolves."

I didn't have the strength to argue or translate.

"I got my shotgun you said I was a deputy in my truck."

Bottom line. There's strength in numbers, and I was short one deputy. One of the werewolves was wounded, and we had the tools for the job, but when Jimmy got his spine snapped, he'd only managed to put his silver bullet into the floor, so there was no guarantee that every one of our shots would count.

Two rakes of the slide, and two silver shotgun shells ejected into my palm. "Here you go, Scotty. Hurry up."

He took them from me with his dirty fingers and dashed out to his truck to get his double-barrel. I headed toward the back office, meeting Tiny halfway.

"I've got five," he said, nodding towards his weapon. "Think that's enough?"

"Give me one. Scotty's getting his shooter, and I've only got three."

He popped a shell out and handed it over. "You really think that's a good idea, letting Scotty..."

Howling. Long, hollow, mocking... and vengeful. Angry. Full of hate.

Tiny's voice lost its center. "That ain't no wolf."

"No, it's not," I agreed, sliding the shell into my gun and following Tiny towards the front door. "Scotty! Scotty, get back in here!"

"I'm in here! I'm in here!" Scotty's voice floated from the front of the station. Tiny and I had just stepped into the room when the front door blasted inwards on top of him.

It fell intact, like a giant Domino, and knocked Scotty to the floor beneath it. His gun clattered from his hands, and something about the way his head hit the floor told me he was knocked out cold.

Then, it was on.

One of them came in through the front door. My mind identified him distantly as Gaul, due to his heavy limp... undoubtedly a result of my shot earlier.

Mostly, though, my mind and body acted in reflex, shouldering the shotgun and sighting down the barrel as the wounded werewolf charged me. He was about eight feet away from me when Tiny's first shot hit him in the gut... Tiny's always been a better shot than I am. My weapon joined in a half-second later, catching Gaul high in the right shoulder. As often happens when firing a pump action shotgun, it took a second to recover from the recoil to aim again. Shotguns buck like a pissed-off mule, and by the time I blew a second charge of homemade shot into Gaul's chest to drop him, my mind had time to realize Sarah Parks had outfoxed us, that she wasn't coming in the front door like Gaul.

I hadn't even finished the thought when the front window blew in and something hit Tiny. No, not something; it was Sarah Parks, and yet it wasn't really her, it was the monster she had become. She hit Tiny like a force of nature; glass shards fell from her hair like sharp snowflakes. It seemed as if the howling wind outside propelled her through the air, until I realized it wasn't the wind that was howling.

It was Bear. He was slamming on the bars, howling at the top of his lungs and frothing at the mouth. It was the violence he saw in front of him; the sight of it drove him into a frenzy.

The werewolf knocked Tiny's gun aside, took it away from him like she was pulling a stick out of the hands of a three year old. I raked my slide and tried to get one off, but Tiny slammed into me from the force of Sarah's attack, and my shot went into the floor. We all went down in a heap, with me on the bottom. I was struggling with my slide to load my last shell in, and Tiny was screaming and trying to hold Sarah off of him with nothing but his bare hands.

Have I mentioned Tiny was heavy? Three hundred pounds' worth of heavy, and while there was panic in me from being smothered underneath him, a sort of guilty gratitude was there, too… he was a human shield, and Sarah couldn't get to me while I was pinned underneath Tiny's bulk.

I don't know how long I was stuck there. Probably only a few seconds, but when I think of that seeming eternity, my skin still shudders over my flesh. I could feel every muscle in Tiny's body squirming, fighting, seeming to scream the same way his mouth screamed as she tore him apart right on top of me. His entire body shook when she pulled and tore at him, his struggles turned him into a quivering, crushing mass. I could hear the wet sounds she was making as she tore through cloth and skin and finally muscle and sinew. I heard ribs cracking, and soon, Tiny's desperate screams and struggles soon turned to gurgles and spasms.

Maybe there was something I could've done, but the entire time that my body wanted to claw its way out from underneath him, to recoil from Tiny in horror and disgust, my terrified mind kept me cringing beneath him, desperate for the protection his body afforded mine. It was a sickening feeling, one that seemed to turn my bone marrow to spoiled milk, but I had lost all rational capacity; all I knew was that for as long as Tiny was being torn apart on top of me, I was safe.

My faculties finally came back to me just as Sarah lifted Tiny's gutted corpse up off of me and tossed it aside like a sack of grain. I still had one shell left, and this time, I was faster than she was. No sooner had the shotgun's slide *shunked* shut than thunder roared. Sarah stumbled backward, away from me, and fell on her ass; but no sooner had I seen the shot hit her than I knew she wouldn't stay down. I had aimed too wide; only a fraction of the pellets hit her in the flank, and although she was very likely in pain and probably slowed down a bit, she wasn't through with me yet.

Both of our eyes spotted Tiny's shotgun, but she got there first, keeping my hands from reaching it by swiping me casually with her right arm. Her talons caught in my heavy coat; didn't get through, luckily, but they acted like fishhooks dragging in a trout's mouth, and she slung me to the floor with her terrible strength.

By the time I picked myself up, she held the shotgun in one hand by the barrel. With a wildcat's screech, she slammed it against the floor like a hammer, and the weapon splintered under the blow.

It was a show of power, and when her feral, leopard-like features twisted into a facsimile of a smile, I lost it. In my mind, I could feel her swing me against the floor like that, shattering my skull like the shotgun. Images of Jimmy's spine getting snapped trickled through me... but this time I felt it, as if it were happening to me, as if I were enduring a dry run for what was certain to come.

I lost it, I ran in a wild panic back toward Bear's office, some distant part of me illogically thinking I would be okay if I got to the silver. Some part of me hoped against hope that maybe, just maybe, Tiny had left a forgotten shell on the reloading press that I could use against her. I drew my service pistol as I ran and fired four useless shots... more wishful thinking... and I swear she was laughing at me, the way a mountain lion would laugh if it could.

She loped after me casually at first, then suddenly her shoulders hunched and her body changed into a speeding torpedo. Sarah was done playing. Now it was time to eat.

She threw me against the desk with the impact of her body. I was spared her jaws only by shoving the shotgun's barrel into her mouth with my left hand. Frothy saliva spattered against my cheek; the musty smell of her wet fur was in my nostrils. There was the strangest feeling; not so much panic, more of discomfort, annoyance at her invasion of my personal space, as if she were a subway commuter standing too close rather than a nightmare come to life. The reality of the situation came back, just for a second, and with it came the panic. Almost without thinking, I jammed the barrel of my service pistol to her head and hammered a half-dozen rounds against her skull.

They weren't silver bullets, but I think the force of their impact stunned her just enough to throw her off her game. She flailed wildly, once, knocking both pistol and shotgun from my grip. I fell to the floor, no longer pinned against the desk by her body, and landed amongst a pile of spent shell casings and half-melted silverware that had been knocked to the floor.

She was on me before I could prop myself on my elbows, and this time, there was no reprieve. Her arms wrapped around me in a deadly embrace… I could feel her claws breaking skin even through my jacket… and her jaws clamped onto my left shoulder, where the jacket had slid away to leave only my uniform covering the skin.

Sharp needles bored into my muscle, heedless of my screams. The pain fueled my panic into frenzy; I thrashed about, I was a drowning man with leaden boots, I was smothering in a collapsed cave, I was burning alive. The harder I struggled, the more I lost it. I couldn't stop staring at the fluorescent lights in the ceiling, all the while thinking *No! No! No! I can't die like this!* and at the same time knowing *I'm dying! I'm dying! This is how I die I'm dying!*

It was very much like drowning, I suppose. Quiet, just like

underwater, because I was deaf from the gunfire. All I could hear was Sarah grunting, and I actually only *felt* that through vibrations in my shoulder. There was that strange, dissociated feeling you get when you're underwater looking up, and the panic… but I've told you about the panic.

What pulled me out of it was a sharp stinging in my hand. It didn't make any sense to my numbed mind; I could feel where Sarah's claws were, where her teeth were, feel the coarse fur of her scalp rub against my neck. There was nothing that should be injuring my hand. It took my mind a moment to process what my feeling fingers told it… that in my thrashing, I had cut my palm open on a jagged edge of half-melted silverware.

It cut you Cut it You're not dead Go Go Do it Do it fluttered like flashes from a strobe light through my mind; I remember wrapping my fingers around what turned out to be the handle of a fork. Its tines had been melted off, leaving only a jagged tip, and with a sudden, savage shout, I drove it like an ice pick against Sarah's leopard-like skull.

It didn't punch through, so I began to dig with it, scraped it around and around like I was mixing thick dough, and when she screamed in her inhuman way, I knew she had let go of me with her jaws. I was still hazy, but now it was in a triumphant, Neanderthalish brutality, and I shoved the point of the fork into her left eye as hard as I could.

Her spasms of pain threw me away from her and face-first to the floor. I pushed myself up with my right arm, the only one that was working, and fled out of the room without looking back. I wasn't thinking anything at all, I was simply hauling ass, putting as much distance between myself and the monster as possible, until the sight of Scotty's shotgun lying near his prone body stopped me short. I lurched for it like a drunk, grabbed at it like a drowning man grabs a life preserver, and once it was in my hand, I turned to face the monster, filled with a sudden, grim determination to destroy her.

The she-wolf came out of Bear's office like a boxer hit hard enough to dull his senses. I could see blood running freely from her ruined eye and more matting the fur on her scalp; she also hunched a bit over the flank where the silver shotgun pellets had hit her... maybe I'd hit her harder than I originally thought.

The werewolf had to look left and right before her remaining eye caught sight of me. She paused for just a second, in the manner of a street fighter who is completely exhausted, but is set on finishing the fight.

I didn't give her the chance. Propping Scotty's shotgun against my right shoulder, I gave her a blast to the head from about ten feet away. The left half of her face disappeared, uncovering the mottled mass of red and white hidden underneath the skin and fur, and she did drop, but she wasn't done. She flopped around for a bit, until I finally hobbled over to her... I was pretty exhausted myself. I stood over her body with the gun inches from her head.

"Let Bear go, you bitch," I said, and blew the rest of her head off.

That gun blast seemed to mark the end of the evening the same way starter pistols mark the start of a race. Bear was back in his seat, quiet. The whole place was suddenly, deathly quiet.

I sat down on an undamaged chair after that, and stared numbly into space for a long, long time. After a few eons had passed, I sensed something moving out of the corner of my eye.

No, no, I thought. *I'm done, it's over, no more, I give up.*

Then, the voice, which should've made me laugh, but I started to cry instead.

"Hey get me out the door I'm stuck under the here..."

Scotty. But like I said, I didn't laugh, I just sat there with hot tears streaming down my cheeks as Scotty fought his way out from under the front door and Sarah Parks' body changed back into that of a human. I never really knew her any more so than anybody else in this town, so I didn't feel much of a sense of mourning. It was just that... there was something wrong about her damaged body, something about the way she lay splayed and broken and naked on the ground, that seemed somehow inappropriate. She looked more like a victim of this insanity than the perpetrator.

Perhaps it was just that a sense of loss from the entire situation had finally taken hold... Tiny and Jimmy gone, Sarah and her once-human family gone as well, and Bear and I stuck with wounds that might or might not end up continuing the night's madness.

It was that thought which galvanized me. I picked the last two loaded shells from the shattered remnants of Tiny's gun and loaded them into Scotty's double barrel. The weapon snicking shut is what caught his attention; he had been staring at Matthew Gaul's now-human body.

"Hey he doesn't look like a Holy Cow your arm is all fucked looks all normal like a person," he chattered quickly, eyes wide at the sight of my mangled shoulder.

I must've looked quite a sight, because Scotty looked as if he thought I was going to shoot him as I gestured with his gun at the open front doorway. "Scotty. Get the hell out of here. Go and don't come back, not for anything."

"No but I you're hurt..."

"Scotty!" I snarled, fixing him with a Sheriff Stare that I suspected might have some werewolf in it, "Get the *fuck* out of here!"

He went, tripping over the debris by the front door in his haste, but I didn't pay any attention to him. Instead, I was fixated on how I seemed to be able to feel my blood as it sped through my veins and arteries, how it felt like every red blood cell was tingling and sparkling with electricity. The more I thought about it, the worse it seemed to get, and the more I wanted to chase down Scotty and beat his dumb white trash ass into the ground for daring to question me for one second.

My blood began to boil. Fucking white trash, that's all he was, that's all they *all* were, all of these racist motherfuckers here in Rambling, looking at me with those shitty sidelong glances, and then, when I pull them over on a traffic stop and they're reeking of whiskey and we both know it, *then* they want to be all cool with me. What the hell was I doing here? Sworn to protect and serve, I faced down a nightmare that would've sent most people running, and now I could be doomed to a living hell of an existence, and for what? For stupid white rednecks like Scotty. Racist, ungrateful, unworthy pieces of shit.

My fists clenched, my entire body clenched. I started to see red, the fire in my blood burned out of control. I slammed a fist against Bear's cage. I should take this shotgun in my hands and blow some fucking sense into these people, that's what I should do, I began to think, when Bear's voice came from behind me.

"Don't feed into it, Andy. Don't listen to it. Just breathe in and out. Don't fight it, don't push it away, don't struggle. Just relax."

I did as he said, and the buzzing energy in my blood subsided until I felt fatigue and cold and pain again. It was like a drink of water to a man dying of thirst; all of a sudden, I was thinking clearly again, shuddering at what my own traitorous thoughts had almost set me to do. *This is what it's like*, I thought, thinking of Bear's sudden and terrible rant earlier. *This is The Werewolf Effect.*

Bear looked at my shoulder wound as I sat down in a chair next to the holding cell. He didn't need to say anything; we both knew what it meant.

"Just because I feel it now doesn't mean it has to stay," I said slowly, staring at the now-human body of Sarah Parks. "It takes time to take you over completely; it must take time to fade completely, as well."

I sensed Bear's nod rather than saw it. "And if it doesn't fade, if killing the one who infected you *doesn't* make it go away?"

My answer was a glance down at Scotty's shotgun. I had one shell left for each of us.

"We'll just sit," I said. "We'll just sit, and wait, and see what happens."

We didn't speak after that; after that, there was only the tangle of ruined furniture and torn corpses tossed around the room, and the cold wind howling through the open doorway.

That, and the sound of snow falling.

The Long Drive Home

When I was still working on my doctorate in Atlanta, I used to drive home to Shillington, Pennsylvania several times a year to visit my family. It was a twelve hour drive, and I'm too Type A to do anything other than make it in one go. Somewhere around the seven to eight hour mark on a long drive, you go batshit insane. You run out of music and things to talk to yourself about; your brain is fried and tired and your body thinks it should be sleeping because you've been sitting still for so long. In that state, the bizarre and unlikely seem a lot more reasonable to believe in, and at night, a ghost breathing down your neck in the back seat seems a distinct possibility.

Andrew C. Piazza

It was dark and quiet and lonely, and Gavin Hawthorne felt like he'd been driving for eighteen days rather than eighteen hours. The inside of his eyelids seemed to be made of some sort of heavy sandpaper, begging to close over his eyes and scratch his corneas along the way. Everything about him felt stale; his clothes, his hair, even the air he dragged into his lungs. His headlights showed him the same endless stretch of yellow dashes he'd been following ever since dawn and all the way through dusk, and almost as an excuse to stop staring at them, he glanced in the rear view mirror.

Somebody was sitting in the back seat.

He spun around in a panic, twisting in the seat to get a look at the intruder and get his hands up in front of his face as a shield in case the guy was armed. The car drifted out of the right lane and gravel noisily churned up amongst his tires, and his headlights now lit up grass and trees.

It was nothing. A part of the formless jumble of junk in his back seat had taken on the appearance of a hunched-down killer in the dark and the quiet and the fatigue that buzzed in Gavin's skull.

He jerked the wheel back around, cutting back onto the road just before his tires hit the grass. His heart was bumping a panicked rhythm against the inside of his ribcage, and his limbs felt like an electric jolt had just shot through them.

"Stupid!" he said, shaking his head and then the rest of his body, ridding himself of the trickling fingers of fear which still tickled along his skin. "Almost ran off the damn road, genius!"

He stuck his fingers into the paper bag sitting next to him and dug out a few French fries. They were cold, but they gave his mouth and his mind something to do other than think about the shape his mind had conjured in the back seat.

He looked back again, shaking his head one more time at his own foolishness. There it was, right there, a jacket slumped over a box of books, the reality behind the mirage.

After a few more long minutes of the monotonous hum of his tires on the road, though, it didn't seem quite so stupid. Right there, the way the jacket's hood poked up just a little bit, it did look like the top of a man's head, slumped down over his shoulders as if to reduce his profile.

Gavin cracked the driver's side door with his left hand to switch on the interior light. It was a little ritual he'd been forced to learn as a result of his car being an '88 POS edition… Piece Of Shit. By now, cracking the door open to turn on the light was as automatic as hitting a switch, and he laughed a little at his skittishness. There it was. Just a jacket, slumped across a cardboard box.

"Going to need a night light, next," he muttered to himself.

He was just tired and bored and slowly succumbing to road hypnosis, he decided. No, not just tired… exhausted. Beyond bored, as well. His entire collection of road tunes were burned through long ago, and he didn't feel like any repeats just now. Nothing good on the radio, either. He'd been talking to himself for the better part of an hour already, and there was nothing left to say.

That asshole back at the last truck stop hadn't helped, either, telling him that freaky story about the accident. What had he been thinking, telling that story to an obviously road-weary and susceptible guy with circles under his eyes and at least another three hours to go?

He rolled down his window, letting the cold air blast his face and stir him back to reality again. Not far to go, now. Three hours. After eighteen, he could do three standing on his head.

Five minutes after he shut the window, Gavin began to feel a strange pressure fill up the car. It was more than just the stillness of the air; it seemed like the sides of the car were closing in on him like the close walls of a coffin. His skin itched and felt like it was covered with grease, like he should scrape it off with a shard of sharp metal.

On top of that, there was the feeling of somebody watching him.

That unsettling pressure of someone reading over your shoulder, or staring intently at you from a nearby table in a restaurant. He could feel it creeping up on him, filling up the back seat like a noxious gas.

He cracked the door to turn on the interior light again and looked in the rear view. Just a jacket, slumped across a cardboard box. Nothing.

The light chased away the feeling for only a few moments. It crept back in, slowly, like a dog chased away from a table scrap but determined to get at it eventually.

Don't make me go there alone.

"Stupid jerk," he muttered to himself, but this time, it wasn't himself that he was rebuking but the guy behind the counter of the truck stop he'd left an hour ago.

Terrible accident, that guy had said. One car swerved, another car swerved to miss it. First car, nothing happened, family of four's Dad hit the brakes hard and brought them to a shuddering stop in the middle of the highway just past the truck stop they were sitting in. Second car, well, that guy wasn't so lucky. He'd been thrown out of the window when he hit hard in the bottom of a ditch. By the time the ambulance got there, he was pretty much done for.

"I knew the guy riding that ambulance," the storyteller had said. "He said when they got there, this guy, he was all torn up and bloody, piece of his skull busted open and you could see his brains and all that. Anyway, he said when he came up on the guy, he was just staring into the night, breathing real shallow. But his eyes were focused, you know, not dull and all that. You know what he said?"

"Who, the paramedic?" Gavin had asked.

"No, the other guy, the one who died. He said, 'Don't make me go there alone'. Then he died. Creepy."

No kidding. Too creepy to tell to a man who was already fighting off the effects of road hypnosis. Not half an hour before he'd stopped, for gas and food he really didn't need, Gavin had made up and spoken out an imaginary argument between he and his uncle, the one who was always pointing out how he'd screwed up his life lately. For twenty minutes, he argued at the air, imagining what his uncle would say, yelling his retorts to the mute, slanted glass of his windshield. It was after that little episode that he realized he needed to get out of his tiny wheeled metal box and walk around a bit.

And then that guy had to go and tell him a story about a recent accident out in front of the truck stop, and now his mind was going batty.

Not even an hour. Not even an hour after he'd stopped, and his mind was already playing tricks on him. But he couldn't stop now. Only three hours to go, nothing at all, but he'd never get there if he kept stopping every time his mind got a little fuzzy. Better to just push his way through it.

His tires continued to hum their quiet monotone on the road, and he was just settling into a nice daze when he heard it.

"Don't make me go there alone."

Real, an actual voice, and Gavin twisted once again in his seat, and there he was, torn to pieces and sitting in the back seat of his car, reaching out with a beckoning hand.

No. No! Gavin forced himself to turn around and steady the wheel before his car hit the gravel again. The interior light came on, dissolving the figment of his imagination into the air.

Just a jacket, slumped over a cardboard box.

In the hushed dark of the back seat, though, good God, did that jacket look like something else.

"Come on, Gavin," he said loudly, chasing the last whispers of that imagined voice out into the night. "Let's get it together, here."

He slapped himself lightly on the face a few times and switched on the radio. Some tunes, a little music, a little whistling in the graveyard to keep the spooks away, that was the ticket.

Except, of course, if there really was something in the back seat, he'd never be able to hear it over the music until it was too late.

"Yeah, right, Gavin," he said, even as he clicked off the radio, "like you picked up a ghost back there with your gas and your french fries."

He considered pulling over at the next rest stop. It was probably a good idea, especially considering how he was coming apart at the seams like this. But he was so close to home, and stopping at a rest stop was just a speed bump at this point. It wasn't like he could stop to spend the night, waste the money on a motel room to only drive a little over two hours the next day. He could never justify that.

Almost reflexively, he cracked the door to click on the interior light and checked his rear view mirror.

Just a jacket, slumped over a cardboard box.

The light clicked off. He squirmed in his seat a little bit, to chase away the touch of sciatica that was beginning to spread down his right leg. It woke him up a bit and he made a mental note to remember it the next time he heard a dead guy whispering in his car.

Better, now. The idea of a spectral hitchhiker seemed a lot more foolish, even if he did glance up into his rear view more than usual. He even stopped using the interior light after a bit.

The darkness, though, seemed to close back in around him, wrapping constricting arms around his shoulders and his throat. He breathed out loudly, just to hear something other than the tires humming along, but the sound seemed swallowed up by the stale air.

Roll the window down, he thought, and when he leaned into the door to do it, caught sight of him out of the corner of his eye.

He didn't over-react this time, none of that spinning around and driving into a ditch for him. He just froze stock-still, keeping his eyes forward while concentrating on what his peripheral vision was picking up. It was a man, about his size, in the passenger seat. He was leaning toward Gavin.

"Don't make me go..."

"No!" Gavin shouted, and cracked the door before spinning to face the ghost.

It wasn't there. Only his reflection in the passenger side window.

Gavin checked the rear view to be sure. Just a jacket, slumped over a cardboard box.

"I gotta pull over," he decided aloud. "The hell with this. I'm going nuts, here."

He didn't feel nuts, though. He felt watched. He felt aware of influences and entities most people laughed at the mere mention of. He felt like someone was gazing intently at him, with more than mere curiosity in mind.

He scratched at his head with his hands, shaking himself to chase away a shudder which always seemed to want to come but never did. He tried the radio again, but turned it off in a second when he heard something in the back seat.

No interior light this time, and no looking. He didn't want to tip his hand. If it was there, really there, he wanted to see it in full, no tricks of the light, no playing with his mind, just the fully bared face of the thing that stared at him from the back seat.

The radio clicked off. His entire body focused in on his ears, straining for any tiny disturbance in the stolid air of the back seat. There was nothing, and he strained further, practically ignoring the road which passed by in little yellow dashes.

Perhaps... there. It was there. Breathing. Slight, so slight it was almost indiscernible. It was the breathing of a man who could barely breathe.

Gavin fought down the urge to hit the interior light and spin around on his tormentor. Instead, he kept his eyes front, allowing himself to look in the rear view mirror with only his peripheral vision.

This is so stupid, he told himself, but his internal voice seemed wavering and unsure. *What do you expect to see back there, dummy?*

What he saw, was a vague shape move slowly toward him from

the back seat, as if a passenger might do if he wanted to speak to the driver more clearly.

His teeth began to tingle; his heart pounded out a feverish rhythm on the inside of his chest. Adrenaline poured into his bloodstream; it made him feel like he'd been up for days and had just drank a pot of coffee. His seatbelt chafed across his shoulder, and he unlatched it so he could spin and face his tormentor that much faster.

It's almost right on top of me, he thought. *Right on top of me!*

He couldn't move, though. Couldn't spin and crack the door for the overhead light and end up just staring at a jacket and some cardboard boxes. He had to see it. He had to see it for real if it were really there, and finally put an end to these mind-games it was playing with him. Maybe he could say something to it, communicate somehow.

Maybe it doesn't want to just talk, he thought, forcing his hands to grip the wheel tightly and keep his body steady as the shape moved closer to him.

Now it was past where he could see it in the rear view mirror. He became acutely aware of the skin on the right side of his neck, where the face of the thing in the back seat would now hover. If it had a face. If it were really there. Moving almost of its own accord, his hand cracked the door handle... not opening it enough to click on the light, just enough to give him a head start on it.

He thought through the story of the accident, of the man dying alone. That man hadn't been able to see that he wasn't alone when he had to face whatever he had seen with his dying eyes.

No, that wasn't right. He had known there was somebody there with him, otherwise he wouldn't have spoken. They just weren't dying with him.

That was what he was after. Somebody to die with him. Somebody to accompany him on that long drive home.

"Don't make me go there alone," the thing in the back whispered to him, and when Gavin felt the warm tickle of breath on the edge of his neck, he recoiled away from the voice with a scream. The already-cracked door gave away under his weight, and the next thing he knew, he was falling out into the whistling night air, his neck still tingling where hot breath had caressed it.

*   *   *

"Ah, Christ!" the paramedic exclaimed, once he got a sight of the corpse. "This guy looks like a chunk of hamburger!"

The state patrolman who had been first on the scene looked up from his clipboard, where he was currently taking notes on the accident scene, and said, "Yeah, it's a messy one, isn't it?"

"Where's the other car?"

"No other car," the state cop answered. "Just this guy. Ran off of the road."

"Here?" the paramedic looked around at the long, straight stretch of highway. "What was he, drunk or something?"

"Won't know until the tox screen comes in from the Coroner's office," the patrolman said.

"I'll tell you what it looks like to me," he added after a moment. "It looks like he tried to jump out of his own car, something caught on to him, and he dragged along the road and then the underbrush until the car finally hit this tree."

The paramedic looked the body over. "That's some crazy shit. It was probably the seat belt. Tangled around his foot."

The state cop nodded. "Yeah. Probably."

A Fine Cigar

Another of my early stories written while I was still living in Atlanta; those who lived in that city in the late '90s might recognize some of the Buckhead clubs that Robby finds himself in throughout the course of his adventures. This story is also a bit of a warm-up to an as-yet unpublished novel using these particular baddies. I'll let you know when it's ready.

Andrew C. Piazza

"There's nothing quite like a fine cigar."

Robby Jenkin's clichéd statement was made to no one in particular; it was more of an oblique compliment directed toward the smoldering tube of tobacco pinched between his thumb and forefinger. He rolled the cigar slowly back and forth, as if to add a tactile dimension to the cigar's cherry-wood aroma.

Robby was sitting alone… not lonely, just alone… reclined in the best couch of his favorite cigar club in the trendy Buckhead neighborhood of Atlanta. The couch he practically melded with faced a large, plate glass window overlooking the street, adding another dimension of sight to the aromatic and tactile sensations the cigar was providing. From his perch here, in the second-story club, Robby could observe the teaming traffic of half-drunk pedestrians walking, stumbling, and rushing to one or another of the dozens of bars and clubs each within a stone's throw of each other in this section of Buckhead.

The swirling sea of pedestrians laughed, pontificated, discussed, argued, and sometimes even fought, creating an intricate complexity to their movements, an unlikely choreography in which each individual's movements were unique but the sum total of the group always added up to *moving on*. Bar-hopping wasn't just a pastime in Buckhead; it was more like a necessity, the way these people moved. It was as if they would stifle and choke if they remained in one place too long, as if they migrated in the constant fear that somewhere, somehow, they could be having a better time than they were having now, no matter how good 'now' happened to be.

    Robby smiled at them, amused in a detached sort of way, blocking out the overload of the Latin band belting out a tune in the wide room adjacent to his. The dance floor was in there, packed to the hilt with men nearly identical to him… dressed classy but casual, demure enough to be comfy but flashy enough to advertise. Those men moved with women who were largely female variations on the same theme; young, trim, gorgeous in a glamorous, dare-you-not-to-look fashion, most of them well experienced in plastic surgery, all of them dressed to thrill in sprayed-on miniskirts constantly threatening to pop up over their tiny waistlines if they moved their legs the slightest bit too far apart.

    The dance floor wasn't Robby's scene, however, even though he would've fit in perfectly with the other twentysomethings in his tailored suit and shirt with no tie. He simply liked a good cigar, with all of the high-class accoutrements that seemed to surround them, which was why he lounged in the VIP room set apart from the dance floor and main bar area. It was a bit quieter here; he could ignore the band if he concentrated, and he loved the view of Buckhead he could enjoy from this couch. So he sat, smoking his cigar, running the index finger of his left hand around and around the rim of his glass, which was almost down to the last bit of his favorite single-malt whiskey.

Excellent cigar, he nearly moaned aloud, as he pulled in the musty, mildly harsh smoke, rolling the vapors around and up to the back of his throat, toying with inhaling it, until at last he blew it out in a reluctant stream that dissipated quickly. *They really do have excellent cigars here.*

He'd burned his way through nearly half of his smoldering companion before he began to notice the unusual change in his thoughts and senses. Robby always felt relaxed, even snug, when he sat on this couch and smoked, and always felt mildly intellectual as well, but this time it was... different. He didn't just watch the people walking and talking and laughing below him in the street, he *felt* them; felt their joy, anger, sadness, silliness, all in the context of the inebriation which intensified their emotions to varying degrees.

He didn't just smell his cigar, either; he experienced it, his awareness floating amongst the scattered molecules of smoke that drifted from its burning tip or blew lazily from between his slightly numb lips. It was as if he could *feel* its smell, join with it, become one with it.

The uneven, coarse surface of the cigar itself suddenly felt like a series of crags and rifts worthy of a lifetime's exploration. His thumb ran along every miniscule crack, bump, and fold, as if he were a blind man reading Braille, but not just reading it, *living* it, finding inspiration in every imagined word found along the rough paper's length.

This is... fucking amazing, he found himself thinking, not concerned just yet with how his senses had become so distorted.

No, not distorted, he decided. *Enhanced, modified, intensified... but certainly not distorted.*

A distant smile curled his lips as he explored this strange new world of sensation. Robby had always been a sensual man; delighting in anything that could stimulate any of the Big Five. This was entirely fresh and exciting to him; all five senses melding into one, and yet also becoming more than themselves, and each individual sense hinting that there were other senses, as yet untapped, which could be revealed in all their complexity if he would just open his mind a little wider and let them in.

"Can I get you a refill?"

The words came languidly, luxuriously; Robby actually felt them slide into his auditory canal, could feel the vibrations on the tiny hairs of his middle ear, and felt the impulses the hairs created on the nerves sending electronic messages to his cerebral cortex. He knew, even before he turned, which waitress had come to offer a refill; her image was splashed all over her words, like a fingerprint, but more intense, more like the scent a dog must recognize when it sniffs a couch its owner has been lying on.

He gazed up at her, noticing in a moment a million discrete sensations emanating from her like rays from a candle. He saw her outer, cordial self, the standard issue bearing of any server in any restaurant. He felt her inner, jaded attitude toward her job, the boredom of the same old, same old, normally easily concealed to the world but laid bare to Robby's newfound abilities.

He felt concern and distaste, mixed nimbly together, directed toward him. She thought he was drunk, he realized, as he waved her off. The substance in his glass, whose harsh aroma he could vividly smell, suddenly felt like... sickness. Given his typical affection for whiskey, he was more than a little surprised to discover that to his newly enhanced senses, alcohol felt like sickness. He felt its potential to dull his senses, dull his experiences, and with a disgusted gesture,

Robby dropped it to the floor.

He felt it fall, felt the ripples in the air that the glass's passage created, and felt it impact with the floor, mostly through vibrations in his feet. He heard the quarter-shot's worth of whiskey slosh out of the glass and onto the carpeting. Then, he sensed the waitress's annoyance, felt her words, heard them in his head an instant before they were spoken.

"Oh, man!"

She'd only whispered them, unwilling to alienate herself from any of the other potentially drunk customers, but for Robby, it was really a shout, magnified a thousand-fold by the intensity of emotion that accompanied it. He saw her walking off to find a bouncer; not watching her with his eyes, as she was behind him, but feeling her mind, feeling her attitude.

Perhaps I should leave, Robby considered, pulling on the cigar yet again, mingling in with the smoke in his mind. His sensual acuity intensified even more, more than he believed possible, and he found himself unable to stand. He felt vaguely high, completely tuned in... but *excessively* tuned in, unable to act, as if his nervous system was so overwhelmed in taking in information that it found acting on that information impossible.

His overloaded mind registered the approach of the bouncer before the man was even in the room. Robby's enhanced senses felt the bouncer's hand on his arm before it actually closed like a vice around his wrist, and he felt himself get pulled to his feet an instant before it actually occurred; but his mind didn't do a damn thing about it, it just registered the occurrences and nothing else.

"Would you come with me please, sir?"

Robby forced himself to ignore the words, ignore the

simmering threat he felt behind them, ignore how the bouncer's heart began to beat fast in anticipation of action. Instead, he focused on forcing his feet to move, step, take him out of here, before the bouncer could act out the aggression Robby sensed lurking behind his superficially polite request.

It wasn't working. Instead, Robby became enthralled with how the blood pulsed through his feet, through its intricate pattern of vessels; the arteries, throbbing slightly, to the capillaries, where nutrients leached out into the tissue, then funneling back into veins...

"Please, sir. Come with me."

A distant fear ate at Robby; a fear that he was paralyzed and would never be able to move again, but would only able to feel in enhanced, extraordinary intensity the beating that the muscle-bound bouncer was about to inflict on him. He realized the waitress was leaving the bouncer's side and felt her intention to inform her manager of the minor scene he was creating. And then, suddenly, his feet moved, and his legs as well, walking him towards the exit, albeit a bit unsteadily.

Focusing on the result was the key, he realized; picturing it in his head, as if the event had already happened. He'd seen himself walking out of the door, and then, it happened.

Robby halted himself just before the bouncer tugged on his arm to stop him. He even felt the manager approaching him before he actually arrived, as he drew in another hit of the cigar smoke merely by imagining it as having already occurred.

He distinctly saw a handful of cigar smoke molecules suck right up the tall, ponytailed manager's nostrils; saw the instant recognition in the manager's eyes, felt the terror that followed said recognition an instant later. Robby could see words forming in his mind, but couldn't quite make them out until they were actually spoken.

"Take him out onto the walkway," slipped into Robby's ear, "and get Frank and Nick."

Once again, he was able to anticipate the bouncer's movements, letting the big doorman lead him out onto a walkway which ran along the length of the second-story club. Below him was a sharply sloping parking lot packed with cars and people weaving their way between them. He could see annoyance on the bouncer's face, could even see himself through the bouncer's eyes; how his wavy black hair fluttered lightly in the night breeze, how the cut of his jacket matched his lean physique perfectly, every detail about himself.

Then, he felt things take a turn for the worse. He felt the bouncer dismissed even before the manager raised an indifferent hand to do it, felt the approach of Frank and Nick, and sensed the mild relief the manager felt as they strode to his side. Frank was just as tall as the manager, easily over six feet, and shared his preference for ponytails and dark suits. They looked similar enough to potentially be brothers. Nick, on the other hand, was short and stocky, with a clean-shaven head and dark goatee. Like the other two, he was dressed in a tailored suit. Both men felt confused to Robby; aware something was amiss, but not sure what, exactly.

"What's up?" escaped Nick's mouth. The words were almost visible to Robby, like a dialogue balloon in a cartoon.

"This," the tall, gangly manager replied, plucking the cigar from Robby's hand and holding it up for display in front of the other two men. Both of them sniffed the smoldering tip carefully.

"Oh, shit," Nick said an instant after Robby saw the words form in his head.

"What do we do?" Frank asked, but Robby already knew the answer to that.

He was still somewhat dazed by the overwhelming effects of the cigar, but the malice he felt evident in Frank's mind began to slowly draw him out of his stupor. They were going to hurt him, maybe even kill him; he could see it in all of their faces, feel it beating in their hearts. They just had to work up the nerve to say it out loud in order to convince themselves that killing him was their only alternative.

"Where the fuck did he get this? Here?" Nick asked. Robby could tell he was trying to skirt the issue of what to do with him.

"How could he? You know we keep them separate from the others. Unless somebody mixed a box in by accident..."

Forget it, Robby felt forming in Frank's mind. "It doesn't matter where he got it. It's obvious he's never used one before, look at him. The only thing that matters is..."

Robby tuned them out; he already knew the outcome of the conversation. The fear growing within him spurred him to send his enhanced thoughts out into the city, searching for some way, any way, to run like hell from these three conspirators.

"Keep your voice down!" one of them whispered, or perhaps merely thought; Robby couldn't tell which anymore. Panic began to swirl through him as he realized the three men were now blocking any possible escape; right or left along the walkway, and even back into the club. He didn't have much time left; he could feel their murderous intentions growing exponentially within them, like wispy clouds gathering together into thick thunderheads.

And then, he saw his escape. He felt it, sensed it, up over the railing he was leaning against, out into the air whose individual molecules he could feel bouncing around merrily amongst themselves. It was at that moment that he understood he could control those molecules of air, merely by thinking about it, by seeing it happen, in the same way that he saw his legs walk him out of the club earlier. He had only to see it as having already occurred, and...

And before the thought was finished, he'd snatched the stubby cigar from the manager's hand and leapt in a single wild move over the rail, his enhanced mind carrying his body higher than his mere flesh-and-blood legs were capable of. The air became thick beneath him, and he floated down to the asphalt on a cushion of air molecules packed tightly together beneath his feet. He landed heavily a few moments later, the condensed air dissipating once he was safely on the ground, and distantly he felt the surprise, shock, and rage of the three men he'd left behind on the second floor walkway.

"Holy sh... did you see that?" a woman shouted, so drunk Robby could feel her inebriation drowning out the other pedestrians' alcoholic auras, like a spotlight drowning out the glow of a birthday candle.

He ignored her, forcing aside the flood of sensations emanating from her and all the other people around him, focusing instead on the image of running across the busy side street before him, down the sidewalk and away from his would-be captors. Once begun is half done, his mother used to say, and in this case, once begun was actually all done, because Robby found himself standing in front of yet another club that was pulsing and thumping with loud music and flashing lights. It was more than merely the music; the walls of the club seemed to throb and pulse like a savagely beating heart. The people inside were pulsing as well; he could feel their... auras, he supposed... pulsing in time with the music's heavy beat.

After him! he felt from the direction of the cigar club. Once again, it came not in discrete words, but as a feeling, an intent to chase, an intent directed toward him. He knew it belonged to the three men from the cigar club, and he immediately spun and found himself disappearing into the pulsating club.

He practically floated past the doorman, barely registering on the big man's mind, and discovered he was staring up at an underage red-haired girl in tight jeans and a tighter T-shirt gyrating suggestively atop the beer-slicked bar. Everything about her shouted the same thing to all of his senses, the girl's drunken mind repeating the same concept again and again, continuously.

They're watching me... They want me... They're watching me... They want me...

Robby pulled himself away, tried to clear his head, but the bar was filled with people, filled with thumping noise, and each sound and light and person and smell had a million stories to tell, all wanting to be heard now, NOW, and Robby found it impossible to concentrate, he was on overload...

There he is! flashed across his mind, a triumphant feeling scented with the image of Frank from the cigar club. Robby managed to visualize himself running down a small ramp to the back room's dance floor, jostling aside sweaty, feverish twentysomethings on his dark, steamy trip to the rear exit. He could feel their thoughts as he passed them; anger, frustration, annoyance, all intensified by alcohol, all directed at him. He could feel his pursuers, as well, caught up in a sudden surge of pressing bodies as the unpredictable tide of club-hoppers blocked their path.

Then, at last, he was free, back out onto the fresh air of the street, far enough away from the overload of sensations to begin to block them out somewhat. He pictured himself running, after driving away the flood of sensations from the people surrounding him as best he could. He was only capable of holding off the thoughts of the other pedestrians for so long, however, and soon Robby found himself leaning queasily up against a telephone pole, perceiving against his will the intentions of everybody on the street.

Urgency... *We have to get there, we'll be late!*

Indecision... *Where should we go next?*

Anger... *How could she do this to me?*

Frustration... *I just want to go home!*

At last, he was able to run a bit further on, encouraged by the distinct lack of thoughts from the cigar club killers in his mind. He rested after a block or two, trying with considerable difficulty to decide where to go, and unconsciously reached out to touch the old-fashioned stone wall of the pub next to him.

A flood of images shot through his mind; he saw the people inside, felt them drinking dark and earthy beer. He could even taste their drinks and feel the smooth cool pint glasses in his hands. The images filled his head to bursting; he felt himself floating from mind to mind, catching snippets of either thoughts or conversations, he couldn't tell which anymore.

Robby pulled his hand away with a Herculean effort and forced himself to concentrate. He experimented with reaching out with his newfound sensitivity, trying to find his pursuers, to no effect. He knew they had to be out here on the streets, somewhere, and when he finally felt a slight twinge (*where is he?*) he shot off down the block, not very far, and ducked into another loud, pulsing club.

He handed off his cover charge before it was even asked for, ignoring the stamp the doorman wanted to mark on his hand.

Instead, he headed for the restrooms, hoping to find a moment's sanctuary in there from the blinding assault his senses now suffered. He almost didn't make it; there were several people on powerful narcotics here, their chaotic thoughts and emotions scraping the inside of his skull with a raspy edge. Finally, though, he pushed his way through the bathroom door, nearly collapsing from the heat and the noise and the feelings.

Three young women, any of whom would've fit in perfectly at the cigar club he'd just left, were snorting cocaine off of mirrors set on the bathroom counter in plain view of Robby and the world. He saw the individual particles suck up their nostrils, felt the instant hit of the drug as it crossed their mucous membranes, experienced the rush of energy and indestructibility each one felt. After a glance over at him, two of the women left immediately, one mostly ignoring him, the other mentally marking him as a pervert before pushing rudely past him. Another moment, and two more women left the stalls they'd just been chatting merrily between and checked their look in the scuffed mirror hanging on the wall, not even noticing Robby until they were almost out of the door. They traded a shocked look (*A guy!*) as they, too, pushed their way out of the bathroom.

Just the bathroom door cracking open was too much. The sounds and smells and thoughts poured in, overwhelming Robby, and he shoved the door shut in the faces of the line of pretty young things hopping up and down in pain.

Hey!

I have to pee!

What the hell is that guy doing?

Robby forced them out and set his back against the door, braced himself against it as some of the girls tried to push their way in.

Hey!

Let me in!

I have to pee!

"Whoa," came from somewhere behind his clenched-shut eyelids, "what kind of shit are you on?"

He was pretty sure it was spoken and not just thought, so he struggled to block out the angry mob beyond the door and open his eyes to examine his new companion. She hadn't spoken harshly; rather, Robby felt bemusement in her words, genuine interest at such a bizarre turn of events.

She was pretty, like most of the other women here; tallish, blonde, with long legs extending provocatively out from a short sundress. Robby suspected her thin legs were the result of the cocaine rather than exercise. He could feel it, feel how her body was used to being high, feel how her nasal septa were so eaten away that they were about to perforate and bleed profusely. She was seriously high now; Robby didn't need the cigar's special endowments to know that. A glance at her glassed-over eyes was enough.

"I just," he heard himself saying, "I just had to get out of there. It was too much."

"Bad trip?" she asked, her curiosity mingling with the distant hope Robby might have some LSD left over for her.

He laughed once. "No. It's... incredible. Nothing like it. Better than E, better than anything."

Her intense interest washed over him immediately, and he felt how she instantly changed from moderately interested observer to intent seductress. Her whole body dynamic changed; she slinked toward him, catlike, smoothing her hands down her dress to draw attention to her long legs as she cooed coyly.

"Really?" she purred, pulling close to him. "Do you have any more?"

Her sexuality was almost stifling. It was everywhere about her; her smell, her look, her feel, the way she stood so close to him he could feel the heat emanating from her gorgeous body. Her intent made his blood boil over; he couldn't take it, he was hornier than he'd ever been in his life, sprouting an erection as hard as a pipe and stabbing the seductress unashamedly in the hip with it.

She didn't shy away, though; in fact, she pressed harder against it, sliding her hands up to his chest. She brought her face close to his, smiling coquettishly, gazing at him with her glassy eyes. The overwhelming pressure wave of her libido completely drowned out the urgent mob outside, the smells of the bathroom, and indeed, every other sensation assaulting him. Robby numbly drew out the cigar he'd secured in his jacket pocket, holding it up in surrender to her.

She frowned, and the aura of sexuality surrounding her wavered for a moment, replaced by a sense of confusion. Robby was able in that instant to distinguish her feeling as seduction, not sexuality. She wanted to turn him on for a share in whatever mystery drug he had, and she'd done a good job of it.

"What's..." she began to ask, when the door behind Robby smashed inwards with tremendous force, flinging them both against a stall's flimsy wall.

Robby tried to orient himself, but there were too many sensations, all flooding in at once.

Who are they?

About time!

There he is! Get him!
Who's she?
Get her too!

Then, he experienced the sensation of being pulled out of the bathroom, into the teeming, pounding club, vaguely aware his cigar-club pursuers had caught up with him at last. He tried to focus, tried to visualize himself fighting back, but the lights and music were pounding him like a jackhammer, the confusion and attention of all the people in the club completely disorienting him. It was too much, sensory overload, and he faded out, drowned helplessly in a sea of sensuality.

* * *

When the world came back, swirling uncertainly into focus, Robby found his enhanced senses were still somewhat intact. They were nowhere near as strong as before, though, and he knew they were fading fast.

He felt without opening his eyes that he was sitting in a chair with his hands tied behind his back. The townhouse he was in wasn't very far from the Buckhead clubs; he could still smell and feel the people reveling there. The residence itself was splashed with the scent of the manager, and Robby could feel all three cigar-club killers waiting impatiently for him to come to.

The girl was there, as well. She was scared out of her mind, crying, every sob an hour-long whimper for mercy in his supernaturally enhanced ears. She was well past frantic, and too high to think of anything but her desire to escape. He could feel in her mind that she was convincing herself she'd do anything, anything at all, no matter how sick or perverted, just to get herself out of this dire situation.

"I think he's coming down," the manager said, as Robby opened his eyes.

"You want to know how much I know," Robby started for them. "How I knew about..."

He frowned, unable to place the name. He could see the plant, see what it looked like, where it grew, how rare and precious it was, but for the life of him, he couldn't read the name in their heads.

"It's called Saishon," Nick said. "That's right, Robby, we can feel you too. We each took a little hit while we were looking for you. Nothing like the dose you inhaled; a fifth of that, maybe. You took in more than most of us do during our vision quests..."

Enough, Robby felt the manager think, and Nick fell silent.

"Please," the girl sobbed, bloody snot trickling string-like out of her cocaine-ravaged nose, "Please just let me go. I don't know anything, I'll do anything you want, you can do me, I won't tell, just let me go..."

"Be quiet," the manager said.

Robby found the girl's panic unnerving. Having such extreme emotions so close to him was like sitting next to a tornado. He turned to ask his captors to let her go, but they were shaking their heads before he'd even spoken.

"No good," Nick said. "We don't know how much she knows."

"What are you going to do with us?" Robby asked, small seeds of dread sprouting up throughout his stomach, watered and fed by the girl's constant, pathetic sniffling.

The three men glanced at each other, and Robby could feel

the conflict between each one and within themselves. They didn't want to, but they had to... kill them both.

"Oh, no, now," Robby said, heart beating faster and faster, as the drug began to fade and he became more and more lucid to his dire situation. "You don't have to, no, I don't... please."

He struggled at his ropes vainly, the tough fibers digging painfully into his wrists. The physical act of straining seemed to throw extra coal onto the furnace of his growing panic; the harder he struggled, the quicker his breath came, the more his mind shouted No, No, NO!

"We have..." Nick said, leaning down intimately, laying a hand on Robby's shoulder to quiet his struggles. "We have to. We *have* to. I'm sorry, really I am, but you were just in the wrong place at the wrong time."

Robby stopped his fruitless attempts at breaking his bonds and pinched his eyes shut tightly as the tears came. For some reason, perhaps because of the contradictory kindness his executioner used to pronounce his sentence, he found himself unwilling to let this person see him cry. He knew Nick was telling the truth, he could feel the remorse within him; and somehow that made it all the worse.

"You... don't have to," Robby said, eyes still clamped shut, as the girl next to him began a fresh bout of sobs and shudders.

"We do," Nick said. "We know how to hide from them, how to conduct our studies in secret, in the shadows. You, though... you're wide open. They'll see you almost instantly. They'll pick up on you in no time at all; find you, catch you, and you'll tell them everything... you won't be able to help yourself."

Who are They? Robby wondered, until a strange twinge distracted him from his would-be killer's obtuse explanation. The enhanced senses imparted from the cigar were fading fast, but he could still feel so much, like the remorse and indecision mixing in varied amounts in the minds of the three cigar-club men.

Then, beyond them, farther out in the city, he began to sense... malice. Menace. Anger, rage, hostility, all of the evil thoughts imaginable, just a twinge now, but starting to get stronger.

"...when you tell them everything," Nick was saying when he tuned back in, "you'll tell them about us. We have to prevent that. We have to protect ourselves."

The hate, the rage, was drawing closer, and Robby could tell it wasn't just one person, one source, but several, all headed directly for them, intent on...

"...never intended to hurt anybody, kill anybody... well, anybody *uninvolved*, that is... but..."

"There's something... no, some*things*... coming," Robby said.

Nick glanced over at the manager in alarm. Robby could feel sudden fear explode within them, the fear a jackrabbit feels when it knows it's been spotted, and he sensed their urge to run from this place, immediately.

"It's bullshit," the manager said, shaking his head, drawing a wicked-looking serrated pocketknife from his pants pocket and flicking it open demonstrably. "He's saying anything he can think of to stall us."

"No, I don't think so," Frank said, examining Robby closely. "I don't feel any deception..."

"Do you feel any of *them*? Hunh?" the manager asked, moving slowly toward the girl, fingering the edge of his knife experimentally.

"No, but we didn't take very much..."

"*What the fuck is happening?*" the drugged-out, panicked girl shrieked, making all of them, including Robby, jump. "Get me out of here! Somebody! Get me out of here! Help! Help me!"

"Shut her up!" the manager said, as the twinge came back to Robby, this time with a vengeance. He could feel *them* coming, feel their murderous intent, feel what they wanted to do. He felt them as dark forms hurtling towards them, to eventually run *over* them, with tearing claws and flashing teeth...

It was too much. The death he felt at the hands of the cigar-club men was at least humane; the things which raced toward the townhouse would rip his screaming body limb from limb, laughing the entire time, reveling in his pain and fear and...

"Listen!" he shouted desperately, voice cracking in undisguised terror. "There's something bad coming, really fast, really close; they want to hurt us, kill us all..."

"Shut up!" the manager said, which only drove the girl to scream even louder than before, and kick wildly at her chair in a useless attempt to break free.

Her screams were bringing them faster, drawing them like moths to a flame, but Robby knew he'd never be able to quiet her. Her panic felt like a wildfire raging out of control; even if she lived, she'd probably end up in a padded cell after this.

"Please!" he pleaded toward Nick, who was watching him curiously, perhaps trying to sense what Robby felt. "Listen! They're almost here! They're like... hate, rage, murder, all in one... thing..."

Robby shook his head, trying to clear it of the terror created by the feverishly intense wave of the faceless evil's bloody intentions. He could taste their desire to rend all five of them apart, rip them to shreds, make them scream, beg, bleed...

"Now!" he screamed, nearly knocking his chair over in his hysteria. "Now! We have to go now, they'll kill all of us, they want us all!"

"Shut up!" the manager shouted again, slapping the girl across the face savagely.

Robby wasn't sure if the manager was talking to him or to the girl, but the girl's screams slowly simmered down to moans and squeals. She rocked herself back and forth in her chair as much as her restraints would allow, murmuring terrified nonsensical phrases over and over again. He envied her, really; the mounting terror he felt, the intensity of the horrors he knew *they* wished to inflict on him, was like an unbearably loud jet engine, coming closer and closer, deafening him, threatening to drive him out of his mind.

"We're out of time! Come on!" he said, again to Nick, who seemed like he might be picking up on the bad vibes himself.

"I said, shut up!" the manager repeated.

"No, wait," Nick said, then shook his head. "Fuck this, I'm getting my gun."

No! No gun! Must run! Robby's mind screamed, laughing giddily at itself and the little rhyme it had just created. *No gun! Must run! No gun! Must run!*

They weren't going to run, though, and even if they did, they wouldn't be able to stop to take him and the girl along with them. He had to figure a way out on his own, now, before *they* came crashing down on him.

But how? he wondered. His hands were tied fast; the ropes solid, tight, unyielding...

Or were they?

He could feel the individual molecules of the rope, feel them just as he'd felt the air an instant before he'd jumped from the second story cigar club to escape his captors earlier. It was harder to feel than before; the cigar's effects were fading fast, and he really had to concentrate, block it all out, block out the overwhelming sense of impending violence, to feel the core building blocks of the ropes.

"Where are you going?" the manager said, gesturing wildly with his glittering pocketknife.

"I said," Nick answered, almost to the front door, "I'm going to get my gun. It's in the car."

Too late! They're here! Robby knew, as the looming freight-train of violent emotions derailed him mentally, nearly knocking him out. There were three of *them* headed straight for the door, and another one coming up on the front plate glass window, behind the curtains which hid Robby and the girl from the view of the streets.

He forced himself to clear his mind, to let the jet-engine fear go, and then...

Part.

Robby didn't think it, he *felt* it, and immediately his hands swung around to his thighs, free of restraints, as the burst ropes fell to the floor.

He stood up just as all hell broke loose. The front door seemed to explode inwards as if under the impact of a gigantic shotgun, throwing Nick back a half-dozen feet, riddled with wooden shrapnel and splinters. The stocky man was still alive, though, struggling to his feet painfully as three figures dashed through the destroyed front door so fast they seemed to fly. They were on Nick in an instant, rending him open from stem to stern with the long, sharp claws sprouting from their fingertips.

They were human, or at least a facsimile of human; human-sized, human-shaped, even dressed like typical human Buckhead club-hoppers. But the claws, the now-bloody claws that tore chunks of Nick away from the rest of his body and flung them carelessly around the room, those were certainly not human. Nor were their eyes; all jet black, entirely black, like a shark's eyes. Those eyes were soulless, heartless, and saw all things as prey.

"Fuck me!" the manager shouted shrilly, ignoring Robby, who staggered back numbly, disbelieving what his sight and other enhanced senses were telling him. They moved so fast, so terribly *fast*, it didn't matter if he ran, they'd be on him in an instant...

The living room window exploded inward under the weight of a fourth monstrosity. It landed directly on Frank, pinning the hapless man face-down onto the floor. Immediately, the black-eyed, half-human monster began tearing at him, ripping away skin and muscle with its awful claws, snapping off ribs with grim determination as Frank screamed and flailed and emptied his bladder and bowels involuntarily.

The girl started screaming again, louder than Robby thought possible; he was sure if he kept watching, he'd scream too, scream until his lungs burst, scream until *they* tore him apart like the others. His mind couldn't wrap itself around the way the monsters looked; just human enough for him to recognize the looks of savage glee on their faces as they tore their victims open mercilessly.

They were enjoying themselves, loving every moment of it, loving every ounce of their victim's terror, pain, and horror. Robby's mind could easily feel the intense charge they were getting out of reveling in pure evil.

The manager broke into a run for the kitchen, drawing the attention of one of the murderers, who abandoned the still-twitching

Nick to the hands of his two companions to take off in pursuit. He was fast, incredibly fast, and a full twelve feet away, he leapt inhumanly far onto the manager's back, knocking him to the kitchen floor and partly out of Robby's sight. Robby could still hear, though, and feel the manager's shrill, piercing shrieks, hear the tissue being torn from his body, and see the blood and gobbets of flesh flung across the kitchen walls from the violence of the monster's assault.

Go, go, go now! Robby gulped, backing away from the ripping monsters, unaware he was also backing away from any possible exits. *Get the fuck out of here before they set their eyes on you!*

Too late. One of the duet busy yanking loops of Nick's entrails out of his gaping abdomen raised his blood-splattered face and looked straight at Robby, and in a frantic heartbeat, he was up and on top of...

...the girl in the chair, who'd already screamed herself hoarse, but still belted out a dry, coughing rattle, the ghost of a scream, a scream in spirit, if not reality. The shark-eyed monster stood triumphantly over her for a moment, surveying her, admiring her drop-dead looks, which were evident even through the smeared mascara and tears and terror marring her complexion. Robby realized that her terror actually made her all the more attractive to the creature, who grinned wide, showcasing a mouth full of awkwardly jutting fangs.

"Mmmm, you're pretty!" the fiend said, as best he could around his misshapen teeth. "I could just eat you up!"

Robby could feel the girl's heart practically burst as the monster bent down and bit her savagely on the cheek, shaking his head grimly as his fangs drove into her muscle and bone. His claws tore at her, tore away her dress, ripped open her skin, and with a savage gesture, he yanked her bodily out of her chair and tossed her face up onto the ground.

Her hands were still tied behind her back, yet she squirmed uselessly, blood pouring out of her mangled face and a dozen superficial wounds. Her assailant leapt on top of her, tearing away the remnants of her sundress, bending over to bite deeply into one of her exposed breasts.

The girl's voice somehow returned as she struggled underneath her murderer, who Robby knew intended to rape her, take her by force at the same time he tore her ravaged body apart. He forgot her instantly, though, forgot them all, all of the screams, all of the ripping, tearing sounds he could hear, all of the horror and terror he could feel coming off of them, forgot everything when he realized the last monster was finished tearing Nick to pieces and was now staring greedily at *him*.

He felt its savage anticipation, the certainty of an imminent kill flooding the mind of the monster staring at him. He knew he couldn't run and certainly couldn't hope to fight this creature; he was doomed, and just as the monster leapt for him, clawed arms spreading wide, he felt...

I can fly.

He *felt* it, just like the feel of 'Part' which had released him from his ropes. He felt it, felt the idea of flying, and before his mind could register the event, his stomach surged with the sensation of hurling backwards through the air. Through the smashed living room window he flew, until he landed with a thump on the lawn.

It took a moment for Robby to realize he was still alive, that he hadn't been thrown backward by the monster, but had flown backward of his own volition using the same strange, fading powers which had saved him twice before that evening. The wind was knocked out of him, and there was an ache in his ribs he knew wouldn't soon fade, but he dragged himself to his feet all the same and stumbled across the dark lawn. He slowed only long enough to climb frantically over the wrought iron fence enclosing the townhouse's front lawn. Then, like a shot, he was off down the dimly-lit sidewalk. He ran back toward the clubs, toward the side street where he remembered his car was parked and waiting.

A crash of glass erupted behind him, and he felt without looking that two of the blood-stained killers were in pursuit. His enhanced powers were weakening, fast; the only reason he could feel their thoughts (*run, little jackrabbit, we can catch you*) was their raw intensity and sheer amplitude.

He knew they were right, too; he had a tiny head start that would disappear within seconds. He had to do it again, had to muster his rapidly fading resources and hurl himself a safe distance away using the fading enhanced powers of his mind.

Fly, he thought, to no avail; the sounds and the feel of his pursuers distracting him.

Fly! he thought desperately, as the flapping sounds of his pursuers' feet on the pavement behind him became louder, and then stuttered, as they both prepared to pounce.

I can fly, he felt, and his body hurled through the air, down the street, for seven or eight blocks at least, before he slowed to a halt. His stumbling feet tried to keep up, but were woefully inadequate for the job, and he fell forward to the ground, scraping both palms open on the rough surface of the sidewalk.

Robby ignored his bleeding hands, crawling to his feet awkwardly and shuffling off towards his car. He was now on the outskirts of the clubs; homes and apartment complexes were gradually giving way to shops and bars. Several throngs of people stared and pointed at his sweaty, haggard form, which had literally flown in from the darkness.

He ignored them as well, trying to feel behind him for any clue about his pursuers. He guessed they wouldn't dare to chase after him through crowds of witnesses in their blood-soaked state, but guessing just didn't cut it this evening, so he searched back the way he came with whatever cigar-imparted powers he might have left.

Robby's special senses were gone now, however, spent entirely by that last, desperate flight from his predators. At least his mind was clear, now that it was unencumbered by the overload of sensations accompanying the cigar's smoke.

He came upon his dark blue Range Rover almost before he knew it, leaping inside and tearing into traffic within a few reckless seconds. A black convertible nearly broad-sided him, and in his haste, he scraped along several parked cars as he sped off down the street. Robby laughed; at this point, he could care less about dents or dings on his car. One positive effect of the horrors he'd seen that night; they certainly put the little things in life into perspective for him.

He drove for several blocks at break-neck speed, visions of the inhuman killers still skipping his heart's beat. At last, he calmed himself enough to slow to a normal pace, once he was convinced imminent death wasn't visible in the rear view mirror.

Another two miles, and Robby's stomach began doing back flips around his abdominal cavity. He cut wildly across a lane of traffic to dart into a parking lot, with barely enough time to throw the vehicle into Park and get the door open before emptying his guts all over the pavement. Once that was over, he leaned back into his open car door, breathing out long and hard in relief and exhaustion.

"It's okay," he reassured himself aloud, even though he kept glancing feverishly around the deserted parking lot, all 360 degrees, even underneath the Range Rover, to insure there weren't any shark-eyed killers sneaking up on him. "It's okay, you're okay, it's all over."

Well, not quite, he admitted to himself, reaching into his jacket pocket to draw out the secret he'd managed to keep from Frank and Nick and the cigar club manager.

He'd bought three cigars at the club that night, identical triplets born from the same box. He looked over the two he still had left, miraculously unbroken in spite of the evening's adventures, and found a smile curling his lips in curious defiance of the terror still clenching its fist in his stomach.

He'd always been a sensual man, after all, and this was the ultimate in sensation. He understood now how junkies kept coming back for more and more of the drug, even though they knew that it was killing them. He was about to take that same risk, wasn't he? In spite of his fear, in spite of his horror, he knew he couldn't pass up what these cigars could give him.

Besides, what choice do I have? he quickly rationalized. *Those things might know who I am, and if I don't get some answers, what I don't know probably will kill me.*

He studied his strange cigars more intently, running one lengthwise under his nose, inhaling its essence. Robby could feel the powers stored within its rough brown wrapper, just a hint, just a tease of what waited for him, and found the desire to indulge nearly unbearable. The cigars weren't much, not much at all in the face of the horrors he'd just witnessed, but they'd be a start.

Nick had let an awful lot slip. There were more of these

plants, somewhere, and people who knew how to use them to see... all kinds of things, Robby supposed. With the help of the two cigars, which he assured himself he would use sparingly, he could find them, and try to seek out guides and advisors while avoiding the Black-Eyed Men.

And if *they* found him? Well, Nick wasn't the only resident of Atlanta to keep a gun in his car. Robby reached around behind him, found the Glock pistol hidden under his driver's seat, and tucked it into his waistband. He'd stay armed round-the-clock; no need to make the same mistake Nick had.

It's risky, he cautioned himself, *risky beyond comparison to anything you've ever done before.*

But the reward, he answered himself, *is also beyond anything you've ever done before. Besides, be honest... like you're ever going to be able to go back to your normal life after this. You know you're going to, so just... do it.*

Robby studied the cigars in his hand for a moment longer before drawing a silver Zippo lighter from another jacket pocket and flicking it open with practiced ease. Quickly, almost impetuously, he clamped one of the cigars between his teeth and rolled his thumb along the lighter's flint, sparking it to life with an almost imperceptible whoosh as the fumes caught fire.

A flicker of flame, a deep inhale, and Robby felt the rush of his enhanced senses return almost immediately. He smiled as he watched the strange smoke waft up from between his fingers. "That is definitely one fine cigar."

Kept Secrets

Like "A Fine Cigar", this story is what I like to think of as a warm up for a novel-length work. Sometimes, I like to explore an idea tangentially related to a novel I'm working up; it might be a spin-off, it might be an expansion to some event mentioned in passing at some point in the novel, or it might be a completely self-contained story that simply shares the same universe as the novel. "Kept Secrets" is an example of the last.

Andrew C. Piazza

Albert's voice echoed off of the hollow air of the car's back seat. "It's time for you to learn my secret."

I glanced over at John Kilpatrick, my partner of eight years, and caught him trying to prevent a snort of derision from escaping his lips. His features were mostly obscured by the dense gloom enveloping the police cruiser we'd commandeered, the only source of illumination being the muted, greenish glow emanating from the cruiser's console.

He was tall and clean-cut, the way most people picture FBI agents, his dark hair speckled with enough gray that is was time to start calling it 'salt and pepper' hair. His dark gray suit and utterly plain tie were also typical FBI attire; he'd easily fit in at any corporate or law office, except, of course, for his daring fashion statement consisting of a thick, dark blue Kevlar vest protecting his torso.

As for myself? Pretty much a carbon copy, I suppose. My hair is considerably less gray; actually, I have more gray in my beard than in my hair, and my physique is considerably more lean and muscular than John's, but the end result is quite similar: standard FBI issue.

"What do you think?" I asked him, only half-joking.

John shrugged. "You're the expert."

I have always wondered why John worked these cases with me. He was much more suited to dealing with the drug-dealing, money-laundering, white-collar realm of the FBI rather than the hazy region of Behavioral Science. He just didn't take the killers seriously; he had no interest in or respect for their altered realities, so he never really *got* why they did what they did.

I do. I might realize that for many of the far-out lunatics, reality is a bizarre and frightening place, but it's their reality, and for them, it's *very* serious. I suppose you could say I have respect for their beliefs.

"Why this case?" John had grunted gruffly when I first approached him with Albert's case, shaking his head with disapproval over the open file he was leafing through.

"Why not this case?" I'd asked him.

"Same old shit. Guy goes whacko, kills a bunch of random people, yada yada yada. Why do you want this one?"

"It's not the same as the others," I insisted. "Albert Beck kills, yes, but not randomly; at least, not to him. He leaves a note with each one, explaining why he killed them, that's practically a confessional. He thinks he's protecting the rest of us, killing some sort of evil creatures who prey..."

"Whatever," John waved off. "You want it that bad, I guess we'll have to do it."

And so, six weeks and seven bodies later, here we were, with Albert in shackles behind us, driving our commandeered police cruiser through the desolate woods where we'd found him, largely by accident. At least, that's what John would've said, by accident. I'm not so sure.

"You've been wanting to tell us about this for some time now, haven't you, Albert?"

I sensed him shrugging his flabby arms. Thirty-nine years old, I don't believe Albert had exercised a single moment of his life; at least, not since high school Gym class. His only exercise was running his fingers on a computer keyboard, as he stumbled from job to job; programmer, mostly, but also troubleshooter, web page designer, just about anything and everything in the information technology field. Nothing seemed to stick.

"All right, then," I prompted, ignoring the increasing condescension radiating off of my partner, "why don't you tell us?"

There were a few moments of hesitant silence, broken only by the muted hum of the cruiser's engine and the sound of our wheels rolling over the dark country road we traversed. There wasn't even any radio traffic; we were between the smallest of small towns in upstate New York. The leaves had long since completed their autumnal change, most of them already fallen dry and lifeless to the earth.

Of course, it was so dark that I couldn't see most of those sloughed-off corpses; except for the handfuls scattered across the road like spatters from some gargantuan painter's brush, blowing about in the biting wind or kicked up by our cruiser's passage.

Rather, I knew autumn was drawing to a close by the silhouette of the trees against the star-lit sky, barren branches reaching like searching, bony fingers up over either side of the road. In a month or so, those skeletal digits would be fleshed out with tufts of new-fallen snow, lending a Kris Kringle Winter Wonderland sort of aspect to this road, but for now, for tonight, they remained grasping hands clawing up out of the grave.

"I'm not sure how to start," Albert said, his voice ringing hollow in the confines of the car, each word sounding swallowed, dead before it was even born, seeming as if it was spoken within a lead-lined coffin.

Or perhaps I've just been at this for too long.

"Start at the beginning," I suggested. "Start with *them*."

Them is the reason I wanted this case, although I hadn't revealed this to John, of course. No need to complicate things. He never would've understood my interest in *them*.

"You won't believe me."

"Try me," I offered, desperate to draw Albert out of his shell, but keeping my voice even to conceal my emotion.

I could hear him breathe out deeply, and then, at last, he simply dove right in. "You've... read my notes, I'm sure."

"Yes."

"Then you know quite a bit already."

Quite a bit, I agreed, but I wanted, I needed, to hear him tell me personally.

"Tell me again."

"I... I don't know who they are," he began, confidence growing in his voice as he went on. "I don't know what they are, or where they come from. They might be human, or some other, dreadfully similar species. I don't know for sure. All I know is, they kill."

Nothing new so far, I muttered inwardly. There was something in particular, something he'd hinted about in his notes, something that called to me...

But I would have to coax it out of him. That would require patience.

"Go on," I said as evenly as I could.

"I stumbled across them, really. I was just messing around online, and found a bunch of unsolved crimes, which shared certain... elements."

John couldn't hold back his sarcasm this time. "Oh, so you're a fearless vigilante of justice?" he scoffed. "Maybe you think you're a full-blown superhero. Need some tights, Captain America?"

"John, please!" I whispered. He *wasn't* helping.

"You laugh if you want, Secret Agent Man," Albert spat in defiance. "I don't expect you to believe *me*. Me you can easily dismiss; I'm just a loser, a fat computer geek who's blurting nonsense in the back of a cop car like a babbling psychopath. I must seem pretty... pathetic to you. But because of me, there are a few less of *them* out there, one of which might've killed you, or someone you love, so you go ahead and laugh away. I know what I'm doing. I'm not crazy."

John muttered something unintelligible under his breath, which I was able to translate into *Fucking nutcase* by virtue of our long partnership. I hoped he'd keep quiet. This was important to me.

"All right, Albert," I said, "let's talk about that. I mean, let's be honest; it does sound a little strange... them. All of your notes talk about *them*, how *they're* not human, how *they* want to kill us all... you have to admit..."

"Yeah, yeah," Albert said.

"So..." I prodded again.

"So how do I know?" he said. "How do I know they aren't human? I don't know that. But if you saw them, just once, you'd know. You'd know I was right."

"What do they look like, that I'd know?" I asked. I had a perverse desire to hear it all, every detail of Albert's testimony about *them*. I can't explain it, or perhaps I just don't want to, but I thirsted for details, no matter how insignificant.

"Just like you or me, normally," Albert answered.

"Of course," John said, in a barely audible tone.

"But then," Albert began again loudly, in defiance of John's comment, "when they... attack people, their eyes get black, and they grow claws."

No kidding, my mind commented, but my mouth said, "Perhaps they just had dark brown eyes and long fingernails."

"No, no," Albert said, shaking his head. I could see his jowls shaking in the rear-view mirror. "You don't get it. They have *black* eyes, all black, completely black. And their claws look like a... bear's, or lion's, I don't know, something big. It's not a trick of the mind. Their teeth get all big and stick out everywhere."

I thought for a second about what that must've looked like for him. "Pretty scary stuff, Albert."

"Don't condescend to me."

"I didn't mean to," I said. "But..."

"But the bodies, *my* bodies, didn't look like that," Albert finished for me.

"That's right," I said. "Even the ones you shot in the head or burned with gasoline, the medical examiner surely would've found some trace..."

"I don't know about that stuff," he interrupted.

I felt a bit disappointed. Albert's belief system was so... concrete, I have to admit, I was hoping for more well-considered detail.

"If there is no way for us to tell who *they* are post-mortem," I asked, "how are we supposed to believe you?"

Albert laughed. "You could start with their crimes."

Another interesting aspect of Albert's victims: each one lived in an area where several gruesome murders or unresolved missing-persons cases abounded. There was rarely any direct link, but it was clear Albert had come up with some 'evidence' to link his victims with the crimes committed nearby.

"Told you," John said, turning the wheel fluidly as we negotiated one of the endless curves in the dark country road.

I ignored him as best I could. "What about their crimes?"

Albert pish-poshed me. "You've read the files, I'm sure."

"I want to hear it from you."

"Start with the victims," he shrugged. "*Their* victims. You've got a bunch of bodies with bizarre pathologies; severe desiccation, or drying, of unknown origin, electrical burns with no discernible cause, apparent animal attacks without actual consumption of the bodies..."

"And you think... *they*... did those crimes?"

"I know they did," Albert said. "They have... abilities, powers, unlike anything you can imagine. More than just turning into those clawed freaks. They can... I don't know... maybe they're wizards or something."

I stole a glance at John, who thankfully swallowed the comment I knew he was itching to spout.

"I know how that sounds," Albert added quickly, almost apologetically. "But if you'd seen what I have..."

"But you have no proof," I reminded him, disappointed yet again. "Those medical files, which I assume you acquired through your computer skills, could all be explained through more conventional means."

"You have to read between the lines," Albert said. "Separately, each piece of the puzzle is meaningless, but together..."

He trailed off. I waited until the silence became too much for me to bear, until the grasping branches overhead seemed to clench down around the car, smothering it, before I broke the terrible quiet with a question.

"Do you... have any real evidence?"

John shot a curious glance at me, and I wondered if perhaps I should've kept quiet. I had to know, though; because for all of John' skepticism, and my considerable experience in dealing with lunatics and their alternate realities, I saw what Albert was talking about. It was more than just the way I tried to sneak a peek into the minds of the killers I tracked; perhaps, just perhaps, I was starting to make sense of the puzzle behind the pieces.

Was it possible? Was it possible one of these crazy loons could actually be telling the truth, might actually know...

"I'm... yes," Albert finally admitted.

My heart crawled its way into my throat, but I was careful to guard against too much optimism. *After all,* I reminded myself, *Albert is rather crazy.*

So is what you're proposing, I responded to myself. *That Albert might know the secret you've been looking for...*

"What do you mean, 'evidence'?" John said, interrupting my internal dialogue.

"I have proof," Albert said slowly, as if afraid to admit it. Did I detect a bit of optimism, as well? As if he were both afraid to embarrass himself but at the same time dying to display his so-called 'evidence'? I thought perhaps I did, which titillated me all the more.

Can you imagine my excitement? Years, *decades,* of listening to the paranoid fabrications of lunatics, always just starting to believe them, giving them the benefit of the doubt, if you will, until I found the one detail, the one loose string, which unraveled the entire delusion. It had gotten to the point where I *wanted* to believe them, *needed* to, needed to find the one lunatic who really did know about *them* and could tell me...

Everything. And it would all be *true*.

"What proof is that?" I asked, my voice trembling just a bit.

He must've sensed my excitement, because I saw his little teeth gleam in a taunting grin in the rear-view mirror. It was almost all I could see of him in the dark; his bulky, shadowy outline, hints of the contours of his face, and now his white teeth, flashing like bared fangs behind me.

"Wouldn't you like to know that?" he said slowly, almost as a tease. "Maybe I should show you. Show you all of it. Show you how they are, show you how they prey on people, how they even prey on each other. Maybe I should show you their true nature."

There was something in his tone, something which made my desires fade into doubts, fearful doubts. He seemed so over-confident, as if he did have undeniable proof... proof he might even be able to show me right now.

"Quit jerking around," John said. "If you've got something, some evidence you have on one of these 'crimes' you accuse your victims of, out with it, already. I'm sick of your Loony Tunes shit."

"Loony Tunes?" Albert said. "Hmmm. Perhaps something a little more tangible, then."

He's one! I knew at one, realization coming in a desperate flood. *He's become one of them; he's been preying on his own, and now on us!*

I spun quickly, afraid what I must find behind the steel mesh separating John and I from the monster in the back seat, sure I would see his chubby, thin-haired head thrust against the wire, with black eyes and saliva-dripping fangs, and long claws threaded into the mesh. For a second, when he leaned forward, his little pebble teeth glittered just right, and I gasped involuntarily as his face came further into the glow of the dashboard light.

It was just Albert, though, plain old chubby Albert, handcuffed in the back of our car, under arrest for the murders of eleven people he claimed were inhuman fiends. His eyes glittered wildly in the uncertain light, but I'd seen crazy before, and I knew how to handle it.

"I have proof. In the form of tape. Videotape, audio tape, and plenty of it."

"What do you mean?" John asked, all business now, condescension vanished from his voice.

"I mean, I taped them," Albert explained patiently. "Some of them, at least. I won't go into the details of how I found the first two or three, because, as much as Secret Agent Man on the right up there surely wants it, I have no proof for those first few. But they told me about others, the others I've killed. I taped them; audio at first, then video."

"What, they just... told you?" John asked.

"Hardly. It took quite a bit to subdue them; in fact, the first two died of their wounds before I had a chance to interrogate them. But the third..."

He trailed off, nodding, as I began to fidget and fret anxiously. What was he waiting for? He knew the secret, he wanted to tell us, so why didn't he stop torturing me and give it up, already?

"I shot the third in both knees with a shotgun," Albert continued, settling me a bit. "Blew the left leg off, actually. Then, while he was out of it, I managed to handcuff his hands behind his back and duct-tape his arms together. *He* talked. I got it on audio. The fourth one I videotaped."

"What did they tell you?" I asked, not bothering to hide my interest anymore.

Another shrug. "I have almost four hours of each on tape. They claim to be human, but I don't know, I guess only a doctor could figure that out for sure. They kill people, and each other, but I'm not sure why; their explanation didn't make any sense to me."

"What else?"

"They have... powers. Incredible powers. I'm sure some of them see me, are hunting me, but they haven't caught up with me yet. They will, though. Now that I'm caught, they'll easily be able to get to me. That's why you have to believe me."

"Why, to let you go?" John said.

It was easy to ignore my Doubting Thomas of a partner in the face of what Albert had both said and implied. Actual tape! Videotape! This was incredible, real proof of *them*, what I'd been searching for!

Easy, now, I told myself. *He could be talking simply to hear his own voice. You don't know he knows, not for sure, not until some detail he couldn't just invent crops up.*

"No," Albert said, as we stopped at a stop sign guarding a lonely intersection in the woods. We were drawing quickly closer to the tiny burg where we'd officially put Albert into custody.

"No," he repeated, "I expect you'll do your job, and arrest me, and find my body tomorrow or the next day or the day after that in my cell. But I also expect you to do your job and find the tapes and books."

"Books?" I asked. "What books?"

This is it, I thought, or hoped, more accurately.

"Books, they have books. I found three of them. I can't make heads or tails of the writing…I guess you could call it writing… but I think it's how they learn how to do their powers."

"Really?" John said, obviously more comfortable remaining a skeptic.

"What… did these books look like?" I asked, shifting slightly as the car decelerated for another stop sign.

Albert shrugged. "Big books, leather bound, heavy. The writing looks like… I don't know. A big Chinese symbol on each page, more of a picture than writing, but it looks kind of more like Russian than Chinese. Sort of like that."

That's it! I grinned triumphantly, and asked my final question.

"Where are they? The books?"

"I have a key in my pocket to a Greyhound bus locker in Albany…"

I moved then, with blinding speed, while we were still stopped at another of the countless, meaningless intersections strewn throughout the New York countryside. A quick knife hand strike to the nose with my left hand stunned John long enough to let me slip a hand around the back of his head and drive it with murderous force into the steering wheel. Then, before the car could drift very far into the intersection, I slipped the transmission into Park.

It was over in a manner of seconds. Afterwards, I sat still in silence, head leaned back against my seat, luxuriating in the splendid feel of taking such savage, decisive action. The violence was so real, so vivid, so wonderfully intense, I could practically taste it.

But, there was Albert to deal with.

I let out a long, low sigh, and said slowly, "Albert... I think it's time for you to learn *my* secret."

"Jesus Christ," Albert whispered.

"Not quite that profound," I grinned. "But still pretty good."

"You see, Albert, years ago, almost eighteen years ago, as a matter of fact, I was completing my psychiatry residency in Detroit when I got a most interesting case. I was trained as a psychiatrist, med school, the whole business, before I joined the FBI. In any case, this patient presented as a sixteen year old boy, delusions of grandeur, mild paranoia. He claimed to be some sort of cult member, each of whom had special abilities very similar to those you mentioned in your notes."

"He was a very difficult patient, and even attacked me one day in the ward," I continued, staring straight ahead into the empty intersection lit only by the cruiser's headlights. "He looked like... a demon. Eyes all black, fangs jutting out everywhere, sharp claws... I could hardly believe it, even while it was happening to me."

"I managed to escape, but who could I tell? Nobody, of course, or I'd be locked up as well. So, I treated my wounds myself, and pulled myself together mentally. No mean feat, I can tell you that."

"Then, after I'd settled myself, I tip-toed into that boy's room late at night. He was in restraints, thanks to our earlier encounter, which made questioning him that much easier. I didn't use your crude methods; my tools of choice were thorazine and sodium pentathol, and lots of them, believe you me. Once he'd been sufficiently prepared, I hypnotized him to discover the truth of who he was."

I paused in my story-telling, gazing once again at the bony branches stretching up to scratch at the night sky, over the desolate intersection where our cruiser sat idling like an obedient attack dog waiting to spring. At that moment, the trees seemed like grasping hands more than ever, but instead of appearing to drag me down and into the earth, they now gave me the impression that they were beckoning to me.

"I was terrified at first, terrified such a typical All-American boy could turn into that. Into *them*, you would say. He told me about how this so-called 'cult' taught him to become... what he was when he attacked me. He told me there were other, darker, blacker powers to be had, if I could find those to teach me.

"He told me about those books, as well, and in the coming weeks, he taught me to translate that bizarre... what you call writing. Then, at last, he schooled me in his power; how to turn my body into a weapon, make myself strong, fast, and able to grow an animal's teeth and fangs.

"His knowledge had limits, though, and I soon found we'd reached the end of what he could teach me. But, I really couldn't let him live, either, so eventually he died of an 'accidental' overdose of his medication."

What the hell, I didn't bother to add. *His therapy wasn't progressing anyway.*

"I tried to track down his 'cult', but they'd disappeared into the winds, leaving no trace of their passing. I went wild, trying anything I could think of to track them down, and at last, I realized what I had to do. Where better to go if you need to find somebody than the FBI?"

"You're... one of *them*!" Albert gasped.

"Sharp as a tack, Albert, don't let anyone tell you differently. For all these years, I've been searching for more of *them*, more of *me*, talking to every two-bit lunatic in the country, and now, finally, you've led me back to them."

"You're... crazy!" Albert said, looking about wildly like a caged animal realizing that its time has come to be put down.

"See, now *that's* funny!" I laughed, drawing my service pistol and checking to insure a round was loaded in the chamber. "*You* calling *me* crazy!"

"You... can't, you killed your... partner, the police will know..."

"The police will know what I tell them," I said. "Once I shoot you, I'll get in the back and kick the screen in. I can do it, I assure you; *we* really are quite strong. Then, I'll drive this car into a tree... poor John, killed in the crash, and you shot trying to escape. No problem at all."

Albert began to flail about wildly, kicking at the windows, the doors, causing me to burst out laughing. "Go ahead!" I shouted. "Knock yourself out, it'll look all the better!"

"I'll tell you one thing," I said. "I don't know why *they* kill, but I know why I do. After becoming one of *them*, I realized how weak and pathetic you all are. You're a useless nothing, a nobody; and besides, it gives me such a charge to kill... but you know all about that, don't you?"

Albert stopped his thrashes and began to whimper and moan. I considered saying something to console him, but the way his blubber shook when he cried disgusted me too much. I didn't even want to find out how he'd managed to kill so many of *them*. *Probably just luck*, I decided, and shot him down through the top of his head as he blubbered into his hands.

It was child's play to find his key, and carry out my little charade with the cruiser. John was a decent partner, I suppose, but in the end, just another of the meaningless, useless, gray insignificants that I've been preying on all these years. Besides... now both my secret and Albert's will be kept.

It won't be hard to find the bus terminal in Albany, with the locker containing Albert's gift to me. I don't know what powers lie in wait for me in those books, or what secrets his tapes will reveal to me, but I'm nearly bursting with enthusiasm.

Soon, I'll truly be one of *them*.

Then, the *real* killing can begin.

Shards Of Glass

I'm a big fan of the novella; too big to be a story, but shorter than a full-length novel. They allow you to more thoroughly play with a story concept while still allowing for an intensity of experience that doesn't work well in a longer format. I think of "Shards Of Glass" as an out-of-control freight train; it moves fast and hits hard with a lot of weight behind it. It was a joy to write, and I particularly enjoyed working with the shifting perspectives, allowing for a nice mix of action, commentary, and character exploration.

Andrew C. Piazza

It had only been a week and a day since the nightmare mission that took Stephen away from her, but when SWAT called, Cass had to answer.

She parked her car as close as she could to the moat of flashing squad cars and TV trucks surrounding the office building that was involved in this evening's festivities. Slinging her equipment bag over her shoulder, she waded into the moat, smiling with grim irony when she caught sight of the cement blocker naming the building in glittering steel letters: Revival Technologies, Incorporated.

About time it came around to bite them in the ass, she thought.

A small spotlight clicked on in front of her, and she froze, cursing her bad luck. She'd hoped to get through the scattered news crews without incident, but there was one of the enemy, right in front of her, prepping and primping herself for the camera.

"Okay, let's try it again," the cameraman said, settling the camera's light on the reporter's model-perfect face.

"Ready," Cass heard her say.

"Go."

"Ever since the discovery of the so-called 'mage sciences' thirty years ago, magic and science have competed to attract the best and brightest minds available, until the creation of Revival Technologies, Incorporated," the reporter began. "Then, the world saw something as controversial as it was unconventional: the combination of the two arts, magic and technology, to bring the dead back to life."

The reporter raised a plucked eyebrow and continued, until the lights of the nearby squad cars distracted her and made her trip up her lines. "This controversy came into the headlines once again today, when eight hours ago, eyewitnesses reported a pillar of fire that fell straight out of the sky..."

"Heavens," the cameraman reminded. "You're supposed to say 'heavens'. Let's try it again."

Cass tried to slip past the reporter, who was scarring her sparkling Miss America persona by swearing like a pirate. Unfortunately, the cameraman spotted the tight-muscled SWAT team leader, and waved to Miss America urgently, spotting Cass with his spotlight like a deer in the woods.

Miss America snapped back into reporter mode and moved to cut Cass off. "I'm here with Cass Penswith, team leader of Reclamation Squad Four from the Special Weapons and Tactics Unit. Ms. Penswith, you lost one of your team only a week ago, in a particularly violent action against..."

"No comment," Cass tried to side-step Miss America, but the reporter was quick on her feet, and blocked Cass's progress.

"Then how about sharing your thoughts on reports that incidents with Revived or rogue mages are on the rise..."

Cass stopped dead and stared the reporter down with a look that could've shattered granite. "How about you step the fuck out of my way, Barbie Doll."

With that, she elbowed her way roughly past Miss America and into the glittering sea of squad cars. Cass picked out Dread, her gigantic second-in-command, in a heartbeat... no one else came even close to his size... and she headed for him.

He saw her coming, and started his report before she could ask for it.

"Twenty-four story building; Revival Technology, Incorporated's headquarters. Target took control about eight hours ago. Maybe a dozen or so maintenance personnel, janitors, that sort of thing, were caught inside. We got a call, one of the janitors probably, and two units were dispatched."

"What's this about a pillar of fire?"

Dread nodded. "Those first two units on the scene got torched. Column of flame ten feet wide, straight down out of the sky, ran across both squad cars. Boom."

Cass broke her gaze away from the building to look at Dread, raising an eyebrow.

"Hey, don't look at me," Dread said. "It's an eyewitness report."

Cass shrugged and turned back to the building. "That's a new one for me. I've heard about some mages who could pull off a stunt like that, but I didn't think any were still around."

"There weren't," Dread agreed. "The target's a Vive Job, that's confirmed, but we're still waiting on an ID. Shakes and Peter are already on site; I sent them to get outfitted at the weapons truck."

The huge man's report was interrupted by the insistent shout of a man in a blue SWAT windbreaker pushing his way around the flashing squad cars and well-armed cops composing the perimeter. A man in an expensive suit followed closely in his wake, as the cop in the windbreaker waved his arms frantically. "Cass! Cass!"

"Edison." The name sounded like it tasted bad in her mouth.

"He's the boss, Cass," Dread said, laying a familiar hand on her shoulder. He was probably the only man alive, with the exception of her father, who could touch Cass that way and not end up with a broken wrist.

"I'll be nice," she said, sounding as if she was spitting out snake venom.

"Cass!" Edison huffed, somehow out of breath before he even reached them. "What the hell took you so long?"

"It's three a.m." Cass said. "I was asleep."

"Thomas got here fifteen minutes ago."

Dread winced at the use of his family name. "Sir, I live about twenty minutes closer than Cass."

Edison glared at him briefly, as if the big man had ruined his train of thought, then gestured toward his companion in the expensive suit. "This is Doctor Adjani, our liaison from Revival Technology."

"So who is it?" Cass asked the newcomer. "Who's the Vive?"

"You didn't tell her?" Edison asked Dread.

The big man shrugged. "Nobody's told me yet."

Doctor Adjani cleared his throat. "It's Maestro Polonius."

CASS

Unbelievable. They Vived Maestro Polonius. The guy's been dead for the better part of a decade, and they still thought the rotten, decayed gray matter in his skull was going to work just fine once they shot enough dope and magic and God knows what else into it.

I should've seen this coming. I *did* see this coming, ten years ago, when they first started Viving humans. They swore they wouldn't, those bright and eager scientists and mages who'd been working their way up from earthworms to frogs to mice to hamsters to dogs, but once they announced they'd managed to revive the corpse of a sheep, a full-blown *sheep*, mind you, I knew they couldn't resist trying to kick a few dead *people* back into moving around.

I think that they might've waited for a whole year before the ants in their scientific pants (or white lab coats or mage's robes or whatever the hell else they were wearing) got too itchy and they Vived that Elsinore Benes woman. She wasn't anything special, other than that she wasn't too old, wasn't dead too long, and didn't have any next of kin to scream in outrage when the boys in white coats jerked her back from Beyond. She lasted something like four days, before she wigged out and started tearing her own skin off with her bare hands.

Surprise! When people are dead, their brains *decay*, research geniuses! They decay, and the synaptic connections and tissue structures go to shit, so even if you do somehow re-ignite that ethereal spark that makes us walk and talk and breathe in and out, you're going to have to expect a little... Mental Dysfunction, was the original term. Batshit Crazy, is more accurate, once you add in the trauma of telling someone they haven't been asleep, they've actually been *dead*, and that sore feeling they've got all over is their body trying to remove and replace the sprinkling of decayed tissue scattered throughout their revived body.

But wait! the Vive Job proponents cried. *At least it's better than being dead! Sure, they freak out once they realize they're half-rotted, and sure, their mushy brains usually drive them straight to psychosis, but it's better than being dead, right?*

Right?

Besides, it was a Great Step Forward, and we all know how important those are to have, especially with research grant money so hard to come by these days. So, Revival research marched on, and more and more Vive Jobs got up off of the slab and started walking and talking and breathing in and out again, until the boys in the white coats really flubbed up, and Vived a dead wizard.

I wasn't on that op; I'd just started in SWAT that year. Lucky for me. They had no idea what they were getting into. The Vived wizard was no stellar honcho, just some Striker Mage named Tallow, but he managed to wipe out a good chunk of the local population that day. You see, although he was definitely crazy as all batshit, his skills were still five stars... in fact, it was as if his decay-induced psychosis somehow made his powers even stronger. Maybe his whacked-out mind was able to see around some corners a sane mind couldn't; whatever the reason, a lot of cops and a lot of civvies got waxed before they took him down.

And did they stop Viving people? 'Course not! Okay, one minor glitch, no big deal, let's keep going. Tallow was just dead too long, that's all, too much decay. We'll try it with fresher specimens, newer techniques; we'll get it right... you'll see.

We saw. We saw plenty. We saw enough to start forming special squads to handle just this sort of situation. "Reclamation Squads", or "Wreck Squads", which I think is a more accurate term, since we usually end up blowing the crap out of the Vive Job's general vicinity. I'm serious... we operate more like the Marines than SWAT.

And now they've Vived Maestro Polonius, and he was way out there even when he was *alive*.

* * *

"Polonius? *Polonius?* Are you people in some sort of a contest to see who can go the furthest out of their minds?"

Edison bristled. "Hey, Cass, Doctor Adjani isn't here to..."

"The guy's been dead for ten years, Edison!"

"We had him preserved," Doctor Adjani said. "A combination of cryo and certain embalming fluids."

"Oh, my," Cass smiled. "Well, that seems to have made all the difference then, hasn't it?"

"There were no indications he would go rogue," Doctor Adjani said, looking impatient, looking like he was tired of explaining himself for the umpteenth time. "Maestro Polonius took the news of his Revival very well. Indeed, he expressed a great deal of interest about the process, and even offered suggestions on how to improve the procedure."

"I'll bet he did."

"The Maestro was conducting experiments when he died, research that was critical to the next level in Revival technology..."

"Is that what he's doing now?" Cass asked. "Conducting research?"

"Cass..."

"Oh, fine," she waved Edison off. "Who did you send in?"

Edison blinked in surprise at the question. "Hunh?"

"Don't give me 'hunh'. You called me eight hours after first contact; no way we're the first team you called. So who was it? Who did you sent in first?"

"Shakes and Peter are back," Dread said, nodding toward two

men picking their way through the obstacle course of cops and vehicles.

Cass nodded in acknowledgement and turned back to Edison. "So?"

"Two," Edison finally said. "I sent in Squad Two."

"Kerry's squad."

"Unh-hunh. We lost contact with them four hours ago."

Cass snorted. "You mean they're all dead."

Edison looked as if he wanted to make a let's-not-jump-to-conclusions comment, but even he knew it would be pointless. "Probably."

"Six?"

"Six tried to insert by chopper two hours ago. The wreckage is over there," Edison said, pointing to a burned-out hull of an assault helicopter.

Cass looked over the huge, squat building again. It was massive and black and vaguely pyramidal, a man-made mountain of concrete and steel and once-dead nightmares. The rooftop blunted what should be the tip of the pyramid, and looked like the waiting mouth of some carnivorous plant, waiting to swallow whoever was so foolish as to follow Squad Two to face the nightmares within.

Images came to her from a week and a day earlier. Her team was surrounded by Slashers; tall, black, cornstalk-thin creatures with a trio of eyes on the top of their bodies and covered with tentacles. Each tentacle was tipped with a razor-sharp claw, and when the Slashers got close, they spun, whipping their razor-claws out to slice flesh to ribbons. They were everywhere; the team couldn't shoot them, the Slashers were too thin and they couldn't risk hitting each other. The whirling creatures were cutting her entire team to pieces, everybody was wounded...

She shook herself out of her daydream with difficulty, driving off the nightmare. It went, reluctantly.

"So long, Kerry," she whispered, then returned to business once Shakes and Peter were by her side.

"Who's the Vive Job?" Shakes asked, directing his question towards Dread, as always.

"Maestro Polonius," the big man answered.

"Je-sus!" Peter said, tugging at his beard.

"Here's what I need," Cass said. "Floor plans of the building, including any air ducts or ventilation shafts or any other pain in the ass stuff like that. I need a report on Polonius's capabilities while he was alive, and a list of what he's shown us he can do now that he's back."

"It should be a pretty tricked up list," Peter said. "Maestro Polonius was the mage's Mozart for his time. He wrote the book."

"Yeah, I heard."

"I mean it, Cass," Peter said. "He literally wrote the book. I have books he wrote... and I don't understand *half* of it."

Cass tried her best to ignore that and go on. "Dread said he's got a dozen or so janitors in there."

"Yeah?" Edison shrugged.

"So, I need to know who's the priority here; the Vive or the hostages?"

"This guy could wreck the entire city, Cass. Terminate with Extreme Prejudice."

Cass and Dread traded looks as a uniformed cop waved a mobile phone in Edison's direction. "Sir! Sir! We have another contact!"

"That simplifies things, at least," Dread muttered to Cass, as

119

they followed Edison over to the communications van.

"Where the hell are Mike and Tara and Ste..." Cass began to say, cutting herself short just in time. *Stephen's dead, remember?* her mind filled in for her, in the awful half-second Dread paused before answering.

"I, um... I'll send Shakes to go look for Mike and Tara."

Cass bit her lip. "Have him make sure they're geared up and ready to go. We'll have to get Edison to scrounge us up a replacement Healer mage."

"Maestro Polonius," Edison spoke into the mobile phone linked directly into the building's comm systems. "We demand that you..."

"There he is!" somebody yelled, and then BOOM! Every cop within thirty feet jumped out of their skin as a thunderclap of cordite went off at ground level. Cass, Dread, and Peter all whirled and very nearly pounded the offender to dust; Cass and Dread with their autopistols, Peter with a Magespear glowing brightly in his upraised fist.

"I hit him!"

The sniper was fresh-faced, in his mid-twenties, grinning from ear to ear behind his fine-tuned rifle. His SWAT baseball cap was on backwards, and he let his rifle lean forward on its bipod as he beamed toward Edison, "I shot him!"

"You shot shit, trooper," Cass said, holstering her weapon.

"I did! I shot him! I... I..." the trooper's smile faded into a confused and concerned look as he held a hand over a suddenly aching stomach.

"You shot an illusion, kid," Dread said sadly, putting away his sidearm and turning away from the sniper so he wouldn't have to watch. "Tell me when it's over, Cass."

POLONIUS

The first came for me at dusk, as if the last dying rays of sunlight could afford them more power than was theirs. They came with guns and magefire, and I broke their backs on my altar. The memory of their screams still sings a satisfying chorus in my ears.

More gathered about my temple, and some tried to speak with me using magic or technology. When I finally determined the time was right to address them using an illusory copy of my form, one of the crawling grubs below attacks, as if it were that easy to kill me, as if I were a human being.

They do not know, they do not understand what they face. I have returned from the far side of the Styx with my mind stretched wide for the wisdom of the universe to fill. They think themselves powerful because they can bring back the dead with technology aiding their magic.

They are nothing. They know nothing of power. They sit beside their flashing squad cars and think they face a man raised from the dead.

I am no man. I am Demon.

I fill this vessel as a manner of convenience, a vector through which my power can invade the world. God had his Jesus to walk the Earth, and Lucifer now has me. I am the Son, I am the Demon, and now it is time to show those arrayed against me the face of real power.

*   *   *

"Hey, what..." the sniper frowned, holding at his stomach with both hands now.

Cass looked around wildly. "God damn it! Where's Shakes! Shakes! Peter, can you do something?"

Peter shook his head. "Not against Polonius. My Defense array is pretty weak."

"Sir, um.." the trooper began to say, confused, then his dull look sharpened into fear and terror as his abdomen bulged out against his dark blue coveralls.

Cass forced herself to turn away before it happened, but she couldn't shut her ears to the screams. First, they were sharp, accompanied by the sounds of heavy blows slammed into a boxer's midsection. Then, the screams stopped, replaced by a grunting "unh! unh!" timed in sync with the sound of the thumping blows. Then, screams again, shrill fingernails scratched down a chalkboard, and the sound of wet cellophane being twisted and torn. At last, the screams subsided, and all Cass could hear were the shocked gasps and retching from the other cops surrounding the building.

Sooner or later, she would have to look, so she steeled herself as best she could and turned back to the sniper. Her hands clenched involuntarily at her sides, and she swallowed down on top of the contents of her stomach to keep them from gushing out of her mouth.

Polonius had torn the sniper inside out.

She looked away as quickly as she could, but the damage was done, the wet, pinkish image burned onto her retinas for all eternity.

"Good Christ," Edison whispered, staring at the mess.

"Who the hell gave him an order to shoot?" Cass said. "Hunh? Who?"

"I, uh..." Edison wiped sweat from his forehead. "All of the, ah, snipers have orders to fire at targets of opportunity."

"Dread." Cass's order was implied in the single word tossed over her shoulder.

"Got it," the big man nodded, and picking up a headset on the tactical frequency, said, "All snipers, all snipers. This is Central. Green light cancelled, repeat, green light..."

"What's he doing?"

"Fixing your f..." Cass said, then stopped and counted ten, as Dread rescinded the order for snipers to fire at anything that moved. "Look, Edison, you don't want to provoke these guys, okay? They're crazy, by *definition* they're crazy, and you want to keep them quiet for as long as possible. Right now, Polonius is writing Scripture on the walls or eating cat food or maybe even driving nails into the soles of his feet. Whatever it is, it doesn't involve us, and we don't *want* it to involve us. Let him rant and rave and do whatever he wants... as long as it's harmless. We provoke him before the time is right, and what you said is true... he may very well destroy the city."

Edison frowned at her. "Procedure..."

"Sir?" Dread interrupted, setting down the headset. "If I may... the procedures you are expert in revolve around the living. That is, for non-Vive Jobs. We're used to dealing with Vives, and only Vives, so our procedures are going to seem a little strange. Please try to bear with us."

Dread's music seemed to strike the right chord with Edison. "Of course. Yes, you're right, of course. Thank you, Thomas. Do as you need to."

"Thank you, sir," Dread said, as Edison got back on the headset to repeat the orders the big man had already given.

"Unbelievable," Cass said. "The explanation comes from a man, and all of a sudden it makes sense. God forbid he listen to a woman."

"It's not because you're a woman. It's because you're such an angry pain in the ass."

Cass's face darkened, and a boiling hot retort nearly shot from her lips, before Dread's deadpan expression cracked and a ghost of a smile tugged at the corners of his mouth.

Cass's smile was unstoppable, and she punched Dread good-naturedly on the arm. "I'm going to kick your big ass, later."

His voice was the timbre of a tympanic drum. "Unh-hunh."

"Why don't you tell Joe SWAT there that we're going to need more Defense mages around this perimeter, since he seems to only want to listen to you."

"My pleasure," Dread bowed slightly, and turned back to Edison.

"Here comes Shakes," Peter said. "Looks like he's found Mike and Tara."

"All right," Cass nodded. "Dread? Let's rally up and get some prelims set."

"Be right there," Dread said, still talking with Edison.

"About time," Cass said toward Mike and Tara, who were about to offer up their excuses, when Dread stepped into the irregular huddle. Several of the team moved around to compensate for his bulk.

"Edison says they only have enough Defense mages for a light perimeter. More are en route via chopper from around the city, but it'll be a little while."

"No problem. We need time to plan the assault," Cass said.

"Floor plans?"

"Got 'em." Dread spread a large blueprint out on the hood of a squad car, moving slightly so Cass could get a look. It was an odd sight; the giant man was over a foot taller than Cass, and his movements looked a bit like an adult stepping aside so a child can get a better look at a parade.

CASS

Six foot six, and if he wasn't three hundred pounds of rock-hard muscle, he was pretty damn close. Is it any wonder why they called him Dread? I've seen him break people's backs bare-handed, and take more physical punishment than a pack horse.

But there was a brain inside the beefy skull, and a stolid placidity about his personality that fit him to this job perfectly. The same man I've seen fight like an unstoppable juggernaut, I have also seen swallow his pride in the face of guys like Edison. Better than that; he usually swallows *my* pride for me as well, and somehow nudges the superior in question subtly towards our needs.

Perhaps part of it is his size and demeanor which commands such respect. All I know is, when someone who doesn't know my team deals with us, they tend to go straight to Dread for answers, not me. It was the same way with Wreck Squad Four when we started. Only after six months and two ops did the others start actually taking orders from me directly. Even now, when they want rote facts, they go to Dread. But at least they come to me for directions.

There are the usual complications you might imagine when the first and second in command are male and female. And I won't pretend I haven't had my moments of romantic whimsy. I'm in damn good shape, killer shape, you might say, but I'll never be taller than five foot four, or as broad around as Dread. One night, we all got drunk, and I found myself just *touching* him all over; those huge, round biceps, the striated mounds of deltoid, the wide, sweeping lats. It was as if I felt I could crawl inside his skin, be that big, own that body, if I ran my hands across it long enough.

Nothing happened, though. We weren't alone long enough, or drunk enough, or both.

I do encourage the team hanging out together as much as possible, by the way. You can never have too much unit integrity… that certain something, the near-ESP between close friends which lets them practically read each other's minds, and anticipate each other's actions. In my line of work, where success and bloody failure can be decided in the space between heartbeats, you need all the unit integrity you can get. Or, as I like to put it, the team that plays together, slays together.

So, instead of the usual divisions in Wreck Squads; that is, the shooters vs. the mages, and the politics that goes along with such divisions, we were one mind, one body. Shakes the Defense mage tossed back shots with Mike the shooter, who didn't know the first thing about spellcasting, but could shoot an earring off of your ear at twenty yards without touching your lobe. Peter the Striker mage shared pitchers with Tara, a shooter who could toss a few minor Tricks, but always went for a gun before trying to cast. The same went for me and Dread and Stephen, our Healer, who got his throat slashed open on our last op, and who we desperately needed here with us now rather than six feet under.

No point in fretting over that, though. We had to get some plans together, or we'd end up like Kerry and the rest of Squad

Two... swallowed by the wide, squat pyramid Maestro Polonius had claimed as his own.

* * *

"Edison says that most of the magical activity is coming from the twenty-first and twenty-second floors," Dread reported.

"That makes sense," Cass said. "Look at that building... it looks a lot like an Egyptian pyramid; at least, it would to a crazy-ass Vive like Polonius. He probably sees himself as some sort of god or pharaoh sitting up there. Figures he'll go as high up as he can, you know, to lord over us, but not too high up. He needs to leave himself a few floors of defensive insulation."

She turned to Shakes. "I take it he's got a screen up, so we can't just teleport right in?"

"That's a fact," Shakes said. "It's all along the outside of the building like a skin..."

"So, how are you going in?" Edison interrupted, poking his head into the huddle with difficulty.

Dread started once he realized Edison was talking to him and not Cass. "Um, we haven't... probably up through the basement, clear the building floor by floor. Is that right, Cass?"

"Is that what Kerry did with Two?" Cass asked.

Edison nodded. "Okay, good, I've got your Healer, so..."

"We're not going in that way."

Edison stared at Cass. "What?"

"We're not going in that way, not through the basement," Cass said.

"Oh, come on, Edison, do the math," she said once she caught his look. "Twenty-four story building, he's on the twenty-first floor, give or take. It's either fight up through twenty floors of insanity or down through three. Which would you want to do?"

"Two went in through the basement," Edison said.

"And they got wasted, didn't they? How far did they make it? Three floors? Four?"

"Six."

"Six. Well, Kerry was a tough son of a bitch. But he still got taken, because going up from the basement is going to be like trench warfare. It turned into Stalingrad for Two, and I am not replaying the Charge of the Light Brigade. We insert on the roof and hit down."

"Charge of the... there's no way," Edison said. "You can't parachute onto that roof... it'd take an expert jumper, and half of your team aren't jump qualified at all. Six tried to rappel onto the roof and..." He nodded toward the flaming wreckage of the helicopter to finish his sentence.

Dread shifted about a bit, as if he was itching to say something, but not with Edison there to hear it. "Cass?"

Cass frowned and looked the building over. "How far around the outside of the building does the teleport screen extend?"

Shakes stirred and tore his attention away from the blueprints. "Um, I don't know. Maybe about five feet. Just enough so we couldn't teleport next to the building and try to grab on to something."

Cass nodded, wheels turning in her head. "And *above* the building?"

Shakes blew out a breath and smiled. "Damn, Cass, you're a genius. Yeah. Yeah, just five feet."

"What? What?" Edison asked. "Who cares? Five feet or five hundred feet, it's..."

"We can't teleport *into* the building because of the screen," Cass began, looking pointedly at Dread.

The huge man nodded in understanding. "But we can teleport *above* it, above the roof, right above the limit of the screen... and five feet isn't that far to drop."

DREAD

Damn. Wish I'd thought of that. But that's the way it is with me and Cass; I'm the slow and steady pack horse, she's the superstar. I never told her that Edison offered me my own team once and I turned it down to stay with her. I don't know why I never told her. It just seemed like one of those things you keep to yourself.

Maybe it's because she knows the business at a much higher level than me. Oh, sure, I know the procedures, and anything that's been written down or tried before I can learn; but Cass, she's on a whole other level. She understands how these Vives think, and she knows the job so well, she can come up with new tactics on the spot... and they'll work. I could never do that. I would've gone up through the basement, cleared the building floor by floor, because that's the standard procedure when you can't teleport in, and we would've gotten creamed.

Then there's that whole other thing about Cass, that there's no use denying. I'm falling for her. If not love, than close enough to count as love. She's the most intriguing, strong-willed, incredible woman I've ever met, and working alongside her has passed like a dream... almost a year now, gone by in the space between breaths.

I can't tell if she feels the same way. I guess it's only a matter of time before I find out… sooner or later, if she'll have me, we'll get together.

For now… back to business.

*   *   *

"Don't," Edison shook his head, obviously wanting to disagree. "It's not… wouldn't Polonius have thought of that?"

"Why would he?" Cass said. "It's never been done before. Don't be fooled by the magefire he tosses around; Polonius is still just a man. He's fallible, he's beatable. He's smart, but he's not all-knowing. Do you see what I mean? He can't think of everything. There are always oversights, something they don't know or don't anticipate or just plain don't remember."

"Still," Edison said.

"Sir," Dread said, "it greatly increases our chances of success. We'll hit him from an angle he isn't expecting."

Edison nodded at last. "All right. I've got your Healer."

"Who?"

Edison looked at her as if the answer were self-evident. "Your Healer. Stephen Tawnborn."

"Fine… what?" Cass said. "What are you talking about, Edison? Stephen was killed a week ago on our last…."

Cass interrupted herself. "A Vive? A fucking *Vive?* You want me to take a Vive along with me, when it's a Vive who's the problem in the first place?"

"He was only down for a few hours…"

"Absolutely no goddamn way! I am not taking my team into

that funhouse with a half-rotten corpse, who I don't even know if I can trust him or not! What if he wigs out while we're in the middle of something hot? No way! You cannot, can *not*, trust a Vive."

"Cass," Dread interrupted softly, nodding toward her back. Stephen was there.

CASS

Edison was a weasel, a bastard, a slimy, no-good son of a bitch.

That's not true. I was just peeved over getting stuck with a lousy situation, a situation that could get my entire team waxed all by its lonesome; and to make matters worse, a monkey wrench just got thrown right into the middle of the well-oiled machine that was my team.

It would've been bad enough to go in with a replacement, someone who had never trained with us before... remember unit integrity?... but a Vive? Forget it. You can not ever trust a Vive Job. My specialty ought to underscore that pretty well. But to go in without a Healer was suicide.

Okay, you could maybe replace a Striker mage with enough heavy-duty firepower, and no Defense Mage? Well, you hit the enemy fast enough, maybe you don't have to worry about them shooting back. But I've never been on an op, ever even *heard* of an op for that matter, that didn't have casualties... casualties bad enough that you'd lose most of your offensive ability without a Healer. My personal bacon was saved twice by Stephen, Team Four's Healer; and each of the others in Four owe their lives to him at least once over.

And it wasn't that I didn't want Stephen back. On the contrary; Stephen was a five-star operator, and when he bought it, I remembered thinking how Squad Four would never be the same. If he'd survived...

But he didn't. And I don't care what Revival Technology, Incorporated says... all the king's horses can't make the dead as good as new. There's always something off. Always.

I remember reading somewhere that, if you break the crystal creating a hologram, the hologram is still there in each piece... it's just smaller, or maybe faded, I can't remember which. I do remember the time I broke the full-length mirror in my bathroom, though... and even after I'd meticulously glued all of the pieces back into place, I couldn't get rid of the cracks marring what used to be a perfect, smooth surface.

I think of Vive Jobs in the same way. Broken holograms, shattered mirrors, Vive Jobs... no matter how you dress them up or paste them back together, they're still just shards of glass.

So I couldn't help it. I turned around, and the dead was right there, looking a little embarrassed to still be walking and talking and breathing in and out. He was wearing a turtleneck to hide the wound on his neck, the wound that killed him, but Stephen was still a dead man come back, and I couldn't help staring at him like he was a leper. Everything got quiet; it was like the time that racist prick Lawrence from Squad Three was telling Mexican jokes, and Jerry Nons from Five told him he was half-Mexican.

Okay, I admit it, I felt bad about talking about Stephen like that while he was standing right there. But this was life and death, and if I had to step on a dead guy's feelings to save our lives, then so be it.

*   *   *

"Stephen Tawnborn," the short man in the black turtleneck said quietly, "reporting for duty."

After a moment of silence, Cass managed to speak. "Not with me, you aren't."

"He's the only Healer we could find this quickly," Edison said.

"Then we wait until you can find a... live one," Cass said with difficulty.

"Oh, that's great," Edison said. "Hey, why don't we just wait until we can find a Maestro for you to take in with you?"

"Yeah, that's likely," Shakes grumbled under his breath, glancing sidelong at Stephen before lighting up a cigarette.

"Hey, no offense, Stephen, but we are not going in with a Vive," Cass said.

"Yes, you are. There's nobody else, you're going in with him."

"Forget it. Fire me."

Edison looked like he wanted to explode. "Don't think I won't. I'll just put Thomas in command."

There wasn't a moment's hesitation from Dread. "No, sir."

"What?" Edison seemed to stand on his tip-toes, but he barely managed to get below Dread's face, much less directly in it. "You listen to me, all of you! I will not have this insubordination! I expected more from you, Thomas! This renegade Vive is a mortal threat to the people of this city, the people you have sworn to protect..."

"Sir, please step out of my face." The words were calm as a placid sea, but there was a strong undercurrent of implied violence beneath the surface.

Cass folded her arms across her chest. "Getting ourselves killed isn't going to save anybody. In fact, it may set Polonius off worse than ever."

"But..."

"They're right," Stephen said, dragging Edison's protests to a halt.

"What?"

"They're right. There's no point in going in unless you're sure, and frankly, if the situation was reversed, I wouldn't take a V... Revived person... in with me, either."

There were a few moments of silence, people looking at their shoes, fiddling with hands that suddenly seemed to need something to do. "It's nothing personal, Stephen," Cass said at last.

"I know."

The hand-wringing silence returned, filled with stolen glances at the no-longer dead.

"How, um... how you doin', Stephen?" Peter asked, as if compelled to break the silence.

Stephen seemed about to answer, but a chorus of excited voices drew everyone's attention.

"What's all that commotion over there?" Shakes asked, nodding over toward the command vehicle.

There were a number of TV screens going inside of the vehicle, and the evening news was running on one of them. The words LIVE REPORT spun slowly around near the bottom of the screen.

Squad Four couldn't hear the voice-over, but they caught the gist of the report quickly enough. Maestro Polonius had struck again.

The live feed showed a burned-out apartment building, burning brightly enough to make the TV screen's image shimmer like a will o' wisp in the faces of the nearby police officers. Bodies were scattered everywhere; emergency personnel swarmed over the ground surrounding the flaming building, trying to decide who was gone and who was salvageable.

Cass walked closer to get a better look at the TV report, watching as terrified tenants trapped inside of the building leapt from the sixth story windows in their desperation to escape the flames. Someone was saying her name, but Cass couldn't hear it; she was focused on a scrap of burnt blanket, covered with pictures of cartoon animals, left by some child to be trampled underfoot. Her nephew had one just like it.

"Where is that?" she asked.

"Just off Bryant Street," Dread answered from her side.

She breathed out her relief. That wasn't her sister's street.

"That's not all," one of the SWAT troopers monitoring the various TV screens said. "Check this out."

The image shimmered and shifted, and began moving in reverse as the recording ran backward. Bodies stood up and ran backward into the building, emergency personnel fled the scene in reverse.

"We got a call from some reporter, said he heard a voice in his head ordering him to get to this building. Here it is."

A sudden flare of flame, then the camera angle pulled back, shrinking the relative size of the apartment building in the image, and the flames were gone, banished through the magic of technology. The video image shifted and stabilized, and proceeded to roll forward in normal time. The apartment building Cass had just seen completely burned out now stood unmarked, unknowing, unsuspecting of its imminent demise. Shadows moved past windows... the same people who would soon be leaping from those windows to escape smoke and fire... and then it happened.

A column of fire, a brilliant pillar of flame, reached down out of the sky, smashed through the roof of the apartment building, and began running along its length. It forced its way to the first floor and began to spread out, like a hungry liquid licking at every wall and window and surface. It seemed to drain into the building as if it were a drink poured from high above. The tail of the pillar fell into the apartments, and the attack was over... but the damage was just beginning.

"Polonius." She turned away from the screen, as the trooper switched the image back to a live feed.

Dread's eyes were locked on Cass. "Looks like he's not going to stay quiet."

She wanted to argue with herself, to wrestle with the decision, but she knew every second of deliberation was another second closer to Polonius's next attack on innocents. She couldn't afford to wait.

"Shakes?" Cass asked loudly.

"Yeah, boss?"

"How long will it take you to prepare for our teleport above the roof?"

"Minute or two," he said.

"Good. We go in fifteen." Cass began walking toward the weapons truck, pausing when she passed Stephen.

She looked the walking dead over once, her face inscrutable. "You coming?"

CASS

Some people want to know every detail of a Wreck Squad, down to our equipment and procedures, as if they can become a surrogate trooper or otherwise vicariously experience an op if they study the details.

It's pretty basic. Body armor, submachineguns with flashlights mounted underneath, ammo, knives, sidearms, grenades, charms for the mages, radios, medical supplies, and various entry tools. On this op, we'd each carry a heavy rucksack full of equipment… spare ammo, specialized hardware, that sort of thing… which we'd drop and leave on the roof once we inserted. I know, it sounds wasteful, just leaving it behind, but we've got to move fast when we're on. Still, we might need a resupply, and I was pretty sure nothing was going to teleport in after us. Polonius was too smart to get caught twice by the same trick.

We were geared up and ready to go in no time, and after that, it was time to teleport. We got in a circle facing outwards, with me on the designated twelve o' clock position. Shakes was on my right at three o' clock, Peter to my left at nine o' clock, and I put Dread on six with one of those belt-fed F-shok assault shotguns. For those of you not well-versed in weapons, trust me when I tell you, a belt-fed autoshotgun can tear an entire mob to pieces. They're awfully heavy, but Dread was a monster, and would've carried an anvil into battle if I asked him to.

I found myself staring up at the building like a little kid looking down from the high dive for the first time. Last week's op was still fresh in my mind; we should've had weeks to recoup from that one before getting thrown back in front of the cannons.

The images came back, unstoppable this time. I was there again, surrounded by the Slashers. They were everywhere; we began shooting like crazy, trying not to hit each other. I got cut pretty bad and dropped. Dread flew into a rage, attacking the Slashers with a fire axe he'd found somewhere, splitting them down the middle like firewood. Stephen knelt by my side, patching me back together with his magic.

Then, disaster. A Slasher moved in, and spun close enough to Stephen while his back was turned, and his throat was sliced open. He just stopped and stared at me, holding a hand to his neck, staring at me as if to ask what just happened, and all I could do was stare back, wondering what I could do, when the answer was nothing, of course there was nothing I could do, *he* was the damn Healer, for God's sake, what could *I* do?

I would've stayed there all night, staring at that building, lost in that too-recent memory. Dread saved my ass. A little cough to catch my attention, and he tipped me a broad wink, as if to say, hey, fuck it, another day at the office. "Ready, boss?"

I gave Shakes the go and braced myself… teleporting is very weird. There's no transition; one instant, your mage is counting down and hits "one", and then, you blink. You always blink, everyone blinks, it's like some sort of natural protective reflex of the mind. I often wonder what that fraction of a nanosecond would look like if our minds could register it. I know teleporting is faster than the speed of light, I've read all the magazine articles, but there has to be *some* sort of time elapse. In any case, you blink, and then you're there. Talk about jarring. It takes a few trips just to take the edge off, and even then, you never really get used to it. It's too unnatural. But it works.

So, Shakes counted down for us, and hit "one", and we blinked.

*   *   *

"Twelve clear."

"Nine cle..."

"Contact! Contact seven!" Dread's voice shouted. Thunder, crash, rumble, roar, a jackhammer's rattle seemed to split the rooftop as Dread hammered out a lethal tune with his shotgun. A submachinegun joined in, and Cass was tempted to break formation so she could check out the seven o'clock arc of the circle, but then Shakes shouted, "Contact! Contact two!" and started firing himself.

There were four creatures running her way, just to her right at the two o'clock position. They were short and bipedal, and as soon as she spotted them, their ugly faces gave them a name in her mind... goblins. Shakes's gun blew the legs out from under the closest one, and Cass shouldered her weapon and tore off three bursts almost before she knew what she was doing. All three goblins fell, headshot, and Shakes finished off the downed goblin and waved his flashlight over his arc of the rooftop.

"Two clear."

Another heavy rattle from Dread, and his deep voice announced, "Seven clear."

"All arcs?" Cass asked, and after each of her team reported "clear", she gave the official "All clear."

They dropped their packs in the center of the circle, keeping their weapons at the ready and their eyes on their respective arc of the circle. "All right," Cass asked, "who's got the stairwell?"

"On mine," Dread answered.

"Okay. Dread straight up the middle, Shakes and Peter on either side, Mike and Tara on the flanks, I'm right behind Dread, Stephen in the rear. Just one thing," Cass said, pivoting to point her weapon at Stephen.

Stephen froze. "What the..."

"Your weapon," she ordered.

Stephen balked. "Hey, no w..."

Five other flashlights converged on him as the rest of the team leveled their weapons at his chest. Cass's face was granite.

"Give your weapon to Dread, now," she said. "Until I know I can trust you."

Stephen's face fell, and he nodded, looking like he was accepting a guilty plea. "Fine, Cass."

"Your sidearm, too."

Submachinegun and pistol were handed over to Dread, who secured them without a word and turned back toward the doorway leading to the access stairwell. The others fanned out in an inverted V, with the mages on either side of Dread, and Mike and Tara the furthest out.

"You're leaving me defenseless, Cass," Stephen said, taking his place with her behind Dread.

"You're surrounded by an entire Wreck Squad armed to the teeth," Cass said. "You're hardly defenseless. Take that rucksack with you."

Stephen snorted and shouldered one of the heavy packs. "Might as well."

Their V formation skimmed across the rooftop, past the half-dozen goblins Dread had laid out with his shotgun. The formation came to a stop at the stairwell's doorway, and paused as if to draw breath.

"Cass?" Dread asked.

"Shakes."

Shakes let his submachinegun hang in front of his body on its sling. He blew out a breath, cracked his knuckles, and put both hands out palm-forward in a STOP gesture. "Ready."

"Peter."

The Striker mage let his weapon hang as well, and twisted his fingers into an arcane knot close to his chest. Sparks and crackles of energy zipped and popped amongst his fingertips, lighting his face like dim flashbulbs. "Ready."

"Dread."

The enormous man shifted his grip on his F-Shok and closed his eyes for just a moment, taking a measured breath. He looked like an athlete preparing for the start of a race, or a karate master preparing to break a board with his fist. His body seemed to relax and tense at the same time, as if he were a thick coil of wire being depressed, ready to spring.

Another slow inhale, his eyes flicked open, and the coil sprang. A short trio of bursts from his shotgun, one for each hinge, the third for the lock, and he stomp-kicked the door into the stairwell with a shout. It fell flat, like a Domino, and slid clattering down the steps into the darkness.

Dread was almost on top of it, aiming his weapon down into the blackness, finger on the trigger, ready to tear an army to pieces if need be. Shakes and Peter crowded in as best they could next to the huge man, Tricks on the tips of their fingers to match whatever horrors came screaming up out of the stairwell.

Nothing.

A beat passed, as Dread and the two mages stared down at the empty void, as if refusing to believe there wasn't anything lethal coming up for them. None of them breathed. They couldn't; the hollow air of the stairwell reached up and closed a fist around their throats.

"Dread?"

Dread shook himself and managed to inhale. "Clear, boss."

"All right," Cass said. "Down we go. Dread on the point with Shakes and Peter, then me and Stephen, Mike and Tara on our six. Go."

They slid into the stairwell, picking their steps with care. There was no sound; only their shallow breathing, which seemed amplified into gasps in the enclosed space. Throats went dry and palms began to sweat, and Cass began to suspect they were climbing down a mile of steps, not just twenty feet, when Dread finally came to a stop.

"What is it?" Cass asked, her voice croaking traitorously.

"Last couple of steps are under water," Dread said.

She craned her neck around, struggling to get a look around his mile-wide back. Sure enough, water filled the last few feet of the stairwell, up to the fourth step. One end of the door Dread shot out was poking out of the top of the water, the other end submerged and out of sight. Its twin was still standing, closing off the stairwell from whatever was on the twenty-fourth floor.

"Do you think the whole twenty-fourth floor is flooded?" Shakes whispered.

"Only one way to find out," Cass said, shifting her grip on her weapon. "Do it."

"I'm not sure I can blow off the bottom hinge through the water," Dread said.

"Don't. Take the top one and the handle. The door will swing open partway, and slow down anything trying to come up."

"Right." Dread breathed out again, and aimed his weapon at the top door hinge. "One...two..."

B-B-BAM! The shotgun blew the door from its top hinge, and

then tore the handle assembly to pieces. Two steps into the water, and a booted stomp from Dread, and the metal door twisted and fell half-way open, blocking the doorway diagonally. Dread squatted down, so he could aim his weapon's flashlight around the twenty-fourth floor without getting too deep into the water.

"Whole floor is gutted out and flooded," he reported after the first sweep of his flashlight. "Water's clean, and looks to be... waist deep, maybe."

"Waist deep on who, Godzilla?" Shakes said, trying as best he could to get low with Dread without stepping foot in the water. "There could be anything in there."

"Yep," Dread nodded.

"All right, Peter, trade; I need to have a look," Cass said, sliding in next to Dread once Peter stepped up and behind her. "Keep a flashlight on the water right in front of us and watch for waves disturbing the surface. It'll at least give us a second or two of warning if anything's moving under the water."

"What do you think, Cass?" Dread asked, keeping his eyes and the muzzle of his heavy shotgun sweeping over the surface. "We've got to get across it."

"I'll tell you what *I* think," Shakes muttered.

"We know what you think, Shakes," Cass said, frowning. The water's surface was perfectly calm, broken only by the top of an occasional desk poking up like a desert island in the Pacific. "How did he do this? All of the walls are gone, just the support struts left, and not even that many of those... how is he containing it, keeping the water from spilling down onto the lower floors?"

"He's a Maestro, Cass," Shakes said, daring a single step into the water. "All bets with reality are off."

CASS

All bets with reality are off. Wasn't that the truth. Well, at least the challenges at my job are always new and exciting.

"Maybe we can get Control to send up an inflatable raft..." Dread began.

"Forget it," I shook my head. "Polonius is on to us. The screen's probably up to... what, Shakes?"

Shakes seemed to consider it for a moment. "Um, feels like a hundred feet or so above the rooftop. Nothing is teleporting in."

"So what do we do?" Dread asked. "Just wade through? God only knows what's in there, and how are we going to fight with... Cass?"

His words were a million miles away. I stared at the water, across its still surface, as if daring something to rise up and shatter its placidity. Random thoughts began to skip through my head. They may have seemed irrelevant on the surface, but I've been at this long enough to trust my instincts. Somewhere in that mental flotsam and jetsam was the key to this puzzle.

It's smooth like a mirror... a pane of glass... desktops like icebergs... a pane of glass... sliding down a sliding board...

"Cass?"

I frowned, trying to block out Dread's insistent tone and also drown out the latent fear of whatever was waiting for us in that magically created pool of the twenty-fourth floor. Something was in there, all right. Something big and ugly and covered in claws, probably, and we once we waded into that water, we'd be sitting ducks. It... or they... would drag us underwater and tear us apart as we struggled and screamed and drowned.

A little shake of my shoulders to chase those thoughts away, and I went back to trying to hear my inner voice. Thinking around corners is hard enough in the safe and comfortable daylight; it's damn near impossible in the dark when very real nightmares are anxiously waiting for their chance to pounce.

Lobsters in a tank, taped claws tapping on the glass... sliding down the water chute... tapping on the glass... slipping on the ice... walking on the water...

"Cass?" Dread sounded as if he might start shaking me; in fact, he was pulling back from the doorway and was probably planning on taking the whole team topside when the pieces finally fell into place for me. "Cass?"

"Shakes," I said, "remember when you put up that wall of fire between us and those ugly fuckers that Conjure mage sent after us, what, maybe, eight months ago?"

"The Knoors? Yeah, sure."

I nodded slowly, looked out at the water, then back at Shakes. "Could you do it with ice?"

"Sure, but there needs to be a water source..." Shake began to say, when the answer dawned on him. "Damn, Cass. I've said it before, and I'll say it again... you're a genius. Yeah, I can freeze the top of the water, maybe a couple of inches deep."

"Will that be enough to hold us?" Dread asked. "And hold... them... below the surface?"

"We're about to find out," I said. "Mike, Tara, get topside and fill a bag with any kind of gravel or shit like that you can find. Dread, back up out of the water. Let's make this quick. Where's the main stairwell?"

"I'll go up," Stephen volunteered. "You may as well send me up with Mike. I'm de... useless baggage to you in this stairwell."

I traded a look with Dread and nodded. "Go."

"Let's toss some grenades in to soften up whatever is in the water," Dread suggested once they'd left.

Shakes shook his head. "Bad idea. The more we agitate the water, the harder it'll be to freeze it. We want this ice to be *thick*."

"Right," I said. "Peter, can you hit the water with a bolt of lightning, fry out whatever is in there?"

"No can do, boss. I fire one off into a body of water, maybe it comes back and nails me as well."

"It can do that?"

"Unh-hunh."

How about that. You learn something new every day.

"All right, then, let's get started. Do your thing, Shakes," I said, gesturing towards the pool.

Shakes rubbed his hands together, as if to warm them up, and knelt down on the stairs by the edge of the pool. He lowered his hands until his palms hovered just above the surface of the water.

I knelt down next to him and pointed my flashlight across the pool. "There's the door we need to get to. Remember to make the ice thickest where we're going to cross."

Shakes nodded. "I'll try."

The stairwell went dead silent as Shakes fell into a near-trance. Below his hands, tiny ice crystals spontaneously formed on the surface of the water, stretching spiderweb-like out and around until they met and knitted together.

"Unbelievable." Dread shook his head.

I tended to agree, but this was business, so I whispered, "Shhh. Let him concentrate."

The tempo of crystal formation sped up exponentially, until the web formed a solid sheet of ice. The sheet began to spread out from the pool's edge, stretching out of the stairwell and extending itself toward the door on the far end of the room. There was a crackling sound, the sound of butcher paper being crumpled, as more and more of the water froze solid. We all marked the progress of the ice bridge with our flashlights, each of us mentally urging it further and deeper, until it reached the far door at last.

The six-foot-wide bridge then began to expand laterally, widening to the left and right simultaneously, until it reached the walls and covered the entire floor. Even then, Shakes didn't stop, but kept concentrating, driving the ice deeper, piling layers on as thick as possible. His breath began to show in puffs of frost, and at last he stopped, almost falling forward onto the ice in exhaustion.

Dread caught him by his body armor vest and pulled him back onto the stairwell.

Shakes looked like he might pass out. "That's all I've got."

"You did good, trooper," Dread patted him on the shoulder.

Peter tested his weight on the ice. "Good, nothing! He did great! You covered the whole floor, Shakes, damn!"

Lovely. Now all we needed were some ice skates.

* * *

"Cass?" Stephen asked, returning with Mike. "I brought down some ropes, figure we can use them for something."

Cass nodded. "Do you have the gravel?"

"Right here," Mike hefted a small rucksack. "What are you going to do with it?"

"*You*," Cass said, "are going to sprinkle it on the ice as you make your way across the room, to give yourself some traction. That ice is going to be as slippery as greased owlshit."

Mike nodded. "That's good thinking."

"Let's do it. Mike and Dread first, trailing this rope. That support strut there is about halfway across the pool and on our way; tie the first rope off there and anchor another one to trail to the far door."

Cass tied the rope onto the stairwell's steel handrail before handing it off to Mike. "No sudden movements. We don't know how thick the ice is, so don't take any chances. If it sounds like it's going to break, get back over here. Shakes and I are next, then Peter and Tara, and Stephen is last."

"Cass," Shakes said softly. "I, uh, need a minute, here."

Cass patted the exhausted mage on the shoulder. "Okay. I'll go solo; you take a minute and bring up the rear with Stephen. Cool?"

"Cool. Thanks."

Cass gave Dread the nod, and he and Mike stepped onto the ice, gingerly at first, then more confidently. By the time they ducked through the half-filled doorway, they were moving as fast as they could on the slick surface, the rope trailing along behind them.

"It seems pretty cool," Mike shouted back to the group. "Plenty thick enough."

Cass took her turn, taking a few steps to get used to the new surface, careful to stay on the path of scattered gravel left in Mike's wake. She stayed to the left of the rope, on the same side as Dread, and took a second to look back before ducking through the doorway.

"If something happens, pull on that rope like crazy," she said. "Wait until Dread and Mike are almost to that strut before you leave, so we don't all get caught out there."

Then, she was through the half-filled doorway and on the twenty-fourth floor, stepping carefully across the slick ice which seemed to stretch into forever. She tried shining her flashlight down into the pool, to see if there was anything under her, but after a second or two forced herself to give it up. She needed to concentrate forward, not downward, or she'd never get anywhere.

She followed about twenty feet behind Dread, seeing his form mostly in negative from the contrast with his flashlight beam in front of him. She stole a quick glance back at the stairwell and cursed herself for it.

Eyes ahead, Cass. Keep your eyes ahead.

It only took a few more quiet steps for paranoid thoughts to creep in. The water beneath the ice seemed filled with such silent, brooding potential, she almost would've preferred hearing something, seeing something, anything, just to break the silent stalemate which seemed to strangle her.

There's got to be something, she thought. *No way this room is empty. No way Polonius just filled up a floor with water and didn't put something in it.*

Images started forming in her mind, imagined shapes of the twisted creatures Polonius could have conjured to lie in wait for them. Each creature was worse than the last; black carapaces, sharp claws, gnashing teeth...

"Fuck!" Mike shouted, taking a quick step backwards and nearly slipping.

Cass's gun was up before she knew it. "What? What?"

"I saw something!" Mike said, pointing his weapon at the ice.

"Don't shoot the ice!" Cass said.

"Something moved, I'm telling you!"

"What?"

"I... I don't know, but it was big and it slipped past quick!"

Cass's breathing picked up. "Um... okay, let's back off."

"We can't, Cass," Dread said. "We have to cross this sooner or later. We're almost at the strut; we should at least try to tie this rope off before we think about a retreat."

"All right. Hurry," she said, walking as fast as she dared toward the strut marking the halfway point.

Something big under the ice, she thought. *Maybe more than one something big.*

Dread and Mike reached the strut and tied off the rope. Cass forced herself to slow down. They couldn't start bunching up... too easy to wipe out the entire team in one attack. All the same, she kicked herself for volunteering to cross the ice solo.

"Should've sent the Vive across first," she muttered to herself, feeling a little guilty the moment after she'd said it.

"We're tied off, Cass," Dread shouted back to her. "We're going for the far side."

"Watch yourselves."

Cass stole a glance backwards. Peter and Tara's waving flashlight beams danced wildly out of the half-filled doorway, and then they ducked out and around the half-broken door, visible in the spilloff from their lights.

When I reach the strut, Cass thought, *that's the time to hit us. Two groups caught on the ice, me in the middle...*

"Shit! Contact!" Mike shouted again.

"What?"

"I saw it again!"

"The same thing?"

"Uh, yeah, I think! I don't know!"

Dread shook his head, keeping the muzzle of his shotgun trained on the ice. "I don't see anything."

Mike's hands were shaking, sending his flashlight beam skittering across the ice. "I'm telling you, I saw it!"

Cass knelt down, wiping away a film of frost so she could see a little better. The ice was clear, almost crystalline, but she could barely make anything out; maybe she could see through to the floor, maybe she was just fooling herself.

A shadow broke her flashlight beam, a phantom through the crystal, a black mass which was gone as soon as it appeared.

Cass shouted and jumped back involuntarily, losing her footing on the slick ice and slipping backwards. For the split second as she fell, she knew she'd crack through the ice, fall through, fall down to where *it* could get her and drag her down into the icy prison Shakes had created...

"Cass!" Dread shouted, and started to run toward her, as if he could make it on time.

Then, she hit the ice, but the ice held, and she merely scrabbled backwards in a panic a few feet away from where she'd seen the creature. The strut was there, marking the halfway point, and she grabbed onto it like it was a life raft.

"Cass?"

"I'm okay, I'm okay!" she waved off. "Just bruised my ass... and my pride."

By the time she pulled herself together, Dread was by her side. "You all right?"

"Yes, yes," she said. "I feel like a damn idiot, is all."

Across the ice, Peter and Tara were halfway to the strut, using the rope as a guideline. Peter stopped, glanced back at Shakes and Stephen peering out of the doorway, and grinned like a kid about to pull his favorite stunt.

"Check this out, Tara," he said, and laid flat on his back on the ice. Pulling himself hand over hand along the rope, he zipped along the ice quickly, sliding like a sleigh.

"Oh, great," Cass said. "Now Peter's showing off."

"See?" Peter said as he went. "Easy!"

"Quit screwing around, idiot!" Tara shouted at him, stopping for a moment.

Peter slid up to the strut in no time and sat up next to Dread with a smile. "Pretty good, hunh?"

"You're amazing," Dread dead-panned. "How about walking your amazing ass over to Mike and keeping him company?"

"No problem," Peter said, hauling himself to his feet and walking fearlessly toward the far side.

"Peter!" Shakes shouted from the stairwell. "Stick close to the rope! The further you get from it, the thinner the ice is!"

"Gotcha!" Peter said, already almost caught up with Mike.

"What's Tara waiting for?" Dread asked.

Cass frowned. Tara's feet seemed frozen to the ice, as if she were afraid movement would draw the attentions of whatever was beneath it.

"Tara?" she shouted. "Come on!"

Tara looked up to wave her off, and then a fierce thump from under the ice made her eyes go wide and her feet hop involuntarily. She jumped back slightly, managing to keep her feet underneath her, and the ice began to hairline crack, from another and another and another blow from underneath the surface.

"Contact! It's right here!" Tara shouted, and lowered her gun toward the cracking ice.

"No don't shoot..." Cass began to warn, but it was too late. Tara blazed directly into the ice with her weapon, at the dark form trying to smash its way to the surface. The bullets catalyzed the monster's assault; the ice cracked loudly and suddenly gave away like a trap door.

Tara screamed as she fell through, reaching out for any kind of purchase, but the edges of the trap door broke away underneath her weight and she fell on top of something wide and slippery and misshapen. Long, clawed limbs reached up for her, wrapped around her, tried to pull her off her feet and under the water. She fired her weapon blindly beneath her, heedless of the possibility she might blow her own legs off, desperate to drive off whatever was pulling her down to her death. The bullets kicked up splashes of water, driving down into the creature, and then the clawed limbs slipped away, off of her, and retreated below the surface.

"Tara? Tara?" Cass shouted, heading toward her.

"Hey, is she all right?" Peter yelled from the far side of the room.

"Just get across the room and tie that goddamn rope off!" Dread ordered, louder than he needed to, debating on whether he should follow Cass or cover the team from where he was. He should stay put, so he could cover as many people as possible, but he found himself following Cass over toward the hole in the ice.

Shaking with wet and cold and mostly terror, Tara shrieked, "Somebody get ME THE FUCK OUT OF HERE!"

"We're coming!" Cass said, when more ice-straining blows cracked the ice on the far side of the room.

"Contact! They're coming up over here!" Peter said.

"Dread!" Cass pointed toward Peter, the order to assist implied rather than spoken. She moved as quickly as she could toward Tara; Shakes and Stephen were on their way out, too, but as fast as these things could move...

"Tara," she said, "grab the rope, and try to jump and slide up along the ice so you don't break it!"

Gunfire thundered from the far side of the room. Something screeched before splashing back into a hole in the ice. Cass forced herself not to look, not to split herself onto two fronts, and kept on toward Tara.

"Damn it!" Tara shouted, breaking off another section of ice as she tried to climb out. "It's not working... ahh!"

Her body toppled backward under the impact of something heavy hitting her legs. The submachinegun fell from her grip, slipping with a splash under the water. She grabbed onto the edges of the ice to stay on her feet, screaming in pain as sharp fangs bit down hard on the inside of her thigh. She tried to hold on to the ice with her left hand while drawing her pistol with her right, but the creature was pulling, tugging her down with immense strength, and her hand began to slip off.

STEPHEN

Having your throat slashed open is a hell of a thing.

When I first began studying the mage arts, I knew right away I wanted to be a Healer. It wasn't just that it was considered the most challenging of the basic Disciplines; Healing just resonated with me, the idea of being able to treat the injured and repair what was often irreparable through natural means.

At the time, the only way for me to afford school was a military scholarship. As you might imagine, the military was all too eager to pony up a couple of bucks to get their hands on a combat medic who could not only save the lives of fellow soldiers, but get wounded men back into the fight within minutes, rather than in weeks or months.

It was a good fit. I've always had an aggressive streak; well hidden, usually, but it was there. Early on, it was clear I could hold my own with the other soldiers with weapons and even hand to hand fighting.

On the battlefield, though, I rarely fired my weapon. Usually I was running around like a madman, answering that desperate call, "Medic!", that's been used by soldiers to plea for help for over a century.

Madman, is an understatement. I swear, there are no sane people who become medics. You run right into the teeth of a firestorm, not guns blazing, but oblivious to the gunfire around you, focused completely on your injured comrade. And you work feverishly to save them, ignoring the death whizzing by your ears, as if the act of ignoring the danger would dispel it somehow.

God loves medics, I suppose. I was never seriously wounded as a military combat medic. Once I did my five years of service, got out, and ended up in a Wreck Squad, I still never took that bad of a hit, even though I was right in the middle of things, rushing about, patching everybody else together without a thought for my own safety.

That night, That Night, it was no different. The Slashers were dangerous, certainly, but most of the wounds they were inflicting were not immediately life-threatening. Painful, bloody, gruesome, yes, but a slashing wound is usually nowhere near as deadly as a penetrating wound. Think about it. We use bullets to punch holes into people, rather than launching circular saw blades or some other nonsense like that. You have to cut through quite a bit of tough tissue to reach something vital; it's much easier to punch a hole in order to disrupt that which counts in a body.

Still, deep cuts can disable, especially psychologically. People who are cut badly often fall and give up even if the damage inflicted wasn't enough to physically drop them. That was the real weapon of the Slashers... fear. They were too thin to shoot; they zipped around the room like insects, and they cut people to ribbons. Such an attack induces panic and gets a team to shoot each other by accident or simply freeze up from either not knowing what to do or the terror of facing a whirling forest of straight razors.

People shrug off just how seriously a deep cut can terrorize you. I think of it much the same way in which people secretly shake their heads at drowning victim. *Hey, just keep swimming, you dummy*, they think... *that's what I would do*. Then they get into a swimming pool for the first time in a few years, and barely make it two laps before they clutch onto the lane rope for dear life before they suck a gallon of water into their lungs.

In the armchair, everyone thinks they're invincible. Everyone thinks they'll keep their cool. Everyone thinks the cliché can't happen to them.

And yet, it does and it did, and I'm hardly an armchair warrior. I ran from person to person that day, patching together the gory lacerations that made my teammates bleed like crazy. Each time, I slapped them on the back hard after I'd put them back together, shouting "Go!". I had to snap them out of that *I'm hurt I'm hurt I can't do anything* shocked state of mind that comes with a painful and gory injury. Otherwise, they would stay stuck in a dazed, deadly haze.

I jumped from casualty to casualty, patching my friends back together, and came to Cass, who was sliced up badly enough that she was in danger of passing out without quick attention. I did what I do, and just as I straightened up and gave her a smile, her eyes went over my shoulder and like an idiot I turned right into it.

I've heard some people describe getting sliced by a sharp blade as being almost as if they didn't feel anything at first. That wasn't how it was with me. I felt the tip of the hooked claw catch in my skin, and then dig in. There was a tearing, pulling sensation; it was quick, but it was there, just long enough for me to think, of all things, *Wait…*

The pain was terrible. Worse, though, was instantly knowing I was a dead man. I could feel wet and warmth across my neck and actually saw it spray away from me in a red mist.

It was the carotid artery. A million thoughts shot through my head in that instant. *What do I do, I'm a dead man, I can't die not like this, stop the bleeding somehow, I can't die yet*, all came at light speed, the thoughts tripping over themselves in a rush to be expressed before the end.

After a person's carotid artery is severed, the supply of blood reaching the brain drops dramatically. You pass out quickly, often within seconds, and then die within about two minutes. I felt myself getting fuzzy almost instantly; shock, most likely. Everything became remote and muffled and somehow brighter and then I felt my legs going out from underneath me.

Then, nothing. Just nothing. Everybody wants to know if there was a bright light or out of body experience and I always have to disappoint them.

I opened my eyes and I was lying in what I thought was a hospital bed. *Just a nick*, I thought. *My artery was just nicked and I passed out, they got to me in time.*

Not exactly.

Being told I'd just come back from the dead felt very much as if they'd told me that I had an untreatable, fatal disease. Ironic, I suppose. And I've tried to intellectualize it, look at it as an experiment, distance myself from the awful reality of it, but I just can't stand to look in the mirror and see those swirls of pinkish skin on my neck.

I feel trapped in my own skin, like it doesn't fit right. Every breath feels strange, like there is a mild irritant in the air that I can't identify. And then there's the thoughts.

Not the awareness that I'm the walking dead; although there is that too. These thoughts are… unhinged, is the best word I can think of. Disjointed is also a pretty accurate description. It's like a mild hallucinogen kicks in at random times and makes me see the world just a little off-kilter.

I remember looking into a mirror and knowing… not thinking, *knowing*… that I could reach right into it and touch my own face on the other side… and I would feel it here, on this side of the mirror. I'd stretched my hand halfway there before I stopped myself.

That's what terrifies me the most. Take my life, destroy my body, but don't let my mind turn against me. Don't take away my soul, if there is such a thing.

The upside is, every Trick I knew before works twice as powerfully and ten times more easily than… well, before. And I pick up new ones at a dizzying rate; I've blown through most of the Healing array and I've even got a decent Defense array going at this point as well. You'd think I'd be thrilled, but mixed with the satisfaction of learning a new skillset is the creeping knowledge of why it's so easy, and a fear of what the cost will be.

Please…just not my mind. Just not my soul. But it's coming. I can feel it.

And then the call came in tonight, and I almost didn't answer. But in the end, loyalty to Cass and Dread and the rest of the squad won out. I can hold it together a little longer. I can. Just long enough to maybe make a difference. And if somebody has to die, let it be me.

Before those… other… thoughts become too strong to fight.

* * *

Across the ice, Stephen checked the distance between himself and Tara and decided he'd never be able to make it on time. He grabbed Shakes by the arm, bringing them both to a halt, and after a moment's deliberation, sat down on the ice with his back toward Tara and his legs straight out.

"What the hell are you doing?" Shakes asked. "We have to…"

"Hit me with a pressor wave," Stephen said, drawing the machete-like Kukri knife from his belt sheath.

"That could break your ribs, Stephen…"

"No, it won't," Stephen said, clamping the knife in his teeth and putting both hands in front of him in a Stop gesture. A two-foot wide circle of air shimmered just in front of them.

"Hey, when did you learn to make a shield…" Shakes began, but after an urgent look from Stephen, shrugged and put his own hands out like he was pushing a cart. "*Shah*!"

An invisible pulse of force slammed into Stephen's shield, hurling him backwards across the ice. He grimaced under the impact, but the spell did the trick; he slid the distance to Tara in a manner of seconds, reaching her just as Cass did.

"Get it off!" Tara screamed, losing her grip on the ice. She started to slide under, but Cass darted forward and grabbed a hold of her a moment before she disappeared. Whatever was under the ice was strong; it tugged on Tara with teeth and claws, and Cass was pulled to the very edge of the hole in the ice. She dug her heels in, but it was no use; the ice cracked under her weight and she fell in, losing her grip on Tara.

Stephen leapt in after her, grabbing on to Tara and taking the knife out of his teeth. The monster pulled back, and Tara screamed as the creature's teeth dug deeper into her thigh from the tug-of-war.

"Cass, hold her!" Stephen said, raising his Kukri.

"It's fucking killing me!" Tara screamed, as Cass dug her heels in and pulled Tara back.

"Die, you fucker!" Stephen shouted, chopping at the water in front of Tara. "Fucking die! Die!"

He cursed again and dug for Tara's sidearm, unable to slash with any effect through the water. Cass shouted and handed him her submachinegun, using both hands to hold on to Tara once she did.

There was a fleeting moment of doubt in Cass's mind, in which she could see Stephen turn, grinning in delight, and shoot Tara and herself with glee, but it was drowned out by the rattle of her weapon, blazing into the water rather than into her. Whatever was holding Tara released her abruptly, and Cass almost fell over backward before regaining her balance.

"Up and out of the water!" Stephen said, setting Cass's gun on the ice and forming a step with his hands.

"She's bleeding, bad."

"Up and out of the water, then we'll take care of it."

Cass stepped up into Stephen's interlocked hands and pushed off onto the ice. She thought for a second it might buckle, but once she realized it would hold, she waved Stephen on.

"Pull her on first," Stephen said, picking Tara up like a groom carrying his bride across the threshold. She was dazed, barely conscious, but he managed to slide her on to the ice with Cass's help. Her mangled leg trailed streaks of blood behind her.

"Hurry, Stephen, before any more come... Shakes, give me a hand here."

More gunfire and magefire crackled on the far side of the room. Shakes reached the hole and held out a hand for Stephen, careful not to get too close to the edge.

"Go help them," Stephen waved off. "I'll get out on my own."

"Yeah, whatever, tough guy," Cass said. "Take our hands, and slide onto the ice, now."

Stephen smiled and waved her back. "Just slide back out of the way."

He stared at the ice for a moment, looking like a high-diver preparing for a difficult jump. Cass realized he was about to pull some sort of a Trick and slid out of the way.

Stephen blew out a breath and jumped. His legs kicked up behind him, as if a gymnastic spotter picked them up for him, and he slid forward onto the ice as if thrown.

Cass shot a look at Shakes. "What..."

Shakes shrugged. "He put up a little shield just a minute ago, too."

She ignored Stephen's newfound capabilities for now, pointing down toward Tara. "All right, superstar, see what you can do for her. Come on, Shakes, we're moving toward the strut. Dread! Report!"

Another loud blast from his F-Shok, and Dread shouted back, "They're breaking up through the ice, out away from the ropes about twenty feet, where it's thinner!"

Cass paused a second to take it all in; a half-dozen holes in the ice on either side of the rope, with several spider-like bodies each the size of a Rottweiler, splayed on the surface, leaking green blood. Dread, Mike, and Peter were in a semi-circle next to the far door, spent shell casings and empty magazines littering the ice at their feet.

"Peter!" she ordered. "Blast a goddamn hole through the top of that door and get off of the ice and into the stairwell behind it. Is that rope tied off?"

"Yeah!" Dread yelled back. "We...shit! Look out!"

Cass spun, weapon shouldered. Something began smashing through the ice underneath Stephen and Tara, something larger than the creatures Dread and the others had shot. Stephen grabbed a hold of Tara by the collar and drug her away, Shakes and Cass lending a hand once he was clear of the splintering ice.

"Go! Go go go!" Stephen said. "It's going to get through!"

A monstrous limb crashed up through the ice, a dozen yards behind them. It was long, a foot thick, and shaft-like, jointed twice before ending in a saw-toothed claw. Another identical limb broke through, and another, and together, they broke out a ten foot section of the ice.

Cass waved the others off as she turned to face the nightmare. "Pull yourselves along like Peter did! Now!"

"What about Tara?" Shakes asked.

"I'll worry about her! Go!"

They were off, sliding hand-over-hand along the ice, and Cass trained her weapon on the fresh hole in the ice as she pulled Tara toward the far side of the room with her free hand. A heavy, lumpy mass began to emerge from the water, along with another half-dozen of the saw-toothed limbs. Stalk-like appendages covered the fleshy body, some ending in eyes, some ending in organs Cass couldn't guess at.

She'd hoped the ice wouldn't hold under such a heavy creature, but another few limbs emerged with the rest of the bloated body, and distributed the weight across enough surface area to prevent its breaking through. A beak-like mouth shivered and snapped underneath the body, and all of the creature's eyes were on Cass.

Cass set her jaw and fired a burst one-handed into the mass of the creature. The slugs smacked into the black flesh, tearing pieces of it away, and the creature shuddered and backed up a few steps; but before Cass's eyes, the bloated body began to grow back into place, and the creature trudged toward her again, slowly, tentatively, testing its limbs on the strange, slick surface.

Cass tried to fire again, but her weapon clicked on empty. She took a half-second to reload, and began dragging Tara toward the support strut with a desperate strength.

"Peter! That door better be open!" she shouted.

More crashing from beneath the ice, about ten feet away on either side of her. Some of the smaller creatures began breaking their way through, as the large one increased its speed, bearing down on her like a locomotive.

The gigantic monster was only ten feet away when she cut loose on it again, emptying almost an entire magazine into it. Tissue tore away, eyestalks disintegrated, green blood splattered on the ice in sprays under her barrage, but Cass knew it would only be a temporary reprieve. She saved the last two bursts for the smaller spiders coming out of the water on either side of her, then pulled Tara the last few feet to the support strut.

She drew her knife and cut the rope leading to the doorway with Dread and the others, tying the free end with nervous fingers around Tara's harness. Another second to reload, and she waved to Dread.

"Dread! Pull her in!"

"Hurry, Cass! It's right on you!"

Tara's inert form slid away, pulled across the ice by Dread's titanic arms, and Cass trotted after her as fast as she could without slipping. The huge monstrosity was faster, though, gaining ground quickly as it regrew, using its multiple legs to churn forward. Two saw-toothed limbs lifted off of the ice and swept her legs out from under her before she could turn and fire. She fell on her back with a thud, the wind knocked half out of her, but she managed to trigger off a long burst point-blank into the creature before it could get on top of her.

She tried to gain her feet, but the ice was too slippery, and she fell on her face. Cass almost laughed in bitter irony; there were her six friends at the door, armed to the teeth and desperate to help her, and none of them could risk a shot with the giant creature so close.

Cass rolled onto her back. She pushed along the ice with her heels, slowly drawing away from the regenerating creature. More small spiders were on the ice now. Gunfire and magefire from the team tore apart a few. The rest would have to wait their turn; the big one would easily catch her before them. It pushed itself up off of the ice with its dozen legs again, beaked mouth jibbering as its eyestalks swiveled toward her.

Cass fired the last of her magazine into the creature. The monster barely slowed this time. She dug her heels into the ice faster, the scrabbling tempo of her feet matching the thumping beat of her heart. She let the submachinegun fall into her lap on its sling, thought about her pistol, and pulled an incendiary grenade off of her belt instead.

Fuck it, she thought. *If I'm gonna go, you're going with me.*

Something slapped the back of her head, just as the spider pulled close enough to kick, and Cass nearly dropped the grenade in surprise. It wasn't another spider, though... it was the rope.

"Cass, grab on!" Dread shouted, and Cass didn't need to be told twice. Wrapping her hand around the rope, she kicked away a probing claw just as the rope whipped tight and she slid toward safety.

With a curse, she slid the grenade back along the ice toward the monster. The giant spider charged after her, beak chomping greedily, but Cass sped away along the ice in a frantic heartbeat.

She reached the door; the half of it above the ice had been blasted in with magefire. Her team was behind it and in the stairwell leading downstairs. Dread pulled her through the hole and down below the level of the ice just as she shouted "Fire in the hole!"

The entire team ducked behind the bottom half of the door, the dam that somehow held all of that water in place, just as Cass's grenade blew. A brief spout of fire bloomed over their heads, gone as soon as it was there.

They rose from behind the half-ruined door, looking across the surface of the ice. The giant spider was broken apart, blown into a dozen flaming fragments that twitched and tried to regenerate, but could not. The burn wounds were cauterized, beyond repair, and all the creature's flesh could do was twitch out the last of its life.

The half-dozen smaller spiders came on, ignoring the burning wreckage of the giant. They scrambled across the ice, straight for the door.

"Kill them all," Cass said.

Machineguns rattled, magefire flew, and soon nothing was left moving on the ice.

"Think that's all of them?" Dread asked, smoke still rising from his weapon.

Cass shrugged. "Shakes, you and Peter boobytrap this entrance so nothing can come down after us," she said, indicating the blasted top half of the doorway.

"Right."

They carried Tara down to the landing, leaving a trail of blood along the way. Stephen cut her pants leg away with a pair of scissors. There were fifteen holes in her leg, spread out along a semi-circle. The flesh around each wound was blue-black, with dark streaks stretching toward her heart.

"Poison," Cass said, and looked at Stephen. "Can you help her?"

"I think so," Stephen nodded, and placed his palms an inch above the bleeding wound.

His eyes fluttered and he winced briefly, and black slime began to ooze out of Tara's leg along with the blood, and the streaks receded back towards the wound and finally disappeared altogether. By the time it was done, Tara's wound was still red, raw, and bleeding… but no longer poisoned.

CASS

Looks like Stephen picked up a few new Tricks while he was dead.

Two weeks ago, seeing him pull a new Trick would've been a relief... one more weapon in our arsenal. But now, this week, it was just a reminder of how he'd been Vived. Mage's powers always increase when they're Vived. God only knew what other changes had occurred in Stephen's gray matter when he came back.

Still, he'd taken a serious risk jumping into the water after me and Tara, so after he healed up the rest of Tara's wound, I told Dread to give his sidearm back to him. His submachinegun I gave to Tara, once she'd taken a few experimental steps on her now-flawless leg and announced she was as good as new.

Almost as good as new. Almost flawless. When a Healer seals up a wound like that, the new skin over the area is slightly pinker than the undamaged flesh. It isn't quite a scar, and it fades to normal within a week or so, but it's a tell-tale sign of a Healing Trick, and a temporary reminder of the misery you or somebody else had sustained. In Tara's case, there were fifteen little pinkish spots visible on the stretch of her thigh visible through her torn pant leg.

But, she said she could walk just fine, which was good, because sometimes even Healed limbs are disabled for a little while, as if the body remembers the recent trauma and refuses to believe that it has resolved so quickly. Tara was soaking wet and shivering a little, more from her nerves than from the cold, so I told her to stick next to Stephen and I, in the center of the group.

"Just like in the stairwell from the roof," I ordered. "Dread out front, with Shakes and Peter flanking, Mike will pull up the rear."

Down we went; thankfully, this stairwell's lighting was still working, so I didn't have to worry about the team getting spooked. Crawling around in the threat-filled dark with only the flashlight under your weapon for comfort gets old pretty quick, I'm here to tell you.

We bypassed the twenty-third floor, mining the doorway with explosives and Tricks, and continued down to the twenty-second. Stephen said he could sense some magical activity on that floor, so we got set and went in.

The whole time, I kept glancing from Tara's leg to Stephen's neck. Not in suspicion; I'd gotten past Distrust and was somewhere in the middle of Uncomfortable, but I couldn't keep my eyes off of Stephen's black turtleneck, couldn't help but wonder what sort of pinkish pattern was hidden there, where that neck wound had killed him a week and a day earlier.

I managed to shake myself loose and focus on the matter at hand when Dread blasted the door to the twenty-second floor off of its hinges. It can be a real problem, zoning out on the quiet moments of an op. Your mind wants to cut the tension by occupying itself with something, anything, minutiae. Right now, I needed my mind to stay tense... I had a rogue Maestro to kill, and the battle had only begun.

* * *

The twenty-second floor, like the stairwell, was well lit, so the team switched off their flashlights to spare the batteries. The hallway was wide enough to accommodate the same formation they'd used coming down the stairwell, so they stayed in it, moving on only after mining the doorway they were leaving behind.

The carpet floor sucked the footfalls from their boots, and once again, their breathing seemed amplified in the silence. Occasionally, someone's harness would creak or rattle, fending off the feeling of a pent-up breath, but Cass found herself breathing shallowly through her open mouth, as if she thought the whistle of air through her sinuses would betray them all.

They approached a four-way intersection. With hand signals, Cass orchestrated the advance: Dread and Shakes took the left hallway, while Peter and Mike took the right. The rest stayed just before the intersection, in reserve, waiting to see which side would be hot.

Neither.

"All clear."

"All clear."

Cass blew out a bit of her tension. "Stephen? Any idea?"

Stephen frowned and looked around like he'd lost something. "I'm not sure. Maybe right."

"Shakes?"

Shakes shrugged. "Maybe. It's hard to tell so close up. I think Stephen's right, though."

"Okay. Back into formation."

From behind them... *click*.

Boots pivoted, weapons were shouldered, laser sights activated, and they all very nearly blew the tarnation out of the light bulb which had just burned itself out.

"Jee-eesh!" Peter shook himself like a dog shaking off water. "I hate when that happens."

Cass lowered her weapon, feeling like a fool for the second time today. "Let's go. Back into formation."

They crept down the hollow hallway, ears strained for any clue, fingers begging for permission to pull triggers just to break the silence. The carpet, the walls, the air itself, all seemed to draw in and crush any noise they made. It was like stalking through a graveyard, a mortuary, where the hush seems more than natural, the quiet more intense, the sounds swallowed by the presence of the dead.

Cass stole another glance at Stephen, at the black turtleneck covering his mortal wound. *Does he feel the same way?* she wondered, as a slight twitch pulled along the skin of his face. It was gone as soon as it had come, but Stephen seemed a little off-set by it, as if he had shorted out for a second, and then came back on-line.

I wonder if he's thinking about a graveyard now. I wonder...
Focus, Cass.

Dread came to an abrupt halt. Everybody froze; there was nothing in front of them, only empty hallway, but nobody dared move, as if they could become silent and invisible simply by freezing in place. Dread held up a fist, the signal to stand still, and took a few cautious steps forward.

Boobytrap? Cass thought, but couldn't see evidence of anything like that. Dread stopped a few feet in front of the group, looking all around the hallway, seeming to sniff it like a bloodhound.

Cass was desperate to ask the question, but the hallway seemed to demand silence, so she waited until the tension through Dread's shoulders relaxed and he turned back to them.

"Well?"

"Nothing," he said. "It just felt..."

Thunder. Gunfire. Smoke. Explosions. Peter's head exploded into red and there were bullets tearing the air past Cass's ears and everything went to hell she could see Dread spin and start blasting into the wall before something came straight out of the wall and hit him she was firing too and pulling the trigger she couldn't see anything her lungs seemed caught in her throat she couldn't breathe and something hit her shoulder and she fell back against the wall her left arm wasn't working she couldn't get it to move so she fired one-handed and something wet hit the side of her face and someone was shouting "Illusion! Illusion!" but she could barely hear over the roar of the weapons and just kept shooting to her right into the wall straight into the wall until her weapon clicked on empty and things started to get too hazy for her and she sank to the floor.

CASS

Oldest trick in the book. Find a T-intersection, pile up your troops just inside the long part of the T, and cover the entrance with an illusory wall. Your target bops along, never realizing there *is* an intersection, until you're pouring gunfire and God knows what sort of ugly monstrosities into them.

People always want to know what a moment like that is like. That foo-fooey princess strutting around in front of the TV cameras out there, with her painted-on face and deeply concerned mask of an expression, she wants to know.

Strike that. She doesn't want to know what it's like, not *really* know, not know like I know. She wants to hear about it. She wants to stare at the scene of the accident while driving by in her warm and cozy car. She wants to live it secondhand, and feel all worldly and wise now that she's got the exclusive.

There is no way to accurately depict that kind of battle. I can only approximate it for you.

Have you ever been caught out on a mountaintop in a storm? I mean, a really bad one? The lightning crashes down so close, you can't even see it anymore, and the thunder is right on top of you, deafening, right in your eardrums, and it rattles your spine like a tuning fork. There's nowhere to run, no place to hide, and your heart's slamming against your chest like it wants to burst out and run screaming through the trees. You can't think straight; shock numbs your mind and makes your skin feel like it's stretched away from your body.

It's sort of like that. Add in the smell of cordite, and the snap of bullets as they shatter the air around you, and the feel of blood splattered across you. You don't know if it's yours or not. People are shouting and screaming, but you can't hear them, or if you can, half of it is drowned out or unintelligible. Hands, or maybe claws, are reaching and grasping and tearing and sometimes stabbing or chopping with makeshift weapons, and if you're not careful, you'll believe the illusion your own mind creates; that it's not real, that none of it is real, you're just floating through a bad dream and you'll wake up soon.

People want to know, "What do you do in a situation like that?" Like there's some mage's trick or training manual procedure that can stop an ambush once it's started. There is only one thing to do: fight. And that's how we have to train, or we'd all fall into that mental trap of dissociation and disbelief. We react by fighting, a knee-jerk reflex of killing, and the rest is up to Lady Luck as to who gets killed and who goes home. Your odds are poor; which is why the ambush is such a popular tactic and why Wreck Squads suffer such terrible casualty rates.

In this particular ambush, it wasn't until I'd been hit that my mind even processed the idea of AMBUSH. And it wasn't like I said to myself, oh gee, an ambush, they must be behind an illusory wall to my right, so I'll just shoot in that direction. I didn't have time to process that. I just burned my magazine in the direction the enemy seemed to be firing from, and hoped that I hit something important.

Other than that, I didn't know shit. I was on the floor, half-passed out from wound shock by the time it all actually dawned on me. Somebody pulled me out of there, dragged me down the hallway by my harness. I didn't know who. I knew it wasn't Peter; my half-numb mind replayed the sight of his head blowing off enough times for that fact to sink in. Other than that, I didn't know who was dead, didn't know who was alive, didn't even know if it was a friend or a foe who was dragging me away. Quite frankly, I didn't have the strength to care. All I could do was concentrate on breathing in and out, and trying to stay conscious, which believe you me, is not easy when you're hit that hard. It's like trying to stay awake during a quiet stretch of road at midnight on a twenty-hour drive. There's no drama; it's really deceptively boring, which is what makes it so deadly. You just start to unfocus, and if you let your guard down for one second, just one second to rest your eyelids or check them for holes or whatever other excuse seems reasonable at the time, you're gone.

The dragging stopped and a million years or a few seconds later, somebody was calling my name, telling me to hold on. My shoulder started to feel a little itchy, and by the time I grumbled and tried to lift my arm to scratch it, the world was back in focus. My mind was wide awake, if slightly off-balance, and I felt as good as new. Almost.

It looked like my savior was Stephen Tawnborn, the living dead.

* * *

"Don't move too quickly, Cass," Stephen said, helping her to a seat and leaning her back against the wall. "I've patched you up, but let your body get used to the idea first."

"Who... who's with us?" Cass asked, blinking through a momentary surge of dizziness.

"Nobody. It's just us."

Cass blinked hard again and shook her head. "What? Where's... I saw something hit Dread, and Peter..."

"He's dead. They're all dead, Cass. Can you stand? We can't stay here too long."

He offered her his hand, but she shook her head, refusing his hand, refusing his words. They couldn't all be dead. Not all of them, not Dread, nothing could kill *him*...

"They're gone, Cass. Even Dread. He's the reason we made it out of there; he was fighting some huge thing hand-to-hand, and I pulled you past them. I guess the bad guys didn't want to risk hitting one of their own. He ran interference for us, bought us enough time for me to drag you out of there."

Cass still couldn't process it. "Were you hit?"

Stephen smiled and pointed to a bloodstained hole in his fatigues. "Already took care of it. Sorry, I had to take care of myself first; I was losing too much blood to drag you, so I had to stop for a second and..."

"Right, of course, forget it," Cass waved off. "Help me up."

She gave herself a moment to test her balance once she was on her feet. "Where's my vest, my harness?"

"Had to pull it off you. You were too heavy with it."

"My weapon?"

"Attached to the harness, remember? I didn't think to stop and grab it, I was just hauling you out of there like crazy and hoping I wouldn't bleed out too soon."

Cass checked her thigh holster. "My sidearm?"

Stephen shrugged. "Dunno. You must've lost it during the ambush, maybe drew it and dropped it."

"Great. At least you still have yours."

Cass gave herself another moment to collect herself before nodding. "All right. Let's move... Stephen, wrong way."

Stephen shook his head. "No, Cass, it's this way. Polonius is pulling some Trick; I can feel exactly where he is now, come on."

"What are you, nuts? We can't take on a Maestro with one dinky handgun between the two of us! This mission is a wash, Stephen, we're getting topside!"

"Cass, we can't just walk away from this guy! Not after what he's done!"

"We're not. Believe me, we're not. Two of those rucksacks on the roof are full of plastic explosives; we spread them out, rig them up, rappel down to the ground, and blow them. The top floors cave in and collapse the rest of the building and we crush that crazy motherfucker under a million tons of concrete."

Stephen didn't seem to want to buy it. "Revival Technology will never let you do that. Not destroy their own building."

"Yeah? Well, fuck *them*. We're here, they're out there, so let's go."

"Can't let you do that, Cass."

His laser sight was on her chest. Cass froze, not wanting to believe it, not after he'd done so much so *right*, but the pistol was pointed at her and there was no denying it.

"Don't do this, Stephen. Not now. Not after..."

"Don't have a choice. Come on."

"Who is it? Is it Revival Tech? Do they have some sort of implant on you, some way they can shut you down unless you..."

"It's not Revival Technology. Come on. This way."

Cass risked balking for another second. "You're not going to shoot me. You wouldn't have healed me just to turn around and kill me."

Stephen's face was blank, ice, lifeless. "I won't kill you, Cass, you're right. But I *will* shoot you. Shoot out your kneecaps and drag you if you won't come quietly."

Cass looked into his eyes and saw nothing. They were a doll's eyes, a shark's eyes, a corpse's eyes.

"All right. Where are we going, Vive?"

Stephen winced at the word. "To see the Maestro."

POLONIUS

It seemed fitting, in this house of resurrection, to use their own people against them. They harbor such hatred in their hearts, ready to turn on each other for the slightest insult, real or imagined. It was appropriate to bring back the first squad sent against me, and send them against these new transgressors.

Fools, to fear me. They should fear each other, fear themselves, the way they hate, the way they vacillate. They know not who they are, what they want, what is right.

I know. I am Wisdom, I am Power, I am Ultimate Authority, and this is why they fear me. My certainty makes them nervous, turns them to rash actions against me, when such power and clarity could be theirs.

All they must do, is worship me.

They are a prideful people, though, and I will have to drag them to their knees, as they will not fall prostrate on their own. Very well. It shall be done.

But I feel myself fading; this damaged body I am trapped in will be insufficient for my needs. A replacement is in order; I was hoping for the big man, but the one called Cass will have to do.

It was not an easy prospect, to take one alive. I needed a confederate, and I found him in one who knew what it meant to come back from Beyond. He feels what I feel; he has seen what I have seen, and my quiet whispers into his mind have finally taken hold and bent him to my will. He has done well.

Bring her to me, my son.

* * *

"Who'd you hit us with, Stephen? Where'd you get the guns and heavy enough ammo to punch through our body armor?"

Stephen waved into the stairwell with his handgun. "Just g-g-g..."

His lips tripped over the word, and his head tilted a little to the left, as if he were working a kink out of his neck. It was over in an instant. "Just go."

"You all right there, Stephen?" Cass asked. "Is a wire getting crossed? Maybe that turtleneck is a little too tight."

Stephen stopped his self-conscious hand halfway up to his neck. "Knock it off, Cass."

"No, really. Is there a big steel bolt sticking out of your neck there, or..."

He moved with blinding speed, shoving Cass backward through the open doorway to crash into the concrete wall. She almost came back at him, snarling, but his pistol was up in her face, holding her back like an invisible hand.

"Go on, do it!" she shrieked. "Do it, you rotting motherfucker! Pull the trigger!"

"Shut up!" Stephen shouted back, tiny muscles quivering in his face in rage. "You shut up! I saved your ass, you ungrateful piece of shit! That last op, you were torn to pieces, and I stopped to save your ass, and *that's* what got me killed! I didn't ask to come back, I didn't want..."

He finally just shook his head.

"Yeah, well," Cass said, "that doesn't mean shit now."

Stephen seemed to settle a bit. "I guess not."

"Why are you doing this? Whatever he's promised you..."

"It's not... like that," Stephen's body seemed to sigh. "If you could see the things he's shown me..."

"Oh, for God's sake, Stephen, don't you see what's happening?" Cass said. "He's got into your head!"

"No, you don't understand, I don't have a choice..."

"The hell you don't! You can f... ahh!"

A shape blurred with motion, tearing past Stephen, knocking Cass down half a flight of concrete steps to the landing. Stephen jumped down next to her, a reflex to a forgotten loyalty, and put himself between her and the blue-uniformed shape pointing a submachinegun down at her.

"Get out of the way," the shape said.

"Back off, right now," Stephen said from behind his pistol. "I'm taking her to the Maestro... intact."

Cass groaned and pulled herself to a seat. "Oh, that's sweet of you, Stephen..."

Her mouth stuck into a fixed O, refusing to form any more words. She stared at the blue-uniformed shape with the gun, and at last, managed to say something.

"Kerry?"

The uniformed trooper glanced at her briefly, dismissively, and then back at Stephen. "That was my intention all along."

"Then lower you weapon," Stephen said.

"Lower yours."

"Kerry?" Cass said again, gaining her feet. "But... they said you were dead."

"They were wro..." Kerry's face seemed to stutter a step, just for a moment, and then Cass saw it... pink flesh, pinker than normal, covering his face and neck in crazed, swirled patterns. "They were wrong."

"Doesn't look like it. Looks like they were right on target, Vive Job."

"Cass," Stephen warned.

"Watch yourself, Cass," Kerry said, taking a step down towards her.

Cass's face was tiger's snarl. "Why don't you come down here and see if you can take me without that pop-gun, Vive?"

"The Maestro wants you undamaged," Kerry said, his voice now emotionless, hollow.

"Aren't I the lucky one."

Kerry lowered his weapon at last. "Yes, you are."

"Just come on, Cass," Stephen said, taking her by the arm.

"Don't make this hard."

"It's already hard," Cass said. "Tell me something, Stephen… when you said everybody was dead, was that just more bullshit, or were you actually telling the truth?"

Stephen shrugged. "Close enough to the truth. Anybody who survived won't be around for long; the Maestro will take care of that. But I can't imagine anybody could've lived through *that* ambush."

DREAD

When the ambush hit, I let the Demon loose.

That's how I think of it. Normally, this job demands an infinite amount of patience; you lose your temper or your nerve, and disaster is bound to strike.

Some tight-ass administrator gets in your face? Keep your cool.

It's dark, and everything is far too quiet, and you've only got your lonely flashlight beams for company? Keep your cool.

You're backed into a corner by things that aren't human, and don't know where to go or what to do next? Keep your cool.

But once the fight is on… it's time to get hot.

I worry sometimes that I'm in this business for all the wrong reasons… that for all my pretensions about protecting the innocent, the real reason I'm on a Wreck Squad is for the moments where I can let my aggressions free to crush, kill, and destroy anything that opposes me. Everybody thinks I'm this endless storehouse of patience and calm, but the truth is, I've always had a problem with my temper. I call it the Demon, and ever since my teens, I've had to keep the Demon sealed in a deep, deep vault. I keep myself cool, because I have to… at my size, a reckless punch thrown in a moment's anger could do some serious damage, maybe even irreparable damage. So, I keep cool, until it's time to get it on, and only then do I let the Demon loose. Afterword, I always feel strangely satisfied and also guilty at the same time, as if I'd just had sex with the wrong woman.

I'm not sure I like who I am at that moment. I'm not sure I like what those feelings imply.

Once it gets hot, though, there's no use debating. I'd stopped in the hallway because something didn't feel right; I couldn't put my finger on it, but it was there. Then, they hit us. I was shooting before I knew what had happened; some part of me registered Peter's head getting blown apart, and that's when I let the Demon loose. The shotgun was rattling in my fists; I was shooting into what seemed to be a solid wall, but I've been on enough ops to know that you can't always trust your eyes.

Something flew out of the wall and hit me; something big and covered with fur. It was vaguely humanoid, probably seven feet tall, and almost as a reflex, I shoved the shotgun up and cold-cocked it across its dripping jaws. It was stunned just long enough for me to stomp-kick it back a meter or two, and then the Demon really kicked in, just as somebody started shouting "Illusion! Illusion!"

My mind left me, and I fell into a red haze. I drew my kukri knife from my belt, and chopped the creature across the side of the head, skinning off its left ear and a chunk of its scalp. It turned and snarled, and that's when I realized what it looked like: a hyena. Broad neck, dog-like ears, and jaws that could break soup bones.

It jumped me. I let the kukri's heavy blade slip into its stomach… it impaled itself in its leap. Blood ran over my wrist, but the hyena-man kept coming. Its breath reeked, a dog's breath when it's been at its own feces. The dripping jaws snapped close enough to my face that the creature's fur slid along my cheek; it had me pinned down and was trying for leverage. The whole time, I was digging in with my small machete of a knife, ripping upwards, snarling much like my enemy.

At last, the strength went out of the creature and its eyes began to dim. I bench-pressed the bastard up and off of me, recovered my shotgun, and just laid on the trigger in the direction of the illusory wall.

Strange thing about illusions. Once you see enough evidence to disbelieve in them... such as creatures leaping through an illusory wall... poof, they're gone. No fading out, no on-again off-again, just pop, as if your mind reaches a critical mass of disbelief all at once.

The illusion disappeared for me when a hand grenade came out of the wall. Luckily, Shakes had a shield up, and the grenade bounced back into the illusion, and poof. I could see our enemy. Eight or nine of those big hairy bastards, the hyenoids. Couple of bodies on the ground... and Ed Wycheck and Sonny Carlisle from Squad Two, blazing away at us with their guns.

"I can't hold it!" Shakes shouted, and we all rolled away from the now-visible hallway entrance, just as the grenade blew.

I was up and my weapon was in my hands in a flash. The Demon was loose, and was not yet satisfied. Most of the enemy were dead, dying, or dazed from fragmentation wounds by the time I rounded the corner, but I laid into them anyway, laid into them with a vengeance, kept firing and firing until my fingers went numb with the vibration of the weapon's recoil. Gunsmoke was practically blinding me; my weapon clicked on empty, and I charged them, smashing the butt into one of the hyenoid's heads again and again, until Shakes finally grabbed my arm.

"Damn it, Dread! They're dead!"

The Demon left, with reluctance. It was time to see how badly we'd been hurt.

"Are you hit?" I asked.

Shakes shook his head. "Peter took the brunt of it, and then when that thing..." he pointed at the first hyenoid, "...jumped on top of you, you both knocked me down and out of the line of fire."

I looked around, saw some were dead, some were hurt, but the center went out of my soul when I saw two were missing.

"Where's Cass?"

Shakes shook his head. "She got hit, and Stephen started dragging her away. I thought, you know, it was just to get her clear, but..."

"He would've come back by now."

Shakes nodded.

I wanted to run off after her, damn the mission, damn the others, find her and get her out of the hands of that fucking traitor.

You see, I'd had an epiphany. It hit me in an instant, a flash of realization. Like the illusory wall... poof, gone... my epiphany was the opposite... poof, there.

Wreck Squads rarely encounter gunfire, usually only when a Vive has some sort of human cult following. Wizards can conjure monsters, throw magefire, but they almost never arm their creations... those monsters don't *need* firearms. But we'd been hit hard, with serious firepower... and the answer was right there when the illusion disappeared.

Polonius had Vived Squad Two somehow and sent them against us. And if he could control those Vive Jobs, he could control

Stephen.

And now, that Vive had Cass.

Running recklessly after her would've been gratifying, momentarily; a way to fight off that feeling of helplessness, a way to assure myself I was doing something, taking action, rushing to the rescue. But the truth was, it would've been rash, stupid, and counter-productive. Who knew what other traps Polonius had, or if Stephen had met up with friends? I counted four Squad Two bodies... which left Kerry and one other still at large.

We had to re-group, work out the best move, and play it smart.

Peter was gone... there was no doubting that. Even without the headshot, he'd taken a dozen rounds to the body. Mike was history, too... magefire had nearly torn him apart. Shakes was okay... he always was lucky... but Tara had bullet wounds in her thigh and stomach, and would have to be carried.

Still, it could've been worse... if Shakes hadn't gotten that shield up so fast, we all would've been Wrecked.

*   *   *

"Your ear," Shakes pointed at Dread's left ear.

Dread's hand touched and came back bloody. "Is it bad?"

"No. Your scalp's a little torn up on that side, but it's not ripped off or anything."

Dread shifted his attention to the bullet wounds scattered across Tara's body. "How you doin', troop?"

Her face was pale, and she looked like she was about to start shivering again. "This ain't... my day, Dread."

"Shakes, what kind of Healing array do you have?"

Shakes shook his head. "Nothing for this. I have a Blood Expander trick; it'll buy her some time, keep her from going into hypovolemic shock..."

"But only temporarily," Dread said. "And she still won't be able to walk."

"She probably couldn't even if I was able to heal her," Shakes said. "I gave her some morphine against the pain; that's why she's been so quiet."

Dread nodded. "Okay. Do what you can... and dress her wounds while you're at it."

Shakes broke open a medical kit. "What are you going to do?"

"Salvage whatever weapons I can," the big man replied, fitting a fresh belt of twelve-gauge rounds into his shotgun. "I wish..."

He stopped. Shakes could almost see the gears turning in his head.

"What?"

"We've all got these..." Dread pulled an earpiece out of his ear and held it up, "...sub-mandibular comm units. We haven't activated them yet, because we haven't needed to split up..."

"And we always maintain radio silence as long as possible," Shakes said. "So what? Even if we activate them and try to talk to Cass, Stephen has an earpiece too; he'll hear everything we say."

"Maybe not," Dread said, clipping a wire into his earpiece which led to a cellular-phone-sized radio on his belt.

Pressing a button, and holding the earpiece in so he could hear better, Dread said, "Control, this is Squad Four. Control, this is Squad Four."

A voice crackled in his ear. "Control here. What is your sitrep, Four?"

"Communications compromised, Control. We need you to remotely shut down the following personal receivers: four, five, and seven."

Dread shrugged and took out his earpiece so he could tell Shakes, "Might as well shut down Mike's and Peter's, too. I don't like the idea of their earpieces talking into... dead ears."

The earpiece crackled again. "Standby, Four. Roger, following receivers down: four, five, seven. Should we activate the others?"

Dread grunted. "Damn right you should."

CASS

I'd never seen a Vived Maestro up close and personal without a gun in my hand. It took me about half a second to decide I preferred to experience them while armed.

Physically, Polonius was a disappointment. I suppose I was expecting a colossus, or a hideous mutation. He was just a guy, medium height, pot belly, gray hair, wearing those ridiculous robes that mages and professors wear during their respective graduation ceremonies... the kind with the funny hats and the braided cord knotted around their shoulder. Frankly, he looked soft. He looked like I could walk up and kick his ass with my left thumb.

Then, the air around him shifted, shimmered, just a bit, as if there were a powerful heat source at his feet. It was a distortion I knew well. A Defensive Shield, the kind that keeps out just about everything except harsh language. Polonius was just shy of invincible behind that barrier.

Kerry's Striker mage... or ex-Striker mage, I suppose... was there with him, his face and neck covered in the pinkish swirls which seemed to be all the rage today. He looked smug when he saw me. They all did; they looked as if the game was already won, and frankly, they were right. I was screwed. I tried to stay strong, tried to be the classic all-American hero, laughing at death, but the truth was, my knees were starting to feel weak and my hands were starting to tremble.

Then, salvation.

My radio earpiece, which I'd completely forgotten, crackled with Dread's voice.

"Cass, Dread. Do not respond, repeat, do not respond. Break squelch if you read me."

I can't ever express how I felt at that moment. A half-second before, I was alone, surrounded by insane Vive Jobs and looking down the barrel of a gruesome fate. Now...

Now I had a fighting chance. Dread was alive, *alive*, God bless the gigantic bastard, and if I knew him at all, I knew he was on his way with the mindset of a wrecking ball.

I broke squelch in my comm unit by tripping it with a pair of short coughs. Stephen didn't seem to be picking up Dread's transmission, thankfully, so I started figuring out how I was going to transmit intel without anybody catching on.

"Okay, Cass, here it is," Dread reported into my ear. "We know Stephen's gone rogue; we've cut off his comm unit. This is our sitrep. Peter and Mike are gone. Tara's shot up, and her clock is ticking. Shakes and I are intact."

Then get your ass down here! I wanted to shout. I kept my cool, though, looking around the room for any pertinent data. Maestro Polonius picked that moment to speak.

"Welcome, Cassandra."

A Hollywood hack couldn't have come up with a more predictable line. Vive Jobs are always suckers for a cliche'.

"Well, well, well, Polonius," I said loudly, picking my words with care. "Here we all are. You, me, Kerry, Stephen, and I think Kerry's Striker is named..."

"Wentworth," the dead man in question finished for me.

"...Wentworth," I said. "Nice cozy spot, too... the twenty-first floor boardroom, I take it?"

"It seemed appropriate," Polonius said, but I was listening to Dread.

"Copy that, Cass, you and four hostiles on the twenty-first floor boardroom."

"Rather impressive shield you've got around you," I nodded toward Polonius.

The Maestro smiled. "A necessary precaution. Your friends outside might decide to rocket the building."

"We can't do that, Maestro, and I think you know it. Posse Comitatus law keeps the military from stepping in, and SWAT doesn't have that sort of firepower."

"If you say so," he said.

Dread's voice came again. "Damn, he's got a shield up? Okay, we're working on it... hang on."

"Very well..." Polonius said, and my mind whirred, desperate for any stalling tactic.

"So why here? Why Revival Tech?" I asked quickly. Vives love to hear themselves talk, and I needed to buy as much time as possible.

Where are you, Dread? my lips begged to ask, but I had to keep quiet.

"Why this place?" he began. "Why, it was..."

I tuned him out. I didn't give a shit about his psycho reasons; I was waiting for Dread's next report, straining whatever vestigial muscles I might have in my auditory canal to detect the tiniest peep out of Dread.

When it came, his voice nearly burst my eardrum. "Shakes! Get a shield up!"

Oh, no, Dread, my mind started to fret. *Come on, don't get caught up, you've got to get down here and save my ass, these guys are planning to do some seriously bad hoo-joo to me...*

I could hear gunfire coming from the floor above, the deep rumble of Dread's F-Shok followed by the sharper stacatto of a submachinegun.

Dread's voice. "Just keep them off on that side!"

Shakes' voice. "Three more your side! Three more your side!"

More gunfire. I was finding it difficult to pretend I was calmly listening to the Maestro's pedantic rambling, instead of wishing I was on the twenty-second floor with a flamethrower.

Shakes' voice. "Are we clear?"

Dread's voice. "Just keep that shield up on your side, I'm going to carry Tara."

A grunt, presumably from Dread, and then his voice. "Come on!"

Shakes. "They're going to break through soon!"

Dread. "Then come on! Cass, we're being over-run by more of those seven-foot hyenoids... no, damn it, Shakes, *this* way... they're all over the damn place... Contact! There!"

More gunfire, and now I was really starting to worry.

DREAD

Those damn hynena-men. They charged us out of nowhere, and we barely got out of that hallway intersection alive.

Shakes held them off with shields and pressor waves on his end, and I burned through half a belt of twelve gauge before clearing an exit route. Then, I carried Tara out of there on my shoulders, praying I could handle any hostiles with her bleeding to death over my shoulder.

The whole time, I was thinking about Cass.

Thinking about where she was, what she was thinking, wondering if she was hurt, scared, panicking. Promising myself when this was over, we were going to sit down and I was going to spill my guts to her.

We got to a corner of the twenty-second floor, and bam... the hyenoids were gone. They disappeared, gave up their pursuit.

I kicked the door in on an office and laid Tara on the floor. There were two doors into the room. We barricaded the one with a heavy desk and stood guard at the other.

"Now what?" Shakes asked.

Good question. I was about to suggest we move out, head for the stairwell while we could, when it started.

Laughter.

Not human laughter, but a twittering, jibbering giggle which, for all its strangeness, sounded vaguely familiar. It took a second before I realized where I'd heard it before... on a TV documentary about hyenas.

"Jesus, listen to that," Shakes said, as the twittering cacophony got louder. "There must be dozens of them."

The radio broke squlech, just as another series of twitters began... over by the barricaded door. It was a second group, coming up on our other side.

"I can't talk right now, Cass," I said, when the radio broke squelch again.

"What do we do, Dread?" Shakes was starting to sound a little jittery.

"I don't know."

"Don't tell me that!" he whispered harshly.

I felt like snapping back, but like I said before, in this job, you have to keep your cool. It wasn't working very well... there weren't any windows to escape through, they were coming up on both sides of us, and we were slowed down by an unconscious casualty.

I didn't see a way out. I started thinking out loud. "Maybe we can make a rush through them."

"Through those things?" Shakes said. "Carrying Tara and with hardly any ammo? I don't think so, Dread!"

The twittering laughter continued to swell, and the louder it got, the more I lost my cool. What the hell did Shakes want from me? There was no way out, couldn't he see that? They'd backed us into a corner, and now they were closing in for the kill.

Sorry, Cass.

* * *

"Why me?" Cass asked. "Why did you take me alive?"

Polonius shrugged. "To be honest, I wanted the one you call Dread. But, the fortunes of war are fickle, and the hyenoids are difficult to control. So, Stephen took you instead."

"What for?"

"I am going to make you a part of the next stage of human development," Polonius said, his shield making him appear to wobble just a bit.

"Oh hey, thanks, but no thanks."

"Don't be so hasty. You have no idea what you're saying no to."

Cass glanced around at Stephen and Kerry. "I think I have an idea. I've taken down enough of you Vives to figure out how your rotten heads think."

"Really."

"Your body's not what it used to be, is it, Polonius? Falling apart at the seams? Shame. Really. Looks like I won't have to wax you after all; you'll just rot away to mush all on your own."

"Watch your tone," Kerry said.

"Fuck you, Kerry. Fuck all of you," Cass looked around the room. "You're all a bunch of traitors. All that crap, all those guilty looks about how we should trust you, Stephen, and you turn on us."

"You don't understand," Stephen said.

"Explain it to her," Polonius said.

"Yeah, explain it to me, Stephen," Cass said. "Explain to me how you can turn your back on every ideal you've ever... you know what? Screw that. Explain to me how you can turn your back on us, on *me*. The team is gone because of you. Explain *that*."

Stephen winced and didn't meet her gaze. "I didn't want it to go that way, but it had to. A few lives, Cass, of people who would've given up those lives if they knew what it meant. What *he* means."

"What does he mean?" Cass asked.

Polonius stepped forward a bit, arms held wide. "I am Wisdom. I am Power. I have so much to offer the world... consider it. How many different factions, loyalties, contradictions, exist in just one person, much less a thousand, much less a million, much less a city of millions? How much conflicting energy, how many conflicting purposes? I can unify the world with my wisdom. I can take away all that separates us and make us one, make us united.

"Look at the contradictions in yourself. You are a woman, a nurturer and creator; and yet here you are, drawn to violence, drawn to death, as if you feel compelled to deny what you are. Your entire existence is a contradiction. And you aren't the only one. This city teems with those just like you, who contradict themselves and each other each and every moment of the day. This is what I can remedy. This is what I offer.

"Think about it," he continued. "Without those chaotic thoughts separating us, there will no longer be conflict. No violence, no greed, no suffering... just peace. Just wisdom. Just one."

"Just *you*," Cass said. "If peace is all that's on your mind, why did you torch that apartment building?"

The Maestro shrugged. "I needed to get you in here. You see, I can control those who have returned..." he gestured to the Revived troopers, "...because I share their situation. To control the living, I need to be the living. I need to be you."

* * *

"He's going to possess her," Shakes said, listening in on his earpiece.

"I know," Dread said, trying to ignore the increasing tempo of the hyenoid's twitters.

"We've got to do something, Dread..."

"What?" Dread shouted, the gibbers of the swarming hyenoids unhinging him. "What are we going to do, Shakes? Leave Tara here, for those things to tear apart? Even then, we wouldn't make it ten feet. We don't have the ammo and you don't have the strength to hold them off. And even if we could, we'd never make it in time. Figure it out, Shakes! We're screwed! We can't go through walls, we can't go through floors, and we sure as h..."

He stopped. The anger left his face, like snow blown away in the wind, replaced by a look Shakes had seen earlier that night on Cass's face, when she'd knelt by the pool on the twenty-fourth floor. It was the look of epiphany.

"Dread?"

Dread nodded, the cackles of the hordes of monsters momentarily forgotten. "I've got an idea."

"Don't leave me in suspense here, Dread."

"When we dropped in..." he said slowly, as if he was still working it out in his head. "Polonius has a screen up along the outside of the building, nobody in, nobody out."

"Right."

"The screen is like... an invisible skin or membrane around the building. You can go all around it, but not through it."

"Yeah, but how..."

"What about *inside* of it?" Dread asked. "What about teleporting around inside of the building? We never cross the membrane, never cross the skin of the building."

Shakes' jaw hung slack. "Goddamn. I am in the presence of greatness. We should... we should be able to do just that. How come we never thought of that before? How come *Polonius* never thought of it?"

"Because it's an oversight," Dread grinned humorlessly. "For all his pretensions, for all his powers, Polonius is like us… he's fallible, he's human, and human beings fall prey to oversights."

The twittering increased exponentially, and they caught sight of heavy shapes from their vantage point at the open door.

"Inside, close the door and lock it," Dread said, when heavy blows began shaking the far door on its hinges behind the desk.

Shakes cut loose with a long burst, ending the assault just for a second. There was a squeal, and then the pounding resumed, brown shapes visible through the bullet holes in the door.

He raised his gun again, but Dread stopped him with a hand on his shoulder. "Don't do their job for them," the big man said. "Stay in front of Tara."

"So what do we do? Teleport down, all of us? What about Tara?"

Dread shook his head. "Only I go."

"Dread…"

"Shakes, you're falling apart. You don't have many more Tricks left in you. You send me down, I nail Polonius. Polonius drops, the teleport screen goes down, and Control can swarm this entire place with reinforcements."

Shakes didn't want to buy it. "I still think I should go with you. You need me."

"*She* needs you," Dread pointed toward Tara. "To hold off those things until help arrives."

Both doors were shaking under the impact of heavy blows now, and dozens of misshapen throats giggled their desire to charge in and tear and rip. "All right," Shakes nodded. "There's just one problem."

CASS

My hands were starting to shake. Hey, sue me; I'm not some granite-nerved movie hero. A Vive Job has me at his mercy, and he's talking about stealing my soul. I was terrified.

I was terrified because I knew I couldn't stop him. There's no way for a non-mage to fight that sort of power, not for very long, anyway. Throw me in the middle of a firefight, send ugly creatures after me, fine; that I can handle, that I can fight, even if the odds are poor.

These odds were zero. They were going to hold me down, Polonius would tear my soul out of my body, and use me to do to the entire city what he'd done to Stephen and Kerry. Better for me to die.

I'd just decided I couldn't wait for Dread any longer, that I was going to have to do something crazy to get myself killed before Polonius could possess me, when Dread's voice came back to save me.

"Cass, Dread. Listen up; I can get down there, I can teleport down there, but you have to get his shield down. Do you read me? You have to get his shield down."

Yeah, sure, no problem, Dread, I thought. *I'll just bat my eyelashes and ask the dead guy nicely, he's sure to do it.*

"Cass, it's Shakes. He's got to drop his shield to work the Possession Trick. Just tell us 'now', and Dread will be there in three seconds."

Now. Beautiful. And if the good Maestro could work his Trick inside of three seconds, then what?

Dread's voice again. "Hurry, Cass. We're about twenty seconds away from being overrun."

"You know what, Polonius?" I said, pushing up my sleeves mentally. "You're full of shit."

He didn't laugh. "Really."

"Really. All this talk about wisdom, and peace, is so much delusional Vive Job crap. If all you needed was a live body, why didn't you just take a janitor that was working here tonight? You didn't... you killed them all, didn't you? And as for drawing us in with that attack on the apartment building...why didn't you just request a hostage negotiator to come in here? Or leave one of Squad Two alive on the first assault?"

Polonius was silent. I could actually see my words cutting into him. Vive Job Psychology 101... They Are All Batshit Insane. Absolutely insane... but they can't stand to admit it. They can't stand it when a mirror gets held up in front of their face and they see how flawed and pathetic they are.

"What was that?" I continued. "Whoops? Killed 'em all again? I don't think so. The truth, the real truth is, you could've taken a live body anytime. You did this all just to show off."

He sneered. "Hardly."

"Hardly my ass. Pillars of fire torching entire buildings, ripping people inside out, hell, taking over this building of all buildings... you were practically daring us to come after you. You don't want to spread wisdom or peace or any other noise like that... you want to be worshipped. You want to be awed. You want to be revered."

Muscles twitched along his face, and he looked at me like he wanted to strip me of my hide with a whip. "Gods should be revered."

"There it is," I said, walking slowly to the board room table and leaning up against it. "Every Vive I ever met has the same lunatic story… God Complex. So you play your pitiful games, killing and destroying just so someone claps their hands, pays you some attention and makes you forget for a while that you're nothing but broken shards of glass. Take a good look, Polonius. You're no god. You're just a rotting chunk of meat who knows a few card tricks."

The Maestro's eyes narrowed. "Then let's do something about that. Gentlemen."

I managed to kick Kerry in the crotch and crack Wentworth on the nose once before they pinned my struggling limbs down and hoisted me face-up onto the table. I managed to lift my head, and saw Polonius approaching slowly, smiling smugly, ready to take me, take my soul.

But the shimmer was gone. No shimmer, no glimmer, no shield… he'd finally let his guard down.

"Do it *now*," I said, staring him down in defiance.

*   *   *

Three.
Two.
One.
Dread blinked.

*   *   *

Polonius was just opening his mouth to say something when there was a pop. It sounded like a large light bulb breaking; it was the sound of a six foot six, three hundred pound mass displacing an

Strange Days

equal amount of air as Dread appeared in the room.

The Maestro turned and said "What?" just in time to catch a burst from Dread's F-Shok that tore open his abdomen and shredded his right arm to the shoulder. He staggered and fell, knocking over a chair as he tried to stop himself on the way down.

Dread pivoted on one foot and leveled the shotgun at the three Vives pinning Cass to the table. "Down!"

Cass didn't need to be told twice. As soon as her captors let go of her to reach for weapons, she rolled off of the table and fell heavily to the floor.

Thunder roared. Kerry was torn to shreds before he could get off a shot, but Wentworth fired a handful of bright darts of magefire from his fingers before taking a round to the hip.

The darts smashed into Dread's upper chest and left shoulder; the F-shok blew apart under a pair of them. Dread dropped the damaged weapon, somehow managing to keep his feet despite the grave wounds trailing smoke from his body. He began struggling to draw his pistol as Wentworth mustered enough strength to fire again.

Stephen rose up from behind the table and aimed his pistol. The shots went wild; Cass recovered from her fall and slammed into Stephen in a tackle that threw the dead man into the wall. She chopped the gun out of his hand with a knife hand strike, and followed it up with a quick stomp to the knee that dropped him.

"Dread!" she shouted, dashing for Stephen's pistol, but she was too late. Dread had lost the race.

Another salvo of magefire flashed into the big man, punching holes through his armor and sending him to his knees. Dread managed to stay upright only by hooking on to a chair with his right arm, the only arm that was still working.

Cass screamed and snatched up Stephen's pistol, firing half of the magazine into Wentworth's head, sending the renegade Vive back to the Earth.

"Dread!" she said, moving around the table toward him. He was shot to pieces; bloody, burnt holes trailing smoke all across his torso, left arm, and shoulder. His eyes rolled toward her and he opened his mouth, trying to gesture behind her.

Gunfire from behind Cass punched a pair of holes out of her abdomen; it was more surprising than painful. Then, shock came crashing in a wave, as she stumbled forward and caught herself on the desk, staring down at her own blood and tissue blown across the wood.

What? Where? she wondered, wound shock taking her mind away.

She was mostly numb now, but she knew that would change to pain in a second; severe pain, crippling pain. For now, she turned her head and saw Stephen holding a pistol, the barrel still smoking.

Took it off of me when he dragged me away from the ambush, she realized. *'Where's my sidearm?' 'Dunno.' Yes, you did, Stephen, you stuck it inside your jacket.*

Stephen shook his head helplessly. "It didn't have to be this w..."

Bullets tore into him, a half-dozen across his left side. He staggered to his left, firing blindly into the table, and another long burst tore the top of his chest to hamburger. His pistol slipped from nerveless fingers, as a third burst caught him in the throat. Stephen held a hand to his neck briefly, staring at Cass, staring much the same way as he had a week and a day earlier, when a similar wound had killed him the first time around. Then, his already-dead eyes rolled back, and he fell, returned to the Earth.

"Cass?" Dread mumbled, his sidearm still pointed at the air Stephen had recently occupied. "Cass..."

He fell off of his armchair support, collapsing to the floor just as Cass's wounds got the better of her. She slid off of the table and to her knees, one hand trying to hold in her insides. Blood soaked her hand and dripped onto the floor; her limbs were trembling in pain. Her stomach was a lump of white-hot lead, burning straight back through her guts to scorch her spine, and when her knees hit the floor, it felt as if someone had kicked her in her bullet wounds. She almost passed out; consciousness throbbed once into a white flash, but she held it together, shuffling around the table to Dread as best she could on her knees.

I can't do this, she thought. *I can't take this, it's too bad, it's too much, it hurts so fucking bad I can't take it just lie down and rest that's what I've got to do is rest...*

He needs you, Cass.

Oh, no, no, rest. Can't help Dread, can't, too hurt.

Get up, Cass.

Get up!

"Get up!" she shouted to herself, snapping out of another unfocused stare. "Get over there! Go on, Cass!"

She could see him now, his body lying inert, face down on the floor. Blood leaked from innumerable wounds, pooling slowly around him. Blood was pooling around herself as well... she almost vomited when she saw the smeared blood trail she was leaving. Luckily, she held it off, or she would've passed out for certain.

"Cass."

She blinked hard. Dread wasn't talking; in fact, it didn't even look like he was breathing...

"Cass."

He was alive. Lying in a puddle of gore, one arm shot down to a torn-up stump, barely able to move his lips, was Maestro Polonius.

I can't shoot him, Cass thought. *The gun's recoil, it'll hurt too bad, it hurts bad now, I can't.*

"Cass."

He was getting stronger, slowly. Color was returning to his face, he started to speak more clearly, and his body started to shift around a bit.

He's healing himself, Cass realized. *He can't do much, because he's so bad, but soon, as he gets stronger...*

Shoot him!

I can't, it hurts...

"Cass." It was a full-fledged whisper now, getting steadily stronger. "Cass, I can save you. I can save him. I can heal you both, heal us all, if you just... join with me. Join with me, Cass, it's the only way, it's not too late..."

Will moved her arm. Hate moved her arm. Pure, stupid stubbornness raised her arm, and put her pistol's sights on Polonius's forehead.

The Maestro began to plead. "Cass, don't do this, you can still save yourself, save Dread, it's not too late..."

Blood flecked out of her lips. "It is for you, fucker."

She passed out almost instantly after firing.

*   *   *

Cass's eyes fluttered briefly, and she awoke. She was lying in a hospital bed, a tube leading from her arm to a clear plastic IV bag. Her whole body ached. It felt like she'd taken the beating of a lifetime.

Edison was there, a stupid smile on his face, like he actually thought he was the first person she'd want to see. "Welcome back, Cass."

She frowned at him. "How bad am I?"

Edison seemed about to answer, but Cass amended her question. "Is Dread okay? What about the others?"

"Peter and Mike were killed in the ambush," Edison said. "Nothing could be done for them. Tara... she'll recover, in time. Shakes is okay."

"Dread?"

Edison shrugged toward the wall. "Next room over."

Thank God, Cass thought. *Thank God for that.*

Something on Edison's face bothered her. "What is it?"

He fidgeted. "Cass, your injuries were pretty extensive..."

"I've got residual damage, something the Healers couldn't fix," Cass finished for him.

She supposed that wasn't such a shock, considering. So, she'd have to make some dietary changes, or maybe...

"It's not that."

Cass waited, and when Edison didn't continue, snapped, "Well, Christ, Edison, what the f-f-f..."

Her tongue seemed to catch, stutter, as if it had forgotten how to form words. A brief twitch of her facial muscles, and the catch disappeared.

She stayed perfectly still.

"Cass..." Edison began.

"Oh my God," she whispered. "You didn't."

"Cass, we had no choice, the facilities were right here, you weren't down very long..."

Her hands scrambled at the sheets, tearing at them, searching through them, until she found what she was looking for. It wasn't a hospital bed she lay in.

Stenciled on the sheets were the words REVIVAL TECHNOLOGY, INC.

CASS

I tried to kill him, but coming back from the dead takes the fight right out of you. Edison made it out of the room, shouting in through the little window mounted in the center of the door something about how he had to bring me back, that I was too valuable to lose, how I was only dead for a little while before they managed to Vive me.

"Was I down longer than Stephen? Hunh?" I shouted.

Edison's face was blank. "Reviving Stephen was a mistake, I admi..."

"They're all mistakes, you stupid prick! You should've left me dead!"

Edison couldn't say much to that. "You take a few days. Think about that," he finally said, and left.

There wasn't much to do at that point other than crumple up into a ball and weep.

Sometimes your worst nightmares come true. How many renegade Vives had I taken? How many lives did they take before I got to them?

How long before I went that way?

What sort of psychosis did I have in store for me? I could already feel it, physically; the inside of my skin felt itchy, as if it didn't like the feel of the muscle it covered.

Now I knew why that first Vive tore her own skin off. Just the idea of it, the idea of my skin, my dead skin, rotten underneath and chafing the rest of my no-longer-dead body, made me want to claw at myself, tear at myself like an animal who won't let a scab heal. How long until that compulsion became overwhelming?

How had my mind been altered? You don't Vive somebody without mis-crossing a few synapses, *that* much I did know. Who was I now? Not Cass Penswith, that's for sure. Now I was some sort of circus freak zombie, doomed to insanity and self-destruction.

I refused to see any visitors for the next two days, until they released me. A few "doctors" came in, told me I was as good as new, and if I hadn't been in a half-catatonic state, I would've ripped their lungs out.

Good as new. Just like Polonius. Just like Stephen.

How long? How long did I have?

They released Dread and I together. We rode the taxi home in silence, staring out of the window, lost in our respective hells. He started to fidget about; I could feel him wanting to say something, desperate to say something, but what was there to say?

"Revival Technology," he finally said, the words sounding like a cheap excuse for what he really wanted to say, "says that they've made a lot of progress since Polonius and Stephen..."

"I love you, Dread."

The words were out before I could think twice. Dread's eyes closed and a long, slow breath eased out of his chest.

"Ever... ever since I met you," was all he could say.

"Come home with me," I said, and took his hand in mine.

I couldn't help but notice the pinkish blotches of skin covering his forearm.

We tried to make love, but the act was doomed from the beginning. Too many pink stretches of skin reminding us what we were now, I guess. We couldn't even hold each other close; the same bulges of muscle I had wanted to meld with not so long ago were nothing but chunks of spoiled meat now. No matter how hard I tried, Dread's body still felt like a carcass to me. I looked into his eyes and knew he felt the same about me.

It's a sad, stupid, sappy cliche', and it's true. I'd hoped we could use this as a second chance, a new lease on life, an experience to set us free from the stupid psychological restraints keeping us apart. But the truth is, there are no second chances... there is only one go at life and there is no coming back, not really.

Every chance we had at a life together, we wasted. Now, we're just shards of glass.

We were laying side by side on our backs, staring at the ceiling, so we wouldn't have to look at each other, when he said it. "I'm not going out like Stephen."

It was decided that easily.

We'll be able to get our hands on what we need much more easily than you'd think. A couple dozen kilos of plastic explosives, detonators, and a sixty second timer. Not enough time to get out of the building, but enough time to say our goodbyes.

Revival Technologies, Incorporated, is about to be cremated.

As for us... Dread was right. It's only a matter of time, and I'm not going out like Stephen. Dread and I, we knew the risks and took them, saw our chances to be together and squandered them, convinced that we were invulnerable, invincible; that there'd always be another day, another chance, another life.

It could be worse. Some people never get the chance to say it, even if it is just a kiss before dying. I may not be able to fool myself for long, but my imagination is strong enough that for a little while, I can pretend he's the old Dread and I'm the old Cass.

I can pretend for sixty seconds.

Independent Study

Fans of HP Lovecraft will very quickly recognize this story as a homage to one of my favorite authors. For those of you unfamiliar with ol' Howie's work, HP Lovecraft was a writer in the '20s and '30s who published a very particular brand of horror. His monsters were unconventional, to say the least, and his horror was often focused around the idea of the human race being a puny and insignificant species adrift in a cosmos filled with massive, alien creatures who haven't wiped us out simply because they haven't noticed us yet.

On a side note, my fellow PSU alumni may recognize some settings and locations for this story that I borrowed from the four excellent years I spent at Penn State University.

Andrew C. Piazza

I brought this on myself.

No whining, no complaining, no laying the blame on others' shoulders when it belongs solely on mine. Curiosity killed the cat, and now it's come for me.

I can hardly be blamed, though. After all, I'm a graduate student in philosophy; at a university that will go unnamed on the off chance that I actually survive long enough to have to concern myself with potential legal entanglements from… well, we'll get to all of that. As I was saying, I'm a philosophy student, and we're supposed to be curious, right? Love of knowledge, and all that?

Perhaps that's all just an excuse. I've always been a snoop. There, fine, I confess.

Don't tell me you've never felt the thrill of peeking into some secret vault of information, whether it is someone's diary or a text message you weren't supposed to see or a letter delivered to your address by mistake. People have secrets, and they go to pretty significant lengths to hide them from the world. It's a serious thrill to peek behind the curtain and see what somebody thinks you shouldn't be allowed to see.

Sometimes what you see is ugly. Most of the time it's just silly or trivial. Still, it's all stuff you're not supposed to see, which makes it as good as gold.

It's even better when there's a challenge in getting to that gold. Peeking through windows is for perverts and amateurs. Getting around passwords, accessing rooms or files that you shouldn't be anywhere near… now, we're talking. That's how you get a really good glimpse into the secret world that lies hidden behind a wall of passwords and encryptions and other locked doors.

And there is a secret world, make no mistake. There is the world that people allow us to see, and there is the world that people keep hidden from the rest of us. So much truth is hidden in those secret places. In those places, people are honest; they allow themselves to be laid bare, to genuinely be who they really are. The world is unfiltered behind the curtain, in that secret world; there is no fear of embarrassment or the need to meet the expectations of others to cloud the true nature of reality.

People confess to their sins and inadequacies. They admit the loss of hope or faith. They reveal their loves and obsessions and desires and dreams, both foolish and otherwise.

They reveal the truth.

Sometimes it's mundane, sometimes it's astonishing. It's all gold to me; just in varying quantities. And it isn't always details about someone's personal life; imagine what truths you could learn about the world if you could read classified files about the real reasons we go to war, or what dangers and transgressions massive corporations hide from us in order to go on raking in millions from an unsuspecting public?

The truth is laid bare in those secret places. Pure, unadulterated, unfeeling… honest. Real. Raw. Golden.

That's how I got pulled in to this disaster. The irony is, there wasn't any obvious indication at first that I was on to anything this… monumental? Horrific? Even now, I have trouble coming up with the right words to characterize my experiences. Sometimes, the truth is awful beyond imagination, and more destructive than a hurricane.

It was during an excruciatingly boring stretch in my classes when I saw him. Thanksgiving break was approaching, and I'd already completed all of my assigned coursework up to break and even beyond; I'm mildly obsessive once I get going, so much so that I end up getting far ahead of the rest of the class. That's what leads to the quiet times that I end up filling with poking my nose into other people's secrets. Idle hands, and all that.

So much of my coursework was structured, spoon-fed tediousness… how can I be blamed for spicing up my life with a little independent study?

In any case, I saw him in the library, and in a second, I could tell he was hiding something. He was tucked away in a low traffic area; our library is gigantic to the point of monstrosity, but with as many students as there are running around campus, you have to go really deep into the stacks to avoid any contact with other people.

This guy clearly wanted to be left alone and hadn't hidden himself far enough away. Every time somebody walked past him, he jumped with a little start and looked all around with little twitch-like movements, as if he was trying to look in every direction at once.

Talk about cheese in a mousetrap for a guy like me. Here's a handy little tip from a snoop… if you have something to hide, the worst possible thing you can do is to keep looking around, wild-eyed, desperate to determine if somebody knows you have something to hide. All you do is tip your hand. If that big, bearded guy with the thick-rimmed glasses and giant stack of ancient looking books had simply sat still like he was slogging through boring nonsense, he would've simply disappeared. People filter out the boring. It becomes invisible. It's the unusual and novel that catches our attention… catches *my* attention.

Now, I wish that bastard *had* sat still with his damned books. I wish he'd blended in to the scenery like bland wallpaper. Then I wouldn't be sitting here, mostly deaf, covered in bruises, with a gun in my hand and surrounded by goddamn gasoline… but I'm getting ahead of myself.

As I said, I'd spotted my latest bit of cheese, and I immediately began to figure out how to snatch it out of the mousetrap. It was practically a reflex; I slipped into it with such practiced ease that I didn't even realize I was doing it until I was halfway done.

Right away, I spotted my way in. The big guy had two empty cans of Mountain Dew sitting on his desk and a third one in his hand. A man drinks that much soda, that fast, he's going to have to drain the snake sometime.

So, I settled in a short distance away behind a row of library books and pretended to be looking through them. There was a little gap above the filed books that allowed me to keep an eye on my quarry, and any time somebody walked by, I looked as enthralled as possible with the copy of Soils Of The American Northwest that I kept in my hand as camouflage.

It didn't take long. Mixed in with his twitching obsession with looking at whatever was over his shoulder, the big guy began a little pelvic shimmy and shake which told me that all of that Mountain Dew had travelled south and wanted out.

My spine began to tingle. This was exactly the moment I live for. Believe me, it takes a lot to cross over that threshold and trespass into the places someone has designated as Off Limits.

Imagine it. If you were walking down the street, and saw a house with the door left wide open, how easily could you walk into it? You have no idea who or what's in there. You have no idea if you'll be caught. All of that uncertainty mixed with the social conditioning of a lifetime's worth of *You're Not Allowed In There* creates an invisible barrier, a membrane that is nearly impossible to break through. It sits across that open doorway and dares you to push against it.

The first time I did it up at school, I got into the access tunnels that snake underground all over campus. There's nothing special in there, just wiring and pipes and some storage rooms, but it was off limits, and the entire time I was in there, I felt like a generator was wired up to my body. Electricity tingled and tickled and teased its way across my skin and along my vertebrae; it felt like the air in my lungs was charged with it.

Now, the old tingle was back, and it pulled me further in. I didn't know exactly where the bathroom was, but I had the general sense that it wasn't particularly close. My caffeine and sugar-addicted friend had chosen his study spot poorly. He realized it soon enough. He began to look back and forth, leaning out into the aisle and frowning, as if that was going to magically conjure a closer bathroom.

I couldn't help laughing a little to myself. It became comical, the big bearded guy's dance of bathroom desperation. A look at his laptop, then down the aisle, then at his books, then the aisle, and so on, and so forth. At last, it looked like he might pack it all up to take to the bathroom with him, but then he shook his head, closed his laptop, and just took that with him on his scurrying flight to release the floodgates.

It was too bad that he'd thought to take his laptop with him, but I'd take what I could get. A quick glance around told me nobody was in sight, so I casually walked over to where my target's books were set up and took a seat. Why not? Anybody walking by would just think that I'd been the one sitting there all along. Unlike my bearded friend, I was able to keep my outer shell calm and collected, even though inside I was a buzzing, crackling live wire.

He could come back at any second and catch me; that was the thought that made it exciting. In reality, though, no, he couldn't do that; he was on a mission and I had a solid two minutes before it became probable that he would return. Two minutes is a surprisingly long time. Try holding your breath.

Still, my heart was pounding and a slight smile played across my lips as I looked over his book selection. Eclectic, to say the least. A bound copy of *Annals of Physical Chemistry* from the late '50s. *Pagan Religions of the Dark Ages*. Some giant tome written in Latin. *On The Nature Of The Soul*, by an author I didn't recognize.

I didn't waste much time on that. Whatever he was looking for in those books, he would've distilled down and wrote into the old-school leather journal I'd spotted on his desk… the kind with the leather strap that wraps around the whole thing. Mr. Mountain Dew had taken along his laptop, but he'd left behind his journal.

A moment to mark just how the journal had been left, so that I could return it to that state after I was done, and then I flipped to the end of the entries. My free hand pulled out my cell phone, and my fingers got the camera working with practiced ease. I'd done this plenty of times before. My laptop is full of files from my little excursions over the years; mostly pictures taken with my phone of whatever secrets places or things I'd uncovered. They're my trophies. I'm a snoop, not a thief, so I don't take objects out of those secret places... only pictures.

There were all kinds of notes in the journal that didn't make much sense, since they were essentially fragments that were linked by whatever secret Mr. Mountain Dew was keeping. Perfect. That's what makes this sort of thing so much fun.

The first thing that caught my eye was a Latin phrase: *Voracis Unum*. Then the word "Emitter?" followed by the notation 74.45 EHz. There were actually several numbers, but most were crossed out and that last one, 74.45, was underlined, so it wasn't a stretch to guess which one was the winner. Another seemingly random number series... X090 D54B1787. I had no idea what that was, but it looked pretty important, and I was thinking password or perhaps two passwords.

The electric buzz sparking through my nervous system started to concentrate on the back of my neck, becoming a pressure that felt like somebody was looking over my shoulder. It was the feeling I got when I felt like I was almost out of time. I shook it off and finished clicking the last of my pictures.

There were several groups of names, with the notation "no amalgam" in the margin next to the last series. I had to shake my head at that one, but I kept snapping pictures before the pressure on the back of my neck become almost intolerable. I was really pushing it; Mr. Mountain Dew could be back any second, so I closed the journal back up just so, with the leather strap as it was when I started, and then I stood and started to walk away.

Two steps, and Mr. Mountain Dew practically ran into me as he charged around the corner. I actually had to backpedal quickly to avoid getting knocked over by his bulky frame. My eyes went wide and I thought I was caught, but I just gave him a little smile and nod, and he scurried around me with barely a second glance.

Of course, I still had that stupid book about soils in my hand, and I was about to toss it on a nearby desk and leave it when I realized it gave me an excuse to retrace my steps and get a second glance at my new target. For a few minutes, I pretended to read, and then wandered back to where I'd started, looking very intently at the numbers on the ends of the rows of stacks. I was just another student, trying to remember where to re-shelve his boring book, and I don't think Mr. Mountain Dew even recognized me as I went past him.

His cell phone rang as I stuck the soils book back amongst its brothers and I lingered long enough to catch bits and pieces of the conversation.

"…well, he's going to have to," Mr. Mountain Dew said, his voice rising enough for me to hear it. "You know we only have, like, two days until we can get to the emitter again…"

I lost the rest of it, but on the way back out of the library, I got a quick glance over Mr. Mountain Dew's shoulder. It was only a glimpse, but I got a taste of what he was looking at on his laptop.

It was obituaries. Local obituary listings. As I passed him, he wrote down one of the names in his journal.

This was getting weirder and weirder. I was in Heaven.

Another one of the pieces clicked into place for me as I pushed my way out of the library's revolving front door and practically skipped down the steps to the sidewalk.

When I'd gone back to peek over Mr. Mountain Dew's shoulder

the second time, I had pantomimed looking for the right place to re-shelve my stupid book on soils. I'd been staring at all those Dewey Decimal numbers like I actually cared where I re-shelved that book, and now I practically kicked myself for not realizing it earlier. That's what that strange series of numbers was. A Dewey Decimal classification.

I mentally patted myself on the back for working that out and began scrolling through the pictures on my phone to pass the time on my walk home. The phrase "no amalgam" was the first thing to catch my eye. An internet search on that phrase brought up a series of pages on mercury poisoning and dental fillings. *No amalgam.* No amalgam fillings, perhaps?

Something crawled along the length of my spine. This guy was looking up obituary listings of the recently deceased, with a reminder to himself to avoid amalgam fillings? For what possible reason could he care what sort of dental work these people had done to them while they were still breathing?

* * *

Things took a turn for the creepier later that night while I was at home. It was an idle comment from my roommate, who was reading through the paper on the couch while we were watching TV.

"Did you see this?" he asked. "Sick."

"What's that?"

"Some lunatic stole a body from the morgue. Who the hell does that?"

Something clicked in my mind, and I snatched the paper out of his hand. The article didn't offer much in the way of details, but it did provide a name: Martin Banks. That was the name of the man whose corpse had been stolen.

I looked through the pictures I'd taken on my phone, but I already knew I what I would find there. Several pages into Mr. Mountain Dew's journal, was the list of names... including the name of the stolen corpse, Martin Banks.

The room spun a bit. Clearly, I'd stumbled onto something much, much bigger and stranger than I'd realized. Thoughts of contacting the police floated in and out of my head, but I knew I'd never go down that path. First off, what exactly would I tell them? That I had a good idea of who stole that body? What would happen when they asked how I knew? A lot of uncomfortable questions about my activities and a lot of unwelcome attention.

That was only part of it. This was *my* mystery to solve, *my* secret to uncover. This glimpse behind the curtain belonged to *me*; I couldn't have the police or somebody else ruin it for me. They would bash down the door and trample through those secret places, ruining them before I'd had a chance to see. I just wanted to see. I needed to see. So I kept it to myself, and moved another step closer to looking behind the curtain… and another step closer to this fate that's befallen me.

My roommate was a grad student in electrical engineering, so I asked him, "If 'MHz' is the shorthand for 'megahertz', what's 'EHz' shorthand for?"

"Um, exahertz. Ten to the… eighteenth power, I think."

"Is there anything special about that frequency?"

He shrugged. "Depends what you mean by special. If we're talking EM fields, that's up in the ionizing radiation range… X-rays or gamma rays, I'm pretty sure. You'd probably want to check with somebody in physics or P Chem."

P Chem…Physical Chemistry. One of Mr. Mountain Dew's books was *Annals of Physical Chemistry*. "What would create that sort of thing?"

"Gamma rays?" he said. "That's like, astronomical events, nuclear fission, that sort of thing. Severe thunderstorms, too, if I remember right."

Something else clicked in the back of my head. The cell phone call… Mr. Mountain Dew had mentioned using 'the emitter'.

"Is there something on campus that could generate a gamma ray like that? An emitter of some sort?"

"Not sure why you'd want to. Gamma rays are dangerous, way worse than X-rays. You'd need shielding… there might be some doo-hickey or another up on the P Chem labs that could do it. What's this all about?"

"Oh, nothing," I lied. "Something I overheard in the library. Just made me curious."

"Curious," my roommate said. He didn't sound convinced.

I changed the subject quickly, to whatever trivial and meaningless garbage we were watching on TV. It was half-hearted at best, though; the reality was, I could barely sit still. It took everything I had to feign interest in that stupid glowing rectangle that sat in front of our couch and was supposed to keep us entertained and numb from what was going on in the real world. I felt like Mr. Mountain Dew, squirming in his chair, looking again and again at the door in desperation.

I might've lasted ten minutes. It was getting late, but the library was still open, and once I mumbled some lame excuse about forgetting a project that was due the next day, I practically ran out of the house and back to the library.

*   *   *

The Dewey decimal number was the next piece to the puzzle. The library's information desk was manned by a work-study student who barely glanced at the slip of paper I'd handed her and never looked up at me at all.

"Rare books room," she said.

"Where's that?"

She sighed, annoyed as hell with me that she had to tear her eyes away from her constant text messaging. "Elevator's around that way. Down three floors. The sub-basement stacks. All the way in the back. You'll need your ID and you have to sign in."

I thanked her and left her to her texting. The rare books room? I didn't even know there was an elevator, much less a rare books room, and I kicked myself a little for never having discovered that little secret about the library.

The elevator to the sub-basement looked like it had been built in the age of steam engines. I felt it wobble slightly as I stepped inside; I pictured the steel cable holding up the elevator as a frayed rope with only a handful of intact strands left. The whole compartment vibrated as I slowly slid downward toward the sub-basement.

My idle mind began to wander. I imagined the big bearded guy out in a cemetery in the dead of night, standing up to his thighs in a grave he was doggedly digging up by the light of a lantern. In my mind, he dug and dug, until he finally hit something unyielding. With a gleeful smile, he ripped open the casket, and taking a pair of pliers from his pocket, he knelt down over the body. *Let's have a look at those fillings*, he said. Pushing the corpse's lips back with one hand, he dug into its mouth with the pliers, and began to pull and yank with everything he had, grunting with exertion until the tissue finally gave free...

There was a lurching shudder, and the elevator finally stopped its slow descent, pulling me out of my gruesome daydream. For a moment, nothing happened, and I began to have a creeping concern that the doors were stuck and I'd have to yell and scream for hours in my ancient metal coffin before somebody would come and dig me out... if they ever came at all.

Even when the doors finally did open, I didn't feel at ease. The long, narrow corridor leading out of the elevator was lined with rows and rows of dusty, moldering books. The lights overhead were dim, sparse in number, and flickering.

This was a mausoleum, not a library; a place for long-dead and forgotten things. Every step I took, every sound I made, seemed somehow amplified by the quiet and then simultaneously swallowed up by it. It felt like I was underwater or in a soundproof room; the air seemed to press against me from all directions at once and clog up my throat like cotton.

That old urban legend of a student being strangled in the stacks and left there, undiscovered for weeks, came back to me. It didn't seem like a legend in that quiet corridor of flickering, uncertain light and deadened sound. Murder seemed a likely occurrence in that place.

I actually slapped my hands against my thighs to shake myself out of those thoughts, and began to whistle softly like a trembling child crossing a graveyard in the middle of the night. A little sound and movement to chase away the phantoms hiding in the dark, that's what I needed; but still, I found myself walking faster than usual toward the end of the corridor, with many side-flung glances into the rows of books to ensure no hidden killer was waiting for me there.

The rare books room itself was a bit of a let-down after feeling like I'd crawled through a haunted cave to get there. It was well lit, had plenty of desks and chairs, and was guarded by a wizened old librarian dead asleep in her chair.

I almost woke her up before it occurred to me that I could put a name to a face for Mr. Mountain Dew if he'd signed in. There, on top of the counter that the sleeping librarian sat behind, was a clipboard with a pen on a chain. Names were scrawled on one side, with the call sign of the book that the visitor was interested in on the opposite side.

My eyes scanned down to find X090 D54B1787 on the right side, and once again, I felt that old, excellent charge of electricity when I spotted it. Another step closer.

The name of the visitor corresponding to the call sign was James Boston. The writing was shaky, as if written by a nervous or trembling hand. Mr. Mountain Dew had a name now.

A little cough woke up the sleeping librarian. She didn't seem surprised, annoyed, or embarrassed at being caught napping; she took it in stride and gestured for me to hand over my ID and sign in.

Once that was accomplished, she gave a little snort when she checked the call sign. "Popular book lately," she said.

I shrugged. "We must have the same class."

"All the same to me. Don't know what the fascination is with that ugly old thing."

It seemed strange to hear a librarian talk about a book that way, but once she brought it out, I understood. It *was* ugly. Old, partially burned, stained by being soaked with water at some point; even the title was mostly obliterated on the cracked and mangled leather cover. The lower right portion looked as if it had been hacked at with a knife.

The first few letters of the title were ARC with the rest obliterated. I afraid to try to open the thing; it was so cracked and splintered and ancient that it felt like it would fall apart with the slightest touch. Why they let anybody with a student ID handle something so fragile, I'll never know. Maybe it wasn't considered valuable. Maybe it had just been forgotten in that tomb of a sub-basement like everything else down there.

The first few pages had been torn out, but there was a partial table of contents left. Among the listings, I found one for *Voracis Unum*, which I recognized from Boston's journal, so I gingerly spread the old book open to the corresponding page. Much of the interior of the book was in the same shape as the exterior: horrible. Dark stains obliterated passages, pages were stuck together or ripped out in wild chunks, and much of the ink was faded into near-nothingness.

What little was left read somewhat like an encyclopedia, with the stilted language and strange double-S that characterizes books printed back in the 1700s. *Voracis Unum*, read the heading:

VORACIS UNUM

(The Voracious One, The Ravenous, The Eater of Souls)

The rest of the entry described some sort of entity or creature which it described as "otherworldly". Like the rest of the book, most of it was obliterated by neglect and violence, but certain passages jumped out at me.

...the entity is known to come in the presence of great discharges of lightning and the most violent of storms; indeed, many of the rituals of the Maya...

...filled with unstoppable hunger. Voracis Unum will continue to consume the souls of the damned so long as additional...

...body of the deceased may be up to seven days since passing, but the greatest response seems to come from those who have most recently...

....cannot tolerate the presence of quicksilver....

To be honest, my initial reaction after reading the book was to grunt and laugh a little in skepticism. I mean, come on. A creature from another world which consumed the souls of the dead? It appeared my little hunting expedition had uncovered a bearded weirdo obsessed with an old fairy tale, a bogeyman written out in some 18th Century book of occult nonsense. And in the well-lit, clean Rare Books Room, it did seem just that; a silly old wives' tale that James Boston had bought into due to an overactive imagination or lack of female companionship or both.

Once I'd left the light behind and began the walk down that dark, too-quiet corridor back to the elevator, however... it didn't seem so funny. It didn't seem so ludicrous. Murder seemed a likely occurrence in that place, I said before, and now, the sheer amount of information that Boston had gathered together, the dry nature of his notes, and his twitching obsession with secrecy, began to lend a certain gravitas to the entire affair that became hard to shake off.

Such a specific frequency, of a dangerous and difficult-to-create radiation. An obsession with recently dead people with no amalgam mercury fillings, matched to the passage in that old, battered book about an intolerance to quicksilver. And, of course, the newspaper article about the stolen body.

There was the cell phone call, too, implying that others were involved. Other people, who had seen the same things Boston had seen, and they still believed in the existence of the bogeyman.

It was lunacy, preposterous, and yet, Boston and his friends were taking it very, very seriously; seriously enough to steal a body, and, it appeared, to get into the Physical Chemistry labs to use some of their equipment for some highly unorthodox experiments. And as much as I wanted to laugh it all off as fanciful nonsense, the truth was, I knew I had to see if it was all for real.

How could I not? If somehow, some way, these body snatchers were right and this creature they called Voracis Unum really existed… how could I not be there to witness it? It would've been anathema to everything I am. I live for glimpses behind the curtain into secret places, in search of truths about life that are hidden from us… and this was the mother of all secrets. If any of this was true, if Boston and company were on to something real and not just a fanciful delusion, then their bizarre experiments might reveal truths about the nature of reality that would re-write our understanding of physics, the soul… maybe everything about our existence.

I had to see it. It was unavoidable. My truth, the truth of my being…the part that I hid from everybody else…demanded that I see it.

So, I had an idea where this would happen…the Physical Chemistry labs…and I had a vague idea of what would occur; now the only question left to answer was *when* would Boston try what was looking like a colossally insane experiment to bend the nature of our reality?

We only have two days, he'd said during his cell phone call, and I had my answer.

*   *   *

Thanksgiving break. Of course. It only made sense; better than ninety-nine percent of the student body…including my roommate…would desert the campus like rats fleeing a sinking ship. You could practically get away with murder when school was on Thanksgiving break. The staff, the students, the faculty… all gone. Campus became a ghost town. There would be no better opportunity for someone looking to conduct a little independent study out of sight of any witnesses.

I knew it all too well. Every Thanksgiving, I made up some story to my family about how I couldn't make it home; some impending doomsday test or colossal project with an imminent due date from a ferocious, unforgiving professor.

Instead of working on that phony project, I would have a field day. In a quiet little college town like mine, people are trusting. Doors are left unlocked. Keys and passwords are left forgotten in drawers by faculty and graduate assistants eager to bolt out of the door and get home before somebody tells them they have to stay and re-run their statistical analysis or some damn thing.

I never stole anything; like I said, I'm a snoop, not a thief. I just wanted to look around, see what was hidden away behind those locked doors and in those secret places, collect a few more trophies with my camera phone.

Which is why I had a good idea of where the Physical Chemistry labs were located. Underneath three of the science buildings… one of which was the Bio labs, the others I wasn't sure of… was an underground tunnel connecting all three. Access was restricted. Of course I'd been in there.

The tunnel was wide, industrial-gray painted cement, lit by unfeeling fluorescent lights. It sloped slightly downward and then back up again along its length. Emergency pull showers…the kind with a triangular metal handle that you see in high school and college chemistry labs…were scattered along the sides of the tunnel.

The doors were mostly unmarked. I guess if you were allowed down there, you were supposed to know what was what. The P Chem labs were marked, though; big, fat stenciled letters spelled out PHYSICAL CHEMISTRY and NO UNAUTHORIZED ENTRY. Normally, the latter warning would've only drawn me in, but next to it were the symbols both for biohazard and radioactive threats. That had kept me away.

Up until now.

Now as I made my way into that tunnel, the old tingle in my spine, usually a welcome charge, became amplified until it was an uncomfortable burning along the entire length of my nervous system. The tunnel seemed filled with a thick, invisible fluid that pressed against me, kept me from moving forward, kept me from being able to breathe anything but shallow, hollow gasps of air.

Still, I had to go. I knew I had to. Haven't you ever been faced with something that compelled you, something that you knew was a bad idea or even well past a bad idea… and yet, you kept stepping forward into that tar pit, knowing that every doomed step took you closer to the kind of trouble that you don't easily walk away from?

But, how could I stay away? How could I stay away, and live the rest of my life wondering what was happening in that room, what secrets were being revealed? The shadowy ghosts of what I might have discovered would haunt me to my grave.

The truth is a dangerous drug.

So I crept towards my doom, pushing myself down the tunnel through that thick, too-quiet air and the harsh fluorescent lights toward the Physical Chemistry labs. At last, I reached the heavy wooden door with the hazardous materials signs warning me away, and after a quick glance through the small window centered high on the door, my hand gave the knob a hesitant, hopeful twist.

Unbelievable. They'd left it unlocked. How very, very typical.

All the same, it took an enormous act of will to finish twisting that knob and opening that door. Crossing the threshold into the labs was the point of no return; up until now, I could more or less talk my way out of being someplace that I shouldn't be. But once I was in the labs, it would be plain as day to Boston or any of his confederates as to why I was there. And if they were willing to steal bodies to feed to their creature, who knew what else they were willing to do?

I cracked the door and began to ease it open by degrees, waiting for an inevitable creak or squeal of the hinge to give me away. There was nothing. The door slid open surprisingly easily, and before I could think about it any further, I slipped through and let it shut gently behind me.

The first room was large and full of long desks topped with black slate. Each had various metal knobs and attachments and couplings, with a hood for ventilation over each. A typical chemistry lab set-up; but for some reason, those black slabs looked to me like crypts scattered around a cemetery. I guess it must've been everything I'd encountered recently about dead bodies and souls.

There were doors to the left, right, and straight ahead, and I was just starting to wonder which way to go when the sound of muffled voices shot an arrow of adrenaline through my heart. I ducked down behind the closest desk, feeling my heart pounding in my throat, feeling it beg to burst free of the constraints of my ribcage. I nearly lost myself to panic and rushed for the exit before I realized that as muffled as the voices were, there wasn't any immediate threat.

The voices were strained, passionate, urgent… and behind the door to the right. My nerves were still charged beyond capacity, but the urgency in those voices compelled me towards that doorway. Had they begun already? Finished already? Was it even Boston, or just some other unfortunate graduate student stuck here over break?

Once again, there was a window centered in the doorway, and a stolen glance through it told me the hallway beyond the window was empty. This door opened as easily and silently as the first one, and I glided through it towards the voices, which became louder and more distinct as I approached the end of the hallway.

Radiation hazard signs were everywhere, mixed amongst the doors scattered along the length of the hallway. Boston and his friends…if it was indeed Boston…were behind the last door on the left. I could hear them much better now, catching muffled bits of heated conversation:

"Not so fast! You'll…"

"…doesn't have sufficient resonance, it won't…"

"…that thing out of the way…"

The window on this last doorway was much smaller; thick glass about six inches square. Still, it was enough for me to get a good view of the room beyond without exposing myself too much to whoever was inside. I slid up to the window from the side, slowly moving across the door to catch more and more of the room in my view.

What I saw beyond the door was some sort of antechamber, a control room perhaps ten feet across, with a large desk-like console covered in knobs and dials and switches set against the far wall. Above the console and extending most of the width of the room was an observation window made of heavy glass, which looked on another, much, much longer room. To the right of the console, a metal door led into that larger room.

I saw them. Three of them; two wearing some sort of protective orange suits standing by the console and arguing over it, and a woman in her mid-twenties fiddling with a small camcorder.

"No, no, slower, slower!" one of the orange suit-clad men said to the other. "The intensity can't go up too quickly; I'm telling you, if its senses are like ours, an intense burst would be like screaming in your ears. Slow down!"

There was a low hum, rising in intensity, coming from some sort of large device mounted on the far side of the barrier. I could feel the vibrations in my feet, in my spine, even in my teeth; as the intensity rose and rose, I felt panic swirling in my midsection, increasing in intensity along with the hum. A sudden need to run, turn tail and sprint flat-out at top speed out of that place came over me, and I had to actually grip the side of the door frame to resist it.

Something began to stir on the far side of the room. I could barely see it, through the glass of the door and then the thicker glass of the barrier, but the air began to… swirl, is the best word I can think of to describe it. It was similar to the hazy shimmer caused by heat rising off of asphalt on a hot summer day, but much more intense and in a random, chaotic pattern rather than straight up.

The men in the orange suits began to look at each other in either alarm or exhilaration, and when sparks of electricity began to arc and jump within the swirling air, they looked as if they didn't know what to do with themselves in their excitement. Their hands gestured about, slapped each other on the back, tapped impatiently on the console, anything to stay in constant movement.

I was so caught up in the haze of the surreal that I'd completely forgotten what I came here to do. Cursing myself for an idiot, I dug my phone out of my pocket and got the video camera working with fumbling fingers. I almost dropped the damn thing before I finally got it recording and held up to the glass.

The arcing of electricity began to increase in intensity and tempo, the hum of the machinery nearly driving me insane, when there was a sudden crash as the doorway flew open and slammed into me. I was hurled across the hallway, too surprised and dazed to do a thing before heavy hands grabbed me and threw me to the ground.

"I knew it! I *knew* it!" growled a voice belonging to the large shape standing over me. It was Boston, his lips tight in a feral sneer.

"What are you doing?" the woman shouted from within the room. "It's coming though, Jim!"

"Don't stop!" Boston shouted back, to be heard over the intolerable hum of the machinery. He had my jacket held tight in one large fist, tightly enough that it pinched and tore at the skin underneath. I winced, but forgot all of that when I saw he had a gun in his free hand.

"Hey, hey…" I gasped out, trying to catch my breath from being knocked over backwards.

"Come on!" he said, dragging me effortlessly to my feet and pulling me into that awful room.

The others were still frantically moving around with excitement. The woman kept the camcorder pointed at the swirling air on the far side of the room, which looked thicker than water at this point, with constant bluish arcs of electricity shooting across it.

"Who the hell is that?" she asked.

"I told you there was somebody snooping around after me," Boston said. "You thought I was just paranoid. This little sneak has been after me since I was in the library. I spotted him sticking his camera phone up against the window. I guess he didn't see me way back in the corner over there."

"What do we do? Should we abort?" asked one of the men by the console.

"No," Boston said, shoving me into a corner and keeping the gun pointed at me. "He wanted to see, let him see."

"I don't think that's a good idea, Jim…" one of them said, but the woman interrupted him with a loud cry.

I saw it then, and forgot everything else. Up until now, everything I'd seen could be explained away in terms of phenomena I'd seen before… hazy hot air warping my vision, arcs of electricity like tiny lightning bolts leaping through the air. But this… this had no precedent, and all I could do was stare like a wide-eyed infant at the impossible.

It seemed to force its way into the world, push through some unseen hole in the air and expand instantly into existence. It happened in a fraction of a second; first, it was just the swirling air, and then, an enormous mass the size of a city bus shoved itself outwards from a point in the air and filled the far half of the room.

"Jesus," one of the men behind the console whispered. "Jesus, look at that."

"Turn that down!" Boston said, pointing toward the large knob his two friends had been arguing over earlier. "It's getting agitated!"

My mind began to actually recover from witnessing the impossible and process what was coming into my eyes. The creature, Boston's creature, was huge, as I said before, and a vaguely ovoid, reddish-purple mass that constantly ebbed and flowed and undulated like ink flowing through water, defying any attempt at classifying its true shape. Its skin, if it had skin, was somewhat transparent, and I could see tiny arcs of electricity arcing and zipping through the deeper mass of the creature. Its surface was in constant motion and limb-like stalks extended and retracted and waved about in a seemingly random fashion.

"Are you getting it this time?" Boston said toward the woman.

"I'm getting it, I'm getting it," she said, camcorder trained on the creature.

The humming reduced, and with it, much of the creature's motion. It seemed to settle into itself, and as it began to settle, I found my senses returning to me somewhat. Boston and his three friends were all enraptured by the sight of the creature, but the big man was standing between me and the exit, his gun held at his hip and vaguely pointed in my direction.

I had no illusions. By the time I picked myself up from where Boston had tossed me into the corner, that gun would be pointed at my heart or my head and that would be it. I began to look wildly around the room for anything I could use to distract them or defend myself, and suddenly, Boston knelt down and dragged me to my feet.

"There. You wanted to see? Now *see*," he said through gritted teeth, pushing me toward the glass barrier… toward the creature, which was now searching along the floor with thick tentacle-like extensions.

"We weren't ready for it the first time," Boston said, his grip on me tight, but his eyes on the creature. "Didn't really know if it was for real. It was all just a... a joke, I guess, a kind of distraction in the lab to keep the four of us amused."

"A little independent study," I said, staring at the creature.

He glanced at me briefly. "Something like that."

I saw it then. The body. It was in the center of the room, not far from the edge of the creature, and as I watched, one of the creature's searching, tentacle-like appendages found it.

"No mercury fillings," I whispered, mostly to myself.

"That's right," Boston said. "That's the mistake we made the last time... the body had mercury amalgam fillings."

"They're toxic to the creature, somehow," the woman said, her eyes never leaving the camcorder screen.

"Well, probably more of a physical insult, like acid is to us," one of the men in the orange suits said, nodding toward a large glass flask sitting on the console filled with a silvery liquid. "That's why we brought that, as self-defense in case..."

"Shut up, Bill," Boston said. "Watch."

Up until now, the creature's searching tentacles had moved slowly, almost lazily, but now the one that found the body moved like a striking rattlesnake. With a sudden, startling speed, the tentacle shot up to the dead body's face and spread across it. We all jumped at the sight of it, and then the one named Bill said, "Yes! I *knew* it!"

"Shut up and pay attention!" Boston said.

The little arcs of electricity deep within the creature began to multiply, travelling down its appendage and across the face of the dead body. Almost immediately, the corpse began to twitch and jump, an eerie dance of shaking limbs which increased and increased until the body looked like a living person having an intense seizure.

"You ever wonder if we really have a soul?" Boston said lowly into my ear, as if afraid of disturbing the creature... or perhaps drawing its attention. "You ever wonder what it would actually look like?"

The frenzied spasms of the corpse reached a sort of crescendo, and then, larger, brighter sparks of electricity began to travel along the creature's limb and back into its mass. The entire bulk of the creature seemed to throb and pulse as the arcs shot throughout it, sometimes co-mingling to form even brighter arcs that lit the semi-transparent mass of the creature from within. Its color even began to change, to a much more brilliant hue, and in its ecstasy, the creature's limb began to actually pull the corpse up off of the ground before the sparks stopped coming out of it. After that, with a shake of that ugly, misshapen limb, the massive creature dropped the corpse back to the floor.

"I still don't get it," Bill said, tugging uncomfortably at the neck of his orange suit. "That guy was dead for days."

"Some religions believe the soul doesn't leave the body right after death," I said, amazed I could speak after what I'd just seen. "Some say it lingers, perhaps for days, before it... moves on."

Boston gave a little grunt. "I'd say they were on to something."

I found myself staring blankly at the creature, at the corpse, forgetting my danger in unbelieving fascination with what I was witnessing. There I stood, staring at the impossible, mind whirling with the implications of what I'd just seen. I would've stood there all night, staring numbly, but one of Boston's friends said something that broke the trance.

"Okay, that's it. That's it."

"Not quite," Boston said.

"What are you talking about?"

"We should replicate the experiment."

"Replicate?" Bill said. "But Jim, we've only got the one body."

"Not true." Boston's grip on my jacket got tighter. "Let's give it something fresher."

The two at the console looked at me with alarm.

"Hey, hold on…" Bill said.

"Shut up," Boston said. "We can't let him walk out of here."

My eyes got wide and I struggled briefly, uselessly, against Boston's grip. "Listen, listen… you don't have to do this," I stammered. "I'm not here to create any trouble for you guys…"

"Save it," Boston said. "There's no way we can let you leave. The things we've done…"

"Not murder, Jim!" Bill said. "We never… I mean, stealing a dead body, that's one thing, but I never said…"

Boston's gun came away from my ribs and pointed at Bill. "I said, shut up! I told you why I was bringing a gun, and you didn't say a word about it."

"Do it," the woman said, stepping forward to open the metal door to the right of the console with her free hand. Her eyes never strayed from the camcorder's screen. "Go ahead and do it. I want to see."

I want to see. How many times had that very thought propelled me towards this fate. Such a simple, innocuous, natural thought to have, and now it was killing me.

Panic rose back up in me, and I acted without thinking, grabbing at the gun now that it was momentarily pointed away from me. It was a futile effort and I knew it; Boston was far too big for me to hope to fight off, but I was desperate, and desperate strength mixed with surprise allowed me to get both hands onto the flat black pistol that Boston held.

He fought back immediately. His arm twisted and turned with the strength of a python, and it was all I could do to hold on to the gun for dear life while we wrestled about.

"Christ, Jim, be careful!" one of the men at the console shouted, and then there was an explosion that numbed my hands and made my ears ring.

The pistol had gone off, sending a shot wild and ricocheting around the room. Boston's confederates ducked and cringed, unsure which way to run to hide from the waving pistol. Still I held on, until a second shot went off and something bit the inside of my right forearm. The gun fell clattering to the floor and skidded a short distance away.

Boston shouted something at me, but I was momentarily deaf from the report of loud gunfire in a confined space. I was a little dazed from it, barely resisting as Boston threw me against the console so he could go after the gun. Bill had fallen into a chair, screaming, grabbing at his leg. The other one in the orange suit was wringing his hands, next to him, unsure what to do, and the woman just stood pressed flat against the far wall, as if she thought that was somehow cover from the bullets.

I thought I'd been shot, but a glance told me that whatever had bit my forearm hadn't been a bullet. Soon enough, that would happen, though; Boston was already diving across the floor for the gun, and I couldn't hope to beat him to it or even try to tackle him before he got to it. I looked around desperately for anything to grab and throw at him, anything at all to buy myself another second of life, and ended up with the large glass flask of mercury in my hand.

I was too late. By the time I'd grabbed it and cocked my hand back, Boston had recovered the gun and had it leveled at me. He saw what I held in my hand and gave a little laugh at my pathetic attempt at a weapon.

I should've charged, or ducked, or done anything, but instead, I was frozen, and even after I saw him pull the trigger, still I was frozen.

Nothing happened. No loud gunshot, no explosion of pain in my guts telling me I'd been shot, nothing. Boston frowned at the gun and tried again, with no effect, and when he began digging at the slide, I knew what had happened.

His gun had jammed. When it went off the second time, what I felt bite my arm was the slide of the weapon moving back and forth, hitting my arm as it went. That must've interfered with the gun's action just enough to make it jam.

My ears were still ringing, but I could vaguely hear Boston shout "Get him!" as he gestured toward me. I tried to back away, but the hand-wringer in the orange suit was on me too quickly, and as I struggled with him, other hands joined his…the woman's, or Boston's, maybe, I'm not sure…and they pushed me through the open metal door and into that room of nightmares. The metal door clanged shut beneath my desperate hands, clanging like a bell tolling for the death of my soul.

A slow turn, and not ten feet away was the creature. Ten feet is an awfully close distance. The lane on a road is about ten feet wide. Imagine standing on the edge of the street with an elephant stepping up to the double yellow line. That's how close, and how big, this inhuman, undulating mass of reddish purple was. This close, I could see even further into its semi-transparent depths, where the bluish arcs of electricity snapped and popped and snaked their way throughout its interior.

It wasn't sitting still, either. As I stared, frozen in place, the mass began to slide closer toward me, two tentacle-like appendages extending out of the main body and toward me.

They waved slowly through the air, looking like lazy charmed cobras following some piper's music I couldn't hear. A quick glance at the body on the floor, however, reminded me just how lightning fast those limbs could move when they wanted to.

Still, I was nearly transfixed by the sight of the thing, barely able to back away slowly as one of the tentacles began to rise up closer to my face, drawing back like a serpent preparing to strike. Another second, and who knows what it would have done to me; perhaps it would have seized me by the face just like it had done with the corpse.

It didn't get the chance. My back bumped up against the metal door, and something in that physical contact snapped me out of my unbelieving haze. Instantly, everything changed for me; the reality and enormity of being shut in with this inhuman thing from beyond our reality drove me into a wild panic, and I spun toward the door, dragging at the handle desperately with my free hand.

Boston laughed at me from beyond the glass, holding the door shut from his side. His gaze shifted behind me, and I turned to see the horror that they had conjured sliding even closer toward me, tentacles reaching out and searching.

There was only one thing to do. In his gloating, Boston had forgotten that I had grabbed his self-defense against the creature; the flask of mercury. I didn't know what it would do, or if it would do anything, but anything was better than waiting for the same fate as the corpse on the floor.

With a shout, I turned and threw the flask as hard as I could, not at the creature, since I didn't know if the glass would break against what looked to be a soft surface, but above it. The flimsy glass broke musically on the hard ceiling, letting the silvery liquid shower down on top of the creature.

It shrieked. That's the closest word I could use to describe it. The entire mass of the creature shuddered and flailed about wildly, and the sound of a locomotive's horn multiplied a hundredfold erupted out of it. It was beyond deafening. The shock wave of sound rattled my teeth, my spine, everything down to my soul, and I dropped to the floor in agony as my eardrums burst.

That's what saved me. As I rolled on the floor, dazed with pain, I saw dozens of waving tentacles shoot out of the creature, slamming against the walls so hard that the concrete cracked under the blows. One smashed the glass barrier to the console room; thick protective glass fell in heavy shards all around me, as I was backed up against the bottom of the barrier.

The devastating shriek of the creature erupted again. I shrank against the wall, hands wrapped around my head, but I saw flashes of light even through my clenched eyelids. I risked a glance.

Massive electrical discharges were arcing out of the creature. The lightning bolts lanced and looped around the room randomly, matching the roiling, spasmodic movements of the mass of the creature. A large bluish arc shot close over my head and into the console room, and even as deaf as I was, I could see hear a scream of either pain or terror.

I had to move, but there was nowhere to go. It was death in that room, everywhere; the creature's wildly thrashing appendages, the foot-wide discharges of electricity slashing the air like some whip wielded by the god of thunder.

Finally, the creature shrieked again, which spurred me into action. I leapt for the door, dragging at the handle like a crazed man, and incredibly, it opened without resistance. I was through it in an instant, chased by one of those swinging, heavy appendages, which slammed into the door with a thud.

It was carnage in the console room. The shattering of the glass barrier had thrown fragments into Boston and his associates, and they were dazed from the creature's shrieks just as I was. One of them, the woman, managed to climb to her feet, only to catch a whiplash of electricity directly in the chest.

Her eyes went wide and her teeth clenched together involuntarily as her whole body shook and jerked with the current. Her hair caught fire and the skin of her face began to blacken and split and I had to turn away when her teeth shattered and her eyes exploded from the heat.

I stumbled toward the door. Something grabbed my leg, and I kicked in desperation, screaming out in terror now that the creature had me in its grip.

It was only Boston, though, bleeding from deep cuts in his face. My kick sent him sprawling, and another close electrical discharge made us both dive for the floor.

His gun was there, dropped from a dazed hand and forgotten in the chaos. In a second, I scooped it up and pointed it at him, at his friends, warning them to stay back even though I knew none of us could hear a damn thing.

They didn't know what to do. Everything was falling apart around them; the lightning had started small fires all around the room, and still, deadly arcs of electricity shot through the hole where the glass barrier had been. The only safe place was behind the cover of the console, and that's where I left the three of them; huddled behind the console, two of them dazed and bleeding in their protective orange suits, Boston looking like he wanted to tear himself apart in impotent rage, as the god they had summoned from another reality destroyed the room around them with titanic blows and blasts of electricity.

I stayed low, to avoid any stray lightning, and scurried toward the door. Something else had been dropped and left forgotten on the floor—their camcorder, and I snatched that up before practically crashing through the door and into the hallway.

After that, it was a sprint. A blast of electricity followed me out into the hallway, practically singeing me with its close passage. A last shriek from the creature, barely muffled by the walls between us, but I paid it no attention, just ran, ran like the Devil was chasing me, out between the black slab crypt-like desks and finally into the tunnel connecting the three science buildings.

I didn't stop. My sprint carried me down and out of that tunnel, bursting through the last set of doors and out into the cold night air, and still I ran, halfway across campus, lungs burning, legs burning, until I finally stumbled and fell into the soft grass.

*   *   *

On my dazed, stumbling, exhausted walk home, I couldn't get the image out of my mind of that body held fast around the head by the one of the creature's limbs; that fat, bloated thing shuddering in ecstasy as it drew... something... out of the poor damned person

Boston had dug out of the ground or stolen from a mortuary or whatever he'd done.

You ever wonder if we really have a soul? Boston had said. *You ever wonder what it would actually look like?*

By the time I finally stumbled home, the aftermath of my evening's adventures was all over the news. The campus was on fire.

The three science buildings connected by that quiet tunnel were all engulfed in flames on the TV screen, surrounded by fire engines which seemed to set the rest of campus ablaze with their red and white flashing lights. Water poured into the buildings from innumerable hoses; men in protective gear ran about like desperate worker ants.

Don't go in there, I thought. *It might not have left. It might not be hurt anymore. It might still be hungry.*

That's the thought that got me moving. I took a second to clean off my face and change my ruined clothes, so as not to attract any unwanted attention, and then I was off on my errands, collecting everything that's lying scattered around me now.

I saw one of them die… the woman whose eyes never left the camcorder. But Boston and the other two… who knows? They could've survived. It's not impossible. And if they did survive… Boston has my cell phone. He took it from me when he caught me peeking through the laboratory door. Take it from a snoop, if they have my cell phone, it'll be child's play to track me down.

I don't know if that thing they conjured up from Hell or whatever you want to name the other dimension managed to survive. I don't know if Boston and the others are dead, or alive, or coming for me, or not. But I need to be ready.

Gas cans. Eight five-gallon cans of gasoline, to be accurate, and road flares within arm's reach of just about anywhere in my house. I still have Boston's pistol; I'm hardly an expert, but I'll be damned if I go down without a fight. And I'll be damned if I let them take my body back to that disgusting abomination and let that thing do to me what it did to the corpse in the lab. Maybe there is such a thing as a soul, and maybe it does linger for a time after death, and maybe it can even be extracted and consumed by something that doesn't belong on this Earth... but it won't happen to me. All this gasoline should burn up my body completely, should it come to that.

    I held the dead woman's camcorder in my hands and stared at it for quite a while before doing what needed to be done. It felt like ripping my own heart out. There it was, in my hands, the last trophy for my laptop, the greatest secret imaginable unlocked and all mine, and I smashed it against the floor until it was shattered into pieces.

    Oh, I'd flirted with the idea of uploading it to Youtube and exposing Boston and his secret for all the world to see. And then what? Then someone else would try to call that damned monster into our world again, or maybe several someone elses, and maybe this time things would truly get out of control.

    This whole time, I'd been in search of the truth... and the truth was, it was better to keep this secret buried.

    Take it from somebody who's done a lot of independent study on the nature of truth: the truth is dangerous. It's a live wire, a poisonous snake, a primed explosive waiting to blow. It's better to live in blissful ignorance, and let the wall of secrets I've been obsessed with protect you from what lies beyond.

    I used to believe that barrier, that wall of secrets, kept me out, kept me away from the truth. In reality, that wall kept the truth in, kept the lethal monstrosities penned away on the other side of the curtain.

Better to never sneak past that wall, better to never peek behind that curtain. Better to walk on, oblivious, lost in a rapture of reality TV and talk radio and other banal, superficial distractions, and hope that the monsters overlook you… rather than dare to look them in the eye, and have them see you in return.

You see, there is another, far more terrifying possibility than revenge at the hands of James Boston. That thing, that terrible thing from beyond reality, which I wounded so badly that it shattered the air with its inhuman shrieks of pain… perhaps *it* will be what comes knocking at my door. Voracis Unum, the Ravenous, the Eater of Souls, might just hold a grudge against the puny thing which showered it with what it would call concentrated acid. If it can find me, it could come, at any time, defying any walls or doors, pushing its way through a hole in the air just like I saw it do in the lab.

If that happens, God help me, I hope I can get this gasoline lit quickly enough.

Andrew C. Piazza

Promises, Promises

I used to love to watch "The Twilight Zone". For me, it's the best example of speculative fiction; fiction without limits. With a brief episode of television, or a short story, a writer can explore a fun, quirky concept without having to develop too large of a plot. They're nice bite-sized chunks of the imaginary, easy to swallow without too much investment of time. Along with "The Last Pencil", "Promises, Promises" is one of the stories I can best classify as "Twilight-Zone-esque"; not quite science fiction, horror, or fantasy as most people think of those genres, but something beyond the ordinary all the same.

Andrew C. Piazza

Frank C. Applebaum had a real problem with promises. He kept making them.

He dished them out by reflex, handed them out like candy at a bank, thanks for coming, here's your lollipop, come again. Promises were a part of his exhalation process; along with the carbon dioxide and whatever other toxins needed to come out, a vow to do the dishes or hand his reports in on time or take out the trash. Every time he breathed in, a promise was bound to come out.

The real problem was, he never kept them. His promises were phantoms, facsimiles of the real thing, make-believe. It was as if Frank believed the promise was kept simply through the promising itself, as if the words that blew out in those exhales would take care of business for him.

They didn't, of course, which was why Frank collected animosity like lint in a trap. His voicemail was constantly clogged with verbal nasties such as today's:

Beep… "Frank, where *are* you? I'm at the airport, been here for an hour. You'd better be on your way, or stuck in traffic, because if you ditched me I swear to God I'll…"

Oh, crap, Frank thought, pressing the button for the next message. *Forgot about that.*

Beep... "Mr. Applebaum, this is Doctor Doral's office calling. You've missed your appointment again. This is the third time in a row, Mister Applebaum, and we will have to bill you for..."

Damn, Frank frowned, pressing the button again. *Really have got to get myself organized.*

Beep... "Frank? Adam Westmore! Frank, way to go, buddy! You really came through!"

Eh? Frank wondered. That didn't sound right.

"To be honest, I was kind of worried; I mean, well, I'm not going to mention any names, but some folks at the office had said that you tended to be a bit, um, unreliable, but I don't know what they're talking about! The Michelson report is perfect, and two days early? You're a miracle worker!"

Frank stared at his phone, as if expecting it to explain the last message further. Michelson report? He didn't even know what that... oh yes. That Westmore guy had asked him to speed up some report or another, and since Frank had been breathing out at the time, a promise was bound to occur.

But he hadn't done it.

Hadn't done a lick of it, hadn't even started it... hadn't even thought about it, actually. All the same, there was the message of gratitude, mixed in with the angry messages like a single white marble in a bag full of black ones.

Maybe he'd done it and had just forgotten. No, that wasn't it. Creating a report that size isn't something that slips your mind.

Frank snapped his fingers. "Somebody did it for me," he nodded to himself. "Did it for me, and I got the credit. Heh.

Thanks, pal, whoever you are."

His phone rang then, and Frank thought about letting it go to voicemail, let his Caller ID act as his doorman, to avoid any direct contact with the next verbal nasty that was sure to be on its way. It was his girlfriend, Jane, and after carefully examining his recent memory for unkept promises, he gave himself a green light and picked up.

"Oh, you're home," Jane said, not sounding all that surprised.

"Yep."

"So I'm off at seven. What are we going to do?"

Frank's lips opened and shut, desperately wanting to blow out a promise.

Jane's voice got a little harder. "You do know what today is?"

"Of course," he lied.

"I was gonna say! So, what? Have you made plans for us yet?"

Nope, was the answer, but the lips said, "Yep. Don't worry about a thing, sweetheart. I pr…"

"Don't promise. Just… don't do that."

Frank laughed, as if she were making a joke, which of course, she wasn't. "See you tonight."

It was close enough to a promise, an implied promise, which meant that within an hour, he was out of the door and on his way to… a pub. A very nice pub, to be sure, but it was definitely *not* his girlfriend's place of work.

He'd worked his way through three and a half pints, drinking well past seven o' clock, when a heavy hand clapped down on his shoulder. Frank froze, a deer in the headlights, sure a verbal nasty was about to become a physical nasty.

"Hey, Frank."

Frank swallowed his mouthful of beer and started to turn, trying to place the voice to the promise. A sizable fellow leaned up against the bar next to him, but he was smiling, and when he clapped Frank on the shoulder again, it was a slap on the back between friends.

"Thanks for lending me that copy of Fahrenheit 451," the old friend said, just as Frank identified him as Chris Whittlescope. "Been meaning to read it forever. Have it back to you in no time, I promise."

You promise? Frank frowned. *Fahrenheit 451? Do I even have that book?*

"Um, yeah, sure," he said. "Any time."

Frank began hoping it would end there, but instead, it was the pebble that started an avalanche. Barely-recognized acquaintances clapped his back, shook his hand, bought him drinks. At first, Frank was confused, and then terrified, trying to figure out who these people were and what he had promised them, and even more importantly, who in the world was keeping these promises.

It was too much to be coincidence; the report, okay, somebody else could've done it, and Adam What's-His-Face mistook it for his work. The book; well, maybe that guy got it from somebody else, and some synapse got crossed in his brain, and he thought Frank had given it to him. But all of these people...

"Frank, thanks for the heads-up on that project over in West Reading..."

"Frank, thanks for coming through with that mechanic. He's really a five-star kind of guy..."

"Frank! You are a Godsend! If you hadn't made those reservations for us... let me buy you another... we would've been in it deep!"

He fended off the undeserved praise as best he could, drinking faster than he was used to in order to clear his stretch of the bar for more thank-you drinks. They kept coming; promises were being kept to a level unheard of in history, and Frank's mind was soon dulled enough that he began to embrace the strange evening rather than fight it off or figure it out.

A man finds a winning lottery ticket, he doesn't wonder why, he decided, and dove right in.

"Of course! Glad to do it! My pleasure! And if there's anything else I can do for you... any of you... just let me know, and it's as good as done! I promise!"

His fan club kept him lubricated with pints well into the evening. At last, he managed to drag himself away, letting loose a promise here, a promise there, and one more just for luck before he made it to the door, finding it mostly by chance.

A chorus of happy farewells propelled him into the street, and a short cab ride later, he was aiming his key at three blurred, swirling identical triplets of a door lock. Four tries, and he struck dead-center, lurching into his apartment and only remembering to remove his keys from the door through Divine Providence.

"Ibedammed," he slurred, staggering toward his bedroom. "One sheeriously weird night."

That was his final thought on the evening. He passed out, fully clothed, keys still in hand, and would've slept half the day away if the phone hadn't rung.

He was hung over and off his game, so he answered it before letting his Caller ID/doorman check who it was.

"Hey, sweetheart," Jane said, and his first pained thought was, *Oh, shit.*

"Um..."

"I just wanted to call you and say that last night was the most wonderful... the best... listen to me! I can't even say it! You really went all out, and I just wanted you to know how much I appreciate it."

His head felt like a rotten melon. "Unh?"

"Are you okay? Sweetie, it's so late! You're still in bed?"

"Um," he licked his dry lips. "I'm a little hung-over."

"Well, I'm not surprised, all that champagne you drank!" she laughed. "Still, I'd better let you go and get back to work. Happy six months, sweetie."

Her words were clanging off his skull like a steel pipe hitting a gong, barely registering, and she had clicked off before the first inklings of comprehension trickled into Frank's swollen, tender brain.

All that champagne I drank. Yeah.

No!

Frank sat bolt upright, cringing as his brain sloshed and banged against the inside of his skull. What the hell was Jane talking about? Last night? He'd spent all last night at the pub...

"This," he said aloud, shaking his aching head gingerly, "this is not right."

It took him halfway into a wake-up shower to reach a theory. Perhaps it was an elaborate hoax, a trick concocted by Jane and others he'd failed in the past in order to teach him a lesson.

Yes, that might be it, he had decided by the time he was done scrubbing the night's excesses off of his teeth. He smiled and laughed once at his reflection in the mirror. Quite a stunt to pull off, lots of preparation, lots of confederates to recruit, but Jane had a point. It really was time for him to start shaping up.

He whistled his way to the office, washed clean of the mystery, and even managed to swallow down a promise that almost snuck out of him a mere two hours later. Everything was going well, until Adam What's-His-Face came around his desk in the early afternoon.

"The word is coming back positive on that Michelson report," Adam said, rapping on Frank's desk as if to indicate applause. "Great work, Frank."

Frank smirked and couldn't resist. Looking around to make sure nobody was listening, he winked conspiratorially at Adam and said, "Hey, you can knock it off. I know."

Adam's smile barely faded. "Know?"

"You know, Jane. The whole show. And, I get it, really I do. I'll do better. I'll shape up, really."

Adam shook his head, bewildered. "Shape up? Frank, I just told you…"

"I know, I know, you can drop the act. I figured it out."

Adam's bewilderment turned to suspicion. "Are you saying you didn't do the Michelson report?"

Frank stopped himself just before another word could slip out and betray him. What Adam just said… it didn't sound right. If he had been a confederate, in on a hoax, he just would've denied any knowledge, re-affirmed that Frank did do the report… but not question it.

"Frank?"

The mystery was back on, but Frank didn't have time to solve it right now. "Um, I… yes, of course I did, I meant…"

He rubbed at his head, as if his hangover was worse than it was. "I'm sorry. I'm not thinking right. Jane and I had a big night…"

The suspicion left Adam's face, replaced with a nod of

understanding. "Yeah, sure, man, no problem. Hey, you should maybe take off a little early. You don't look so good."

Frank didn't feel so good. No hoax, no conspiracy, no answers. "Yeah."

"Hell, take the rest of the day, figure you earned it!" Adam winked, rapped once more on the desk, and was gone.

I'm not so sure about that, Frank thought, but decided that he would head home early. He wouldn't be much good today, anyway… not until he got some answers.

He paused only long enough to dig the tiny bottle of aspirin out of his desk. Then, it was down the elevator, out to his car, and home, chewing aspirin along the way, wincing against the bitter taste.

The entire trip was made with his shoulders stooped and head down, as if Frank expected to find clues on either the floor or sidewalk along the way. He stayed head-down until he reached his bedroom, and oddly enough, didn't even see the tarp until he was standing right on top of it.

Tarp? he wondered, freezing in his tracks. *What the hell is a tarp doing covering my bedroom furniture?*

Frank stayed as still as possible, turning his head by minute degrees to look around the room. He briefly considered burglars, but dismissed that notion quickly. Why would burglars put down a tarp?

"You promised to paint your bedroom, Frank," said a familiar voice from behind him.

His heart began to leap out of his chest in fright, then stopped in mid-leap and quickly returned to normal. With a voice that familiar, so similar to his own, it could only be…

"Dad…" Frank said, turning, then froze again. Standing in the doorway, leaning up against the jamb in exactly the same way he would, was not his father... it was him. A carbon copy, a mirror image, a doppelganger, him, he, Frank C. Applebaum, same face, same height, same body, even the same suit, down to the loosened necktie.

Frank, the real Frank, the original Frank, couldn't move. His brain was locked up, stuck in place, overloaded. The twin Frank nodded toward the tarp and began again.

"Remember? Two months ago, you promised her you'd paint the bedroom. So now you are. We are. I am."

Original Frank began to stammer. "But... you... I... don't have a twin."

"I'm not a twin. I'm you. I'm we. I'm us. You know what I mean."

No, not really, Original Frank thought. "Who... you did all those things?"

Twin Frank stepped into the bedroom, onto the tarp. "Kept your promises? Yep. I've been keeping all of your promises lately."

Original Frank's brain whirred out of control. "But... who are you?"

"I told you, I'm you. I'm us."

"But..."

"I don't know where I came from. I just sort of... was... about two or three days ago. I have memories, your memories, I suppose, but I also have this need to... well, keep your promises."

Twin Frank saw that wasn't quite enough, and continued. "Plato used to talk about Forms... ideal concepts we can only approximate. For each imperfect triangle we draw, there is a perfect triangle, a Form, somewhere out there. So maybe I'm your Form, your Promise Ideal, created by all those imperfect promises you made."

Original Frank sat onto the bed, gravity overpowering his jittery leg muscles. Impossible. No way. No how. This was the really real world, and twins didn't magically appear to quote Plato and do your dirty work for you.

Hey, Frank, his mind popped up. *Roll with it. A man finds a winning lottery ticket, he doesn't ask why.*

"I know what you're thinking," Twin Frank said. "You're thinking you can keep firing off your promises, more than ever before, and I'll run around like some sort of butler, cleaning up after you. Forget it."

Original Frank's face fell. "What?"

"I said, forget it. I'm not a captive genie granting you wishes, Frank. I despise you. You're an empty man; your words are hollow, your feelings are hollow, you're hollow. You don't deserve what you've got. You don't deserve a woman like Jane."

Puzzle pieces clicked into place. "Jane! Hey! You took her out…"

"…last night, that's right," Twin Frank nodded. "And that's when I decided there's going to be some changes around here. I'm doing all the work, so I'm going to get all the credit. I'm going to be Frank, for real, the only Frank, and live my life instead of watching you squander it."

"Forget that. I don't know who the hell you are or what you're doing here, but this crazy nonsense is over," Original Frank snapped, pulling open the nightstand drawer, fingers already itching for the pistol kept there.

The drawer was empty.

The gun was already in Twin Frank's fist, pointing toward Original Frank's midsection. "You promised her you'd get rid of it, remember? And you will, later today, after it goes off once by accident."

The tarp, Original Frank realized. *The tarp's pulling double duty today, catching more than just spatters of paint.*

"Nobody hurt," Twin Frank said, "at least, nobody of consequence."

"You can't do this. I... I made you," Original Frank said, almost pleaded.

"Sure I can. You see, I finally made a promise last night, after making love to Jane. I promised myself I would get rid of the dead weight in my life... you... and never let anyone be the wiser."

There was a snick-click as the gun's hammer cocked its lethal arm back. "And unlike you, Frank, I keep my promises."

Bang. Thump. The tarp rustled briefly.

Twin Frank was as good as his word.

Andrew C. Piazza

The Last Pencil

John Gardner wrote that good fiction should create a "waking dream" for the reader, a sort of semi-hypnosis that makes the world go away for a little while. It's certainly what happens to me when I'm writing. I have to be very careful setting up my writing time; if I'm not, I will lose track of time completely and "come to" hours and hours later. The worst example of this was when I still wrote with pencils, much like Pop's No. 2 Berols in this story. One time, I began writing at about nine o'clock at night. Later, my hand started to cramp, and my eyes were squinting, which seemed odd, until I realized that I was squinting because the sun was coming up and peeking through my window. Scattered around my feet like spent cartridges were dropped, dull, pencils. I'd written maybe sixty, seventy pages, which was why my hand was cramping up. I never noticed the passage of time. As this story's narrator would say, I'd gone there. It got me thinking about just how far into that fictional space one could go.

Andrew C. Piazza

I found magic while my father was dying.

Pancreatic Cancer; the worst, they told me, 'they' being any one of innumerable self-proclaimed experts on death and dying. I'm sure these experts would have assured me Pop's diagnosis was 'the worst' regardless of what it had been; bone cancer, Lou Gehrig's disease, even an upset stomach.

I didn't need this consensus of uninformed opinion to know the situation was grave. Pop had always been a relatively thin man, but by the time he was hospitalized, he looked like a bona fide Holocaust survivor. His ribs jutted awkwardly from his skin, like outstretched fingers pressed up underneath a tablecloth, and his facial bones stood out so prominently they seemed to cast long shadows across his pained face. He was a wretched apparition; a vibrant man laid waste by an uncaring, unfeeling, unstoppable demon named Cancer.

He'd laughed when, eight months before, his doctor had suggested chemotherapy. "Son, I'm seventy years old," he'd said, when I, too, took a hand at convincing him of the benefits of therapy. "Old enough to see you grow up, old enough to see you get married and raise a family, and old enough to bury my wife. There's no damn point in poisoning myself slowly to death with chemo; the cancer will take care of business soon enough."

I hated him for saying that, hated him for his stubborn, simple fatalism, hated him for giving up just because Mom was dead. I hated him because I was most likely going to lose my wife, too; the demon Cancer had struck the same family twice. Rachel had been diagnosed with breast cancer a little earlier than Pop, and trying to prop up her soul while coping with the very real possibility of her death was bad enough; I didn't need Pop giving in like this.

But he did, living blissfully in his self-imposed ignorance, playing with his grandchildren, trading lies about his past accomplishments with friends over pints of beer, and, of course, writing.

You've probably read some of his work, just by the law of averages if nothing else. Over fifty years of writing at his trademark breakneck speed creates a lot of material, most of which has found its way onto the bookshelf under one pseudonym or another. Writing has been the one constant in Pop's life, which is why it was no surprise to me when he asked me to bring some paper and a box of pencils to his hospital room.

A very certain box of pencils, to be exact. He was very adamant on this point. In his battered-to-hell leather satchel, inside an inner pocket, lay a box of No. 2 Berols, sans the yellow paint. A lone, unsharpened pencil rolled hollowly inside that box, the last of its clan. I couldn't imagine Pop would need more than one, considering the pain he must've been in, but it never hurts to be sure, so I picked up a package of yellow No. 2's on the way back to his room.

"Thanks, Steve," he said, taking the lone Berol and pushing the other package back towards me. "You can keep those."

I shrugged. Old men, particularly when they are my dying father, are allowed their share of bizarre idiosyncrasies.

"Why that pencil, Pop?"

"Because it's magic," he said, reaching reflexively toward his pocket for the ancient pocketknife before remembering he was wearing a hospital gown, and, therefore, had no pockets. "Could you..."

"Yeah," I said, recovering his knife from the closet and rolling a portable tray over to his bed. Immediately, he clicked his knife open, and with expert fingers, began sharpening his pencil to a fine point.

"How's Rachel?" he asked, eyes never leaving the pencil.

I didn't have the strength or the temperament to dull the truth. "Not good. Doctors say the cancer may have metastasized; probably has, in fact."

"You should be with her."

You're dying faster than she is, strayed into my mind, and I stomped flat that ugly Judas of a thought. I didn't want to talk about that, think about any of it, just for one night. For one night, I simply wanted to be alone, with my dad, and not have to worry about how the demon Cancer was tearing my family away from me.

I took advantage of a muscle twitch, betraying Pop's pain, to change the subject. "You know, Pop, I could get you one of those electric sharpeners, set it up right on..."

"Bah," he said, waving me off. "In all the years you've known me, son, have you ever seen me use an electric sharpener?"

"Nope."

"Nope," he said, nodding.

I tried to keep my eyes on his hands, on how they worked carefully over the pencil with that old, sharp knife, so I wouldn't have to look at how gaunt his face had grown. "Nope, it's always that knife."

He nodded again. "This knife, these pencils."

"So how come?"

I sensed his smile, rather than seeing it, as my cowardly eyes were still firmly fastened onto his hands. "I told you. Magic."

"Pop."

"Oh, fine, then; ritual, superstition, whatever the hell you want to call it. Rudyard Kipling only ever wrote in black ink; I only use these pencils, and this knife to sharpen them. It's all a part of going there."

'Going there' was his pet term for the complete trances he would go into while writing. It was almost funny, how oblivious he would get to the entire world, when he 'went there'. He would lose track of time; Mom would have to bring a sandwich into his den, which he'd promptly ignore for hours on end, and then suddenly look at it with a start, as if wondering how on Earth it got there in the first place. I was warned many times not to disturb Pop while he was in his den writing, but even when I defied those orders and invaded his study, he never noticed me. Oh, I was quiet, and clever; at least, as quiet and clever as a young boy can be, but the real reason he didn't see or hear me was... he'd gone there.

"Your doctor says you're refusing pain medication."

"Damn straight," he said, eyeing the pencil's point one last time before setting it aside and closing his knife with a satisfied nod.

"Pop..."

"Son, how in the hell am I supposed to go there if my old noggin is soaking in morphine or opium or whatever other gobbledigook they want to pump in me?"

"Pop, don't be stubborn..."

"I'm not..." he said, frowning as he began to search around his immediate area. Reading his mind effortlessly, I crossed the room to hand him a small stack of paper, which he accepted with another satisfied nod.

"Good. Remembered the right kind of paper, too."

"Pop, I'm serious..."

"So am I," he said sternly, then his bony face relaxed and he began again more softly. "Look, son, I know you're worried, and I know I'm being an old goat, and a Grade A pain in the ass, and making an already tough situation miserable. But, please, just.... respect my wishes on this one. I can deal with the pain. It's awful, yes it is, and I do believe it's going to get unbearable, but as long as I can go there..."

I nodded. Maybe yes, maybe no, but as long as Pop could go there, he just might stay oblivious to his pain along with the rest of the world, wrapped instead in the protective blanket of a fictional universe. And if he could, than that *would* be magic, wouldn't it?

"How come you quit writing?" he asked suddenly, staring at the paper, waiting patiently to go there.

"Pop, come on."

"Don't 'come on' me," he said, eyes still fixed on the paper. "You used to go there all the time as a kid."

"Well, kids have to grow up," I said, and immediately regretted it.

It was a lie; a black, soulless, cowardly lie, made all the worse by the fact it debased Pop's passion by labeling it as childish. I saw the lie sink into him, saw his gaunt features sag for just a moment, and then, thankfully, he went there, after saying one last thing to me.

"Go be with your wife."

I felt like killing myself for saying that lie; I would have, except I couldn't think of a horrible enough way to do it. I'd insulted a dying man, my father, just to hide my own insecurity. The truth, the real reason I never took up writing like my old man, was... fear.

Simple as that. Pop's talent was incredible, amazing; I used to sit enraptured by his words for hours on end. Still do, as a matter of fact. He 'went there' when he wrote his books, I 'went there' when I read his books, but when I first started my own fledgling attempts at creating those worlds, those stories... I failed. I would read the horrid, stale garbage I'd written, then read his effortless mastery, and knew I could never, ever compare to what he'd done. Oh, sure, Pop patted me on the back, and praised my stumbling sentences and clichéd plots, and offered gentle criticism, and assured me that I was getting better, but the truth is, I never felt I could measure up. So... what, what was I supposed to do? It was a foregone conclusion that anything I wrote would be compared to my father's work; mercilessly crucified, in other words. I could practically see the critics' words in my head, whenever I thought seriously about writing: "Steve Jackson is no substitute for his father. He was obviously conceived by the milkman, for he certainly didn't inherit any literary genes from his father."

So, I quit. I ran away, ran straight to electrical engineering, about as far from writing as I could get, so I would never have to see that imagined criticism come alive. And as I sat there in his hospital room, watching him go there, watching him die, I searched for the strength and resolve to tell him the truth.

I didn't find it. He wouldn't have heard me anyway; he had already gone there. His face relaxed; I was surprised how much baseline tension had been in his features this entire time, and I had never recognized it until it was gone, banished by his going there.

Strong magic, indeed.

I watched him for a little while longer, feeling like a kid again, feeling like I was five years old, spying on him in his den. For that short time, I forgot the weight of the world pressing on my shoulders, forgot the impending loss of my father, forgot the fear of losing my wife, forgot the anxiety of facing life with no parents, no partner, and three children to whom I'd have to explain it all. In a way, I guess I went there too.

Then, the world came back, and I left his room, listened patiently to his doctor tell me again about how little time he had left, and went home to my wife. Once the kids were asleep, her cheerful facade cracked and split, and I had to hold her for several hours as she mourned the loss of her left breast, and God knows what else, until at last, she, too, fell asleep.

I couldn't sleep, however. I kept thinking about my father, kept thinking about going there, and before I knew what I was doing, I'd scrounged up a pencil and some paper.

I only wrote for a little while, two and a half pages, before my old fears managed to bubble up and destroy my concentration. I looked over what I had written and was disgusted. As my mind transferred thoughts to my hand, it had seemed perfect, natural, perhaps even magical; but once that foolish glow had faded and I could examine my work in the harsh light of reality, I knew it could never measure up, knew it would never be worth anything. So, I burned my stillborn creation in the fireplace... destroying the evidence... if you will, before finally and fretfully falling to sleep.

I had to leave work in mid-afternoon the next day due to an emergency with my father. The worst part was, the hospital refused to tell me what was wrong; all they told me was to get to the hospital and hurry.

Hurry. As if I wouldn't, normally. I won't bother to recount the thoughts racing through my head; any of you with a whit of empathy can imagine what goes through a person's mind at a time like that. Suffice it to say I broke land speed records driving to the hospital and foot speed records on the cruelly long dash to his room.

"We're sorry to have bothered you, Mr. Jackson," a nurse told me, as I came barreling down the hallway. "I'm afraid we've brought you down here for nothing."

I almost skidded to a halt. "Nothing?"

"We lost track of him for a bit, thought he might've coded, but it turned out his monitor had some sort of power failure or glitch of some sort for about sixty seconds or so. It's unusual… you don't usually get all of the monitoring equipment to hiccup like that at once. It was probably just a power surge. There was just no sign of him on the monitors; it was like he'd disappeared. I actually thought he might've disconnected all of it for some reason, but in the shape he's in…"

She paused, aware that she had said far too much already, that she'd probably be in deep shit trouble if her bosses knew how much she was telling me about their unreliable equipment.

"It's nothing to worry about, though… just a glitch."

"He's all right… he's awake?" He could hardly be all right.

"Yes. Will you be…"

"Yes, I'm staying," I said, and ambled into Pop's room.

He was asleep, pain tightening his features even while unconscious. Sitting on his tray was a stack of thirty or so handwritten pages, about five or six hours' worth of writing for Pop. I pulled a chair next to his bed, and began to read through his scrawled handwriting, once again feeling like a kid sneaking into Pop's study.

Faraway

"What do you see?" the man in the black metallic armor, Lord Halifax, asked.

"Danger," replied the old, crippled, nearly blind man who huddled with Lord Halifax in a dark chamber of the castle. He stared with rheumy eyes into a column of reddish smoke rising from the floor like a rippling curtain. "Darkness. Evil. Faraway is in great peril. There shall be an invasion."

"An invasion?" A shiver rippled through Lord Halifax, but he quickly remembered himself and straightened up. "Surely you are mistaken, Elder. There hasn't been an invasion of Faraway for centuries. Even then, it was a disaster for the invading army. Our geography is our best defense; the distances necessary to travel, and the way our coasts are protected by mountain ranges, makes it impossible for an invader to sustain and supply an army."

"I didn't say it was an *army*," the Elder hissed. "I said it was an *invasion*. You speak of one as if it must be the other."

The old man rose as best he could, joints groaning in protest. "Even you knights, with your sharp steel and clever horses, will not be ready. This geography, our geography, of which you speak, has made us soft. It cradles us in its bosom and protects us from any serious threat, and like hands never worked in the fields, we have become soft and uncalloused as a consequence."

The old man pulled his shawl around himself a bit tighter, as if trying to embrace himself, and sighed. "Faraway is not ready for what approaches; it will come at night, always unseen, just around the corner, just inside the shadows… for the shadows is where it belongs. Evil is coming to Faraway, my Lord, and Faraway is not ready for it."

I read on, about the mystical land of Faraway, and how it was populated with all manner of men and mystical races, all of whom lived together in harmony. The wise men of Faraway could perform miracles with their magic, crime and social discase were nil, and the denizens lived under the rule of a benevolent king. All in all, a far better reality to live in then ours.

Pop's handwriting had just began to relate the nature of Faraway's peril when a voice stirred me from my sleep.

"…you think?"

I started visibly, jarring back to reality; rather reluctantly, I must say. Pop's writing took him away from his pain; reading it took me away from mine, and I wasn't quite ready to come back yet.

"What, Pop?"

"What do you think?"

"Oh, um," I stammered, feeling like a trespasser. Pop *hated* when people read his rough drafts.

"No, no, it's okay," he said. "How far did you get?"

I glanced back down at the story before answering. "Um, the elders, or one of them, was having a vision of a man, warning them of the evil that was coming."

"Read almost all of it, then."

"How are you feeling, Pop?"

He waved me off, as if the question were irrelevant, and began sharpening his pencil with his pocketknife again. It was significantly worn down, almost a third of its length used up, and seeing it made me think of my own abortive attempt to go there the night before.

"I..."

"What, son?"

I tried to write last night, danced across my tongue, begged to burst from my lips, but I just couldn't seem to set the words free. "I was... wondering about... the pencil. And the knife."

Pop looked the instruments in question over, fondly, and shrugged as if to say, *why the hell not tell him about it*. "Two different stories. Which do you want first?"

"Either, or."

He held up the knife. "When I was eight, my dad gave this to me. It wasn't my first pocketknife, but it was the first one he gave to me. I remember thinking it was the coolest gift ever. It felt special, and not just to me, either; my dad admonished me not to ever lose it, so I could give it to *my* son one day. So, I kept it in my pocket, and promptly lost it not too long thereafter."

"Really?"

"Oh, yeah. I was mortified. Then, almost six months later, I actually cleaned underneath my bed for once, and found it lying there. I swear, I almost cried, I was so happy. And, over the years, I formed a consistent pattern of keeping the knife nearby, losing it, getting all worked up over losing it, and just as I'd given up hope on ever finding it again, it would show up in the damnedest of places. It's far beyond a mere good luck charm; it's magic. Magic, infused by the love and worry and gratitude I've showered on it for over sixty years."

"And the pencils?"

"Your mother," he said. "Many, many moons ago, she made

fun of how I always used the same pencils, refused to use any others. I'd run low, and she'd get some more, the wrong ones, and I'd refuse to use them. Drove her nuts. Then, my birthday rolls around, and she'd wrapped a whole pile of big boxes of Berol No. 2's, my brand, and said, 'Well, that ought to hold you for a while, you pain in the ass'. And it did, too; I've never used any other pencils but those she gave me, and they've lasted until this day. Until this pencil."

"That's the last one?"

"Yep. So it's probably good that I'm checking out, or I'd have to retire. My books only started getting worthwhile, really worthwhile, after I started using these pencils and this knife."

"Magic," I said.

"Magic," he agreed, then waved me off yet again, if perhaps more painfully than before. "Now get the hell out of here and go be with your wife. It's time for me to go there."

I smiled and set his story back in front of him. I wanted to say something before I left, something about how I was going to miss him, something about how spending time with him like this, listening to stories like that of his pocketknife, was far beyond priceless to me, and most of all, something about how I'd never be able to get along without him. But, I was too tired, too emotional, too off-balance, so I just told him I loved him and left.

"Son?" he said, as I paused in the doorway.

"Yeah, Pop?"

"Always remember, even when I'm gone, I'm here for you. You can always find me in *here*," he said, setting his palms on his manuscript.

I thought about a lot that night, as I told Rachel the story of Pop's Last Pencil. I told her about how I did believe it was magic, about how pouring nostalgia and love and emotion on an object can make it magical, at least for us. They say haunted houses are like storehouses of negative energy; batteries charged with the intense energy of horrific events. I told her I believed the same could be true for positive energy, how the emotions invested in an object can indeed make it a magic talisman. I told her about how Pop's magical Last Pencil and ancient pocketknife were able to take his pain away, without drugs, without doctors, and as I told the story, I realized the magic of the Last Pencil had struck yet again. You see, for the first time in months, my wife didn't cry herself to sleep in fear of her future. The story of Pop's Last Pencil had taken her away from all that, enraptured her, focused her thoughts on the possibility of a miraculous reality. It opened her mind to ponder wondrous possibilities, and drove away the visions of dark storms blackening the horizons of her future. When I held her that night, it was as husband and wife, man and woman, not caregiver and patient.

Strong magic, indeed.

After Rachel had fallen asleep, I found myself once again with pencil and paper in hand. I'd seen the effects of the story on my wife, and finally realized part of the magic was in *me*. A story, by itself, can only be so special; the manner of its telling is what creates the majority of its magic. Comedians call it delivery, and they know it makes or breaks the joke, but whatever you call it, something in *me* helped Rachel forget her troubles, something in *me* made the story come alive. If I could just capture that something, refine it, maybe...

Ten pages later, my euphemistic feeling had faded and my old nemesis, Fear of Failure, set in, destroying my focus. I read over what I'd written; garbage, compared to Pop's tale of Faraway, but this time I didn't destroy the substandard pages. Instead, I set them in my desk drawer, promising myself to return later to try and improve on the rough draft.

The clock told me in unfeeling digits that I'd been at it far too late. A smile crept across my face. I hadn't noticed the passage of time; I'd gone there.

At five-thirty that morning, I got the call I'd been dreading.

"Mr. Jackson?" a tight voice said, barely penetrating my bleary mind, "It's your father. You'd better get down here."

Once again, they refused to give me any more information over the phone, so I kissed my wife on the head, told her to go back to sleep, and dressed as quickly as I could. She'd curse me for it later, but she looked so peaceful, I just couldn't take her first good night's sleep in ages away from her.

I forced myself to keep the car from going to warp speed on the way to the hospital. *Probably just another glitch*, I told myself, but I knew deep inside it wasn't.

It wasn't fair. He wasn't supposed to go yet; I was supposed to have weeks left of talking with him about last pencils and old pocketknives and going there. Weeks yet; the doctors all said so.

But then, Pop never did have much use for doctors.

I reached his floor at a slow trot and was intercepted once again before I could reach his room, strangely enough by the same nurse as before. "Mr. Jackson?"

It went mostly as you'd expect. They told me he was gone, and I lost it. I yelled and cried and cursed and spluttered, and finally accepted the large envelope full of Pop's personal effects before leaving.

After that, I went home and woke up my wife, and told her a story. I also spilled my guts, which is sometimes the same thing. I told her about how I'd been hiding from Pop's legacy all these years, how I'd neglected writing because of my insecurity and fear of failing to measure up to him. I told her about going there; about how Pop did it, and I did it, and what it meant to both of us. I told her about Pop's last story, Faraway, and how its magic had shielded him from his pain. I told her about how he must've been writing it until the very end, as there were now just over one hundred pages covered in his scrawled script; and I told her how I intended to finish the story for him.

Here's what I didn't tell her. In those hundred pages, Pop had woven a story of a blissful country; a place in which demons like Cancer could be defeated with the wave of a mage's hand, a place where wives didn't have to sacrifice one of their breasts in a desperate bid to stave off that ravenous demon, a place where a man didn't have to stand helplessly in place while those he loved died around him.

There was more, though; towards the end of those hundred pages, a strange old man had come to Faraway, a sick man whom the elders healed with their magic, and who in return warned them of their impending danger. This old storyteller also promised the imminent arrival of his son and family, who would save the mystical land and protect its peace.

I didn't tell her Pop wasn't dead.

I should've seen it the first time, when the well-meaning nurse apologized for calling me out for no reason. It was like he'd disappeared, she'd said. She had thought equipment failure was to blame, but I think Pop's last pencil had more to do with it.

When I got to the hospital *this* time, I found his bed empty and assumed the worst. They told me he was gone... not dead, but *gone*... lost somewhere, obviously transferred to another room or another floor by some clerical error. Once I'd stopped frothing at the mouth, they assured me up and down, left and right, that they would solve the mystery.

Not bloody likely. They aren't going to find Pop in that hospital, or anywhere else on this Earth, for that matter. He's finally, truly, *gone there*, gone to Faraway, gone to the other side of the looking-glass.

I've begun writing in earnest. Every day, hours on end, I go there, trying to find the door to Faraway. I'm on a deadline; the doctors give Rachel about a year, and so I have quite a bit of time to make up. Pop wrote for fifty-odd years; I need to go there in six months if I'm going to save my wife. It's a hell of a ways to go; but I've got dozens of Pop's books to learn from, and his first hundred Faraway pages, and I have other allies, as well.

My wife just bought me a box of pencils to kick off my new career. Berol No. 2's, no paint on the sides; she's seen Pop write and has an excellent eye for detail. Plus, I have what Pop left for me in the envelope.

It was a torn slip of paper, scrawled with the words GO THERE, wrapped around an old, worn pocketknife, first handed down from father to son sixty years before. It's sharp as hell; I've already cut myself twice while sharpening my Berols. It may not seem like much, not much at all in the face of the demon Cancer, but the magic in *it* might be just enough to awaken the magic in *me*.

Wait for me, Pop. Wait for *us*.

We're going there.

Harry's Ride

"Harry's Ride" began as a sort of writing exercise ("Doctor Insanity Vs. The Sparrow", a comedy written under my Christopher Andrews pen name, also started off this way). So much of speculative fiction is epic and broad; think big Hollywood budgets and highly technical special effects. After all, one of the great things about the written word is that there are no financial or physical limitations that venues like film or theater have to contend with; the sky's the limit. The exercise began as a challenge to write a science fiction short story that could be done as a short play. No budget, no effects, the old idea of two people talking in a room. This story of a futuristic revolutionary and an Imperial torturer having a ride in a small starship is the result.

Andrew C. Piazza

"This is the one?"

Harry Connors peered up at the voice, trying to focus through the haze created by the neuropacifier attached to the base of his neck. It was difficult; everything was fuzzy and indistinct, as if he was being mildly electrocuted while drunk and smoked up on a THC cigar. Reality bent and folded and twisted, always warping just to the left or right of center, always staying just out of his mind's reach.

"Yes, Advisor," another, more familiar, voice answered.

"He doesn't look like much... doesn't look like much at all. Certainly not the nightmare everyone has made him out to be."

"No, Advisor," the second voice agreed.

Harry clenched and unclenched his tingling hands, which were shackled fast onto the bench next to him. His feet were shackled and tingling as well, but he ignored them, concentrating instead on the two blurry images in front of him. His eyesight was perfect, normally, but with the neuropacifier operating, he'd be considered legally blind. Now, he could barely tell one man was taller than the other, and he was pretty sure the shorter one wore the uniform of a Royal Fleet officer. It was hard to tell, though; mental functions were impaired by the neuropacifier along with sensual acuity.

"Thank you, Captain, that will be all," the taller form said, then added a moment later, "You will, of course, remember in the future to do me the same courtesy as the rest of the Empire by addressing me as 'Your Eminence'."

Harry wasn't sure, but the taller man's words didn't sound like a request. Advisor... Advisor. What did that mean? He couldn't remember; he couldn't think straight. If his head would clear, just for a second, just for a single damn second...

"Here now, I don't think we need this anymore," the voice said, as the blurry figure loomed large before him, and the hazy nature of existence briefly intensified almost to the point of uncontrollable nausea.

Then, the haze cleared instantly, the world snapping back into focus with a jarring jolt that nearly made Harry throw up onto his shackled boots. There was a man standing before him, a tall man, older, lean, with a hawk-like face and a powdered white wig atop his head. His clothes were expensive, stylish; and yet, reserved enough to fit in flawlessly with the long, sleeveless steel-gray robe of office which seemed to act as the tall man's center of gravity. Every move he made seemed to originate there, in the robe; it was his axis of rotation, the core of his being, his beginning, his end, and everything in between.

"Besides, how could we ever hold a conversation with *this* unpleasant technology in effect?" Gray-robes said, holding up the now-detached neuropacifier in one hand.

Harry managed another glimpse at the white-wigged scarecrow before another wave of queasiness overcame him, doubling him over at the waist and nearly driving a panicked scream from his throat.

The nausea was exquisite, so intense that unbidden tears spilled out from between his squinted lids and splattered on the same boots he was certain he'd soon be covering with the contents of his stomach. Soon, though, the nausea passed, and Harry was able to finally straighten up and tilt his head back for a few gasping breaths, tears now running in rivulets down his cheeks.

"My goodness," Gray-robes said. "How long did they have this on you?"

Harry took a few deep and steady breaths before croaking his answer through cracked and bloodied lips. "What time is it now?"

The tall man reached inside of his robe with a deliberate move that drew attention yet again to the flowing garment, and drew out a small, flat device. "It is now fourteen hundred thirty hours, Earth Greenwich Standard Time."

"What day?"

Gray-robes chuckled as he tucked the computer pad away with another grandiose gesture. "Let's not be too dramatic, Harry. It's still Friday, still only... what, seven hours since your capture this morning."

Harry closed his eyes and concentrated on his breathing yet again, feeling his senses begin to even out steadily. The bruises on his face and body were the first sensations to come fully into focus, but his hearing, eyesight, and equilibrium all seemed to be almost entirely back to normal. His olfactory senses were still a bit off, though.

"I smell... burnt copper," he said.

"Yes, an unfortunate side effect of the pacifier. You'll have that particular smell stuck in that broken nose of yours for several months, I'm afraid." Gray-robes said. "Still, a small price to pay for keeping a prisoner under control."

"Especially when *you* don't have to pay the price," Harry said, finally straightening himself up now that he felt like himself again.

The tall man smiled mirthlessly and sat down on the bench across from Harry, fluffing his robe out carefully as he did so. His long, gaunt arm reached out to the intercom unit built into the wall next to him.

"Are we ready for departure?" he asked, depressing the TALK button.

"Yes, Ad... yes, Your Eminence."

The gaunt man smiled. "Then get us under way, Captain."

"As you wish, Eminence."

Harry examined the cylindrical room in which he was confined. It ran only about fifteen feet long, eight feet wide, and wasn't much more than a tube with a pair of opposing benches straddling a walkway between them. There were no windows, no adornments, and few consoles other than the intercom unit next to the gaunt man. The concave walls were painted a dull, light beige, fitting in perfectly with the drab and spartan surroundings.

"This isn't a prison transport. This is a Fastdash," Harry said, mostly to himself. "The passenger section of a Fastdash."

"Correct," Gray-robes said. He nodded almost imperceptibly as the craft trembled slightly and the engines, somewhere past the steel door to Harry's right, began to whir and whine. "We had to make a few modifications, of course."

Harry glanced down at the manacles binding his feet and ankles as the intercom barked harshly yet again.

"We have departed Mars Orbital Platform Twelve, Eminence," the Captain's voice announced.

Gray-robes rolled his eyes in frustration and pressed the intercom button. "Thank you, Captain. I don't believe I'll be requiring any more interruptions, if you don't mind."

"A lieutenant commander," the gaunt man said, as he shook his powdered wig in exasperation. "Can you imagine? A *lieutenant* commander, not even a full commander, captaining the vessel in which I must ride… even if it is only a Fastdash. How insulting."

"It's awful," Harry said. "A real tragedy."

Gray-robes didn't seem to notice; instead, he just continued to frown and shake his head slowly. At last, he sighed and slapped his hands on his bony knees, drawing attention once more to his robes, as if indicating it was time to get down to business.

"Well," he said, "enough of that. I am Advisor 341 to His Majesty, the Emperor August Tempor. You will address me as 'Your Eminence'."

That explains the robes, at least, Harry thought, adding aloud, "Advisor? You mean you're an interrogator."

Advisor 341 scoffed. "Oh, please, Harry, what a limited view. I may call you Harry, may I not?"

Harry shrugged, as best he could in his condition. "Why the hell not? You're going to be torturing me to death soon, we might as well be on a first name basis."

Harry's casual remarks belied an increasing terror gnawing at his gut. *Jesus, an Advisor*, he thought. *They put an Advisor on me, this fast. What is he going to do to me? How bad will it get? Will I scream? Will I talk?*

"Harry," the Advisor said, "you're being melodramatic. I was saying, I have myriad and varied responsibilities in my service to His Majesty."

"Myriad and varied duties which include interrogation and torture."

The Advisor shook his head noncommittally. "I have never tortured anyone in my life."

"Of course you haven't. Just as the Emperor has never ordered anything so unpleasant as, say, genocide."

"Genocide?" the Advisor said. "I think you have an overactive imagination, Harry."

"You're probably right. I probably imagined those mass graves I found on Pelosi 4. I probably imagined sinking thigh-deep into the half-disintegrated and burnt bodies of the colonists who lived there."

"Pelosi 4?" the Advisor said. "Pelosi 4? Oh, yes. Admiral Ishiharu's action against the insurgents. An unfortunate conflict, but the Admiral's conduct was exemplary. Really, I should think you would be grateful. After all, for a commanding officer to be so gracious as to take the time and effort to bury the bodies of his enemies, the same enemies who viciously murdered hundreds of those under his command, shows him to be a man of the deepest sympathy and compassion, does it not?"

"Oh, yes," Harry said. "I'm sure the four and a half million farmers who were slaughtered there would be very grateful to know Admiral Ishiharu bull-dozed whatever scraps of them were left into a bunch of bomb craters and then covered them over with a few inches of topsoil."

"Don't be insensible," the Advisor said. "It was a rebellion. You make it sound like a concentration camp."

"They were farmers!" Harry shouted. "They didn't have any strategic weapons, any warships... They were harmless! They got pushed too far, and they shot up an Imperial garrison. For that, you destroy a planet? You said they killed hundreds? Ishiharu killed millions!"

"Numbers are irrelevant. In order for the Empire to survive, all of the outlying districts *must* comply with..."

"Sometimes I wonder what it must have been like," Harry said, not looking at Advisor 341, but off into space instead. "A massacre like that, what could it have been like? Orbit-to-planet missiles hitting everywhere, wiping out entire square miles of territory. Then the atmospheric fighter-bombers come in, strafe the populated areas; streets, buildings, terrified mobs of people being torn up mercilessly. Then the ground assault..."

Harry's voice trailed off for a moment before he could continue. "What could it have been like? Four million lives, four million bodies. The numbers, the horror, it's... too big. Too terrifying to really understand, to really *get* on a gut level. I was even there; I saw the ruined towns, the bombed-out settlements, the heaped-up bodies, and I still can't accept it as something that actually happened."

"But I guess it's just my imagination," he continued. "You mentioned concentration camps. I imagined one of those, too. I imagined one on Triandos, on that so-called planetary way-station."

"Triandos *is* a way-station," Advisor 341 said, "what used to be called a 'cow town' centuries ago on North America. It exists only to funnel people to other systems. How could a concentration camp possibly exist there?"

"It doesn't, now," Harry said. "But you know that already; in fact, it's one of the charges you'll bring up against me... if I survive my interrogation. It was there, though. I saw it. I saw how people were killed there... or perhaps they were just killed as an afterthought."

"I saw, Advisor 341," he said, leaning forward to stare the taller man in the eyes, "I saw people infected with the common cold, and then have every single antibody that their body produced to fight that infection extracted and saved for use by the prosperous. They called it a clinic, but it was really a slaughterhouse. People kept in a perpetual state of illness, their immune systems sucked dry, never allowed to defeat the normally inconsequential organisms that infected them, until their ravaged bodies just couldn't take it anymore. I wonder if people know that the so-called miracle drug that the Imperial Society of Medicine advertises so heavily really comes from..."

"I think I've heard enough of your fabrications," the Advisor said. "*Fabrications,* Harry, that's all they are. Yes, there was a Clinic on Triandos, and yes, most of the research and production of the ISM's Universal Antibody came from it, but not because of any ridiculous death camp. Triandos is a way-station, the largest in the Empire, with thousands of travelers from dozens of systems; where better to study all of the vast numbers of new germs, all of the varied microorganisms that Imperial citizens will come into contact with as a result of our interplanetary exploration? We need to keep on top of these concerns, Harry; and Triandos Clinic was the perfect location to study that concern, keep our citizens safe and their health assured. Until you blew it up, of course, and *fabricated* the story of the fictitious Triandos Concentration Camp. You did more harm to the citizens of the Empire, whom you so arrogantly claim to protect, on that day, than any other individual in the history of Imperial rule."

Harry leaned back, sneering at Advisor 341 in contempt. "Must've just been my imagination, then."

The Advisor shook his head irritably. "Be realistic. How could the Empire possibly commit these atrocities and not incite immediate rebellion? How could anyone possibly stand for such horrible abuses of human rights?"

"Apathy," Harry answered. "Ignorance. Distraction."

"That simple?"

"That simple. I've already told you *I* have trouble believing in the Triandos Clinic and Pelosi 4, and I've been there; saw it, smelled it, experienced it up close and personal. What about a bunch of well-fed, comfortable, middle-management middle-class Earthers or Martians a year's transport or more away? They don't believe, because they can't or don't want to. Do you really think Susie Housewife in plush North America wants to know the reason Little Johnny can get over the flu in a half-hour or less, with that ISM Universal Antibody, is because somebody on the far-off frontier was killed slowly and their immunity extracted from them? It's too much, it's too big. Four and a half million dead on Pelosi 4. That number, it just doesn't compute, it doesn't make sense, so people choose not to believe it.

"If they even hear of it. It takes seven or eight months to get to Pelosi 4 from the nearest system of any consequence. Who's going to know about what happened there, except for what you and the government tell them? Me? What can I do? Take vidcam shots of it all, Pelosi 4, Triandos, all the other dirty little secrets, and then the Empire scoffs and tells everyone they're digitized fakes. Hell, they even have experts 'prove' they're fake. So people get a choice; believe in something impossible and horrible and dangerous to their lives and livelihoods, or believe something easy and safe and sane, and life goes on as usual. What do you think people will believe?

"And even if they do believe me, how many are going to do

something about it, put their lives, their family's lives, at risk, when they're comfy and their stomachs are full and life is generally good? Not very many, and those few that do... well, that's why you're here."

"And so you, you're what?" Advisor 341 asked. "One of the enlightened few who will save the Empire?"

"No," Harry said. "I'm one of the intolerant. One of the intolerant who will destroy the Empire."

"I suppose you see yourself as a sort of Robin Hood," the Advisor said.

"Who?"

"Robin Hood? You've never heard of him?" the Advisor said. "I'm surprised, Harry, you have a reputation for being well-read. Robin Hood was a folk hero, a bandit fighting the oppressive rule of an evil prince. I suppose that's how you see yourself. Or perhaps it's more than that. Perhaps you see yourself as a messiah or a martyr to your stupid, senseless, powerless cause. Is that it? Is that why you were captured so easily? I mean, really, what on Earth were you doing on a Martian Orbital Platform? You should be hiding in some hole on the edge of the frontier, where it's too much of a hassle for the Empire to come looking for you. You had to know you'd get caught. Is that it? Is it martyrdom you seek?"

Harry stared at the floor, steadfastly refusing to answer. Advisor 341 folded his hands in his lap and began to chuckle.

"How quaint," he said. "Harry Connors, would-be folk hero, bucking for a promotion to martyr. I wonder if your insurgent cronies know the truth about you. Look at you; those ridiculous worn dungarees, the steel-tip work boots, that battered leather jacket... how very proletariat you look. Nobody would ever suspect you were raised a blue-blood in North America, went to school at

Harvard, even worked for the government as a journalist until you saw something you shouldn't have. Only then did you become The Hero of The Common Man. How farcical. I'm sure it'll ruin your chances at that promotion."

"What promotion are *you* bucking for?" Harry asked.

"What do you mean?" the Advisor said, laughter dying instantly on his lips.

"Why are we on a Fastdash?" Harry said.

"What?"

"You heard me," Harry said. "Why a Fastdash, why not a secure prison transport? These little ships are hardly more than an overgrown missile with a giant engine bolted onto the back. No secure brig, barely any defensive systems… it's a poor choice for moving a high-risk prisoner."

"Can't have an escort, either," Harry continued, ignoring the increasingly malevolent stare of Advisor 341. "The only ship that can keep pace with a Fastdash, is another Fastdash. Do we have an escort of several other Fastdashes?"

The Advisor remained silent.

"I didn't think so; I didn't see any other crews hanging around the airlocks. And there isn't much of a security detail on board, either; just the captain and two other crew members."

"And you," Harry added. "But, that's the whole idea, isn't it?"

"You have no idea what you're talking about," Advisor 341 said. "You're on a Fastdash because the Emperor's birthday celebration is in thirty-two hours, and this is the only craft that can get you there in time."

"In time?"

"Time for you to be presented to His Majesty as a prize, for his birthday."

Harry nodded. "So why no escort? Why aren't there half a dozen security guards, armed to the teeth? If I'm such a valuable prize, why isn't the Martian Governor coming along to present me to 'His Majesty'?"

"His Lordship, the Governor, had other concerns," Advisor 341 said.

Harry smiled slightly and angled his head, just a bit, just enough to accentuate the curious look he ran over his less-than-ideal companion. "Advisor 341," he said, as if to himself. "Don't you have a name?"

"Don't condescend to me," the Advisor said. "Of course I have a name."

"But you're referred to by a number."

"For security reasons."

"Of course," Harry said. "And it doesn't bother you to be just a number, anonymous, nameless..."

"I've heard just about enough out of you..."

"It doesn't bother you to be nobody..."

"Shut up!" the Advisor snarled, leaping to his feet. "You shut your damnable mouth, prisoner! You're the nobody here! You're nothing; you're a second-rate criminal with a lot of high-sounding excuses. Oh, you talk a good game, but the truth is you're useless hypocrite. You haven't made a damn bit of difference in the Empire. You're just a nuisance, a thorn in the ass of the Emperor, nothing more."

Harry shrank back involuntarily in his seat. He'd pushed it too far, pressing his luck in a morbid desire to tempt fate, to step on the proverbial sleeping lion's tail. Now, Advisor 341 was in a rage, fire blazing in his eyes and his lips curled back around predatory teeth. This man could kill him at will, inflict the worst pains imaginable or unimaginable without ever having to answer for it. Harry's heart began to beat fast, panicked despite himself, and he began to regret ever having set foot on that damn orbital platform floating above Mars.

"And I," Advisor 341 continued, "I will be the one to remove you. You're on a Fastdash with no escort, you damn fool, so I can be the one to present you to the Emperor; not the idiotic Martian Governor, not the Chief of Security, *me*. Yes, I commandeered this craft so nobody else could take the credit; it belongs to me! I've earned it with nearly half a lifetime of dealing with pisspots like you, torturing them until they blubbered their pathetic little secrets to me. When I drag your stumbling, neuropacified carcass before the Emperor, he will be so grateful, he'll declare me a hero, right there, in front of the cameras, before the entire galaxy. After that, it won't be Advisor 341 anymore; it'll be Senator Dorian, or perhaps even Lord Dorian, with a title and a colony to rule. That is my destiny; yours is to die under my hands in an interrogation room, slowly, horribly, the focus of twenty-two years of experience as an Advisor, as my last official act in that capacity. Yes, that's right, Harry Connors, Savior of the Universe; you're no more than a prize bull headed for the slaughter. What do you think of *that*?"

Harry fought to maintain his composure; his pulse raced, his lower lip quivered involuntarily, all under the assault of the Advisor's outburst of fury. Still, he managed to slow his breathing somewhat, and although his voice cracked and croaked a bit when he spoke, it wasn't *completely* out of control.

"What do I think about that?" he said. "Your Eminence, I have been counting on it."

Almost on cue, the Fastdash shuddered slightly, inertia from the craft coming to a quick stop. The Advisor, still leering angrily into Harry's face, had to take a small stutter-step to maintain his balance.

The gray-robed torturer shot a look toward the cockpit in obvious annoyance, then another back at Harry. Harry felt much more under control, now. He'd been scared to death up until this point, in spite of all his sanctimonious lecturing; scared to death his plan wouldn't work, that he would end up on this Advisor's slab, screaming, straining at the restraints they would use to hold him down...

Easy, Harry, he thought, to calm himself. *You may still be in shackles, but you're in charge of this prison now.*

"What is..." the Advisor said, practically leaping to the intercom console to restate his question fiercely. "Captain! What is going on here?"

"One moment, Eminence, we are taking on two passengers."

"What?" the Advisor said. "I specifically said no stops, especially no passenger pick-ups. Only I am to present the prisoner, no one else! Or perhaps you'd like to spend some time in my interrogation room?"

After a moment, the Advisor depressed the TALK switch again. "Get back here at once."

Advisor 341 straightened up, frustration twisting his already haughty features into a snarl. He didn't move his body from the robe up anymore; now he paced furiously, clenching and unclenching his hands.

"Idiot," he said. "Who could he be picking up? It has to be me, no one else, it has to be *me*..."

"I have an idea who it is," Harry said.

"Oh, really? Why don't you dazzle me with your deductive reasoning, prisoner?"

Harry smiled slightly and watched the Advisor's expression closely as he began. "Let's say there was a surgeon, one who was very high up in the Empire, one who personally cared for the Royal Family, one who had access to their security codes and protocols. Let's say he had a brash, headstrong daughter, his youngest, who took off for the Pelosi 4 colony with her lover to start an adventurous life on the frontier."

"Pelosi 4..." the Advisor said.

"Pelosi 4," Harry nodded, speaking softly now, so the Advisor had to lean over in order to hear him properly. "Let's say after the massacre, he even believed the Royal propaganda that his daughter, with all of the other settlers, had been relocated to a new home, unharmed. But then, after he never hears from her, he goes to Pelosi 4; under the guise of a sabbatical, of course."

"Dr. Hendritch!" the Advisor whispered, eyes flashing in sudden realization.

"Let's say this doctor was met by a certain prize bull," Harry said, "not entirely by accident. Let's say he saw the mass graves, the evidence of massacre, and decided vengeance on the Royal Family and the Empire in general would be his new guiding policy."

Advisor 341 glanced at the floor briefly in thought, then back up at Harry. "Triandos Clinic!"

Harry smiled, raising his voice slightly as he leaned back as far as his shackles would allow. He had to admit, he was enjoying this little display of showmanship.

"Let's say this doctor, with all of those super-secret codes, helps that prize bull destroy a concentration camp called the Triandos Clinic. While there, they rescue a man called Miller..."

Harry's story was interrupted by the *Pssssk!* of the cockpit door opening. The Fastdash's captain was there, followed closely by a short, bald, neatly dressed man, and another, taller man, whose features were clouded by an air filter mask strapped to his face.

"Captain!" the Advisor shouted as he raced toward him, "Your sidearm! Quickly! These men are insurgents!"

The Advisor's rush was halted by the captain's forearm forcibly thrown into his face. The torturer fell back, directly onto his ass, limbs splayed and flailing, twin rivulets of blood instantly pouring out of his shattered nose.

"Shannon," Harry tsk-tsked, shaking his head in mock sympathy over the Advisor's injury…which, coincidentally, nearly identically matched his own fractured nose… "you were supposed to break his nose *after* you changed his face."

"Sorry, Harry," the young lieutenant commander apologized, lungs huffing from the surge of adrenaline brought on by his assault. "I just couldn't take it anymore, his lecturing..."

"I understand," Harry said, then glanced down at his manacles. "Do you mind?"

"Right, of course," Shannon said, and pointed a remote control device at the shackles to release them electronically.

Harry stood up, rubbing his wrists, glaring down at the shocked, prostrate Advisor, who stammered, "Captain! This is treason!"

"And you, Dr. Hendritch," the Advisor said, eyes flashing toward the short, neat man, "I'll see you are..."

Harry raised a hand to halt the Fleet officer's snarling advance. "Time's short, Advisor... Dorian, did you say? In any case, I'll finish my story quickly. Aside from Mr. Miller, Dr. Hendritch and I found several vials of a biological weapon called the Kreston Plague at the 'fictitious' Triandos Clinic."

"The Kreston Plague has been outlawed for over sixty years," the Advisor said, as Dr. Hendritch and Fastdash Captain Shannon lifted him into Harry's old seat, affixing the manacles immediately.

"Indeed it has," Harry said. "But it was there nonetheless, and actually presented us with a unique opportunity. You see, Mr. Miller is dying; his immune system has suffered so much damage that even Dr. Hendritch's considerable skills are useless now. But.... Mr. Miller has an unusual strength of character. Instead of lying down to die in some ratty cot on a remote outpost on the frontier, he has decided to lend his death some meaning."

"You lured me onto this ship... to assassinate me!" the Advisor whispered.

"Ha!" Harry said. "I could give a damn about *you*! I knew *somebody* would pull a stunt like this, try to cash in on the credit of presenting me to the Emperor on his birthday. It could've been anyone, but we knew it would have to be on a Fastdash, otherwise, they'd never make it on time for the Emperor's big celebration, and alone, or they've have to share the credit."

"The Emperor..." the Advisor said, his body now starting to shake, his hands and shoulders trembling nervously. "That man... he's Miller, isn't he? You infected him with the Kreston Plague, that's why he's wearing the mask, because it's airborne..."

"And when the Emperor kneels Advisor 341 down to knight him with that ridiculous sword he always wears, Miller will breathe as much of it into his face, and the Royal Family's faces, as he can," Harry said. "You see, *he'll* be Advisor 341, and just to make sure the

Emperor dies, when he's close he'll detonate the shaped charge explosive he has imbedded in his frontal sinuses. The Emperor will be blown apart, and the rest of the Royals will die of the Kreston Plague, along with all of the highest and most mighty of the Empire, who will of course be there for His Majesty's birthday."

"It'll never work," the Advisor said. "He's not me, he can't pass for me..."

"Sure he can. You're not a person, you're a number... Advisor 341. They won't check; an Advisor with a top priority prisoner to present to His Majesty? They'll take one look at your robes, which he'll be wearing, and knock each other out of the way to lick his boots clean, in the hopes they'll be remembered once said Advisor gets his title. And as for me... well, Harry Connors will die, or at least, so they'll think. You see, *you'll* be standing in for me. Doctor?"

"Oh, yes," Doctor Hendritch answered. "I have the implants ready to go. He'll look just like you. I'll have to remove two inches from each thigh and lower leg, due to his height, but I have a pair of electric-drive braces that will make him capable of ambulation. They'll be easily concealed beneath his clothing. He'll appear to have a slight limp, but no one will suspect."

"You'd better get started," Harry said. "We need to detach in two hours if we're going to clear any Fleet activity by the time the fireworks start."

"I think I'm going to enjoy my vacation," he added after a moment, almost to himself. "My so-called death should give me at least a month's worth of peace and quiet, no running and hiding..."

"The Empire will fall apart," the Advisor said. "No Royals, no one to hold it together, the separate districts will fracture, fight amongst themselves..."

Harry glanced over briefly as the Advisor trailed off, laughing once to himself. "Shannon, once you offload *Advisor* Miller and the all-new Harry, get your ass out of Dodge immediately. You'll be the first one they look for."

"I'm afraid... I neglected to bring any anesthetic along," Doctor Hendritch said, examining his instrument tray carefully as he moved it in front of the Advisor.

Harry frowned, but not too deeply. "Doctor... that's not very humane."

"I believe Humanity will take a back seat to Justice today," the doctor replied, staring with revulsion at the freshly-trembling Advisor.

"Well, we'll at least use this," Harry replied, picking up the neuropacifier and bending the Advisor's head down so he could place it on the back of his neck. "It'll also keep him quiet until it's too late to do anything."

"Actually, Your Eminence," he whispered, leaning in close to Advisor 341's ear, "I *have* heard of Robin Hood. Let me tell you a little something about folk heroes. Every now and again, they beat the odds; they escape, they strike a blow, they somehow manage to outwit their adversary. And sometimes, not very often, but sometimes, they even manage to kill the evil prince."

He fixed the pacifier firmly in place and stood up straight, speaking loudly and slowly so the dazed Advisor would be able to understand him. "Try to concentrate on not throwing up, Eminence," he said, "it'll help to pass the time."

Andrew C. Piazza

Tracks In The Snow

"Tracks In The Snow" is the only story in this collection that is not speculative fiction; instead, it is a grounded-in-reality war story. It stands on its own as a story about trying to cope with loss and overwhelming hardship, but additionally, it allowed me to get used to writing in this setting for my horror novel, "One Last Gasp", also set during the Battle of the Bulge in WWII.

Andrew C. Piazza

"Sarge! Hey, Sarge, look!"

"Hey! Hey...." Sergeant Abel Wicland struggled to remember the name of the replacement who now ran like an idiot out of formation and off of the icy road into the snow-covered field. He wanted to warn the kid to stick to the road, that the Germans sometimes booby-trapped American bodies, but the short guy with the fresh face was already digging at the snow. Wieland noted with disapproval that the brand-new private had dropped his carbine carelessly into the snow, as if it were a walking stick and not his lifeline.

"What the hell is that dumb kid's name?" he asked the soldier next to him in line. It turned out to be the squad's other, equally nameless, brand-new replacement. The private was armed with a sniper rifle, but from the terrified look on the kid's face, Wieland figured the only thing he'd be able to shoot with it was a deer.

"P-Peele," the new sniper said. "Jerry Peele."

"Hey, Peele, you dumb shit!" It wasn't Sergeant Wieland shouting. Private Freddy 'Pep' Culpepper had beat him to it. It was almost funny; Pep would be almost indistinguishable from Peele at a distance. They were both short, wiry guys who looked like they'd been issued gear two sizes too large, but Pep had the grizzled look of a front-line veteran and Peele was a fresh-scrubbed replacement straight off of the boat. "Get out of there! You hit a Kraut mine and I catch any shrapnel from it, and I'll cut your…"

"Shit!" Peele shouted shrilly, falling backwards into the ditch next to the road.

"Oh my God, was he hit?" the nameless private next to Wieland asked.

"Did you hear a grenade go off, genius?" Pep snapped at him. "Sarge, how come we have to get stuck with these two shitheels?"

"Because there'd only be five people in our squad without them," Wieland answered, shaking his head at the private floundering on his back in the road. "Okay, Kemp and Egleston, go check out who little what's-his-name is digging out of the snow over there. Sayles, you stay here with me."

"What about me, Sarge?"

Wieland looked the new sniper over. "Keep an eye on that farmhouse there." He pointed to a two-story stone and wood farmhouse about a hundred yards ahead of them to their left.

There was a few seconds of waiting, as Kemp and Egleston pulled Peele to his feet and checked the two bodies half-buried in the snow. Wieland shivered against an icy gust of wind… there were trees by the farmhouse, but out here they were completely exposed… and pulled his overcoat around himself more tightly.

"Stupid," he muttered to himself, and that about covered his thoughts on the entire matter. Two G.I.s had wandered off to look for eggs or booze or whatever else they could scrounge, and the platoon leader decided that made for a good reason to send a squad out into the middle of nowhere for a combination search party and patrol.

But sir, he'd said. I don't have a squad. A squad is twelve men, one of whom is armed with a B.A.R. for fire support. I have five men, including myself, and no B.A.R.

Here's two replacements, the lieutenant had replied, and you can get along without an automatic weapon, can't you, Sarge?

So here he was, freezing his ass off in the remotest part of Belgium with a trembling brand-new private for a sniper and another psyching himself out by digging bodies out of the snow. It was no way to fight a war.

"It's so cold," the replacement said next to him, interrupting his thoughts. "Is it always so cold?"

Wieland scowled, but Sayles stepped in for him. "Stamp your feet some, Private. It's cold because it's December and we're standing out in the open where the wind can get at us. If those are the two guys we're looking for, we'll stop by that farmhouse and try to warm up some before the sun goes down. Right, Sarge?"

"I heard..." the replacement said. "They, I mean, everybody back home said the war was supposed to be over by now, or soon. General Eisenhower bet General Montgomery five pounds it would be over by Christmas."

"I don't think Adolf heard about that bet," Wieland said, then shouted to the others checking out the bodies, "Well?"

"They're clean," Pep said, waving them over. "No boobytraps."

"They ours?" Wieland asked, adding an order almost as an afterthought. "Don't bunch up, guys."

"Sorry about that, Sarge," Peele said, brushing the snow off of his overcoat. He still hadn't picked up his weapon. "I thought it was just a helmet at first and when I started digging it out, well, I touched his face and it..."

"Forget about it, Private," Wieland said. He knelt next to the bodies to search for dog tags. The bodies were American, all right, and frozen stiff. One of their arms pointed straight up in the air, bent at the elbow, frozen into place.

"They're our guys for sure, Sarge," Egleston said. He was a tall, widely-built man who always seemed to have four or five day's worth of beard, even if he'd just shaved. "That one with the bullet hole in the face is Johnny Trendle from Easy Company."

"All right," Wieland nodded, "let's get them marked for Graves Registration and..."

"Hey! Check it out!" Peele said, stepping away from the group thronged around the bodies and toward the farmhouse. "A couple of Mademoiselles!"

Wieland glanced up long enough to see Peele had left his weapon lying forgotten in the snow. He shook his head. It was sloppy form. "Private."

Peele waved at the two women standing by the side of the farmhouse. "This is a little more like it! They're wearing white... bed sheets, it looks like. Maybe they think they're snow bun..."

A rifle report cut him off in mid-sentence and a bullet punched through his chest and blew his right lung out of his back.

Wieland hit the ground before he did, diving face first into the ditch running along the side of the road. The rest of the squad was down there with him in a heartbeat, except for the two replacements. Peele knelt on the red-spattered road, blinking a few times blankly, and the other replacement stood next to him, trying to hold him up.

"Jerry?" the replacement said.

"Get down!" Wieland shouted, over the sudden snap and whine

of submachinegun bullets zipping close overhead. "You dumb shit, get...down!"

A burp gun, Wieland thought, *they had to have a damn burp gun*. At this range, a burp gun was more terrifying than dangerous, but it sure as hell filled the air with angry hornets that Wieland knew were actually bullets.

It was Sayles who went to go get the replacement, bolting out of the ditch and firing his rifle at the farmhouse as he went. He only had to go five yards to get to Peele and the second replacement, but with all the gunfire in the air from the chattering burp gun, it seemed to Wieland like a million miles.

"Cover fire!" he shouted, firing his rifle at the farmhouse as quickly as he could.

He could see them now; two civilian females with white bedsheets wrapped around their coats as ersatz winter camouflage. One stood just by the corner of the house, using the wall as a rest to help her aim her rifle, and the other was kneeling next to her, rifle propped up on her knee. Wieland guessed the third, the one with the burp gun, must be firing from one of the windows, but he couldn't see her just now.

Wieland's first three shots had been quick and blind, more pointed in the general direction of the farmhouse than anything else. Now that he saw who was shooting at him, he rested his elbow on the road to steady his rifle and aimed at the kneeling woman.

He hit her on the second shot. Even a hundred yards away, he could see the spray of red explode out of her back and stain the white snow before she fell forward, lifeless. He fired the last three shots in his clip at the other woman, still standing by the corner of the house.

The empty metal clip popped out of his rifle with a loud *Ping!*

and Wieland ducked back down into the ditch. He had a new eight shot clip pushed down into his rifle in seconds.

He ratcheted his action forward, and was about to ask who was still with him, when the replacement practically fell on top of him, dragging Sayles into the ditch with him. A fresh bout of burp-gun fire started up from the house.

"Medic! Medic!" Sayles shouted.

We don't have a medic, Sayles, Wieland thought, but he knew it was just a reflexive action on Sayles's part. When people got hit, they shouted 'Medic', even if there wasn't any medic around.

"Son of a bitch! Where's he hit?" Wieland asked. He had to shout to be heard over the rifle fire the rest of the squad unloaded at the farmhouse.

"I, uh, I don't know," the replacement said. "His hand's all messed up, but he fell, so I don't know if he got shot anywhere else…"

"Damn it!" Wieland said. "I thought you were watching the farmhouse!"

"I'm sorry! I thought, I mean, we were all standing around and now Jerry's been shot and he's just lying out there," the trembling private said, on the verge of tears. "We have to get him, we have to…"

"Hang on. First things first, Private," Wieland said, lifting his head up to look along the ditch. The rest of his squad was firing away at the farmhouse, stopping to reload when the empty clips popped out of the top of their rifles with their distinctive *Ping!* sound.

"Egleston! Kemp! You still with me?" Wieland shouted.

"Ready, Sarge!" They each gave him a thumbs-up.

"Okay. We wait until the burp gun goes dry, then when they

reload, we go two and two. Me and Pep go first, you cover, then switch. Our first leg takes us to that clump of trees a third of the way there. Got it?"

"Hang on," Kemp said, pushing a fresh clip into the top of his rifle. "Okay!"

"Pep?"

Pep gave him a nod. "Ready."

"What about me?" the replacement asked.

"Stay with the wounded," Wieland said, then nodded to Pep. "Go!"

*   *   *

Sergeant Wieland was breathing heavily before he'd taken three steps. He and Pep had abandoned their long, heavy overcoats in the ditch, but they were still carrying heavy rifles and ammunition and running through eight inches of snow. Besides, Wieland had found that even the slightest activity created breathless fatigue when performed in combat; it was as if the mere idea of combat was the equivalent of running a marathon. Even lying on the ground felt like he was running hard up a hill.

He stumbled forward at a breathless pace, firing twice with his rifle from the hip. Behind him, Kemp and Egleston fired rapidly at the farmhouse, keeping the enemy's heads down.

It was only thirty or forty yards to the clump of trees, but it seemed like a million miles and the twenty or so seconds it took to get there seemed like an hour during which he could get hit at any moment. *Just not the burp gun*, he thought. The closer they got to the farmhouse, the more the submachinegun became a threat. Inside of fifty yards, they would be outgunned if they were caught in the open, but they had to close with the farmhouse, or they might never flush the snipers out and would have to lay pinned down in that ditch.

There didn't seem to be any cold anymore, and although he was huffing for air, Wieland didn't actually feel any fatigue. Instead, all of his consciousness seemed focused into a funnel, a snowy tunnel that he ran through toward a copse of trees. Snow kicked up about six feet away, but the burp gun was quiet. She must be either pinned down or reloading.

The metal clip popped out of the top of his rifle… *Ping!* Wieland hadn't even realized he'd been firing, and the instant he realized he was empty, he reached the trees. He felt like hugging them, kissing them for the protection they afforded. There wasn't any time to rest and reflect, though; a glance back told him Kemp and Egleston were already up out of the ditch and running towards them.

His fumbling fingers tried to retrieve a clip, dropped it in the snow, then dug out another and managed to shove it down into the rifle's magazine well. Pep started firing to his left, pop pop pop, but the burp gun started up again, kicking up little clouds of snow in front of Kemp.

Wieland cursed and finished reloading his rifle clumsily. Something was wrong with his fingers, too cold maybe, but the bolt finally slammed forward as a rifle bullet punched into the tree in front of Pep.

"Shit!" Pep said, dropping to one knee and ducking behind the tree. "*Too* close!"

Wieland snapped off a quick shot at the woman with the rifle. He missed; he could see even before he shifted sight pictures that she was still up and trying to reload.

"Burp gun's in the lower left hand window!" Pep shouted.

Wieland saw it, then; just the muzzle, really. It was spitting fire toward Kemp and Egleston, who were crowded together behind an old abandoned cart left out in the open.

Fools, Wieland thought. *That won't stop a bullet.*

He fired quickly at the burp gun's window, joined almost immediately by Pep. Splinters of wood exploded from the pane, and Wieland could see the submachine-gun's barrel jerk away from the window reflexively, but he and Pep kept firing until they were empty.

"We got 'em! We got 'em!" Pep shouted toward the two men pinned down behind the cart.

Wieland glanced over toward the one with the rifle. She disappeared behind the corner of the house.

"She's running!" he shouted. "She's running! Go! Go!" he waved Kemp and Egleston toward the corner of the farmhouse behind which she'd just disappeared. "Now's your chance!"

He and Pep fired through another clip each at the lower left-hand window, just to be sure. Once the clips ejected out of the tops of their rifles and they reloaded, Wieland saw Kemp and Egleston were up to the front wall of the farmhouse, pressed flat against it. Each of them covered either side of the house as they crept towards the front door.

"Pep. How's your ammo?"

"Uh, this clip and three more."

"Okay. We're going for the house. All the way. Watch that window. Ready?"

"Ready."

Wieland paused long enough to watch Egleston throw a hand grenade into the window that the burp gun had been firing from.

"Go!"

Another huffing, breathless thirty seconds that felt like an eternity, and then they were pressed up against the front of the farmhouse. Egleston's grenade shattered both of the front windows when it exploded, but Wieland made sure to crouch below their line of sight just in case.

"You two around the house," he said, "and get that one with the rifle. Pep and I do the house."

"Oh, thanks so much, Sarge," Pep said, taking a grenade off of his gear and pulling the pin.

"Ready?" Wieland asked, flat against the left side of the front door. He didn't bother to check to make sure Kemp and Egleston were going around the side.

Pep nodded and Wieland kicked the door inwards. Pep lobbed the grenade inside, towards the room where the burp gun was, and they both took cover behind the wall when it blew. In a flash, they were both inside, Wieland covering the hallway and stairs, Pep charging to the left. Three loud reports thundered out of Pep's rifle into the already-dead body lying on the floor near the shot-up window.

Pep said something, but the close gunfire had filled Wieland's ears with a loud ringing. "What?"

"I said, this one's down!" Pep shouted, kneeling next to the body to make sure and then kicking the submachine-gun away.

They cleared the rest of the house quickly, only pausing when they heard Kemp's and Egleston's rifles pounding away outside. Pep made as if to rush out back, but Wieland stopped him with a hand on his arm. "Not yet. We make sure the house is clean so nobody can shoot us in the back."

Pep nodded and kicked in the last bedroom door on the second floor. There was a man lying on the bed, and Pep nearly shot him before Wieland stopped him.

"Hold it. I think he's already dead."

Pep covered him while he stepped next to the bed. The body didn't have the rotten smell of death on him, but Wieland could smell blood. The man looked dead, too; he had a greenish cast to his skin that Wieland had seen on dead Germans before and had always wondered what caused it.

He pulled away the covers. It was a soldier, Wehrmacht, maybe twenty-two years old or so. There was a gunshot or shrapnel wound in his abdomen that had soaked his uniform and the bedsheets as well.

"Any pistols on him?" Pep asked.

Wieland shook his head. "The women probably would've taken them. Besides, you've got, what, two already?"

"Walthers, yeah, but I want a Luger," Pep said.

They heard shouting from the two men outside. It didn't sound urgent, and there wasn't any firing, so Pep and Wieland took their time getting downstairs.

Wieland noticed for the first time how warm he was. There must be a fire going in the hearth, he decided. He also noticed he wasn't as winded anymore, but fatigue was already starting to make his limbs heavy.

"We got the other one," Kemp said, waving them over to him one they stepped out of the back door of the farmhouse. The third woman lay face-down in the snow. There was a rifle next to her and the snow beneath her was stained red.

"Dead?" Wieland asked as he walked over.

"As a doornail," Kemp said.

Pep knelt next to the body. "Jeez, this kid's all of what… fifteen?"

"If that," Kemp said. He had his helmet off and was raking his fingers through his red hair.

"Man, look at her," Pep said, shaking his head as he lifted up her head by the hair. "She was beautiful. Beautiful."

Blood dripped out of her mouth and into the depression her head had made in the snow. Pep laid her head back down and closed her sightless eyes.

"Damn," he said, straightening up and shivering once. With a wink at Wieland, he said, "Momma said there'd be days like this, but *damn*!"

Wieland snorted once. "Okay, you two, go through the house once more, check it for boobytraps. If that Schmeisser's still in good shape, round up all the ammo for it… we'll take it with us. We could use a submachine-gun. Pep and I are going to go collect Sayles and the new guy, get them inside."

"Roger that," they both said.

*   *   *

"They're inside the house," the replacement said, peering over the lip of the ditch. "Should I go get Jerry now?"

"Forget him. He's dead," Sayles said, wincing through the pain in his hand. He already had a crude bandage on it, but even a cursory glance told him he was going to lose the last two fingers on his left hand and maybe the third. "Get… get one of those overcoats they left behind, put it on the ground near me so I can lay on it. I'm freezing."

"But I really think I should get Jerry, he's just lying out..."

"He's dead, Private!" Sayles said, then settled down. "Look, there's nothing you can do for him, and if I don't warm up, I could go into shock and die, especially in this cold. I've seen it happen. So please."

"Okay."

The replacement laid one of the overcoats on the ground and manhandled Sayles onto it. "I just feel like I should be doing something."

"You are doing something. Keeping me alive."

"You know what I mean."

"It doesn't work like that, kid. The only reason we pulled that frontal charge is because our asshole lieutenant sent us out here without a heavy weapon. If we would've had a B.A.R., or better yet, a thirty-cal machinegun or sixty mortar, we would've just sat here in our nice safe ditch, blown the shit out of the house and the enemy, and only gone in once our ammo had run low. Hell, we'd have called in a bomber mission on that house if we could have."

"For three people? And just armed with rifles?"

"Damn right. They killed your friend, didn't they? Blew a good part of my hand off, too. We don't take chances. This is a job. A dirty, dangerous job, and we get it done as safely and unglamorously as possible. No armchair warrior nonsense."

Sayles caught the replacement looking at his mangled hand and laughed.

"What's so funny?"

"What's so funny?" Sayles repeated, with a wince of pain. "You, that's what's so funny. You probably feel sorry for me for getting shot."

The replacement frowned.

"See, I knew it," Sayles said. "Kid, believe you me, in a couple of days you'll be jealous of me. You'll wish with every ounce of energy in your soul that bullet had taken half of *your* hand off. 'Cause I'm going *home*, and you with your two good hands have got to stay *here*."

The replacement frowned even deeper, mulling that over for a bit. Sayles interrupted his thoughts once again.

"Go ahead and get up, kid. Here comes Pep and the Sarge."

* * *

It was just before dusk when the jeep finally arrived for Sayles. The entire squad was inside the farmhouse, warming up after a day's worth of freezing.

Sayles was laid out on the kitchen table, barely moving. Wieland had given him a hit of morphine, once the shock of being wounded had worn off and Sayles could feel the entire measure of his pain again.

"Where is he?" the jeep driver asked once he was inside, instinctively heading toward the fireplace with gloved hands extended.

"Wounded is on the table," Wieland said, pointing with his cigarette. They were all smoking like it was the first chance they'd had to burn a cigarette in weeks, all clustered around the fireplace, except for the replacement, who sat on the floor away from the rest.

"I heard I had bodies to pick up," the jeep driver said. "I ain't got a medic. We're Graves Registration."

"Yeah, well, we got bodies as well, Mac," Wieland said. "So take Sayles back along with the bodies, so he can get to a medic. Unless you want to tell a guy with half his hand blown off he's got to walk home."

"Okay, no problem," the jeep driver said, holding his hands up in surrender. "I'm just saying, we don't have a medic. Hey, Charlie!" he shouted toward the open front door. "We're taking a live one back with us!"

"Bodies are out front," Wieland said, leading the way.

"How many?"

"Three."

"Oh." The jeep driver stopped once they were outside in the cold. He looked over the three bodies and shook his head. "Don't know if I can take them all *and* the wounded guy."

"Sayles goes with you." Wieland said, his hand dropping toward the flap holster on his belt as punctuation.

The driver's eyes caught his hand's movement. Raising his hands up once again, he said, "I'm just saying, may have to leave a body behind."

The driver's partner, a big private with a towel wrapped around his neck and stuffed into his jacket like a scarf, uncovered the first body. He took it by the feet, waited for the driver to get it by the shoulders, and heaved.

It stayed stuck to the ground for a second, then ripped away with the sound of frozen steaks being pulled apart. The corpse's arm and elbow were still frozen in the air, as if the soldier had been shielding his eyes from the sun when he died.

They lifted him up. The body did not sag, but stayed flat like a wooden plank.

"This stiff is *stiff*," the jeep driver grunted around his smoldering stub of a cigar. He winked at Wieland as he passed and then paused. "Oh, hey, this ain't one of..."

"Not one of mine," Wieland said.

The Graves Registration duo heaved the body unceremoniously onto the back of the jeep, as if it were indeed a plank of wood and not a human corpse. "Whaddaya think, Charlie? Wounded guy in the back seat, strap this one to the back, prop another up in the seat next to the live one?" He tilted his head toward Wieland. "Think he'd mind? Ridin' next to a dead guy?"

Wieland had to laugh. "For a ride home? He'd sit on the stiff's *lap*."

The driver found that funny and returned to the next body with his partner. "Whoa, a fresh one!" he said, when the corpse bent and sagged in the middle upon lifting. "Ah, hell, Sarge, I'm sorry. This guy's probably one of yours, right?"

Wieland shrugged.

"What was his name?"

"How the hell should I know?" Wieland said, watching the two men prop the body in the back seat of the jeep. "I had him in my squad for all of three hours before he got nailed."

"Yeah? Well, tough break, Mac," the driver said, giving the body a friendly pat on the cheek.

"His name was Jerry Peele, and..."

Wieland turned to see who had spoken and saw his other replacement was standing in the doorway, without the benefit of a helmet or overcoat. He was shivering and his voice see-sawed between furious indignation and hesitant apprehension.

"...and I don't think you should be hitting him like that," the replacement finished.

"Take it easy," the driver said, but the replacement had already ducked back inside of the house. "What's his problem?"

"New guy," Wieland said.

"Oh," the driver said. "Who hit you? I don't see any Kraut bodies. You get shelled?"

Wieland shook his head. "Nazi sympathizers. Civilians."

"No shit," the driver said. "That's no way to fight a war, when the damn civilians start shooting at you. Hey, Charlie! I think with as stiff as this other guy is, we can strap the two frozen ones on with the rope and take the third in the back seat. That's enough room for the live one. Think?"

"I'm game," Charlie said, and retrieved a rope from the jeep.

The driver tipped Wieland another wink. "Am I good at my job, or what?"

"You're an innovator. Look…" Wieland waited until they had stacked the second frozen body on top of the first with a thud that made the jeep bounce, "…look, did the lieutenant give you any orders for me?"

"Eh?" the driver said, running the rope around the bodies. "Oh, yeah. Yeah, you guys gotta stay here on outpost tonight. They'll meet up with you, relieve you in the morning."

Wieland glared at him. "Are you kidding? Stay all the way out here? No artillery, no… us, just the five of us, almost three-quarters of a mile from the nearest friendly unit, and no heavy weapons?"

He shook his head. "Son of… did they at least send up a thirty cal or something for us?"

The driver nodded at the jeep. "You see a thirty cal in there?"

"Son of a…" Wieland bit off the curse before he could finish it.

"Hey, Mac, I'm just the messenger. Don't cut off my head," the driver said. "Your lieutenant says stay here until relieved in the morning. Keep in contact with him with your radio."

"Which doesn't work half the time," Wieland said, but the driver didn't hear him.

"Hey, Charlie? All set?"

"I think we're a go," Charlie said, giving the driver a thumbs-up.

"Okay, Sarge," the driver said, "go get your man."

Wieland was already up the two front steps and inside before he'd finished saying it.

"Get Sayles on his feet," he said. "His ride home is ready."

"C'mon, Sayles, up!" Pep said, helping the still-drugged Sayles off of the kitchen table and to his feet. "Up, up! Time to go home!"

"Unh?" Sayles said, blinking a few times dazedly.

Pep took the lit cigarette out of his mouth and put it into Sayles's. "I said, you're going home now, you lucky son of a bitch! Hurry up, before I put a bullet through *my* hand and take your place!"

"Heh," Sayles said, smiling to himself as he let Pep walk him to the jeep. "Home."

Just before he walked out of the door, he paused and pointed at the replacement, who was once again sitting against the wall furthest from the others, his arms wrapped around his knees. "*Home*, Private," he said, and then let himself be led out to the jeep.

Wieland followed him out, made sure he was secure in the jeep's back seat, and covered him with a blanket he'd found in one of the bedrooms on the second floor. "Don't you go freezing to death now that you're on your way home," he said.

"Lucky son of a bitch," Pep added, and then the jeep lurched once and took off down the road toward the rest of the battalion.

"Orders?" Pep asked as they walked back into the house, and Wieland glared at him.

"Not good," he said, then once he was in the doorway, addressed the entire squad. "Listen up, gentlemen. We've been ordered to hold here as an outpost. You know…"

He raised his voice to be heard over the immediate grumbling. "…you know what that means! I want a foxhole about thirty-forty yards out toward the road."

"What the hell for?" Kemp said. "We don't have a machine-gun for it."

"Doesn't matter," Wieland said. "We need to stay spread out in case they shell the house, and some warning if someone comes wandering down the road tonight."

"Ground's frozen, Sarge," Egleston said, turning his spare pair of socks over on the hearth like strips of bacon. "Can't dig in. Take all night."

"Pep's got a half-stick," Wieland said, then catching a look from him, added, "I know you do, Pep. You always keep one tucked away for a rainy day, like a squirrel with his nuts."

Pep dug a half-stick of TNT out of a pocket. "Yeah, well, just quit talking about my nuts, Sarge," he said with a grin.

"Kemp and Egleston, get it started," Wieland said. "We'll trade off every forty-five minutes or so, so nobody gets too cold or too tired. Once it's done, we'll set shifts. Keep it camouflaged, and we can keep a little fire going in here. Hopefully Jerry just thinks it's just his sympathizer buddies keeping hearth and home warm and comfy."

"At least I managed to dry my socks," Egleston said, trading the fire-dried socks for the wet ones on his feet. "Okay if I leave this pair here to dry?"

Wieland nodded, but Pep said, "Hey, be sure to keep those to the side, Moose. I'm gonna heat up some C-rats in a while, and I don't want your stinky foot-fumes in my government cheese."

"Adds flavor," Egleston said with a smile, taking the half-stick away from Pep.

"Flavor," Pep said. "Ought to tie his socks to our artillery shells, blow 'em up over the Krauts. Kill hundreds at a time, burn holes through their tanks... nah, forget it. Probably violates the Geneva Convention, mustard gas or something."

Egleston shook his head and smiled as he pulled on his overcoat. "You're a beautiful man, Pep."

"I like to think so," Pep said, and waved as Egleston and Kemp walked outside into the gloom. "Enjoy the fresh air."

There were a few minutes of silence, with Pep looking at Wieland, Wieland looking at the fire, the replacement staring into his hands, and nobody talking.

"Going to make radio contact?" Pep asked.

"Try in an hour or so," Wieland said, digging for his cigarettes.

Pep nodded, looked back and forth from the sergeant to the replacement, endured a few more seconds of awkward silence, and then, with a slap of both hands on his knees, got up out of the chair he'd been sitting on and collected his overcoat and helmet. "Well, I think I'll lend a hand outside."

"Hey, what..." Wieland said quickly, grabbing at Pep's coat with a look that said *Don't leave me alone in here!*, but Pep dodged his hand.

"See you in a bit, fellas."

"Damn," Wieland said to himself with a glance toward the replacement. "Damn."

The silence quickly became more stifling than the smoke curling up from the logs in the fireplace. Wieland was almost happy when a series of eight rifle shots from outside shattered the air into splinters.

The replacement scrambled to his feet, grabbing at his weapon, but Wieland stayed seated and waved the private back down. "Take it easy, Private. It's okay."

The replacement looked toward the door, didn't hear any more shooting, and settled back down to a seat. "What was it?"

Wieland sighed, as if too tired to explain, then explained it anyway. "Trying to dig a hole in ground this frozen is like trying to dig a hole in concrete. Takes forever. So, you shoot a clip into the ground, and that drills a little hole for you. Stick a half-stick of TNT in there, light it, run like hell, boom. It doesn't dig you a full blown foxhole, but it gets you through the frozen layer and down into the soft stuff where you can dig."

Sure enough, a few seconds later, they heard Pep yell "Fire in the hole!", followed by a muffled explosion, followed by some whooping and cheering from Pep. The replacement kept looking wistfully at the door and the laughter coming from the other side.

Sergeant Wieland looked at him and sighed doggedly once again. *Well, it's my job, I guess*, he thought, and said, "Look, kid, grab a chair and get over by the fire. God only knows when you'll be able to get this warm again."

The replacement seemed to perk up, almost ran over to a chair and slid it near the fireplace. Wieland cursed himself instantly, but forced himself to take another step.

"Take those wet socks off, put the dry spares on and lay the wet ones out on the fireplace like Egleston did. Do that whenever you can. If there isn't any fire, put the wet ones around your neck to dry. Trench foot takes out as many guys as Jerry does, and you can lose a foot to it."

And now I've done my good deed for the day, Wieland thought, and went back to staring at the fire.

The replacement practically tore off his shoes to comply, and once he had, nodded to himself almost happily. "So where you from, Sarge?"

Oh, splendid, Wieland thought. *Now the kid thinks I want some conversation with him.*

"Look, kid… you smoke?"

"Uh, uh-hunh, yeah."

"Then light up and just smoke for a while, okay?"

The replacement found his cigarettes and lit one. "I'm from Wisconsin. A farm. A dairy farm, you know, cows and… I heard you were a farmer. From a farm. Or on a farm. Mine was cows."

God help me, Wieland thought, rolling his eyes at his misfortune. He glanced sideways at the replacement. Wieland still had no idea what the little misfit's name was. He was pretty sure that in all the action today, the kid hadn't fired a single shot. He knew for a fact that Sayles had been taken out with a million-dollar wound because this kid was too stupid to take cover when bullets were in the air.

Sayles, who was worth ten of these God-Awful, know-nothing replacements, that came and went like passing rain showers. And here this one was, staring at his cigarette, practically begging Wieland to hold his hand and talk pretty to him all night long.

Then, despite his better judgment, despite the veteran's solemn vow not to learn the new guy's name until he proved he wasn't going to get killed straightaway, Wieland saw something. He saw himself, six months ago, looking just like this kid, except he'd thrown up in his foxhole the morning of his first attack. His lieutenant at the time, a guy by the name of Fetters, had gotten him up and squared away. He'd told Wieland what to look for, what not to do, and best of all, had him tag along with an old hand so he could learn the ropes by doing. And three days later, after two full-blown attacks and three artillery barrages, Wieland was A Veteran, one of the old guys, and the rest of the company took him in.

He was never sure how to thank Fetters, and when he tried, Fetters clapped him on the back and said, "Pass it on." A week later, an 88 shell tore half of the lieutenant's head away.

Pass it on. He'd avoided it, for the longest time, because the replacements got killed so damn quickly. Better not to learn their names, better not to get to know them…

But now he was a sergeant, and while Pep and the others could afford to snicker and wander off and indulge in the luxury of ignoring the new guy, it was Wieland's job to pass it on.

He looked over at the replacement again, couldn't help thinking *Dumb kid got Sayles taken out*, but then, he swore he could feel Fetter's hand clapping him good-naturedly on the shoulder, swore he could hear his voice in his ear. *He's hurting, Wieland. You were right there not too long ago yourself. We pass it on.*

Wieland groaned inwardly, clenched his fists, but there was nothing else to do.

Oh, fine, he thought, and said abruptly, "Didn't have any cows."

The replacement looked over at him. "What?"

"Cows. The farm I grew up on, back in Ephrata, Pennsylvania, we didn't have any cows on it."

"No?" The replacement sounded almost hopeful.

"Corn, mostly. Some other stuff, but mostly corn."

"Oh." The replacement nodded, positively beaming now, then

quieted down for a few seconds before speaking again. "I used to hate it."

"What was that?"

"Growing up on a farm, I used to... hate it," the replacement said, still smiling a little, as if laughing at himself. Wieland thought he looked like he was hiding tears behind that little smile.

"Getting up so early, everything's dirty, everything smelled," the replacement went on. "There's always so much to do, and you were always so dirty, and... that smell. God. I loved school, you know, because it got me away from that smell and that dirty feeling for a little while. I always swore I would go to college, get off that farm. I hated it. More than anything, I wanted to get off that farm."

"Yeah, well," Wieland said, flicking an ash off of his cigarette, "I bet you'd give anything to get back on that farm after today."

The replacement's response was quiet. "No takers on that bet."

There were a few minutes of quiet, in which they could hear shovels digging at the ground outside.

"It doesn't seem real."

Wieland ground his teeth and kept quiet. He never should've taken those stripes, should've stayed a private so he could ignore the new guys like everybody else.

"Jerry getting shot, you know?" the replacement said.

I know all about it, Wieland thought, but kept quiet.

"It doesn't seem real that he's not going to walk anymore or talk anymore or joke about how the white beans gave him bad gas," the replacement said, smiling bittersweetly at the memory. "He was a real nice guy. You'd have liked him. We came over on the transport together. Every night... every day, too, really... we'd all play poker for cigarettes, and Jerry'd beat the tar out of everybody. You've never seen a poker player like him. So in no time, he'd have everybody's stash. But he didn't smoke, so he just gave it all back with a smile. 'I need something to win tomorrow', he'd say with a big smile. Everybody loved Jerry. He was a hell of a guy."

Wieland watched him stare at his cigarette, watched him hurt, and then he spoke. "What you're feeling now, right now, is why those guys outside don't want to talk to you… why I don't want to talk to you. It isn't anything personal, it's just that you new guys get killed off so *quick*. If we got to know all of you, we'd have to go through what you're going through every day.

"You're a front line soldier, kid. Most of the people you see around you are dead men walking. You really want to get to know Pep, like you knew Jerry? And then tomorrow we get shelled and Pep gets it and you're right back where you are now? You can't do that; you can't take that, day in, day out. Maybe if you last a week or so, and then they see that you're not going to get it right away, maybe then they'll start getting to know you. But not now. Not when you might end up like your buddy. They have to cut themselves off from that."

"But how am I supposed to…"

"It doesn't have anything to do with what you deserve," Wieland said. "Or anything to do with what's fair or right or anything other than that's the way things are. You want it straight? Your buddy got himself killed today, and you helped him along."

That bit into the replacement visibly, and Wieland hurried to explain himself.

"Now, all fair being fair, it's not really your fault. You guys probably got pushed through Basic too fast, and nobody told you anything, and you haven't been here long enough to see that you're playing for keeps. So your buddy drops his weapon on the ground and leaves it there, when if he'd held on to it, maybe he could've opened fire on those women before they got him. And if you would've kept an eye on this house with that scoped rifle, maybe you could've dinged one of them before they could shoot him. I understand that you didn't know. And there's not a one of those guys out there, if the war ended tomorrow and we were all in a nice safe pub drinking beer, that wouldn't shrug and tell you, hey kid, we understand, you were new, you couldn't have done any better. Not a one. You seem like an okay kid, and if we were in Paris or London or…"

He shook his head. "But we aren't. We're on the front lines, and none of those guys will want to get to know you. Your buddy…"

"Jerry," the replacement said.

"…was with us three hours before he got it. Sooner or later it's going to happen to you, and nobody's going to want to be your friend, so that when you do get it, it doesn't mean anything. That's why none of us are torn up about your buddy getting hit. They didn't know him, so he was just some guy who got nailed… see it all the time, no big deal… and then they can act like those Graves Registration guys did with the bodies. All that gallows humor stuff. You thought he was being disrespectful, but… it seems sick and twisted, and it should, because it is. But it's also the only way to get by out here without going nuts."

"But that," the replacement said. "That's not living. That's just existing."

Wieland blew out a drag. "I'll take existing for as long as I can get it, kid."

He waited a beat before continuing. "I'll bet you want to know Why for today. Why about everything. Why did these three women... hell, *girls*... shoot us up? How did they get their weapons? Did they kill those two other G.I.s? Why? What happened to the G.I.s' weapons? Who's the dead Kraut we found upstairs? Why were the girls sympathetic to the Nazis in the first place, when they're Belgian and should want to fight them? Why'd they take us on when there's only three of them and seven of us? Right?"

"Sure you do," Wieland said. "I can tell just by looking at you. You look the type, always looking for the why behind the world. Listen up, Private. *Forget why.* 'Why' doesn't matter to you. 'Is' is all that matters to you. Keep looking for meaning in all of this, and you'll go nuts in no time. There is no why. All that matters is, three people shot at us, we returned fire. That's it. Keep debating about it, and some German is going to shoot you in the head while you're figuring it all out."

The replacement shook his head. "But how can you say that? Are you telling me you don't wonder about this? Any of it? Or wish that you'd met some of these people, got to know them, even if it's just for a little while? You know, think about getting together with them after we go home?"

Wieland stared at him. "Who says we're going home?"

"What?"

"You haven't been listening to a word I've said. You're a dead man, Private. Just like me, just like those three guys digging a hole out there, just like every G.I. on the line. We're all dead men. It's just a matter of when and where and how."

The replacement looked away from Wieland, back at the fire. "I can't believe that. I mean, Sayles..."

"Sayles is crippled," Wieland said, "and that's why all of us old guys envy him. He goes home. Get it? The only way off of this line is dead or wounded; and wounded guys come back to the line once they recover, and stay until they're dead or wounded again, and if they recover again, then they come back again, and so on, until they're dead or they can't recover into fighting condition... like Sayles. You're here until you die, the war ends, or you're so crippled that you can't fight anymore. Get it?"

The replacement thought it over. "That... that doesn't make any sense."

"No shit. But it's US Army policy to keep a front line division in the line continually, and keep it at strength with a constant stream of replacements who know jack shit. No, no, don't take a unit that's just been decimated out of the line to get their heads together and re-organize. Just shove a truckload of Repple-Depples... new guys... into their foxholes until the next disaster. Shell shock? Come out of the line for a day or two, get doped up, a clean shower, then back at it. You know what they say about the First Division? Three divisions in one: one in the field, one in the hospital, and one in the grave. And that's it. Face it, Private, you..."

"Whitney," the replacement said. "Carl Whitney."

"Okay, Carl Whitney," Wieland said, "face it, you rolled snake eyes and got put into a line unit and the only way out is dead."

Wieland ground out his cigarette on the sole of his boot. "We're all dead men, Whitney, and nobody gives a damn. We're a bunch of walking ghosts out here, and the only signs of our passing are a couple of tracks in the snow. Those fade. Those fade awfully quick."

"I can't believe that," Whitney said. "I can't believe that's all that we are."

Wieland sighed and tossed his cigarette stub into the fire, giving up on a lost cause. He'd just settled in to a comfortable stare into the fireplace when a rifle shot cracked his cozy daze into pieces.

Shouts, from outside, and then their nightmare began.

* * *

"Are you gonna dig?" Kemp said to Pep, who was sitting contentedly on the edge of the shallow hole Egleston and Kemp were currently deepening with entrenching tools.

"That'll be the day," Egleston said, and Pep affirmed it.

"Nah. Not my turn yet. I'm just out here so I don't have to deal with the new guy. Let Sarge take care of that. Price of rank. Never catch *me* with any of those stripes."

"You'd have to earn them before they could 'catch' you," Egleston said. "We all know that's never gonna happen."

"Oh, ho-ho-ho, wise guy," Pep said. "Okay, Moose, why don't you go in there, hold the new guy's hand, take a nice long shower with him?"

"Dunno, Pep, it's been a while since I had a shower," Egleston said.

"Jesus! Careful there, Moose! You stepped on my foot!" Pep said. "Look at those boots, the size of those feet! They're like elephant feet! How'd they ever find boots big enough to fit those gigantic hooves of yours?"

"They had to make 'em special," Kemp said. "Took a couple of snow shoes and stretched canvas across 'em."

"Heh!" Pep clapped his hands once. "That's a good one, Red! I didn't think you had it in you!"

"Yeah, well, how'd they ever find boots small enough for you, Pep?" Egleston said, pausing in his digging just long enough to swat Pep's dangling feet. "I mean, is it hard to stay up on feet that small?"

"Oh, ha-ha," Pep said, as Kemp laughed out loud. "Very funny. Keep it up, Moose, and these little feet are going to swat that big hairy ass of yours."

A rifle report seemed to whiplash the air around them. Simultaneous to the report was a sound like an aluminum trash can getting pelted by a rock, and Kemp's body crumpled limply to the ground.

Pep and Egleston dropped to the ground almost as quickly as Kemp's body. They tried to shove themselves into the half-dug foxhole, but bits and pieces of themselves kept poking out.

"Shit! He's dead, he took it in the head," Egleston said, running a hand over Kemp's body. "Right through the helmet."

"Get him out, I can't... fit, damn it, Egleston, move!" Pep said, then yelled at the farmhouse, "Sniper! Sniper!"

Another rifle report, and a slug punched into Kemp's body as they shoved it up out of the hole. It was like trying to move four sacks of grain tied together at the middle; one part kept wanting to slide back in as their hands held the rest up.

"We're sitting ducks out here," Pep said, trying to squeeze his body flat into the unfinished foxhole. His feet and part of a leg poked out; it felt like they had bull's-eyes painted on them in bright orange paint. He felt for a second like a kid convinced the monsters under the bed couldn't get at him so long as he kept under the covers; but his leg was sticking out, exposed, and now the night monsters could and would gnaw it off once he closed his eyes.

If he was having this kind of trouble, Egleston must really be screwed, he figured, and a glance confirmed it. The big man's body was almost half-exposed.

"We'll try to use Kemp as a sandbag," Pep said. He could see Wieland in the doorway of the farmhouse, holding the burp gun. His head barely edged out past the doorjamb. The new guy was right behind him.

"They got Ke... shit!" he shouted, as another bullet thudded into Kemp's body in front of him. "They got Kemp in the head! He's over that way," he held up his rifle to point so the Sarge could see it better than just a finger. "I think!"

"How the hell can he see to shoot this good?" Egleston said, face pressed into the frozen earth. He sounded like a kid calling "No Fair" on a cheating playmate.

"Are you kidding?" Pep said. "With all this snow reflecting that bright moon? It's practically daylight. Bastard's just been waiting out there, waiting for Kemp to dig his own grave."

"I was digging too, Pep," Egleston said, and then another rifle shot ringed Kemp's helmet like a bell as it punched through.

Showing off, Pep thought, but then he heard the Sarge shout.

"There! See it?" the Sarge said, and then, "Just shoot where I do! Pep! Go now!"

The burp gun chattered away at the night, followed by the heavier, hollower thunder of an M1 rifle. Pep didn't deliberate; he grabbed Egleston by the belt, shouted "Come on!" and practically launched himself out of the hole, dragging Egleston with his right hand and clutching his rifle with the other.

He was sure he was going to get hit. He had to; he had thirty yards to cross with no cover, thumping and stomping through heavy snow and dragging Egleston along with him. Wieland was in the doorway ahead of him, kneeling, shooting the burp gun in long bursts at where he'd seen the last muzzle flash. The new guy stood behind him, firing the Sarge's M1 over Wieland's shoulder, pop pop pop until *Ping!* Pep could hear the empty clip pop out even from thirty yards away, except it wasn't thirty yards anymore, it was more like ten, and he realized he still had a hold of Egleston's belt with his trailing right arm, just as Egleston suddenly stopped running and fell and jerked Pep to a halt like an anchor dropped on a slowly moving boat.

Pep turned, saw the blood in the snow from the light cast out of the doorway, and knew what it meant before Egleston could shout *I'm hit*. He felt suddenly outside himself, the terror of an imminent gunshot wound combining with the sudden strenuous run to create a sort of endorphin haze; Pep never thought, he just hauled on Egleston's belt as hard as he could, hauled for the doorway, dragged him the seven yards to the doorway and up the steps before he realized he'd just dragged a heavily clothed two-hundred-pound man like he was a duffel bag.

He lost his grip on Egleston's belt and fell sprawling to the floor. Wieland and the new guy went to Egleston's aid just as a final rifle shot blew splinters out of the right side of the doorjamb.

Son of a bitch I made it, Pep thought dully, before shaking his head to tune back in.

"He's bleeding! He's bleeding all over the place!" the new guy said.

"Whitney!" Wieland said. "Get pressure on it! Hard!"

"Medic!" Egleston shouted. "M… Kemp! Kemp, I'm hit, get me a medic!"

The big man started to struggle to his feet, fighting with Wieland and the new guy when they tried to hold him down. Pep scrambled to his feet and ran to Egleston's side. He took the big man's face in his hands and practically shouted into his face.

"Moose! Moose! It's Pep! Knock it off, man, settle down! You're killing yourself! We can't stop the bleeding when you fight us like that!"

Egleston's eyes blinked and the haze cleared from them a bit. He stopped fighting them, looked down at his leg, where bright red blood pulsed out near the crease of his inner thigh. "Hey… hey, Pep…"

"I know. I see it, Moose."

"It's bad, Pep, it's really…"

"I know, shut up. Hold still."

The new guy orbited around the cluster of Pep and Egleston and Wieland, wringing his hands around his weapon. He looked like he was looking for an open spot to join in with Pep and Wieland in comforting Egleston.

"He needs a, uh, a…what's it, a tourniquet," the new guy said.

"Yeah, no shit," Pep said, barely looking up from where he knelt next to the wounded man. "How are you going to get a tourniquet up that high?"

Wieland looked around wildly for a moment, then said, "Whitney, find a belt or piece of rope, fast." When Pep glanced over at him, he added, "We'll have to try."

"It's bad, Pep, is…iss real… bad," Egleston mumbled. His breaths were getting shallow; it seemed like he was exhausted after a long march and fighting to stay awake. "Pep… Pep…"

"Yeah, I'm here, Moose." Pep laid the big man flat, keeping

Egleston's head in his lap to cushion it. "Sarge, get… his legs up, I think we're supposed to get his legs up."

Wieland looked up from where he was pressing an already-soaked bandage against the wound. "It's… I can't stop it, Pep."

Pep looked at the bandage, up at Wieland, then back at Egleston. "Hey, come on, now, Moose, you've got to stay with me. Stay with me, don't you go into shock."

"No," Egleston shook his head, licked his lips. "No shock. I'm… I'm really thirsty, Pep. You got some water?"

"Sure I got some water, you know I got some water," Pep said, leaning to pull a canteen off of Wieland's belt. "I'm like a squirrel with his nuts, remember? Sarge is always talking about my nuts, I don't know what's going on there."

Egleston smiled weakly. "You're funny, Pep."

"Yeah, I'm funny. I know I'm funny," Pep said, tilting the canteen to Egleston's lips. He couldn't help glancing down at the pool of blood collecting between Egleston's thighs. It spread like a river delta between his legs and out past his feet. There was so much; Pep couldn't believe so much blood was in ten bodies, much less one.

"Careful there, Moose, don't slop this down too quick," Pep said. He saw Wieland's hands were covered in blood, still uselessly clamping the soaked bandage to the pulsing wound. His voice cracked as he shouted, "Where's that goddamn tourniquet, Private?"

"That's it, not too much," he went on, in a soothing tone that surprised Wieland. "Don't want to slop it down like that ice cream last week. You remember that, Moose? Hunh? You remember that ice cream, how you sucked it down?"

Egleston nodded weakly, eyelids drooping. "I like ice cream."

"Yeah, no kidding you like ice cream, I was there," Pep said, cradling the big man as best he could. "Ten below freezing, some jackass sends our kitchen truck out with five gallons of ice cream. Nobody else eats it, just you. Just you, Moose, chowing it down like a horse working on a feed bag. You remember that?"

"I... member..." Egleston said.

"Hey, you got to stay awake now, Moose," Pep said, slapping him lightly on the face. The pool of blood looked more than ever like a river now. "Come on, here... here's the new guy, new guy's got a belt, a tourniquet, see? Fix you right up. You're going home."

The replacement knelt down next to Egleston, an old leather belt in his hand. "I don't know how to do this."

"Just get it around his leg as high up as you can," Wieland said. "Here. Let me help you."

The two men struggled to get the belt around Egleston's upper thigh. The replacement cringed visibly when blood smeared all over his hand.

"Hey now, easy fellas," Pep said, "you don't want to hurt the man. Moose is a delicate flower, aren't you, Moose? Moose?"

Pep twisted Egleston's chalk white face up toward his. "Hey, Moose! No, no, no, don't you do it, don't you give up now, you big sack of shit! Come on! Come on, we got you a tourniquet, you're gonna be fine, now come on!"

The replacement continued to struggle with the belt, but Wieland stopped him.

"Damn it, damn it," Pep said, rocking back and forth a little, still cradling Egleston's head in his arms. The big man's eyes were half-open, sightlessly staring at the ceiling. "Why'd you have to... go and get shot, you big dumb fuck, you?"

Pep's voice cracked and he choked up, sudden tears springing to his eyes. He didn't look at Egleston, as if he could deny his friend's death a little longer so long as he didn't see it. His hands ran over and over the big man's face, like a blind man trying to memorize his features.

"You didn't… you don't… you stupid fuck!" he suddenly shouted, slamming a fist down on the dead man's chest. "You stupid…"

He leapt to his feet, hand clenched into fists at his sides. "Fuck! Fuck!"

Pep tore his helmet off of his head and hurled it savagely against the wall. "You motherfucker!" he screamed at the front door, toward the unseen sniper outside.

The replacement looked like he might get up to try to comfort him, and Wieland held him back with a hand laid on his arm.

Pep stalked around the room, one step this way, another two that way, as if he were determined to pace but had no idea which way he should go. His hands bobbed around, looking for something to grab and crush. A booted foot sent a chair flying with a loud clatter. A few stutter-steps, and Pep kicked over the short pile of logs next to the fireplace. They fell over themselves into a jumble. He scooped up his rifle, moved it around a couple of times like he was going to swing it against the wall like a baseball bat, then he dropped to the floor, rifle cradled between his legs, face buried in his hands. He didn't make a sound, but his body quivered with silent sobs.

Wieland blew out a long, slow breath.

"What do we do?" the replacement whispered.

Pep laughed bitterly, sobs fluttering away. "What do we do? What the fuck do you *want* to do about this, Private?"

The replacement looked down at the floor. "I just meant…"

"What?" Pep said, standing up and letting his rifle fall to the floor with a clatter. "What did you mean?"

"You know, should we do something for him, or for Kemp…"

"Kemp's dead," Pep said. He advanced slowly on the replacement, a slightly wild look in his eyes.

"I know, but the body…"

"He's dead, he doesn't care," Pep said. "What do you think you can do for him now? Make him less dead? That'd be a hell of a trick. He's dead, asshole, he wouldn't care if the entire Kraut army pissed on him. What do you want to do, go out there and get your dumb ass shot so you can take care of a dead man? Hunh?"

"Pep." There was a warning tone to Wieland's voice.

"Don't 'Pep' me, Wieland. This asshole can't even piss in his pants when it gets hot and he wants to go take that guy on. Is that what you want, Private? Go take on an obvious expert, who can hit two men, one of them moving, with a rifle shot lit only by moonlight? When you've been exactly… fucking… *useless*… this entire time?"

"Pep!" Wieland stood up now, as much to stop Pep's advance on the replacement as anything else. The short man looked like he was planning on beating the replacement senseless.

Pep looked up at him, and Wieland was sure to keep his expression neutral, so as not to provoke him. "Go watch the back."

Pep looked down at the replacement, then up at Wieland.

"Go on, Pep. Go now."

"Yes, Sergeant Wieland," Pep sneered, and flipped a grandiose salute before collecting his helmet and rifle and stomping into the kitchen, towards the back door.

"Jesus," the replacement said, once Pep had left the room. He stared at the river of blood running from Egleston's leg and flowing out toward the front door. "How do you do this? Every day, how do you keep doing this, going on like this?"

Wieland nodded his head. "Welcome to the war, kid."

*   *   *

"Say again?"

Carl Whitney shifted his weight so his legs wouldn't fall asleep. For the better part of half an hour, Sergeant Wieland had tried to get a distress call through to battalion, without much luck. The batteries on their portable radio were dying, and for every word that got through, three were garbled.

"No, no," Sergeant Wieland said into the radio. "I said, we're pinned down and... hello? Hello?"

"Damn it!" he cursed, throwing the radio handset down in disgust. "Useless. God damn useless. We need a telephone line."

"What now?" Carl asked.

"How the hell should I know?" Wieland said. "Hunh? I mean, if we had a thirty-cal or even better, a fifty, we could draw the sniper's fire and then machine-gun the hell out of his position. Sixty mortar, same thing. Or if we were in the line like we're supposed to be, with squads on either side of us for support, we could call in fire from them or an artillery barrage from battalion. But we can't do any of that, because our stupid *fucking* lieutenant stuck us out here in Bumblefuck with our asses swinging in the breeze... and he'll be shocked to hear we've lost half our squad. So I don't know what to do, kid."

"Kid" is at least a step up from "Private", Carl decided. "It's getting cold in here."

"Yeah, well, can't have a fire going and give the sniper enough light to see us through the windows and pick us off."

Carl nodded and shrugged into his overcoat. "You want some of that bread I found?"

"Not hungry. Wish there'd been some cognac. I could use a good hit right about now."

Carl noticed Pep's overcoat on the floor. What the hell. It was depressing out here with the Sarge, to the point of making Carl uncomfortable just by being in the same room. "I'm gonna go give Pep his coat."

Wieland looked over at him. "All right. I'll watch your window for a whi… Stay low, Whitney! You don't want to take any chances!"

"Even after this long?"

"Especially after this long," Wieland said, scooting over to one of the front windows on hands and knees. "They wait for you to get sloppy or tired or just sick of it, and then you screw up, and that's when they kill you."

"I can't get over how such trivial details can cost a man his life."

"Nothing's trivial over here," Wieland said. "Except the value of a G.I.'s life to a general."

Carl frowned at that. "I'm… gonna go give Pep his coat."

He crouched low all the way to the kitchen. Pep was next to the back door, peering out of the corner of the window next to it. He turned briefly when he heard Carl come into the room, then went back to his silent vigil.

"I brought you your coat."

Pep looked down at himself, saw he wasn't wearing his overcoat.

"Thanks."

He took it wordlessly from Carl and pulled it on.

Carl waited a few seconds before trying again. "I found some bread in the cellar. Do you want some?"

Pep still didn't look at him. "Is it that black kind?"

"Um, yeah."

Pep shrugged. "Okay."

Finally, Carl thought, and broke a generous hunk off of the loaf. "Here."

Pep only looked away from the window long enough to take it from him. "Thanks, uh… thanks, kid."

"Whitney," Carl said. "Carl Whitney."

Pep nodded, still looking out the window. "Okay."

Carl filled a few seconds' time with chewing some of the hard, black bread, then said, "I'm sorry about your friend. Egleston."

"What the hell do you know about it?"

Carl shrugged. "I lost a friend today too. Jerry, remember? He was shot by the uh, the sympathizers…"

"Oh, yeah, right. The other new guy."

"The other new guy," Carl said.

Pep stared silently out of the window for a few more seconds. Whitney was almost surprised when he spoke again.

"You know him long?"

"Who, Jerry? Yeah… no, I… guess not. Couple of weeks. Seems like longer."

"Yeah," Pep said. "I bet you never shared a foxhole with him, though, hunh?"

Carl shook his head. "No, we… I never had to do that yet."

Pep bit off another piece of bread and ate it before continuing, his eyes never leaving the snow-covered trees beyond the window. "Me and Moose... Egleston, we were foxhole buddies for a long time. Long time," he smiled, shaking his head. "Yeah, it's like you said, it always seems like longer. Me and... Egleston... came to this company together... well, maybe about a day apart. Our sergeant put me with him because he said I was the only one small enough to fit into a foxhole with a big S.O.B. like him."

Pep smiled at the memory. "Hated him at first. Always drying his stinky socks over my C-rats fire. Or trying to snag the last of my chow. You know when you get near the end and slow down a little? He'd take that as a sign that you were done, and start poking his fork around your plate. 'You want that? You want that?' Big goof."

"What changed things?"

"Time," Pep said. "The situation. We spent three months on the line together, almost every night in a foxhole. When you share a hole with somebody... it's like marrying them. Except worse. You're living in a hole in the dirt, freezing cold, never any food, can't move out of the hole or you'll get shelled, hours on end. Time drags on the line. You have to stay alert, because you never know, a German patrol might've sneaked past the outposts. All night, nothing to do but sit and stare.

"Think about it. How many times at home did you lose your cool because you had to wait in line... twenty minutes? Maybe an hour? This is all night, scared to death, can't read, can't play cards, can't smoke unless you lie in the bottom of the hole with Egleston's stinky feet stepping on you. You get shelled every now and again. Whitney, there's nothing like artillery. Awful. And there's nothing you can do, but sit and take it, you and your foxhole buddy."

"And you talk. You talk about anything, to keep the boredom

away. I know more about Egleston than his wife does."

"He was married?" Carl said.

"Sure, to his high school sweetheart," Pep said. "He played football, offensive line. Wife was a cheerleader. All-American, hunh?"

Whitney shrugged. "Yeah, I guess so. You, Pep? You married?"

"Me?" Pep said, turning to look at Whitney for the first time. "Do I look crazy to you? Hell, no!"

"But Egleston was," he continued, looking back out of the window. "He loved it, too. His wife's pregnant. Gonna drop it any day now. Anyway, I took a piece of shrapnel and went back to the rear for two weeks. Came back, and Kemp's his new foxhole buddy. And here we are."

Pep was quiet after that.

"I didn't know Jerry that well," Carl said. "A little bit. He was funny. I liked him. I guess we would've been foxhole buddies, too."

"Then you lucked out, him getting it now," Pep said.

Whitney wasn't sure how to take that, so he changed the subject. "How do you do it, Pep? All the… everything, people dying, our shooting… kids… like we had to do today. How do you do it for so long?"

"I think you answered your own question when you said 'had to'," Pep said. "What's the alternative? Lay down and die? We're stuck in a shitty situation, Whitney. Got dealt a bad hand. What the hell are you gonna do but ride it out as best you can?"

"I'll tell you," he went on, turning again to look at Whitney, "there are some benefits. Like showers. Man, you never had a shower till you've come in off the line for six weeks without a single bath, and eating government cheese for three weeks straight, and haven't shaved for ten days. They take you to the rear, and that first hot shower is like... *Man!* It's like Heaven is one long, hot shower after coming in off of the line. I bet you thought the chow sucked in the rear, right? But off of the line, you never had such a meal. It's like everything's drenched in butter, it's so good. And clean clothes, and a shave... the trivial parts of life become what make it worth living. Like this bread you just gave me."

Carl nodded. "Me and Sarge were just talking about how trivial stuff can get you killed."

"That's a fact," Pep said. "God! It's a fucked-up sort of existence, isn't it? But I guess life in general is, too; people back home die in car crashes or accidents at work or diseases, too, people who don't deserve it. Maybe it's all just amplified over here. Life Amplified. War is Life Amplified. You can quote me on that."

Pep flashed a grin, then, the first Whitney had seen since before he'd gone outside to help dig the foxhole. It seemed to make his face right again, like the last hour or so he'd been wearing a disguise of pain and loss and now it was gone and he was good old grinning Pep again. Whitney thought it might very well be the best smile he'd ever seen. In fact, it was a little contagious.

"I guess you're not a total dipshit, Whitney," Pep said. "Just try not to buy it in the next couple of days, okay? I've already got my spirits down, and it's bad for my complexion."

"Okay," Whitney said. "I'll try. Smoke?"

"Yeah, all right. Just keep your head below the window so he can't see the ash," Pep said, digging out his own cigarettes.

He bent down all the way to the level of the floor to light it, and Whitney mirrored his actions, cupping the flame carefully until his

Zippo snapped shut.

"Whew," Pep said, getting back up to sit cross-legged on the floor. "Talk about trivial things making it all worthwhile. These little babies," he held his cigarette up, "have kept me going for better than four and a half months now. I'm going to have to write the Lucky Strike company a nice letter…"

The window shattered inwards and Pep lurched forwards under the impact of a rifle slug whose report echoed off of the trees like thunder.

"Fuck!" Pep shouted, grabbing at his upper chest. "Get it out… get it…"

"It's already out, it went straight through!" Whitney said, pulling Pep tight against the wall, his hands already clamped onto the sticky wound. "The bullet's not in you!"

"Not the… bullet!" Pep said. "Cigarette…get it… out…"

Whitney realized he still had his cigarette in his mouth, and tossed it away just as another rifle shot blasted through the window. It snapped the air by his face and blew the leg off of a wooden chair sitting nearby.

"Are you hit? Are you hit?" Pep said through gritted teeth. "Whitney?"

"No, I'm okay," Whitney said, ducking lower and pressing against the wall. "How'd he shoot… we were below the window…"

"Son of a bitch climbed a tree… to get the angle," Pep forced out.

"Pep? Whitney?" Wieland's voice shouted to them from just outside the kitchen door. "Talk to me!"

"I'm okay, but Pep's hit," Whitney shouted back. He tried to ignore the sticky, wet feeling his hands had clamped over Pep's wound. "He got hit in the chest. The sniper's in a tree or something so he could shoot down through the window…"

Another rifle shot buzzed through the window and over Whitney's head, forcing him to cringe so low he was practically smothering Pep. A second shot tore up a piece of the floorboards where Whitney's tossed cigarette still glowed.

"I saw him! I saw him!" Wieland shouted, rushing into the kitchen with the submachinegun in his hand. "Drag Pep into the living room! Now, Whitney!"

Whitney grabbed Pep by his overcoat lapels and dragged him like a sack of grain across the floor. Wieland practically slammed into the wall by the window, blazing away at the night with the burp gun. The loud hammering of the weapon seemed to pound inside Whitney's head until he made it into the living room.

The gunfire stopped a second later. Wieland came into the living room just afterwards, barely visible in the dark. Whitney could hear him changing the submachinegun's magazine.

"How bad is he?"

"I don't… know, I can't see," Whitney said.

"Son of a bitch!" Pep shouted. He sounded almost like he was slightly drunk. "Shot me in the… couldn't shoot me in the leg, or the hand like Sayles, and let me just go home. No! Had to shoot me in the chest…"

"Hang on, my flashlight's… here," Wieland said, and a beam of light shone down onto Pep.

"Whoa!" Whitney shouted, covering the light immediately. "The sniper!"

"There's no line of sight from that window to this room," Wieland said, shaking the flashlight free of his grip. "It's okay for now."

The flashlight beam played over Pep's pained face and down to where Whitney pressed his bloodstained hands against the wound in Pep's upper chest.

"Jesus," Wieland said.

"Pretty... pretty bad, Sarge," Pep said. Blood flecked his lips as he spoke. "I'm gonna... I need a medic."

Wieland looked around the room desperately, hands clenching at his side uselessly. He scrambled for the radio, tried it, and threw it across the room with a curse when it failed to work.

"Damn it! Damn it!" He hurled his voice at the walls now, stomping around aimlessly with an occasional concerned look at Pep.

"Sarge?" Whitney asked.

"This isn't... I don't want to die like this," Pep said. His breath was starting to huff through his mouth, and more and more blood-tinged spittle spattered his overcoat as he struggled to keep his lungs filled.

"Hang on, Pep," Whitney said, then to Wieland, "What can we do for him?"

"Nothing," Wieland said, running his hands through his hair as if it were the only thing he could think of to do with them. "Here, just us? Nothing. Nothing! Even if we get the bleeding stopped, as it get colder..."

He shook his head.

Whitney looked from Pep's pale face to Wieland. The Sergeant stared at Pep, nodding to himself, as if resigned to a course of action.

"Whitney."

"Yeah, Sarge?"

"Get your weapon."

Whitney's brow furled. "Sarge?"

"Get your weapon," Wieland repeated, bending down and pressing a bandage into place over Pep's wound. "Hurry. We're moving out."

"Moving out?" Whitney said, looking around for and then recovering his rifle.

"Don't… don't you do… nothing stupid," Pep said, wheezing, grabbing at Wieland's arm. "Don't do nothin'… stupid, Sarge."

"Shut up, Pep," Wieland said. He tied the bandage into place as quickly as he could. "Whitney?"

"Yeah, Sarge?"

"Help me get him up."

"What are we going to do?"

Wieland looked toward the kitchen. "He was in a tree back there. Can't see the front of the house from there. Can't move too quickly, either. Not without exposing himself, right? And he's too good to take that chance. So we've got some time. We haul ass for the road, keep in the trees next to it… and just keep going until we reach our lines."

"That's… can you make it that far, carrying Pep?" Whitney asked.

Wieland hauled Pep to his feet with Whitney's help and draped him over one shoulder in a fireman's carry. "I'll have to. Pep's dead if I don't."

Whitney held the burp gun toward Wieland. "You want this?"

"Leave it," Wieland strained under Pep's weight. "I need to save as much weight as I can. You ready?"

"Sarge… don't…" Pep said over Wieland's shoulder.

Whitney licked his lips and checked to make sure his rifle was loaded. "Ready."

The word was barely out of his mouth before Wieland was chugging out of the front door. Whitney followed in his tracks, out into the dark, out into the cold.

*   *   *

Wieland hadn't even made it to the road when he realized he'd never make it. Not a half of a mile, not like this.

You have to, his mind forced through the burning sensation in his lungs caused by the freezing air huffing in and out of them. *You have to, or Pep's a dead man. You've lost too many already.*

His boots hit the road, and nearly slipped on a slick patch before he caught himself. Whitney was ten yards in front of him, running much more easily without a wounded man on his back, rifle pointed toward the trees to the right of them.

I can't make it, not this far, he thought, already wheezing, already exhausted, but he forced himself to push on.

Just a little further. Just a little further, and it'll all be over.

For tonight, at least, he laughed bitterly to himself. Until the next patrol or the next attack or the next damn fool errand his lieutenant sent him on.

The thought distracted him from his fatigue for the handful of seconds it took to reach the first of the trees lining the road. Wieland's boots thudded into thick snow as he left the road and dove into the cover of the trees. His heart pumped wildly, like a boxer's fists hitting a speed bag, and the cold air burned his lungs with every desperate breath.

One hundred yards, he thought. *I've made it about one hundred yards.*

The trees were still spread out, but another fifty yards and they became dense pines, a perfect blanket of cover. It would be a nightmare trying to carry Pep though it, but the sniper wouldn't be able to see them.

A stray twig caught him in the eye. He shouted and slowed to a walk, blinking tears, which seemed to crystallize on his face immediately.

"Whitney! Whitney, hang on, I can't…"

"Come on, Sarge!"

A few more blinks, and Wieland could make out Whitney against the white snow, waving him on to the pines. Close now, so close Whitney could jump into the lower pine boughs with a good head start.

"Go, Whitney!" he shouted. "Get into the pines, get cover!"

He forced himself to run again, forced his rebellious legs to pump him towards safety. A rest, he could take a little rest once they were inside the pines and out of immediate danger. Maybe even trade up, have Whitney carry Pep for a little, or carry him between them.

Come on, Sergeant! he shouted inwardly. *This is nothing as bad as Basic, now go!*

It was a lie, but it got him into the waiting arms of the pines before he had to slow to a shuffle, breath huffing out in great steamy streams. The first pine boughs tickled his face in welcome.

"Whitney…" he said, and then a rifle shot cracked the cold air and punched into his shoulder.

There was a dizzying moment, in which he wasn't sure which end was up, and then he was lying on his back in the snow, the pine boughs waving lazily up and down overhead. He blinked once, and winced with pain that became suddenly evident to him. The back of his left shoulder felt numb, like he'd been lying in the snow for hours and not seconds, but there was a central core of pain digging straight through the middle of the numb region that seemed somehow both distant and unbearable.

Far away, more rifle shots. Whitney was shooting back, he realized, as the pine boughs continued to wave over him like palm fronds waved over a Roman emperor by the hands of slaves.

You lied to me, he accused the pine boughs in his mind. *You said I'd be safe once I was inside.*

The pine boughs didn't reply, just waved slowly until finally coming to rest.

Wieland shook his head to clear it of the fuzzy haze that seemed to cloud his senses. Had he just reprimanded a pine branch? Shock, he was going into shock, that was it. The impact of the rifle bullet, the blood loss, the cold, all combined to send his body into a spiral of hazy perplexity, his mind coated like a stick swirled around the inside of a cotton candy machine.

Stay with it, Wieland, he told himself, but it was worse than being drunk, the world tipped on its side as he tried to move and he nearly passed out. When his mind caught up with his eyes, he saw Pep was right next to him, staring at him.

"Pep? Pep, I got hit too…" he slurred, oblivious now to the volley of rifle shots Whitney was firing into the dark nearby.

Pep's stare wasn't right. His eyes had a peculiar quality to them, an unfocused glaze that Wieland had seen too many times before. There was a hole in the center of his chest, a big one that Wieland knew was an exit wound.

Right through him and into me, his dizzy mind translated, and he started to huff out sobs, as if he wanted to cry but was so tired he couldn't remember how to.

"Peb? Pe…" he slurred, face slumping into the snow as the world swam too wildly for him to control. He never felt the snow on his skin; he knew nothing more.

*   *   *

When Wieland started to come around, the first sensation to penetrate his haze was the boring pain in his shoulder. The second was the smell of smoke.

Smoke? He wondered dizzily. *Am I on fire?*

Then, his eyes blinked open and saw he was back in the farmhouse, lying on his side in front of the fire.

"Ah, shit," he said.

"Sarge? Sarge, you okay?" Whitney asked. Wieland had to twist his head to see him, and the movement sent fresh daggers of pain lancing through his shoulder.

"Easy, Sarge. I think the bleeding's stopped, but don't move around too much or it might start up again."

"The hell are we doing back in the farmhouse?" Wieland asked, voice croaking. "Is there any water? Where's Pep?"

"Um…" Whitney looked around, as if not sure which question to answer first, then he dug out a canteen. "Here."

Wieland swallowed the water clumsily, since he was lying on his side. Some of it sloshed out of his mouth and onto the ground.

"Pep?"

Whitney shook his head, and Wieland could remember it all then, the vacant look on Pep's face, the second bullet hole in the center of his chest. Wieland suddenly felt an irrational concern for Pep, that he might be too cold out there in the snow, and then a slight shift of his body position sent pain lancing through his shoulder that brought him back to reality.

"The hell are we doing back here?"

"I had to," Whitney said. "I didn't know how bad you were hurt, and I couldn't check you out with that sniper around, so I just grabbed you and ran back in here."

"Should've kept going." Wieland said, wincing as he sat up. "With or without me, you should've kept going, Whitney. Now we're right back where we started."

"I couldn't. You would've gotten too cold and died from shock, like Sayles said," Whitney said. "I had to come back here and start the fire again to keep you warm."

Wieland looked at the fireplace in alarm. Idiot! He'd smelled the smoke, seen the yellow light dancing across Whitney's face, and it still hadn't dawned on his wakening mind that there was a fire lit.

"Put it out," he said.

"No, Sarge," Whitney shook his head. "You'll freeze."

"He'll shoot us both if he can see through the windows, you dumb shit," Wieland said, suddenly losing his patience. "Damn it, Whitney! This was a stupid fucking move coming back here! You should've gone for our lines. Now we're right back where we started, and no way we can make another break for it."

"Stupid," he muttered again, more to himself than Whitney. "Don't know what the hell I was thinking, damn fool move like that. Got Pep killed. Fucking waste of space, that's what I am. Got them all killed, every one."

"Come on, Sarge," Whitney said quietly. "We have to figure out what to do."

"What to do?" Wieland said with a laugh, fresh pain digging into his shoulder. "What to do? What would you like to do, Private Whitney? Hunh? Might as well ask you, I sure as hell can't seem to keep anybody alive."

Whitney looked down at the ground. "It's not your fault, Sarge."

"Oh, I think it is. It's my responsibility. These are... were... my men. I should've refused to stay out here, out on a limb. Should've disobeyed orders and returned to the rest of the company."

Whitney shook his head, and stayed silent for a little while. After a few long seconds of silence, he said, "I'm going out after him."

Wieland looked up sharply. "Like hell you are."

"I have to, Sarge. I..."

"Like hell! Like.... hell, Private! You listen to me! There will be no more damn fool heroics, do you hear me? We are going upstairs, taking the burp gun with us, and waiting for dawn and our relief. Got it? It's four a.m.... actually a little later... and it's going to be light in a few hours. That's all we've got to hold out. We hole up upstairs, and if we hear anything..."

"We can't," Whitney said.

"Whitney, I'm ordering you..."

"No, Sarge, this time you listen to me," Whitney said. "We can't do that. If we go upstairs and wait, that sniper will just hit our relief when it arrives. How many more will he kill, especially since he'll catch them out in the open, in daylight, no idea what's about to hit them?"

He shook his head again. "I can't let that happen. Maybe I was too scared or too stupid or too… new… to be of any use before, but it's my turn at the plate now. I understand that. I'm up at bat, somebody's got to do it, and it's got to be me. Who else? If I don't, then other guys just like me get killed. It's my turn."

"No, Whitney," Wieland said. "He'll kill you."

"Maybe," Whitney said, with a nervous laugh. "Maybe, and I'm scared to death about that. But it doesn't change anything."

"It changes everything. Don't try to be a hero. All the heroes I know are dead, and they died for nothing."

"That's not true," Whitney said. "When I first signed up, it was one-half Save The World and one-half Get Off The Farm. But now… now I don't care about any of that. I don't want to be a hero. I just want to get past tomorrow without any more of my people getting killed. Not you, not our relief… nobody. And if that means I have to go out there and face down that sniper, then that's what I have to do. I don't want to die, but if it means living knowing that other guys died because I didn't do what I had to do…

"Pep said that war is like life amplified. Well, if that's true, then what we do in war reflects who we are better than anything else. Maybe it's when times are at their worst, that we have to be at our best; even if it's not the smart thing or the safe thing to do. Maybe it's just that I don't want to sit in a hole and just take it like Pep said you have to do when artillery comes in."

"War is a reality check, Whitney. Guys who get out of their holes in the middle of an artillery barrage get dead," Wieland said. "They get dead, and just for stupidity. You stay in your hole and stay alive."

"What about the medics? They have to get out of their holes and go help the wounded, even when there's shells coming down, right?"

Wieland shrugged. "That's their job. It sucks, but they've got to do it."

"Well, this is my job," Whitney said, picking up his sniper rifle. "And I've got to do it."

"Whitney," Wieland pleaded once more, "don't do this. You're no match for him."

Whitney looked at Wieland's wound. "You should be able to get upstairs on your own. Get up there, hide out, wait for our relief. Just in case, you know?"

"Whitney…"

"We're doing the right thing here, Sarge. You can't see the difference we're making, because you've been in the middle of it for too long, and all you can see is the pain and the hurt it's caused you. But it's worth it. It's worth the hurt, to keep people free. That's what we're doing here, keeping people free, and that's bigger than you or me. You have to believe that. I do."

And before Wieland could say another word, he was out of the door and back into the night.

* * *

The cold got to Whitney much more quickly this time, since it already had a foothold inside his overcoat and on his bones from their desperate run for their lines. He didn't notice it at first; fear and terror kept the sensation of cold away from him like a phantasmal blanket, until he was kneeling amongst the cover of the trees and conscious thought blew his blanket to tatters.

Where the hell could he be? Whitney thought. His entire body quivered, but he couldn't tell if it was the biting cold or the gnawing fear.

Paranoia overwhelmed him at first. He couldn't seem to look around him fast enough; every time he turned to look for the sniper, it felt as if his enemy were creeping up behind him. When he turned back to chase away the tingling between his shoulder blades, the unseen enemy seemed to be behind him yet again, always behind him, no matter which way he turned, until he was practically spinning like a top to never have his back exposed.

Stop it, he told himself, and forced himself to stay still. Small movements. Slow movements. Patience. All those things he'd been taught. Fear wanted to take them away from him, but he would hold on for a little while longer.

He eased to his stomach in the snow. His body sank into it, and it gave him the illusion of lying in a safe cocoon. He would be hard to see, half-buried in the deep snow and lying next to a tree. Hard to see, even with the moonlight reflecting off of the snow to bathe the woods in a ghostly ambient light, and that gave him the luxury of slowing his thoughts down to stem his panic.

Maybe he should just lie where he was, wait for the sniper here. It felt right in this spot, it felt safe. It was almost like being in a warm bed on a cold morning; he didn't want to get up and move out of his safe place.

It wasn't safe, though, he reminded himself. It was just an illusion of safety. He had to start hunting, because he was already being hunted.

The panic came back, tried to break the dam with a heavy surge, but Whitney closed his eyes and fought through a ten-count to keep the floodwaters of panic back. The German couldn't be everywhere at once. He was just a man. He had to work with the same rules

Whitney did.

It's like a chess game, he told himself. Move and counter-move. Figure out where he'd be, where he last was, where he would want to go, and intercept him without his knowledge.

Except I never played chess, Whitney thought.

He shook his head to clear it of stray mental noise. Concentrate. He looked to where he'd last seen the sniper… or more accurately, heard him. Not far from the house, in the copse of trees Pep and the Sarge had used as their halfway point in their attack on the farmhouse earlier that day.

Should he go out there? Better to wait, be sure nobody was there first. He crawled through the snow through the trees, slowly, until his muscles burned and begged him to either stop or stand up and walk like his body had been designed to do.

He was at the edge of the trees now, with the farmhouse on his left. There was a clearing in front of him, all the way to the road, and the tree line sloped forward to his right on a diagonal toward the road.

The copse of trees was maybe eighty yards away. A dozen trees at most, black skeletons visible against the pale snow. He couldn't see anybody in there. Nothing moved.

Wait. The sniper…

I'm a sniper, he reminded himself.

Right. Better to call him "The German", put them on equal footing in his mind; both snipers, neither better than the other, separated only by nationality. After all, he was an excellent shot. He'd been hand-picked to become a sniper ever since they saw how good his marksmanship was.

Ought to be, he thought, raising the rifle so he could look at the trees through his telescopic lens. *I've shot more deer than I can count.*

Never a man, though. And he never did get around to playing chess, although he'd always meant to. All his life, Whitney could remember seeing two people bookending a chessboard, a pair of nearly identical statues staring at the pieces like scholars solving an arcane puzzle. It seemed like a secret club, with handshakes and meetings, and membership was gained by learning the mystery of how the pieces moved. He'd always wanted to join that club, always meant to; he just never seemed to get around to it.

There was nothing in the copse. Nobody. He'd been lying there... how long? Long enough to see that there was nobody there, that was for sure.

Now what? The German wasn't in the little copse of trees anymore. Where would he go?

Where would I go? he asked himself.

The trees swayed stiffly in the breeze and made a crackling sound, like kneecaps popping after standing up from squatting. Whitney suddenly felt stupid, lost, without direction. He had no idea where to go.

Some sniper I am, he thought, then his eyes narrowed at the stretch of snow between the copse and the farmhouse. *Are those tracks?*

It was hard to tell in the dark, but he swore there was a set of tracks leading away from the copse, crossing in front of the farmhouse, and disappearing on the far side.

Of course, Whitney thought. *He shot at us, I returned fire. He thought I spotted him, so when I carried the Sarge back, he took off back towards the farmhouse... away from us... and put it between us to screen his movements. He's in the woods on the other side of the farmhouse.*

Whitney's entire body relaxed, pressing deeper into the snow.

That little bit of distance made the all difference, and that little bit of information pointing him in the right direction was a Godsend. He didn't feel terrified anymore. He felt like somebody had finally told him what to do, and now he could get on with it.

First I have to make sure those are tracks, he thought, and the only way to do that was to get to the copse of trees.

He should be okay. By cutting to his right, the copse itself would screen him from the far woods, as would the house. There would be only a short stretch where he'd be out in the open, and if he ran, there was no way the German could react quickly enough. If the German was even looking in the right direction at the right time, which was extremely unlikely.

In theory.

So test it, Whitney thought, and pushed himself up out of the snow and dashed across the clearing.

This is stupid, go back, you're a dead man, he thought, chest heaving with freezer-burnt breaths and pounding with a jackhammer heartbeat. He kept waiting for the shot, sure it would come, and was almost disappointed when it didn't. It was like watching a pitcher wind up but never throw; there was a sense of the moment being incomplete.

Screw that, he thought, *I'm alive*. His eyes could easily pick out the tracks now, coming from the tree line near where he'd just been hiding, to where he was now, and leading off in front of the farmhouse.

He sank flat onto his belly again, hitching his elbows into place so he could prop up his rifle and peer through its scope. With it, Whitney could mark the trail of tracks easily, across the clearing in front of the house, looping around behind it and out of sight.

Whitney let the rifle rest forward. Something dark lay in the snow by his left arm. He picked it up and brushed the snow off. It was an M1 clip, eight bullets staggered in a row, dropped by a clumsy hand during the attack earlier that day.

Whitney smiled and tucked the clip into a pocket. When this was over, he'd say "Yeah, got that German sniper... oh, and by the way, Sarge, you dropped this," and hand him the clip. That'd be one for the books.

He looked at the tracks, smiled again at Wieland's defeatism. *Well, Sarge, you said we were just ghosts leaving tracks in the snow*, he thought. *And that's how I'll get him.*

Things started to line up in his mind, slowly at first, so that he couldn't tell what the shape was going to be until all the pieces were in place, then they came faster, until it all crashed down on him like an avalanche of realization. It started with the tracks.

The tracks going around the house.

Around to the back of the house.

The German hadn't shot at him while he'd carried Wieland back to the farmhouse. Why? They were sitting ducks.

The clip of bullets in his pocket. The German was out of bullets.

Out of bullets, and he had gone around the back of the house, where the back door was, leading to the veritable arsenal of weapons now stocked there from the fallen squad. Plenty of rifles, plenty of ammo...

...and only the Sarge, wounded and unsuspecting, in his way.

"Oh, my God," Whitney whispered, then sprang to his feet and sprinted for the front door for all he was worth.

The shot caught him before he'd made fifteen yards. The now-familiar crack whiplashed the frigid air, and before he knew what was happening, Whitney was lying on his back staring at the moon.

What the hell? he tried to say, but someone was sitting on his chest, he couldn't breathe, he could only gape like a fish for air that wasn't going into him no matter how hard he tried.

I'm shot, I'm shot! shouted out in his mind. He tried to pull himself to his feet, get inside before the German could take another shot, but he couldn't feel his legs or anything else below his waist.

Came around the house to double back on his tracks and shot me.

Whitney struggled for air like a drowning man, but it didn't come. He coughed to clear his chest, and blood spluttered out of his mouth.

This is it I'm dying I don't want to die please let me go home

A trickle of air made it into his lungs. Whitney was starting to fade out; the world became a tunnel through which he could see the moon and nothing else. His entire lower body seemed encased in ice; everything from his armpits down was frozen.

"Sa... Sarge..." he tried to shout to warn Wieland, but it only came out as a whisper, which turned into a death rattle, as Whitney's eyes glazed over staring at the full moon.

*   *   *

Wieland's eyes pinched shut when he heard the shot. A small part of him desperately hoped it had been Whitney who pulled the trigger, but the rest of him, the part callused by the war, knew otherwise. Whitney would've shouted out if he'd been the victor. "I got him!" or "It's okay, Sarge!" or both, but there was nothing, only the moaning of the wind, which became Whitney's death knell.

What the hell, Wieland thought, trying to shrug it all off. *It's my turn soon.*

He looked over at Egleston's body, covered with his overcoat in a corner of the room away from the fire. "Looks like it's just you and me now, Egleston."

You and me, Sarge.

Wieland's brow furled for a moment, then he smiled and sat up a little straighter so he could get a better look at Egleston's body. A trick of the mind made him hear Egleston's voice, so why not play along with it? A semi-hallucination or delirium to pass the time as he waited for Death.

That's a pretty morbid way to put it, Sarge.

"Pretty morbid situation, Paul," Wieland said, talking to the body. "Can I call you Paul? It seems like a first-name situation."

Sure thing, Sarge.

Wieland's smile faded. "Pep's dead. Whitney, too."

I know.

"You're dead too, Paul. I watched you die."

There was no response from the body.

"Are you a ghost or something?"

Now, it seemed to Wieland that Egleston was sitting up, propped against the wall just like he was, face pale and bloodless. *Naw, nothing like that. I'm you, is all. Your mind is playing tricks on you, and you're letting it. So I'm you, or what you remember of me.*

Wieland looked away from the image of Egleston for a moment. The sleeve of his jacket caught his eye; the left one, where he'd been shot, was darkly stained with blood. He touched a finger to it experimentally, as if it were a novel kind of ink or paint stain.

Is this me? he wondered. *Could this really be blood, my blood?*

Knock it off, Sarge, Egleston said. *Try to stay focused. That sniper's going to be coming for you. Soon.*

"Let him."

What's that supposed to mean?

"That means, I'm looking at this fire, and I'm thinking I'd like to die down and flicker out just like it. I'm tired, and I'm sick of burning. Maybe I'll just sit and wait for Death and let it all be over."

You don't mean that.

"Oh, yes I do," Wieland said. "I really do think that sniper is Death. I tried to tell Whitney, but he wouldn't listen. Death is always waiting. You can run, but he always waits you out or wears you down. He's worn me down. I'm tired. He's beaten me."

You don't want to die. You're scared of dying.

"Don't I know it. Scared of living, too. That's the problem. I just can't... I just don't want to hurt anymore. I can't take anymore."

You've got a job to do here. We all do. Don't be a cry-baby about it.

"Cry-baby? Cry-baby? You got a lot of nerve saying that, Paul. Nobody who's gone through what I've gone through is a cry-baby. Nobody should have to go through what I've gone through."

Should has nothing to do with it. It's just the way it is.

"So what's the point? Why bother? Why fight Death when it comes? I've got nothing to live for, except more pain, and loss, and misery. I survive this, and it's more of the same, every day, until I do get killed. Why suffer through all of that? Why not just end it now?"

There are people counting on you.

"That's Whitney talking," Wieland said, pointing a finger at Egleston. "Nobility gets used up awfully quick out here..."

He shook his head. "I keep thinking of Pep, joking and grinning and cracking me up."

A good memory.

"Yeah. And now he's dead. Gone. A waste. It's all a waste."

You're lying.

Wieland glanced at Egleston. "What?"

You're lying. You're hurt and tired and broken, and it's turned you sour inside. The truth is, you don't want to die. The truth is, you know why you're here. The truth is, you want to live.

"You don't know what you're talking about."

Remember that farmhouse in France? A lot like this one, really.

Wieland's brow furled. "How could you know about that? It was before you joined the company."

I'm not Paul Egleston, Sarge; I'm you, a reflection of you. You're talking to yourself. Get that straight. Do you remember it?

"I helped an old lady out of her cellar. She was really pale, even though it was August. She said…"

What?

Tears rimmed the bottom of Wieland's eyelids. "She said it was the first time she'd been outside for three years. She was too old to be able to get into the cellar quickly enough from outside, so she had to… her family got out sometimes, for a few minutes here and there, but the Germans killed one of their sons and… when we found them, they cried because they didn't have to hide in the cellar anymore."

So you know why you're here.

"But I'm all used up," Wieland said, shaking his head. "I've got no reason to keep fighting, no… wife at home, no kids, no big-time career waiting for me. I've done my time. I've done my good deeds, now I just want to rest."

That doesn't mean die. And as for wife and family and career, you can still do those things. And the other good things in life, too.

"Hot showers. And soft beds." Wieland's head tilted back and he looked at the ceiling wistfully. "Baseball games and the feel of a woman's skin under my fingers."

And ice cream and blue skies and the smell of springtime. There are good things in life too, Sarge.

"It's like I can't even remember them."

You're just tired and worn down. When you're in the middle of pain, it's all you can think about, until it seems like the whole world is nothing but pain. It's like being under water; everything is distorted. Once you get out, you can see much more clearly.

Wieland stared at the dying fire for a while. "I don't know, Paul. Once a horse is broken, it can't get back up again."

You're better than that. Don't give up now, Sarge. You end the pain by fighting, just like you get out of the water by swimming. Each stroke brings you closer to the surface, and each battle brings you closer to the end of the war. It's the fourth quarter, and you're behind on points. But you can still pull it out. If you want it.

Wieland looked down at his right hand, opened it, clenched it shut, marveled at what potential lay within. Build a house or shoot a man dead, hold an infant close or burn a village to the ground.

"I guess we'll see."

*   *   *

The smoke still curled up slowly from the top of the chimney, and that was what drew the German. The last American, the one with the bullet in his shoulder, might or might not still be alive, but it didn't matter. If the American were already dead, then he would rest a while by the fire, collect what supplies he could, and leave before their reinforcements could arrive. If he were alive…

So much the better, he decided.

His name was Dussel, and he'd served on the freezing Eastern front before being transferred here to fight the Americans and British. Dussel had a first name, but it had been years since anyone had called him anything but Dussel. Even his partner, the scout who lay dead in the cozy warm house he was creeping up on, always called him Dussel.

He preferred fighting the Russians. The Eastern Front was as cruel as it was cold, and that was how Dussel liked it. The Russians were hard, tough, merciless. War should be that way, no quarter asked or given. On the Eastern front, every battlefield he saw made him want to shoot Russians more than ever, until they were piled up in great heaps.

But Americans… Americans were harder to hate. Many of them had German ancestry. They had a reputation for treating prisoners well. They didn't raze villages like the Russians; though they might take over a house for the night and eat whatever food they could find, they wouldn't shoot or rape the inhabitants or burn the house to the ground. There was already talk in the Army: if it all goes to hell, be sure to surrender to the Americans if at all possible.

However, Dussel was a soldier, and he had learned to find a certain satisfaction in his job over the years. True, he didn't hate the Americans, but *five* of them. Five, in one night, and two earlier that morning. Seven within twenty-four hours, and not even on a battlefield. Seven, single-handed. Must be a record.

Dussel almost hoped the last American was still alive. He was still buzzing from the last kill. His second to last bullet. That was why he hadn't shot when the young one, the one with the fresh face and the sniper rifle, carried the other one back to the house. Instead, he'd waited, and as always, was rewarded.

Now, with his last bullet, he crept up to the front door, so slowly, wincing every time the snow shifted and crunched under his feet. He'd been out in the cold for so long that he could feel the warm air coming out from underneath the crack of the door as he eased up the steps. The door was cracked open; flickers of light danced along the edge of the doorjamb from the dying fire within.

Dussel crawled right up to the edge of the door. It took him almost five minutes to crawl up the steps. It took another ten for him to scan the living room for anything living. The shifting shadows made dancing phantoms out of the furniture, but there was nothing. Ten minutes without a sound convinced Dussel of that.

Patience. It always came down to patience. And so he waited another two minutes, enjoying the way the warm air sneaking out of the cracked door heated a small part of his face and a small part only. It was somehow better than being warm all over, like the cold freezing the rest of his body to the bone made him appreciate the warmth on his face that much more. That was when he saw it.

Blood.

A blood trail, leading upstairs. It was difficult to see, considering the uncertain lighting, but patience had paid off once again.

The last one was upstairs. And alive, or had been, at least long enough to drag himself up to the second floor.

Dussel smiled. This would do it. This would put the icing on the cake for him. He would tell the story of this night to his grandchildren. This might even earn him a Knight's Cross.

A full minute to open the door, and another ten to approach the stairwell. A floorboard creaked under his foot, and he froze.

There was a metallic clink from the second floor, and Dussel's blood turned to ice before his brain recognized the sound as a cigarette lighter opening. A second later, it shut again, and once Dussel forced his heart rate to smooth out and settle down, he noticed that he could smell cigarette smoke.

He doesn't know I'm here, he realized, and let the thought warm him like the fire flickering a few feet away. He took his time, eased out of his overcoat and let it lay by the fire, slowly, silently. He didn't want it to make him clumsy as he went up the steps. Another minute, to warm his hands once he removed his gloves, and then he moved for the stairs.

His progress was by inches. A floorboard creaked upstairs… the American was probably shifting his weight… and Dussel used the instant's worth of noise as cover to move a full two feet. Then, inches again, as he eased onto the stairs.

He could see the cigarette smoke curling across the top of the stairs. The American was sitting or lying on the hallway floor.

Dussel took a moment to remember the layout of the house from his visit there the day before, before he'd left to find help for his wounded partner and had returned to find slaughter. The stairs led to an L-shaped hallway, with the short end of the L at the top of the stairs, the angle to the left, and the long end of the hallway leading back toward him, toward the front door. Just at the top was a door on the right, and the hallway was separated from the stairwell by a thin wall.

The cigarette smoke came from the left. The American was sitting behind the thin wall separating the hallway from the stairwell, up and to Dussel's left. As he crept up the stairs, he confirmed this assumption; he could see where the smoke was coming from. When

Dussel was a third of the way up the stairs, he spotted the American… or at least his right hand, resting on the floor, the cigarette between his fingers.

He's been waiting so long, and got bored and maybe even fell asleep, Dussel thought. *Or passed out.*

It didn't matter. It was perfect. The perfect ending to his incredible feat of arms, the perfect shot to end the perfect battle.

He raised the rifle, lined it up with the wall. He could tell from the position of the American's hand where he was sitting, and took his time deciding where to put the bullet.

No rush. Enjoy it.

With my last bullet, he would tell his grandchildren, *with my last bullet I shot the last of them through the wall.*

He smiled and savored the moment a bit longer; not a moment of hate, as he didn't hate the Americans, but a moment of anticipation and satisfaction, of pride in doing his job better than anyone he knew. He thought he saw the American's finger twitch out of the corner of his eye.

It seemed like a signal. Quit screwing around and get it done. It would be light soon.

A final adjustment on his aim, and then his finger squeezed and the rifle thundered in the close confines of the stairwell. A hole appeared in the wall, and Dussel could hear the bullet impact with the American's body on the other side. There was a thump, which Dussel barely heard due to the ringing in his ears from the gunfire, but he saw the American slump onto his right side. His helmet fell off of his head and clattered across the floor.

Dussel nodded to himself and allowed himself a little grunt of satisfaction. He blew out a long breath. It was almost a let-down, to see it all over. The need for stealth now gone, he climbed the rest of the stairs at a regular, stomping pace.

He looked the body over. The cigarette still burned between his fingers. The bullet had hit him just left of center of his chest, directly in the heart.

And with my last bullet, I shot the last American through the wall and pierced his heart.

Dussel nodded to himself again. The cigarette caught his eye. American cigarettes! Like gold, and with as many as he'd killed, there would be cigarettes for a long time. He bent down to the body to search for the pack.

Big one, he thought, struggling to move the body so he could check the pockets.

The sharp, unmistakable sound of a pistol's hammer being clicked back behind him froze Dussel's bones as surely as the frigid air outside.

"His name was Paul Egleston," said a shaky voice behind him.

Dussel clenched his hands briefly around his empty rifle, and then dropped it to the ground. *Well, at least I will surrender to an American*, he thought. *And it will still make a good story.*

He turned slowly and rose to his feet, hands held up in surrender. The American sergeant was in the doorway to the bedroom in which Dussel's partner had laid dying, the one just to the right of the top of the stairs. His overcoat was off; the left sleeve of his jacket was dark with blood, and the pistol shook visibly in his hand. He looked like he might pass out at any minute.

"I dragged him up here with me, and lit a cigarette and put it in his hand when I heard you downstairs. Then I waited for you," the American said. His voice trembled as much as the barrel of his weapon. "Oldest trick in the book, and I knew you couldn't resist it."

At least it's surrendering to an American, Dussel thought again, wondering if their food would be as good as he'd heard. His lip curled into a little smile as he shrugged and said, "Kamerad."

A gunshot cut him off in mid-word, blowing through his right hand to smash into his ribcage. A second followed, exploding in his ears like close thunder, hitting him in the right shoulder like a kick from a mule. He stumbled backwards, tripped over the body of the dead American, and fell just as a third shot punched into his stomach.

He fell hard to the floor, dazed, instantly lost to wound shock. Dussel blinked a few times blankly, wondering what had happened, unable to feel anything. *But my story…* he thought distantly, words formed in a thick mist. Gunshots boomed again and again, four more times, but the sound was muffled like distant thunder heard from inside a house, and he barely felt it when two bullets shattered his spine.

It took him a little while to fade away, as the American sank to the floor and leaned against the wall for support. Dussel's world was rapidly becoming more cloudy to the point of indistinct chaos; random thoughts pushed through the mists for mere moments before fading away… *I'm dying But my story I had cigarettes I surrendered This isn't the way to die*

The American's voice was the last thing to push through the mist before he died.

"Just a man. Just a man, after all."

* * *

"Sergeant? Sergeant Wieland?"

Wieland blinked his eyes once and came back around. He hadn't been asleep; more in a daze than anything else. He'd never noticed when the sun came up, shining early dawn through the bedroom window and on the bodies of Egleston and the German sniper.

"Up here," he said weakly, but didn't move. He'd put a bandage between his shoulder and the hallway wall, leaning back to put pressure on the wound. He thought the bleeding had stopped, but no use tempting fate.

There was a flurry of commotion downstairs, booted feet thumping across the floor, bark-like orders being given. Boots started to thump their way up the stairs, preceded by his lieutenant's voice.

"Hey Sarge, is that you? You up there? Where is everybody?"

The lieutenant came into view by degrees, first helmet, then face, then shoulders, and then the rest of him, over the lip of the stairway. "Is that sniper still around? I brought a half-track... Jesus, man, are you hit?"

Wieland found he couldn't speak, that his vocal cords were tightened up like a noose on a condemned man's neck. His eyes felt dry and sandpapery, and the only way he could communicate was to nod his head yes.

"Jeez... Medic! Get a medic up here! You okay? How long have you been sitting in this hallway propped up like that?"

Wieland shook his head, tried to swallow down on the tight feeling in his throat, tried to squeeze his eyes shut over the tears. He pointed with his empty pistol at the German's body, tried to say *Since that*, but nothing came out but a dry rattle.

"Damn, is that Egleston? Is this the sniper? Where is

everybody, Sarge?" his lieutenant asked. He knelt down next to Wieland and leaned his carbine against the wall. "We found Kemp outside. Where are the others? Are they hunkered down outside? We can't find them, this snowfall is covering up their tracks…"

Wieland couldn't help it then; the sobs wracked his body head to foot, twisting tears out of him as from a damp towel. He brought his good hand up to his face, but it was still clutching his pistol, and he dropped it in his lap so he could cover his face with his hand.

"Take… take it easy, Sarge," his lieutenant said. "It's over now. Medic! M… get that damn medic up here, now!"

The words sounded alien and foreign to Wieland. *It's over now.* He knew better than that.

His lieutenant patted him on the shoulder. "It's okay, Sarge, just take it easy. Couple of weeks in the rear, then you can come back good as new to kick hell out of Jerry."

Wieland's sobs increased in intensity, mingling now with an occasional bitter laugh. *It's over now.*

"We need guys like you, Wieland. You're going to win this war for us."

Wieland didn't say anything, couldn't say anything, could only cry and sob and shake, full of pain, because for the first time in a long while, he hoped to be more than just another fading set of tracks in the snow.

Andrew C. Piazza

As Christopher Andrews

Alley Cats

A Little Vampire Story

The Death Of Armadillo Boy

Andrew C. Piazza

Alley Cats

After "Tracks in the Snow", you're probably ready to lighten things up a bit (if you're reading these in order, that is). Christopher Andrews is the pen name I use when I write comedy; I'd hate for someone to read something as fun and lighthearted as "Doctor Insanity vs. The Sparrow" and then end up picking up something like "The Sound Of Snow Falling", thinking they were getting another comedy. Um, no. This story is darkly humorous; my way of taking an HP Lovecraft story and turning it on its ear. By the way, for my readers who are cat-lovers... I like cats, too, very much so, and I assure you, no actual cats were harmed in the writing of this story.

Andrew C. Piazza

"God damn cats!"

Gary Fitters hopped up off of the couch with a grunt, zipping up his previously loosened trousers. Again! The cats were fighting in the alley *again!*

Bad enough that they had a terrible knack for knocking over the garbage cans in their frenzy, even worse that he had to hear that... screeching. Gary swore, the way the cats yelped when they fought, it sounded as if someone was twisting them out like a wet dishtowel.

It was his neighbor's fault. The way he left his garbage piled up in the alley, it was no wonder the cats kept swarming it like a plague of locusts. The mess was so awful, it was as if his neighbor *wanted* the cats out there, screaming and fighting and copulating all night. Damned irresponsible, that's what it was.

"Mr. High-and-Mighty," Gary muttered to himself, storming over to the coat closet and snatching up the broom secured there. He wasn't going to take this anymore, even if his neighbor did happen to be the mayor of Polk, the small town Gary had been doomed to live in for the past six months.

"Fat pompous jerk," Gary said, moving to the kitchen and

searching through the drawers with overenthusiastic pushes and pulls that turned into slams. "I didn't vote for your garbage-dumping ass."

"Gary!" his wife, Angela, called down from the upstairs bedroom. "What are you doing! Come to bed!"

"I'm.... doin' somethin'!" Gary yelled back. It was as good an answer as any; he wasn't entirely sure *what* he was doing.

"Ha!" he said with a triumphant cry, once he'd found the fat black and green flashlight he'd known was left tucked away in one of the kitchen drawers. "Now you pussycats are gonna get somethin'!"

Gary strode to the side kitchen door, broom clenched tightly in one fist like a Neanderthal's club, and practically leapt into the alley, as if plotting to take the mewling and pewling cats by surprise. He clicked the flashlight on, swinging its wide beam back and forth across the dark alley.

There was garbage piled everywhere; overflowing out of the cans lined up along the Mayor's residence, lying on the ground, torn up and flung about like a garbage tornado had just rolled through. It had always been this way, ever since that lousy day they'd first moved in. Even then, the damn cats had come, every night. Gary had tried cleaning up the alley himself, and the garbage was back the very next day, along with the cats, as if his neighbor had an endless supply of garbage secured somewhere and an insatiable desire to share it with the feline community.

Gary had even tried pleading directly with his neighbor... his August Presence, the Mayor of Polk... all to no avail. The garbage kept piling up, the cats kept coming in, and Gary kept going slowly insane.

For six months, he'd put up with the cats' screeching and yowling and hissing. Well, no longer. A man can only take so much before he snaps.

"Here, kitty, kitty," Gary said with a mirthless grin, stepping carefully around the garbage. "Here, kitty kitty kitty..."

Movement flashed briefly through his flashlight beam, and Gary set the light directly on it, hoping to dazzle the cat until he could get close enough to shoo it out of the alley with the broom. The more he thought about all those sleepless nights caused by the yowling and screeching from the cats, though, the more 'shoo it out of the alley' seemed like too mild of a response. What he really wanted to do was smack the cat like a hockey player firing a slap-shot on the goalie. Heck, if he was lucky, and swept up underneath it just right with the broom, he might get some serious air time for the trespassing pussycat as he launched it out of the alley. That would show 'em.

"Hel-lo, kitty-witty!" he cooed, stalking closer to the cat. It was a great fat tom, yellow with slightly darker yellow stripes running along it, staring at Gary with baleful eyes reflecting the flashlight beam. It was a good ten feet away, but didn't appear ready just yet to abandon its newly-found feast bursting out of a torn garbage bag.

"Aww, is kitty-witty hungwy?" Gary said, stepping carefully towards his nemesis, broom held low and behind him. He wanted to sprint forward and launch the damnable cat all the way to the next town, but he had to be careful, take his time, keep his cool, so he could get close...

Five feet now, and his grip began to get sweaty in anticipation. *I'm going to get him!* Gary nearly said aloud with a giggle. *I can't believe it, I'm finally going to get some payback on these mewling little monsters!*

"I've got something for you, kitty-witty," he said, his tone starting to turn vicious. "I've got..."

Another flash of movement, and the cat shrieked and seemed to leap into midair... and hover there. It happened so fast, all Gary could do was shout "Gaa!", leap back reflexively, trip over one of the countless garbage cans, and land on his ass in a pile of squishy rubbish.

Rather than cursing and climbing out of the garbage, Gary found himself transfixed, paralyzed, rendered incapable of anything but slack-jawed staring. His flashlight beam was fixed on the cat, which wasn't hovering in mid-air; it was being held there.

Held by a tentacle, to be exact.

Not your average, ordinary tentacle, either; rather, a foot-thick, green, and God Only Knew how long tentacle, which had wrapped itself once around the tom and was now waving it about like a strand of wheat waving in the wind. The tip, which was bluntly pointed, flicked along the struggling cat's length, as if tasting and savoring it.

The cat let out a yowl of terror, hideously reminiscent of all the other feline screeches Gary had endured over the past six months, and it raked its back claws across the tentacle, drawing blood, or some sort of yellowish ichor Gary took for blood. The tentacle twitched once in response, and then flexed with tremendous strength, squeezing the life out of the tom. Gary could hear bones crunch and grate together and the cat flailed about wildly, its last screech cut off piteously.

"Wha... da...fa..." Gary stammered at last, unable to stop staring at the sight of the squished pussycat.

Then, the tentacle was gone, retracting between a pair of garbage cans set against the Mayor's wall with the cat corpse in tow.

Gary sat dazed for quite some time in his personal little garbage heap, until the soppy wetness soaking through the seat of his pants jarred him out of his hypnosis. He leapt to his feet, cursing and remembering the anger which had brought him out here in the first place.

His anger was quickly replaced with irresistible curiosity. *What on Earth was that thing?*

Who cares? his wiser side replied. *Get the hell out of here!*

"Yeah," he agreed with himself aloud. "Gettin' outta here. This freaky crap is for the cops or somethin'."

Still, despite his trepidation, Gary found himself taking uncertain, tiny baby steps towards the spot between the garbage cans where the tentacle had disappeared. His mind was mostly numb; no further warnings screamed in his cerebral cortex to stay away, stay away, get back inside and get some help. Instead, he found himself staring down at the twin garbage cans hiding the tentacle's exit, like cheap, small-town versions of the statues guarding the tombs of Egyptian pharaohs.

Gary scratched his belly idly and adjusted his grip on the broom handle. What could that tentacle belong to? Did the Mayor know about it? Wouldn't you need a license for that sort of thing?

He extended a foot towards the trash can on the left, leaning and grunting a bit to slide it to the side. It only occurred to him that probably wasn't a good idea after he had done it; that tentacle could come back, grab him by the leg, and haul him foot-first into...

...what looked to be a window into the Mayor's basement, set into the wall right at ground level. It was two feet by two feet in dimension, but wasn't covered in glass; rather, there was a little wooden door, hinged at the top, covering the alley window. It looked very much like one of the doggie doors conscientious pet owners put on their front doors to allow Fido unfettered access to do their poopy business on their neighbors' lawns.

Do not open that door, Gary, his mind ordered. *Repeat… do not open that door. It's not too late; you can still walk away, still go back to your couch and drink a whole big giant pile of beer and find some way to explain or ignore what you saw in the alley just now. But if you open that door…*

"Right, right," he said, nodding to himself, but found his hand reaching for the door anyway, fingers sliding along the unhinged bottom in an attempt to find a decent grip there.

What if it comes back out right now, right as you're staring in its door? he wondered, finally deciding he would simply have to push the door inwards to get it open. *What then? It could just grab your throat and…*

Then, the door swung open, and Gary's flashlight beam snuck into the half-open basement window. It searched left, searched right, and finally settled on a thick green tentacle, which snaked across the dirty cement floor like a vine from some colossal, carnivorous plant. Gary followed its length with the flashlight, and one tentacle intersected with another, and another, and another, until the twisted multitude of limbs resembled a complex root system.

The "roots" began to converge, and for a fraction of an instant, Gary hesitated, as if unsure he wanted to go on, as if perhaps he regretted coming this far. However, the flashlight beam moved on, seemingly of its own accord, and Gary's eyes finally came to fall on the beast which sprouted the tentacles splayed about on the floor.

It was green, and roughly the size and shape of one of the garbage cans lined along the alley. Around the 'rim' of this organic trash can was a ring of thin, foot-long tentacles, which were currently transferring the squished pussycat from the large tentacle Gary had just seen into the creature's mouth. The mouth itself was two feet across and beaked, located in the center of the tiny tentacle ring.

As Gary watched, the little tentacles held the dead cat directly above the beak, and then SNAP! The cat disappeared into the beaked mouth, and the creature's body began to shimmy about as it swallowed the pussycat down into whatever passed for its belly.

"God... damn," Gary said in a whisper, still staring in shock, as a satisfied belch erupted from the creature.

Okay, Gary! his mind shouted, as the creature's single eye slowly swiveled up towards him and then narrowed in response to Gary's flashlight beam. *Time to go! You've seen quite enough!*

Still, he kept staring, even as the large tangle of tentacles began to move, undulating about like sea kelp in a strong current.

Go, Gary, go now! he told himself, fruitlessly willing his paralyzed legs to move.

One of the tentacles raised up slowly, waving back and forth like a hypnotized cobra. It seemed to regard him for a moment, the blunted tip pointed at him like a finger, and then it froze completely still.

Okay, I think I'm going now, Gary decided, staring at the tentacle a mere three feet from his face.

The tentacle flew, moving with blinding speed, and Gary leapt back again reflexively. He was almost surprised he managed to fall on his ass; he'd felt the tentacle tug on his arm, and he could've sworn he was about to be yanked face-first into that basement window.

However, once he'd plopped ass-first into a newer, sloppier pile of filth, he realized the creature hadn't grabbed his arm at all, but merely yanked the flashlight out of his hand. It waved the light around once, sending the beam swinging about blindly, and then smashed the annoyance into the ground, splintering it.

Gary assumed the tentacle went back into the basement, but he couldn't be sure, so he hauled his soggy butt out of the garbage and sprinted top speed back into his kitchen without so much as a glance backwards. Once he was inside, he locked the door and set his back against it, then decided that wasn't such a good idea after all. What if one of those tentacles was long enough to punch through one of his kitchen windows? He'd be much safer if he got upstairs.

"Gotta... call a... vet, maybe, or a zoo..." he mumbled to himself as he trudged up the stairs, until a green-skinned monster leapt in front of him, drawing a shrill shriek from his lips.

"Honey, what is wrong with you?" his wife demanded, moving her lips as little as possible to avoid cracking the green mud-mask facial she'd slathered on a moment ago. "You scared the... what... you stink! What is that smell?"

"I... was a... there's a... garbage, and the cats, and I think the Mayor knows it's there..." he tried to answer.

"What on Earth are you talking about? Gary Fitters, answer me!"

"There's an octopus in the Mayor's basement!" Gary finally shouted, quite unhinged by the evening's ordeal. "A big, giant octopus, and it eats cats!"

There was dead silence from his glop-smeared wife. She didn't need to say a word. After all the wretched years of their marriage, Gary could read the sneer on her face like the morning newspaper.

"You've flipped your lid," she said at last, but he barely heard her, simply pushed past her and walked the short distance down the hallway to their bedroom. He was exhausted, spent, and couldn't resist plopping down on the bed, garbage-soaked pants and all.

"You get off my bed in those disgusting clothes..." Angela began to splutter.

"Octopus!" Gary said. "There's an *octopus*... in the Mayor's basement... and..."

"It eats cats, yes, I heard you," his wife said. "This is just typical. I mean, what was I thinking, marrying a used car salesman? What happened to the man I married right out of high school? You get drunk, you don't come to bed and take care of me *like a man should*, and then you go completely off your rocker after dragging me out to this Godforsaken butthole of a town..."

"Oh, screw this!" Gary said, leaping up with a snarl. "I've had enough! You can't... keep a thing like that in your basement! It's unsanitary!"

He stomped over to his closet, and rummaged around for a moment. His wife stood a good distance away from him, a trickle of apprehension in her eyes betraying the contemptuous sneer cracking her mud mask. It didn't help when he pulled an ancient, cut-down double-barreled shotgun out of the closet with a satisfied grunt.

"What are you..." she began.

"What happened to me?" he asked, still rummaging, until he found his stash of twelve gauge shells. "What happened to *you*? What happened to the woman who promised to love me 'for richer, for poorer'? What happened to the woman who used to be supportive? She got replaced by a shrieking monster in a green mask who feels the burning need to point out my faults on a daily basis. I don't need that... garbage, Angela. I'm not living like this for one more second."

He shoved two shells into their respective barrels, and closed the gun with a manly *Snick!* After dropping the remaining shells into his pocket, he spotted and scooped up his trusty-dusty baseball bat out of the back of his closet and nodded to himself, believing he was well-armed and ready for his imminent duel.

He shot a look at his wife, who cowered in the corner, groping blindly for the phone with one hand. "I'm... calling the police. I am," she said.

"You go ahead and do that," Gary said, teeth glittering in a maniacal Jack Nicholson grin. "I've got to go kill me a giant land octopus."

With that, he left his wife to her 911 call and headed for the alley. It would be dark; he'd lost his flashlight, but he could turn on all the lights on the first floor, and the spilloff from the windows would hopefully be enough to get the job done.

Once this preparation was accomplished, he stood by the side door, one hand on the knob, the other cradling both of his weapons clumsily. He took a few deep breaths, trying to firm up his resolve.

Are you nuts? his mind managed to sneak in. *You're not really going to do this, are you?*

Damn straight I am, he found himself answering. *I'm sick of being called a loser. I'm sick of those cats getting scrunched every night. I'm sick of the garbage in the alley. I'm sick of the garbage in my life. It's time to take out the trash.*

Testosterone levels now at maximum, he yanked open the door and leapt into the alley, shotgun in one hand, bat in the other, like a modern-day Polk County version of a two-sword-slinging samurai. His eyes scanned the alley, slowly acclimating to the darkness, until he could pick out where the trash cans stood.

Gary stepped around the rubbish with care, using his feet as a sort of probe to determine where the piles of trash lay in wait. It wouldn't do for him to fall ass-first into the garbage again, now that he was set out to fight monsters and do all kinds of heroic stuff.

There was a sound reminiscent of a cabinet door slamming, instantly identified in Gary's hyped-up mind as the Tentacle Doggy Door slamming open. The fight was on.

He reflexively pointed the sawed-off shotgun in the direction of the noise and fired, the recoil nearly tearing the gun from his grip. Instantly, he went deaf from the thunderous explosion resonating throughout the alley, and a large purplish spot sat in the center of his night vision from the flare of the blast.

Idiot! he cursed himself, trying to get a better grip on the shotgun with his now-numb hand. *You don't even know if you hit it!*

He swung the bat around wildly, blindly, hoping to keep any unseen tentacles at bay. The purplish spot stayed stubbornly in place, and the ringing in his ears certainly didn't seem to be going anyplace fast. Gary began to consider a strategic retreat to his kitchen, when something large moved in the far-left reaches of his peripheral vision.

He swung savagely at it with the bat, connecting with something yielding, largely by chance. Gary shouted in triumph, swinging again and again in the general vicinity of his enemy, but was unable to follow up his first blow. Finally, he found himself backed up against the wall of his own house, below his living room window. A large square of light shone into the alley from it, banishing the purple spot from his vision at last.

A hint of movement to his left again; but Gary controlled the impulse to blaze away at it with the one shell still left in his gun. Instead, he took a firmer grip on the bat, intending to daze the tentacle, if that was possible, and then blow it apart once it was down.

Something large loomed towards him, and Gary swung at it, connecting with a metallic clang. He took a step back, confused, swinging out at a second tentacle, again producing a tinny clang. The twin tentacles strayed just far enough into the light to reveal that each gripped a trash can lid like a medieval warrior's shield. The tentacles themselves were difficult to see, but the dull metallic glint off of the two lids was easy to pick out, and the way they seemed to float about, they looked like giant cymbals preparing to be banged together by an invisible poltergeist.

The trash can lid on the left swung in, and Gary smacked it, but that foolishly left him open, and the lid on the right swooped in and cracked him across the side of the head. Gary spluttered and swore, feeling a slow trickle of blood oozing down the side of his scalp.

"Oh, so that's how it's gonna be, hunh?" he said with a murderous grin, raising the shotgun. "How about... dah!"

He grunted as both lids flew in past his guard and smacked on either side of his head, boxing his ears with a gonging sound. The shotgun fired off, almost by itself, sending its charge uselessly into a garbage can and rendering Gary freshly deaf and blind. The hapless used car salesman swung his baseball bat feebly, hitting nothing but the air, until the lids battered his arm, knocking the bat from his fingers.

He staggered dizzily for a moment, the ringing from the shotgun blast combining with the ringing from the double lid-smacking to create a veritable symphony in his ears. *This thing... is kicking my ass!* he thought crazily, as he stumbled for the mouth of the alley.

He was actually rather surprised he made it. Perhaps that second shotgun blast had clipped one of the tentacles after all; whatever the reason, Gary finally came to his senses in his front lawn, swaying unsteadily on his feet. He still had his empty shotgun, but he'd left the bat lying back in the alleyway.

Of the tentacles, there was no sign. The dark mouth of the alley seemed to gape wide, however, practically daring him to come back in, try his luck again, and Gary would have, if it weren't for the flashing blue lights that suddenly seemed to surround him.

At first, he thought he was hallucinating, but then a megaphone-enhanced voice cut through the ringing in his ears. "Mr. Fitters! This is the Polk Township Police Department! Put down your weapon and put your haEEEEE...."

"Damn it!" an un-amplified voice swore, once the sudden flare of feedback from the megaphone was cut off. From the sound of it, the voice was only a dozen or so feet away anyway.

He couldn't be sure, though, because three spotlights and several flashlights were shining directly in his face. They seemed to move and bob about, will-o-wisp's orbiting the swirling blue lights of four police cruisers, as the entire Polk Township police force deployed onto the lawn to surround Gary Fitters, used car salesman and would-be monster killer.

"Put the gun down, Mr. Fitters!" a voice hidden behind one of the spotlights ordered.

"It's empty!" Gary shouted. "But there's a... a thing in the alley, it's..."

"There isn't anything in there, Mr. Fitters!" the voice said. "Just put the gun down and we can..."

"Listen to him, Gary!" his wife screeched from between

several lights, reminding Gary of the feedback from the cop's malfunctioning megaphone. "Listen!"

"But that thing in the alley, it's like a giant octopus..." Gary said, realizing how ridiculous he must sound. Still, he had to convince them. Had to! With all of this firepower, they could surely kill whatever was eating cats in the mayor's basement!

His eyes began to adjust, and he was able to pick out a half-dozen or so uniformed cops surrounding him. Standing behind a police car, next to his wife, was the man with the megaphone, who Gary took to be the police chief. He was fat, with a bushy moustache, and inexplicably still talking into the inactive megaphone.

"I'm not going to tell you again!" the police chief demanded into the mute megaphone. "For your own good, put the gun down and step away from the alley!"

"But..." Gary said, struggling to find the right words to explain the existence of a giant cat-eating octopus in the middle of town.

"Mr. Fitters! Listen to me carefully!" the police chief said loudly, finally giving up on the inoperative megaphone. "There has been a gas leak! If you were in the alley, you have inhaled toxic fumes which may have caused hallucinations!"

Gas leak? Gary thought, as the policemen finally got between him and the alley. *Hallucinations?*

"I repeat! There is no monster! You have taken in toxic fumes and are hallucinating!"

Gary thought that over a bit. His head *did* hurt, but whether it was from fumes or a bonk on the noggin from a pair of trash can lids, he couldn't tell. He'd hate to think he'd been in the alley alone just now, swinging his bat at the air and shooting his shotgun at a fantasy, but it *was* a more logical alternative, wasn't it? He'd heard of people taking LSD and seeing freaky stuff like potatoes playing the banjo and walls melting; wasn't it possible, even likely, he was experiencing something like that, courtesy of some sort of gas leak?

"Honey, do what he says! You're hallucinating!"

"She's right, Mr. Fitters! There is no..."

"Ahh!" the policeman nearest the mouth of the alley shrieked at the top of his lungs. Everyone... Gary, Angela, and all of the police... spun to see the hapless patrolman caught in the grip of a great green tentacle, waving slowly back and forth a good four feet off of the ground.

"Oh, darn it all," the police chief said with a sigh, his shoulders slumping.

"Help me!" the patrolman cried, flailing his limbs about wildly, reminding Gary eerily of the cat squished by the tentacle just a bit earlier. "For Christ's sake, hel...akkk....akkk..."

The tentacle flexed around the cop's waist, splintering bones with audible pops and crackles. It began to shake him vigorously, tossing him about like a rag doll, and then another tentacle came out of the alley gripping Gary's abandoned baseball bat.

"Oh, my..." Angela said with a gasp, before dropping to her knees and vomiting all over the lawn.

"You see!" Gary said, as the tentacle began to smack the mostly crushed policeman on the head with Gary's bat. "You see!"

"It must be pissed," the deputy police chief said to his boss, shuddering whenever the baseball bat connected, producing the icky sound of a sledgehammer smashing an overripe pumpkin. "It never goes for people unless it's pissed."

"Or really hungry," the chief agreed, sighing again and

scratching his moustache idly while the body of the mangled patrolman was dragged into the shadows by the tentacle.

"You see!" Gary screamed again, barely registering it when one of the cops relieved him of his shotgun. "It *is* real! It *is!* You all saw... come on, Angela, get up, you've got to see this!"

"Well gosh," the chief said, trading a knowing look with his second-in-command, "I really wish you folks wouldn't have seen that."

"Wha... hey!" Gary said, when two of the burlier cops grabbed him forcefully by either arm. Two more picked up his wife, after lightly shaking her, as if trying to determine whether there was any vomit left in her.

"What are you..."

"*Really* wish you folks wouldn't have seen that," the police chief said again with a sigh.

"What are you... you mean you knew about it, all along?" Gary said.

"Well, yeah, duh!" the chief said, trading a look and a smirk with his second in command.

"But... how? You let it live in the Mayor's house?"

"Oh, it's not just living in the Mayor's house. It *is* the Mayor."

"What?" Gary said, shaking his head. "That's not possible. I've seen the Mayor. He's human. Ugly, but human."

"Oh, *that* guy," the chief said. "He's just some schmuck we use for public appearances. The Kreigel is the real Mayor of this town."

"The.... Kreigel?" Gary asked.

"That's right, Kreigel," the chief said, then, upon catching Gary's stare, added defensively, "Well, what would you call it, smart guy?"

"What... why..."

"We worship it," the chief said. "Yep, we've got a whole big pagan god-worshipping cult thing going on in this town. We were sort of feeling you out over the last couple of months, seeing if you might want to join up, but you folks aren't really the pagan religion type, are you?"

"No," Angela somehow managed to answer. "We're Lutheran."

"See, there you go," the chief said. "Yep, real shame you saw it, though. Guess we're going to have to feed you to it now."

"We won't tell!" Gary said quickly. "Really, we..."

"Yeah, right!" the chief said, trading another look with his second in command. "That's what they all say! Then you get something like that National Enquirer article back in '88... ugh! No, it's better this..."

"Wait a minute!" Gary said. "Why did you even let us move in if you knew your big secret was next door?"

"What can I say?" the chief said. "Nobody else would buy that property, the owners kept bitching at EVERY cult meeting about how nobody would buy it, and when you folks actually offered to pick it up, we got so excited... I guess we just didn't think ahead."

"Ahh!" Gary's wife screamed, as one of the patrolmen cracked her in the kneecap with his nightstick, producing the sound of a snapping branch.

"Jesus! What is he doing?" Gary said.

The chief rolled his eyes and shook his head. These outsiders sure were slow on the uptake. "I told you, we have to feed you to the Kreigel. He's breaking your kneecaps so you can't run away once we throw you in the alley. Gosh, keep up, man!"

"Help!" Gary's wife screamed, once she found her voice. "For God's sake, somebody help us!"

"Lady, please!" the deputy chief said, as one of the patrolmen stuck a hand over her mouth to quiet her. "You're being rude! It's late and people are trying to sleep! Besides, folks aren't likely to look kindly on your calling on that *other* God."

"You mean they all..." she said, as the patrolmen began to drag her towards the alley.

"Careful, boys, not too close, he's pissed," the chief warned, indicating to his henchmen that Gary's knees needed whacking.

Gary's mind began to whirl desperately, half-formed plans of how to get out of this insane predicament getting pushed about and stepped on by terrified speculations on what it was going to be like to get crushed to death by the giant tentacle. He need to think of something, anything…

"Wait! I have an idea!" he said, trying unsuccessfully to shrink away from the club-wielding policeman approaching him.

"Look, Mr. Fitters..."

"No, wait, really!" Gary insisted. "We could feed it!"

"Gary…." his wife said nervously, as the patrolmen picked her up by the arms and legs to toss her into the alley.

"We *are* feeding it, dummy," the chief said.

"No, I mean we could feed it, my wife and I, on a regular basis!"

The chief held up a hand to halt Angela's imminent sacrifice. "What do you mean?"

"I mean," Gary said, pulling himself slightly closer to the chief and speaking conspiratorially, "look at the system you have here. Big bunch of reeking garbage, to lure an uncertain supply of tomcats to feed the Great Kreigel?"

"*Almighty* Kreigel," the chief corrected.

"*Almighty* Kreigel," Gary said, mind racing to think of the right combination of words to save his life. "But, let us live, like, um... caretakers! Caretakers, and we'll feed it regularly."

"Gary!" Angela said, squirming in the policemen's grasp. "What are you doing?"

Gary bit his lip and ignored her. "And not just cats," he continued quickly, sliding effortlessly into his Salesman tone of voice, "No, sir... eating the same thing every day is no good for a human being, much less a pagan god. We'll feed it a variety; cats, rabbits, squirrels..."

"Possums?" the chief asked.

"Sure!" Gary said. "You name it!"

The chief sucked on his teeth in thought, nodding to himself. Gary had seen this look a thousand times; it was the look that meant his customer was sliding in toward buying the deal. The chief's eyes suddenly narrowed, however, and he eyed Gary sternly.

"No skunks, though. Stink up the place worse than it is now."

"Absolutely not. C'mon, what do you say?"

"Gary, what... you're not trying to help them, are you?" his wife said.

Not now, woman!, he groaned inwardly. *I'm trying to save our asses here!*

"Your wife doesn't seem too thrilled about this," the chief said.

"Don't worry about her," Gary said, even more conspiratorially, flashing a grin and a wink as he added, "If she doesn't come around, we'll feed her to the *Almighty* Kreigel on one of your special holidays."

The chief frowned in thought for a second or two, then his face brightened and he clapped Gary on the back with a smile. "You've got a deal, Mr. Fitters! We'll give it a try for a couple of weeks! But, if it doesn't work out..."

"Into the alley I go," Gary said, shrugging with an Aw-Shucks grin.

"Boys!" the chief called out. "Get Mrs. Fitters over to a squad car and get her knee looked at. We've got ourselves some caretakers for the Kreigel!"

*   *   *

"Hon?"

"Yeah, babe," Gary answered, staring out of the kitchen window into the alley. The garbage was gone, cleaned out weeks ago, and there was a large stretch of chicken-wire covering either end of the alley. There was no way in or out, except for their kitchen door, which Gary now opened slightly, reaching into his Pet Travel Case to draw out a big gray and black striped cat. It squirmed a bit in his arms, and for a second, Gary thought he might lose it, but he managed to toss it into the alley and shut the door on it.

"Rabbits?" his wife asked, limping into the kitchen with the aid of a cane to stand by his side. "Oh, Gary! A cat *again?*"

"Couldn't find any rabbits," Gary said with a shrug, "so I stopped by the SPCA and picked this guy up. Big 'un, isn't he?"

"I guess," his wife said, with a bemused smile at her husband's over-enthusiasm. "I think you just like to hear them yowl."

"Heh-heh," Gary said, still watching intently as the pussycat meandered carefully throughout the alley, sniffing cautiously hither and yon.

Look around all you like, he thought with a devilish grin. *The only lunch in that alley is you.*

"They're saying they may make me a Grand Kagoona at the cult," Gary mentioned off-handedly.

"Honey!" his wife said, beaming. "I'm so proud!"

She meant it, too. The last several weeks had seen a dramatic shift in their marital relationship. He was a changed man; position and responsibility had taken quite a shine on him. As he came to have respect for himself as Kreigel Caretaker… and with luck, perhaps soon Grand Kagoona… his wife came to have respect for him as well.

"There!" he cried happily, as the green tentacle shot out of the basement window and caught the hapless cat in its grip.

His wife sighed again, a sigh of love and contentment, and he gazed into her eyes to recognize a level of affection and adoration he never would've thought possible a few weeks ago. Husband and wife looked back into the alleyway, and as they watched the Kreigel's tentacle crush the life out of the squirming pussycat, their arms slipped around each others' waists with the tenderness of brand-new lovers.

"Sweetheart," Gary said, smiling warmly, as the screeching of the cat was replaced by the musical crunching and crackling of snapping feline vertebrae, "I think we can make a good life here."

Andrew C. Piazza

A Little Vampire Story

I used to work in a Caribou coffee shop in Atlanta, and one night, a regular customer mentioned that I should write a little vampire story. I responded that there were about a billion vampire stories out there, that I didn't really like to work with conventional monsters that much, that I didn't care for how vampires were becoming fluffy romantic creatures, and I began adding some other overly arsty-fartsy type nonsense, and he interrupted me with, "No, no, a story... about a little vampire."

Hell, yes. Now, we're talking.

Andrew C. Piazza

"I am the King of the Vampires," he said, and when I turned to face him, the blood ran cold in my veins.

He was only six inches tall.

The cold of the barren night air clutched at my breast as Minutio, the King of the Vampires, flew through my open window and landed on my bedroom dresser. I had gone to great lengths to discover the dark secrets which would summon the prince of the undead, and I have to admit, I was a bit disappointed. I had assumed Minutio's name was meaningless, but there he was, tiny little cape, tiny little boots, tiny little fangs.

"I see you have set out for me the two things no vampire can resist," he squeaked in his tiny, tinny voice, as he nibbled on a bulb of garlic bigger than his head. "Garlic… and blood."

"The legends…" I said, as Minutio flew into a hover near the rim of the goblet filled with my blood, and produced a proportionally-sized tiny pewter mug from underneath his cape, "…the legends say vampires abhor garlic."

He did not answer at first; rather, he dipped his mug into the lake of blood again and again, drinking with unfathomable hunger, occasionally whispering "mmm... good, it's good," to himself. When he had sated his bloodlust, he floated back down to the surface of the dresser, wiping his mouth with a delicate slip of a handkerchief as he composed himself.

"The legends," he said, smiling evilly, shrill voice tinkling through the air like the fall of broken glass. "I *am* the legend. I *created* the legend. Five hundred years ago, when the nearby villagers began to suspect my dark presence among them, they sought ways to hide themselves from my power. A confederate of mine spread the word that the Vampyr could not stand the smell of garlic, when in truth, we find it irresistible. The villagers gorged themselves on the stuff, hung it around their necks in great bundles, making it all the easier to find them."

Oh, the black genius of the ancient terror before me! Who but the prince of the Vampyr could create such a fiendish conspiracy of tangled lies? There was one part I didn't quite follow, though.

"Find them?"

Minutio's face darkened in irritation. "They didn't have light bulbs back then, girlie! I may be a vampire, but I can't see in the dark!"

"But enough of this prelude," he said, leaping off of the table and flying into a hover in front of my face like a very, very evil Ken doll on the end of an invisible string. "You have summoned me here tonight for a reason. You seek my dark and bloody gift."

"Um..." I stammered.

"Ah, you hesitate? You hesitate?" he squeaked, mocking me. "But you want me, you want to be with me... or you would not have performed the ritual. So come... give yourself to me! Be my victim! Be my lover! Be my eternal companion, and we shall stalk the night like…"

"It's… not that."

He frowned. "It's not?"

"No."

Minutio's beady little eyes searched around the room, confused. "Well, what is it, then?"

"I, uh… are you sure you're the king of the vampires?"

"What? Of course I am!"

"It's just that I was expecting someone a bit… taller."

Feral rage lit his undead features, and the icy hand of fear clenched around my heart, until I realized that if worse came to worse, I could just smack him with a tennis racket. His miniature bloodstained lips trembled, and he shouted as loud as a person of his size could, "I'm the King of the Vampires! Twenty-two centuries I have prowled… no! *Owned* the night, taking what prey I wished, oblivious to the petty concerns of mortality, striking wherever my whims sent me!"

"Oh, screw *this*!" he said, and flew for the window. "Now I'm not going to make you into a vampire, how about *that*?"

"I have performed the ritual," I reminded him. "You have no choice."

Minutio stopped before crossing the plane of the window, staring wistfully out into the night air, the night air which had served as his hunting ground for more centuries than I could imagine. "Damn you," he squeaked. "Damn you and this dark curse which binds me. Very well. I shall give you what you desire."

He turned upon me then, and my knees went to water as the pint-sized lord of the undead flew to a perch on my shoulder. His hot, foul breath reeked of the charnel house, and pattered on my neck like when Mr. Whiskers, my cat, sleeps under the covers with me.

"But beware!" he whispered directly into my ear, tickling me a bit. "It is a black gift I bring, a treachery against all that is good and pure! You will be doomed to roam the night, never seeing the dawn, and forced to drink a daily draught of human blood!"

"But I'll never get old, right?" I asked.

"Yes, that's right."

"Very well," I said, tilting my head to expose my neck to him, giving myself to him, to evil, to death, completely, before I could lose my nerve and damn myself to mortality through my cowardice. "Take me, Minutio. I am yours."

There was the briefest contact on my neck, like one might expect from a hamster's paw. The hand of the vampire, I assumed, and steeled myself for the pinch as my vein was punctured and the lifeblood let slowly out of my body.

"It is done."

My eyes blinked in surprise. There had been no pinch, no lifeblood, nothing.

"Aren't you... supposed to bite my neck or something?"

Minutio looked at me quizzically as he returned to the garlic bulbs scattered around the table. "Are you joking? I'd need a pickaxe to get all the way through to your veins. It's just a touch, that's it. No biting."

"Just a touch?" I certainly didn't feel any different. "Are you sure?"

"Check your teeth."

Long, sharp, murderous canines pointed down from either side of my mouth. My tongue couldn't seem to stop running over them;

the novel sensation was as compelling as when I'd first gotten my braces taken off, three months ago.

"Thank goodness for *that*," I mumbled to myself, adding a curious finger to the exploration of my new fangs.

"What?" Minutio asked.

My answer never came; the door to my bedroom flew open, and there was my mother, blissfully ignorant of the monstrous change that had come over me. "Cass, honey?" she said, "That nice young man from your debate club is on the phone."

Minutio shrieked with rage. "No! She is mine!"

"Jesa-watz!" Mom gulped, backing against the wall in startled surprise. "What the hell is... Ted! Ted! Get up here!"

The distant, muted sounds of my father shouting his confusion up the steps from downstairs faded away as I nearly fell into a swoon. What had I done? Condemning myself to this dread existence, betraying the love of my mother, my father, and my little brother. Okay, maybe not *that* little grub, but Mom and Dad, definitely.

"You are too late!" Minutio squeaked triumphantly. "She belongs to me now! She is the night! She is Vampyr!"

"Cassie," Mom said, eyes still locked on the vampire and wide in amazement, "what is... it...talking about?"

There was no gentle way to put it. "I summoned him using black magic and made him turn me into a vampire. Sorry, Mom."

"It is too late for regrets!" Minutio said, pulling insistently at my sleeve to lead me over to the window. "Come, my new student! We must hunt!"

"Sorry Mom, I gotta go," I said, as I climbed onto the window, a bit awkwardly in my black dress. "I'm one of the undead now."

"But..." Mom said, her mind still to hazy to process what she was seeing, "you've got school tomorrow!"

I wept, for I knew those would be the last words I would ever hear her speak. Never again would she be there when I needed her to straighten up my room or remove a stubborn stain from my clothes. Minutio tugged me out of the window and into the night, and a scream tore from my lips, in the illogical fear I would fall to my death.

Foolish thoughts! I was an immortal now, a vampire, a dark angel on Earth. I no longer had to fear mortal death, and the power of flight was within me; although I did find it difficult to get my bearings and navigate through the trees surrounding our suburban home, and I suffered several embarrassing scrapes before I got the hang of flying.

The air swirled about my face, ran its lifeless fingers through my hair. The world rushed beneath us at a dizzying speed, and I knew true freedom for the first time in my sixteen and a half years. Laughing, I threw my learner's permit from me, and as it floated and flipped end-over-end to the ground, I realized I would never have to endure a driver's license test.

"There is our victim," Minutio said, pointing.

A middle-aged man in jeans and a worn Chicago Bears jacket was stumbling across a bar's parking lot a hundred feet below us. His uncertain feet sent him lurching into cars, bouncing between them like a Ping-Pong ball, and on one of his careening ricochets, a bottle slipped from his hand and shattered musically on the pavement.

It was my Algebra teacher, Mr. Connely.

"Now is the time for you to strike," Minutio said, hovering by my shoulder like a little devil with no corresponding angel to contradict him. "Descend upon him, and fulfill your destiny."

It did seem like Destiny. Sixteen years of a relatively moral upbringing clashed with the memory of the "D" Mr. Connely had given me last year. Was I a murderer? Was I a killer? Who gave a crap about the value of x, anyway?

Before I knew what was happening, the ground rushed toward me, my black dress flapping about my legs as Mr. Connely grew larger and larger. He heard me, or sensed me, perhaps, because he glanced up, jaw swinging slackly, until he saw his death.

"Hoh!" was all he could grunt, before I was on him.

It is much harder than you think to swoop down on your prey like that. It requires a great deal of timing and skill, and most of all practice, which I'd had none of. So, instead of scooping him up and off into the night like a hawk catching fish out of a lake, I crashed directly into him and smashed him backwards into the side of a car.

We were both reeling about dizzily; Mr. Connely from drink, me from hurtling into the pavement. His bloated belly bumped into me, and without thinking, I reached out, grabbed him, and bit him in the neck.

"Ow!" he shouted, jerking away from me and holding a hand to his neck. "Whaddahell you doin'?"

"You've got the angle wrong!" Minutio squeaked, pointing to his own neck. "Up here! Up here!"

Mr. Connely screamed at the sight of the tiny vampire, and struggled to pull out of my grip, but my strength was that of ten men. His feeble thrashings were nothing; indeed, they only served to stir up the flames of rage and hate within me, drawing out my predatory instincts, and I flirted with the idea of beating the crap out of him for that time he made a doofus of me when I was working out a problem on the blackboard.

Then, I kicked him in the nuts.

It was the first time I'd done that, too, and I think I way overdid it. A kick to the jimmies is pretty harsh to begin with, and when you add in the strength of a vampire… well, let's just say he was better off dying at that point.

The algebra teacher's tongue protruded out of his mouth as he gurgled and fell to his knees. In a flash, I was on him again, and this time I did not miss.

Blood squirted into my mouth like a macabre piece of Freshen-up gum; so much, so fast it nearly gagged me. It swirled down my throat, pounded its way into my gullet in a never-ending torrent, and I did not stop drinking until it stopped flowing.

It was gross. The legends all spoke of the euphoria vampires experience when drinking blood, the shared ecstasy for both victim and predator, but the truth was, it just tasted like a salty ass. A dirty, salty ass. I had to force it down, like the time Rob Zelliwig had a party while his parents were out of town, and we all played Anchorman and had to chug a crazy amount of beer, and then that dork Billy Peterman tried to feel me up when he thought I was passed out.

Mr. Connely's body dropped to the ground. He would solve no more equations; he would torment the students of Levante High School no longer.

"Come," Minutio squeaked, tugging at my sleeve, trying to shake my staring eyes from the corpse.

I was a killer. A murderer. I had taken the life of my algebra teacher, and now my stomach was starting to hurt.

"I feel awful," I said.

"Do not agonize over the carcass of this mortal," Minutio

squeaked, misunderstanding me. "You are beyond such trivial concerns now."

"No, I…"

"No more of this!" he squeaked insistently, and pulled me into the air again. "I must take you somewhere!"

A branch full of twigs and leaves nearly swatted me out of the sky, but I was learning quickly, and avoided it. "Where?"

"To my subjects. They have gathered to pay homage to me."

We flew on in silence after that, the lights of the town twinkling fireflies far beneath our feet. I barely noticed; dark expectations of how Minutio's followers would appear stalked my thoughts. Would they accept me? Shun me? Teach me? Torture me?

Oh, what had I done? Giving myself to a breed of murderous immortals, fallen angels, who worshipped a six inch king?

"There," Minutio said, pointing.

The temple was massive, unfeeling stone, shaped by nameless workers countless years ago. Squat, rectangular, gray as the soul of the vampire I now was, it sat aside a busy thoroughfare, watching tens and hundreds of unknowing mortals drive by; waiting, thirsting, wanting.

"We lease the space," Minutio squeaked, pointing out the MASONIC TEMPLE sign as I alit upon the front stair like a black stray cat unsure whether its curiosity would take another of its nine lives. The vampire stayed by my right shoulder as I approached the huge double doors, licking my lips nervously, my bellyache forgotten, paling in comparison to the fear of what unknown horrors lay within the Masonic Temple.

Curiosity won out, aided by the insistent squeaks of Minutio, and with a straining grunt, I opened the doors and met my destiny.

It was horrible.

Dozens of vampires were seated or standing about the massive meeting hall, and not one of them was wearing black. Not *one*. Jeans, sweaters, leather bomber jackets, shirts and ties, even a miniskirt, for Pete's sake, but not one Gothic dreary costume in the whole lot. They looked more like a bunch of twenty- and thirty-something pub-dwellers rather than centuries-old dungeon-dwellers. There I was, in my long black dress, black fishnet stockings, black combat boots, dyed-black hair, black lipstick, black nailpolish, and I'm smack-dab in the middle of a friggin' L.L. Bean convention. It totally blew.

"Oh, Christ, here he is," somebody grumbled, as Minutio flew into the center of the hall.

"Greetings, my subjects, my children," Minutio said, as loudly as he could. "Tonight, we welcome another deathless soul into our ranks. Welcome…"

He frowned. "Um, what was your name again?"

"Cassandra," I said as loud and as boldly as I could, enduring the stares of the yuppie vampires as my voice echoed throughout the Masonic Temple "I am called Cassandra."

"Cassandra? Nice to meetcha. I'm Bill," said a bearded vampire who looked way too much like my guidance counselor, standing up and walking me over to his table. "Can I call you Cassie?"

"Well, I…"

"This is Sally, and Floyd, and Jimmy," Bill pointed around the table. "Everybody? This is Cassie."

"Cassan…" I started to correct, but my stomach really started to hurt again, and a piteous moan escaped my lips.

"You okay?" Bill asked, looking at me carefully.

"It is merely the death of her mortal shell," Minutio squeaked.

"Death of her mortal shell, my ass," Bill said, guiding me into a chair. "She's got an upset stomach. Don't you, Cassie?"

I could only nod.

"Did Minutio take you out hunting?"

Another nod.

"How much did you drink?"

My deathless shoulders shrugged. "As much as came out."

Exasperated groans and sighs erupted around the table. "Jeez, Cassie!" Sally said. "What did you do, kill the guy?"

"Well… yeah," I said. Of course I had killed him… I was a vampire.

"Oh, Cassie," Bill sighed, sounding as if he were disappointed in me. "You don't have to kill them. You must've drank three pints, at least. No wonder you're sick."

"How much should I drink?"

"You only need a pint or so," Sally said, frowning at me with distaste.

"Most of us don't even bite people anymore," Bill said.

"Where do you get your blood from?"

"Blood banks, mostly," Sally answered, laying a loving hand on Bill's with a smile. "That's where I met him."

"Blood banks definitely have the primo juice," Jimmy said. "Score yourself a graveyard shift at a hospital or something ASAP."

"But," I said, "what about being immortal predators? What about the shared ecstasy, the connection between the dying victim and the feeding…"

"Oh, great. Another Goth," Sally muttered.

"Cassie, honey, did you get any of that when you killed that guy earlier tonight?" Bill asked.

"Well, uh... no."

Bill nodded, as if to say, *there you are, then.*

This was awful. For months, years, I had prepared myself mentally for the dark realm of the undead, feeding on the words of Stoker and Rice and anything else vampiric I could get my hands on. I knew what it meant to be a vampire: cold, dark, rotting coffins, orgasmic blood-drainings, eternal torment, all that good stuff. But here was Bill and Sally and Jimmy and freaking *Floyd*, telling me that real vampires work for the Red Cross and dress casual and probably drive Sport Utility vehicles when they don't feel like flying.

"Gawd," I said. "If I knew it was going to be like this, I never would've went to all the trouble of that ritual."

"You did the *ritual*?" Floyd said with a snicker. "What for?"

"So I could become a vampire, duh," I said. "What did you do?"

He shrugged. "Caught him inside of a blanket and whacked him with a hammer until he made me one."

"Floyd!" Bill said.

"What? You're just as bad!"

"What did you do?" I asked.

"I, uh," Bill said, clearing this his throat uncomfortably. "I caught him inside of a glass jar and wouldn't let him out until he promised."

"Why didn't you just have Sally do it?"

"Minutio is the only one who can make vampires... at least, that we know of," Sally said. "Think about it. If every vampire could make vampires, the population would explode exponentially."

"This sucks," I said, the words tasting like bitter ashes in my mouth.

Minutio returned to a hover by my shoulder, having finished whatever stupid squeaky conversations he had been having around the room. "I trust they have not been too harsh with you, Cassandra."

"They suck," I said, sneering at him, my temper lost along with the delusions I'd had about the vampiric life. "They suck, and you suck too."

"And I don't mean suck blood," I continued, standing up to stare down at the miniature lord of the undead. "I mean suck, as in you're a loser, a total wastoid."

Minutio's face twitched in malevolence. "How dare you! How dare you speak to me, your master, in this manner! I… I shall…"

"What? What can you do?" I said, no longer caring what sort of spectacle I was making of myself.

"Cassie…" Bill said, trying to warn me, but the hate and rage and disappointment in me was a festering boil, and it had to be lanced.

"Shut up! There!" I shouted, smacking the little vampire to the ground with my open palm. "There, hunh? What do you think about that?"

"Oh!" I said, as he flew back up, and I swatted him back down again. "Look! I did it again!"

I finally stopped tormenting him, as tiny, tinny sobs floated up from his prostrate form. Rage and hate and disappointment melted into shame, shame at my own meanness and brutality.

"It's true," Minutio wept. "It's all true."

"Oh, boy, here we go again," Sally said, shaking her head.

"You're right, Cassandra!" he squeaked. "I am a sad joke on the lips of all vampires. I am nothing, I am nobody; just a slip of senseless, undead stupidity."

He rallied himself enough to fly up onto the table. "I can endure this existence no longer. This dawn I shall meet the sun, not in my cigar humidor, but in the morning air, where it will burn my freakishly small body to a cinder."

"No, Minutio, no!" Bill cried, standing and moving to my side. "She doesn't know what she's saying! She's just a young fool... you are our lord, our master! We owe everything to you!"

"I don't know," Minutio said, sitting down on the table and hugging his knees. "She made me want to kill myself pretty bad."

"Only one thing can snap him out of this," Bill told me.

"What?"

"Cassie?" Minutio said, lying back on the table and stretching out. "Rub my belly."

"No... way!" I said. "No freakin' w... ow!"

Bill caught my arm in a grip that reminded me how strong we vampires are. "You listen to me, little girl," he said. "He'll kill himself if you don't, so you *will* rub his belly, or you'll find out just how much pain a vampire can take."

"What do you care?" I said. "He dies, and you all become mortal again, freed from your eternal damnation."

"What are you smoking?" Jimmy said, laughing at me. "Being a vampire *rules*! You get to stay up all night, and live forever, and if anybody messes with you, you can totally kick their ass!"

"That's right," Bill said with a nod. "And if having all that means we have to stroke the ego of a six-inch vampire, and rub his belly from time to time, so be it."

A quick look around the room and the steely eyes of my peers convinced me. "Fine."

"Ooo, yes," Minutio squeaked, as I rubbed his tiny belly with the pad of my forefinger. "Up... up... yes, yes right... there... oooo..."

I rubbed and rubbed the vampire, cursing my fate as Minutio rolled back and forth in ecstasy. At last, he rose, waving me off.

"Very well, my children. You have dissuaded me. I will live on, deathless, into eternity."

"But *she* must leave my sight!" he said, pointing at me.

"Fine by me," Sally said.

"C'mon, Cassie," Bill said, leading me toward the double doors leading back into the night.

"But... but..." I began to plead, unwilling to leave the only members of my tribe. There was so much I needed to know, and I didn't want to be alone, not now...

"No buts, young lady," the bearded vampire said, pulling open the doors with his free hand and shoving me outside. "You don't come back until you've learned some manners!"

With that, the massive oaken doors shut, sealing me off from the only social contact left to me. I simply stood and stared at them. No desperate pounding of fists on the wood, no wails or pleading for forgiveness. I was lost; I had no idea what to do, or what to think, or anything, so after a while, I sat down with my back to the doors, trying to collect my thoughts.

Then, I heard it, picked up by my newly-enhanced vampire senses. Laughter.

Uproarious laughter. Gut-splitting, pee-your-pants laughter, practically shaking the cold stone beneath me.

"Did you hear what I said?" Bill's voice cried out chokingly, the sound muffled by the huge doors. "Don't come back until you've learned some manners!"

"That was great!" somebody else shouted.

"I can't believe you got her to rub your belly, Minutio!" another vampire said. "You are the best!"

"I know, it was awesome!" Minutio's tinny voice squeaked with laughter. "She bought the whole thing! What a dork!"

The undead mirth drowned out the words then, as the true horror of my situation dawned upon me. I wasn't a fallen angel; I was a whipping boy, a punching bag for the *truly* evil, and they'd tossed me aside like an empty bottle once they'd had their jollies with me.

"Where do you think she'll go now, Minutio?" I heard a voice ask.

"Who the hell cares?" the tiny voice squeaked. "Bring out that wino! Let's get piss drunk!"

I could take no more; I reeled from the steps of the Masonic Temple, and staggered into the dark and dirty streets, searching for solace, searching for guidance, finding nothing but the chill wind. There was nothing for me, no place to turn, no avenue left to pursue.

That wasn't true. I came to a stop here, in mid-Suburbia, when it occurred to me.

I still know the ritual.

And so now, I go in search of a tennis racket and a glass jar, as evil plans congeal in the back of my undead mind. Plans involving garlic, and blood… and a tiny little stake.

The Death Of Armadillo Boy

Remember earlier, when I wrote that I sometimes like to write little spin-off short stories based on novels I've written? Here's an example of a spin-off from "Doctor Insanity and The Sparrow", born out of a throw-away line used early in the novel when The Sparrow vows revenge on Doctor Insanity for killing his sidekick, Armadillo Boy.

Again, just as with "Alley Cats", please allow me to assure you that no actual Armadillo-human hybrids were harmed in the writing of this story.

Andrew C. Piazza

"**There, Armadillo Boy**," The Sparrow said, his voice becoming heroically baritone as he pointed towards the house. "**Our nemesis awaits!**"

Armadillo Boy didn't say anything. He couldn't; armadillos can't speak, and anybody who says they can is a silly person. However, he could sigh, and in fact, he sighed quite often, using them as a crude form of communication. He used his Here We Go Again sigh now.

"**Yes!**" The Sparrow said, hitching his brown tights up over his soft belly. "**I am excited as well! Let us dispense Justice!**"

As they stalked toward the house, keeping to the neatly trimmed bushes dotting the suburban landscape, Armadillo Boy wondered yet again how he'd gotten himself into this. He never really wanted to be a superhero; he just wanted to root for grubs and stay out of sight during the day.

But Sparrow… Sparrow had charmed him with his extraordinary enthusiasm for heroism, an enthusiasm unmarred by Sparrow's distinct lack of credits in the Archcriminals Caught column of the ledger. For the first time, Armadillo Boy saw more to life than eating worms, curling into a ball to protect his soft abdomen, and the occasional bit of carrion. And so, here they were, sneaking up on the tastefully designed one-story ranch home of the evil genius Doctor Insanity, who Armadillo Boy suspected had never even heard of them.

Suddenly, a gnashing, churning blade whooshed at his head. This surely would've been the end for Armadillo Boy, but he ducked his body into a compact ball and rolled to the side just in time. The growling blade missed him by inches.

But the danger was not past. Out of nowhere, a hideous machine of death, complete with whirling blades, roared out of its hiding place and bore down on the quivering super-rodent. This surely would've been the end for Armadillo Boy, but The Sparrow pushed him out of the way at the last moment and the Whirling Death Machine rushed by close enough to blow an evil wind and grass clippings across them.

"Holy Jeez!" The Whirling Death Machine came to a sudden stop, and Armadillo Boy opened his eyes and saw that it was only a riding lawnmower, whose middle-aged driver was now standing up and looking at them in shock and surprise. "I almost ran you over, buddy! What are you doing down there?"

"He came out of the bushes," a teen-aged boy complete with cracking voice and acne-enhanced looks said, lowering the hedge trimmer that had nearly decapitated Armadillo Boy a moment before. "Scared the crap out of me. I was trying to trim the corner of this bush when he just jumped out with this fat guy."

"Yes, yes, yes," The Sparrow said quickly, forgetting his baritone in his haste. "It's all right. I'm The Sparrow."

The father and son looked at each other in confusion. "Who?"

The Sparrow gritted his teeth. "The Sp… look, this is official superhero business, okay? We're on the job here."

"Oh," the father said, scratching his head and looking quite unconvinced. "What happened to him?"

"What...nothing *happened* to him!" The Sparrow said. "That's how he's supposed to look! He is Armadillo Boy, my sidekick! We have come to stop the evil Doctor Insanity!"

"Speaking of which," The Sparrow continued, lowering his voice conspiratorially, "that is Doctor Insanity's house... I mean, *lair*... right?"

"Yep, sure is," the father said with a nod. "Moved in about six months ago."

"Aha!" The Sparrow cried triumphantly, perfectly ready to scoff at those who had said he was no good as a detective, but another question begged to be asked first.

"Say," he asked, "doesn't it bother you to have a bona fide archvillain living next door to you?"

The father shrugged. "He keeps the place nice."

"He robs banks and kills people and tries to take over the world for a living."

"Yes, but check out that two-tier garden he's put in the back yard," the father said. "And the magnolias out front, and how perfect he keeps his lawn. It's like Pebble Beach over there! My property value has gone through the roof because of him. You should've seen the last bozo who lived there... never mowed his lawn, didn't mulch at *all*, and..."

"All right, all right, I get it," The Sparrow said, then shooed them off. "Now please, stand aside. We're about to get heroic."

Through all of this, Armadillo Boy remained silent. He was, after all, just a sidekick, and so he always left all of the requisite defiant challenges and declarations of justice to The Sparrow. Finally, they were off, dashing through the bushes and across Doctor Insanity's magnificent two-tier garden, much to the chagrin of his lawn-loving neighbors.

"Gaa!" Sparrow cried, suddenly hurled to the ground after being struck across the neck. Armadillo Boy would've cried out too, but as we've already covered, armadillos don't speak, so he just fell down next to his partner.

A boobytrap! A follow-up attack to finish them off while they were helpless was certain. This surely would've been the end for Armadillo Boy, but when they struggled to their feet, they found that no attack was forthcoming. The Sparrow inspected the nasty boobytrap device while fingering his sore throat.

"Ingenious," he said, running a finger along the clothesline, "deceptively simple in design, and fiendishly camouflaged with these damp pieces of clothing scattered along its length."

Armadillo Boy was starting to re-think this entire adventure. His scaly skin was not as impervious as he would've liked. Oh sure, it saved him from the occasional scratch or ugly scrape, as he had discovered once while running with scissors in blatant defiance of his parents' wishes. But it wouldn't stop bullets or chainsaws or riding lawnmowers; he was sure of that.

"All right," The Sparrow said, lying flat on the lawn to stay hidden, which didn't really work out, because the lawn was perfectly level and trimmed to an inch in height. "Here we go. You sneak around the front and wait for him in case he runs. I'll go in the back."

Armadillo Boy sighed, his Can't We Just Go Home? sigh, but Sparrow slapped a hand on the gorgeous lawn insistently.

"No! Come *on*, Armadillo, this is our chance! Now we can show up all those other guys who said we suck and we're losers and we couldn't catch an archvillain if they were shot with a Paralyzing Ray and why couldn't we lose some *weight* to get our *tights* to fit!" Sparrow said with a splutter. "Don't give up now!"

Armadillo Boy sighed his Oh, All Right sigh and lumbered off for the front of the house, never knowing he was on his way to meet with Destiny.

Meanwhile, inside his tastefully designed one-level ranch house lair, Doctor Insanity was fixing up a tuna-fish sandwich.

The half-cyborg whistled while he made it, the LED lights scattered across the metallic half of his face twinkling in time with the tune. His cybernetic eye and robotic brain implants calculated the exact proportion of tuna-fish and mayo to use in order to keep the caloric value of the sandwich reasonable and the fat/carb/protein ratio in proper perspective. After all, he might've been an evil genius, but he still liked to look good for the ladies.

Movement caught his eye through the front window, and Doctor Insanity realized certain disaster was imminent on his front lawn. Cursing his lapse in awareness, he snatched up his handy remote control, which controlled not only the digital cable but all sorts of goodies around the house, and pressed the button corresponding to the front lawn.

"That takes care of that," he smiled, LED lights twinkling in satisfaction.

Armadillo Boy was nestled nicely behind an azalea bush, waiting for his chance to pounce on the evil Doctor Insanity, when a strange metallic noise came from behind him. Before he could react, he was drenched with acid from hidden sprayers, soaked from head to paws. This surely would've been the end for Armadillo Boy, but when he realized his body wasn't being eaten alive by hydroflouric acid, but instead was just moist and clammy, he realized he hadn't been doused with acid, but simply that Doctor Insanity's lawn sprinklers had just switched on.

This sucks, he thought, trudging out toward the sidewalk to get out of range of the sprinkler, whose whisking sounds seemed like fiendish, mocking laughter to the scaly sidekick. He had no idea being a superhero involved so much humiliation. If this kept up, he was going to make Sparrow buy him a cape.

He settled in behind a maple tree, having no idea that Destiny was only a few paragraphs away.

"Curses!" Doctor Insanity snarled, crushing his daily To Do list in his robotic fist. With all of these senseless errands taking up his time, his plans for World Domination were seriously suffering.

But, there wasn't anything to be done about it, so he left his perfectly constructed tuna-fish sandwich on the counter and rummaged in his kitchen drawers for his car keys. As usual, he couldn't find them, and he was just about ready to lose it and poison the city's water supply in frustration when he remembered that they were in his pants pocket the whole time.

"Silly of me, really," he said, chuckling to himself as he headed out to the garage. "But that water supply thing does seem like a good idea."

With a crash, The Sparrow came leaping through the sliding glass door leading to the back yard. With a thud, he smacked into the screen door behind it and bounced off back onto the lawn.

"Criminy!" he said, picking himself up. There was really no way to make that sort of thing look good.

He yanked open the screen door and hopped into the living room, hands on his hips and his arms akimbo as he cried out his challenge. **"Soho, Doctor Insan**... hello? Hello?"

It looked like nobody was home.

Sparrow's shoulders slumped in disappointment. All of the horrors he had braved, and the villain wasn't even home!

He wandered into the kitchen and knocked on the bathroom door to make sure he hadn't caught his nemesis on the pot. Nothing. Nothing at all to reward his heroic efforts.

Well, not quite. There was a marvelous-looking tuna-fish sandwich on the counter.

"Fool!" Sparrow cried triumphantly, seizing the sandwich. "Looks like even an evil genius slips up every now and again!"

It was so tasty, he didn't even notice Doctor Insanity's car starting in the garage.

The coarse whiskers between Armadillo Boy's scales perked up. Something was amiss, his nocturnal feeder's instincts knew it. He crouched low behind the maple tree on Doctor Insanity's front lawn, peeking his head out to keep an eye on the house.

Suddenly, a neo-Nazi skinhead obviously in the employ of Doctor Insanity whooshed by on a motorcycle, heaving a WWII German potato-masher grenade at him. It twirled end-over-end to smack him right in the head. Dazed, he fell onto his back on the lawn, the grenade lying heavily on his chest.

This surely would've been the end for Armadillo Boy, but when he lurched about to heave the grenade off of his chest, he saw that the potato-masher grenade was only a rolled-up newspaper, and Doctor Insanity's neo-Nazi skinhead henchman was really just a reckless paperboy with a bad haircut on a bicycle. He pulled himself to his paws, and sighed his I'm Sick Of This sigh.

Let Sparrow take care of this, he thought, trudging over to the driveway and sitting down next to Doctor Insanity's mailbox, which was built to look like an Iron Maiden. He stretched out across the asphalt, letting the warm sun dry his scales and warm his bones.

Little did he know, Destiny was waiting for him in the very next scene.

"Do de do do do," Doctor Insanity said in time with his favorite '50's tunes coming over the radio. He shifted in his seat so he could watch out of the rear window as he backed out of the garage, pointed the automatic garage door opener, and clicked the button.

His face contorted horribly, lips twitching and eyes crossing. The LED lights on the metallic half of his face twinkled wildly, and sparks began to crackle and pop as smoke rose from his ears.

"Damnable gadget!" he cried, hurling the garage door opener to the floor. He had a bad habit of forgetting what that thing did to him, at least once a week, and this was the inevitable result. Now, he'd be in a lousy mood all day.

He blinked and squinted his eyes, both the cybernetic and the organic one, to try to clear his blurred vision. It seemed to improve a bit, and the evil half-cyborg threw the transmission into Reverse with a bitter oath concerning the murder of the automatic garage door opener's inventor.

As his car lurched backward, Doctor Insanity began to nod in evil glee, his imagination running wild with his latest murder scheme. Perhaps he could electrocute this inventor with a twenty-foot version of his machine, or grind him in the gears of a similarly massive reconstruction of a garage door opener. The poetic murders were always the most satisfying.

"Watch out!" somebody shouted, and a sudden bump shook him from his reverie. With another handful of blinks, his vision finally cleared enough for him to realize he was already out of his driveway and halfway into the street. His idiot neighbors were out on their sub-standard lawn, both father and son green-faced and staring.

"What in blazes was that?" he said, looking around his car until he spotted the squished mass of scales and yuck on his driveway. "Criminy! What was that doing there? I didn't even think they lived in this part of the country!"

The neighbor's son began to vomit copiously, and Doctor Insanity sneered at the father. "What the hell are you looking at?" he shouted, flipping them the bird before he drove off, as he was also evil in addition to being a genius. "You should be working on your lawn! Your grass looks like shit!"

"Does not," the father said, inspecting his grass with additional scrutiny.

The Sparrow rushed out of the front door of the house, half-eaten sandwich in hand. "No, no, no!" he shouted around a mouthful of tunafish.

But, yes, yes, yes, it was indeed the end for Armadillo Boy. Sparrow stumbled his way to the street, plopping to a seat on the curb by his fallen comrade. There, he forlornly munched on his captured sandwich, until he reached the crust, which he didn't quite care for, and then he threw the sandwich to the ground in defiance.

"I swear that…" he began, but then, a large orange truck pulled up and an overweight man in the employ of the Department of Transportation scooped up the remains of Armadillo Boy with a shovel and tossed him in the back of the truck.

"Hey! You want the rest of that?" the DOT crewman asked, nodding toward Sparrow's abandoned sandwich.

"Yes!" Sparrow said with righteous indignation.

The truck drove off, and Sparrow bent and picked the sandwich crusts from the dirty pavement. More emotions than he could count coursed through him, and he worked through them with a heroic vow as best he could, which wasn't very good.

"In the name of this tuna-fish sandwich and everything else that is both tasty and wholesome to eat, I shall avenge you, Armadillo Boy!" he cried, and leapt into the air. Unfortunately, he was a bit too caught up in the moment, and accidentally flew into some power lines, and with a loud crackle of sparks, fell unconscious to the ground, trailing smoke.

Now that it was all over, the teenaged neighbor of Doctor Insanity finally stopped puking and asked, "Dad? That… thing… wasn't a person, was it?"

"I don't know, son," his father said, putting an arm around him. "But it's off our lawn, and that's what matters. Now hose off that vomit before it kills the grass."

ABOUT THE AUTHOR

Andrew C. Piazza is a rotten, no good son of a.... okay, just checking to see if you were paying attention.

Andrew C. Piazza is a writer who recklessly jumps from genre to genre in foolish defiance of any sensible career building advice. Some of his strong influences are JRR Tolkien, Robert E. Howard, Harlan Ellison, Ray Bradbury, Stephen King, and HP Lovecraft. He writes humorous fiction under the pen name "Christopher Andrews", and nonfiction in the field of natural health under the name "Healthy Andy". He currently resides outside Philadelphia.

Join The ARC (Advanced Review Copy) Squad!

If you like what you've read, stop by www.andrewpiazza.com and request to be on the ARC squad to get free advanced review copies.

OTHER BOOKS BY ANDREW C. PIAZZA

One Last Gasp
The Messiah Project
Resurrection Day

AS CHRISTOPHER ANDREWS

Doctor Insanity vs. The Sparrow

Printed in Great Britain
by Amazon